JILLIAND

A STORY OF
LOVE AND FREEDOM

JILLIAND

CLARE GUTIERREZ

RIVER GROVE
BOOKS

Published by River Grove Books
Austin, TX
www.rivergrovebooks.com

Distributed by River Grove Books

Design and composition by Greenleaf Book Group
Cover design by Greenleaf Book Group
©iStockphoto.com/Aaltazar; TeusRenes; SergeyMikhaylov; Sylphe_7
©Elivagar; Canicula, 2018. Used under license from Shutterstock.com

Cataloging-in-Publication data is available.

Print ISBN: 978-1-63299-171-3

eBook ISBN: 978-1-63299-172-1

First Edition

THIS NOVEL IS DEDICATED TO STEPHEN WHITTEMORE, my grandson. Thank you, Stephen, for asking me to tell another story, become a pirate, take trips on our "train," and for generally reminding me to open my mind to the endless possibilities of one's imagination. Our time . . .

ACKNOWLEDGMENTS

AS ALWAYS, I AM INDEBTED to my husband, Beto, for his unwavering support. He never complains about the hours I spend in research, reading, hauling my laptop everywhere, and begging off engagements so I can write (or type).

I would also like to thank the team at Greenleaf Book Group. A special thank you to Sally Garland, Associate Editor; Elizabeth Chenette; Rachael Brandenburg, Graphic Designer; and everyone else who assisted in moving this project forward.

HUSH, HUSH, SWEET PAIN,
lest you shatter night's fragile refuge.

PROLOGUE

TIMES WERE TURBULENT IN ENGLAND, Scotland, and Wales during the eighth and ninth centuries. England itself was a checkerboard of lands held by separate "kings" and lords who needed financial help from their subjects to field defensive armies. The people, struggling with poverty, high death rates, and illness were only able to provide meager funding—if at all. Few infants survived birth, and fewer still lived to reach adulthood. Viking raids made a miserable existence even worse. At the same time, Christianity was spreading steadily. Monasteries sprang up along the routes utilized by travelers, sometimes next to larger settlements and sometimes in rather isolated areas.

Into the middle of the chaos and uncertainty of the times, one soul would step forward, struggling to survive. The odds were against that happening.

The lady looked down into the face of the man. His eyes were locked onto hers. She knew his love for her was something he could never describe. "You will be safe," he assured her.

"I know," she responded softly, wiping away the beads of perspiration from his brow.

"I picked your guard myself," the man added. "They are all good men."

"Yes, I feel protected with them," she murmured. The atmosphere between them was quiet, soft, easy—the way of dear friends, companions, and lovers.

He kissed her hand like he had done so many times before. "I'm sorry," he began, and his voice dropped.

"For?"

"For leaving so soon." He paused for an instant. "You must leave too—tonight. Else travel will not be safe."

"I am ready," she assured him. He nodded, and his face relaxed. The rise and fall of his chest ceased. At last, she bent and tenderly kissed his lips. This was her final parting from her husband. She turned to the page standing near. "Tell his father the prince is dead. It is over." She knew the king was acutely aware that she would not, could not, stay for the prince's funeral. She must leave under the shield of night. Her husband was dead. His younger brother and his brother's Spanish wife would take the crown. The dead prince's wife would be an unwelcome problem. Unwelcome problems were removed.

Moving into her own chambers, the lady stood for a moment and stared vacantly into the room. The impending trip felt as if she were losing her place in life, giving up all she had ever been, and yet, for her safety, there was no alternative.

The lady spoke softly to the guard at her door. He motioned to several other soldiers, and the few belongings she had packed were loaded onto a cart waiting in the courtyard. A somber man, Captain Avila, assisted her into her carriage. The man had served the lady and the prince as the captain of their guard since she first came to this palace. He gladly agreed to remain captain of her guard and escort her and the company of soldiers to wherever she would be safe.

The moon refused to show her face as the lady and her escort left the place she had called home all her married life. The time had come for her to return to her motherland, but her heart would be buried with her husband. *I shall never love again*, she thought. The men with her had been given only an initial destination. If she safely arrived at that first stop, they would be told the next destination, and so on. None but the captain and the lady knew where her final stop would be. Once she arrived there, everyone would be safe.

PART ONE

CHAPTER 1

AS THE AFTERNOON SUN BEGAN to fade, a tall man with a huge gut hanging over his belt coiled his whip and stomped away from the training corral, leaving a bleeding heap on the ground. The corral was near the stables and housing where his soldiers lived. He held the title of "lord," though the honor of the title was sorely misplaced. His lips were set in a permanent sneer. A dirty, matted beard straggled across his face, and his cold pale-grey eyes looked out on the world without emotion. This scene had been repeated more times than could be tallied, but even so, he still had not controlled his cruelty. A path quickly opened for him as the soldiers and other men moved aside, unwilling to risk agitating him further.

When the lord was out of sight, a timid old man named Silas slowly crossed the grounds. Silas limped with the ache of arthritis in his feet and knees. His hair, all white, was nearly gone. What little was left stuck out around his head. His eyesight was poor as was his hearing. His face, covered in wrinkles, softened as he approached the heap on the ground. He picked up the mass of rags, flesh, and bones with an infinitely gentle touch. His frail body struggled to carry the bundle past his wife, Myla, who stood in the shadows cast by a row of ramshackle huts that housed the lord's subjects. Without speaking, Myla followed him into the meager hut they shared. Tucked into a corner of the high walls surrounding their burg, their hut, like all the others, was in need of repair. The lord had neither the money nor frame of mind to be bothered about caring for his people.

Years long past, when the torture sessions first began, the lord had caught Silas rushing to care for his victim. He had descended upon Silas with fury, knocking him to the ground. "What permission do you have to interfere? Leave things be, or you will face the same!" he shouted, standing over him, whip in hand.

Calmly, the old man had replied, "Because you are my lord, I will not permit anyone to speak wrongly of you. Others do not know everything about you." After pondering the old man's words, the lord had turned and walked away. From that time on, he had allowed the old couple to clean up the devastation he left behind.

Myla began to murmur to the bleeding creature that her husband had carried and laid down gently upon his own small bed. "There, there, little one. Easy, now." Myla shook her head sadly as she gently loosened the torn shirt and began to cleanse the wounds. The cleansing and the salve she applied caused nearly as much pain as the whip, and small moans escaped from the victim's lips. The old woman wrapped the wounds carefully, using much more padding, before tying the dressing on securely.

Lately, the punishments were becoming more harsh and frequent. Myla spoke softly, "You must leave. He will kill you eventually, you know."

"Why should I wish to live?" came the bitter reply.

"For your mother," was Myla's quick response. "Your blood runs royal. No one can take that away from you."

"My blood runs onto the dirt where it soaks in, fades, and disappears. Soon, there will be none left." The weak voice was heavy with loathing. Fear had grown into hate. Each encounter with the lord ended the same way.

"You cannot die," the old woman shook her head again. "The time has come." The couple had done all in their power to care for the only legacy of their lady. The lord had been obsessed with using his expectant wife's child to fulfill his desire for money and stature. Those dreams died with the infant's mother. No one really knew who the woman was, nor it seemed, who might care about the child. On her deathbed, the mother had exacted a promise from the old woman who delivered the newborn, "Protect my child." At first, it was not difficult. The lord paid little attention to the child. Over time, he began trying to devise a way he could use the child to his advantage.

On this night, Silas spoke out in agreement with Myla. "My wife is right. We are too old to keep you safe any longer. We have waited long enough, and your hour has come. You must leave this place tonight. Here," he said, as he handed over a small blue silken bag. A fine rope of gold and silver threads closed the top. "This was your mother's. We have kept it hidden for you all these years."

"Where do I go?" Uncertainty tinged the voice, making it waver.

"Where he cannot come for you; leave his lands," Silas replied. "You know where the sun rises and sets. Use your knowledge and travel north. You will find people to help you." He added a warning, "Stay away from places the Vikings raid."

Once long ago, a man had come to the lord begging for help, saying Vikings had been sighted coming upriver, toward his village. The lord refused to help for several days. When he had finally arrived with his soldiers, the scene they came upon was beyond words. The smell of death was overwhelming. Even the soldiers covered their faces with rags. Dogs and other scavengers fed on carcasses. Millions of flies swarmed over the area, creating an audible buzz. The lord made certain his only child saw every detail, thereby killing any possible desire the child might have to run away.

Those memories brought a shudder from the form now sitting up on the bed. "I have seen horrible deaths. Men, women, and children . . . all killed by Vikings." Even though no Vikings had been seen by the child that day, the memories of what they had left filled a young heart with fear. "How? How can I leave? What about the Vikings?" The voice faded away.

Firmly, the old man continued. "You go this night. If you stay, you will die. I would not allow you to leave if I could do anything at all to keep you safe. I cannot. Tonight we go to your room, as always. Find and use what I have hidden under your sleeping place."

Silas gently touched Myla's hand, then took a deep breath, and continued. He understood the risk he and his wife were taking. *God willing, the plan will be all we need.* "While the soldiers eat, you must make your escape. Keep in the shadow close to the walls. On the far side, near the wall beyond the gate, water runs rapidly into the moat that carries away the waste. When everyone has eaten, and the slop is dumped, a spiked gate will be lowered beneath the wall into the water. You must be gone before then. Slip under the wall with the water." He saw his wife's anxious expression but continued. "It will be cold at night; you need dry clothes so take your clothes off before you are in the water. Carry them above you. Move quickly and stay near the bank closest to the wall."

He kissed the dirty hand. "Soon I will die. I can no longer help you. Your wit and God will keep you." His wife wept, as she tenderly touched the face of the child she had cared for these long years. "'Tis the night," the old man continued firmly. "'Tis the night." For the last time, he picked up the bruised body and left his hut with it in his arms.

At that hour, the occupants of the old blockhouse were settling down, anticipating the darkness that would soon cover the land. The lord's house staff joined the soldiers, while groups of men were wandering across the grounds to join others gathering at a large hall set for their evening meal. The courtyard was slowly emptying for the night. Just as he had done for years, the old man carried his bundle past soldiers and guards to a cell that had been built near one side of the compound. The floor space only allowed room for a single makeshift bed and a small area in which to move about. The ceiling was twenty feet above, with open windows near the top on two sides. Silas pushed the cell door open and stepped inside. Once in the cell, the old man carefully deposited his burden on a raised board that served as a bed in an otherwise bare room. The old man's eyes filled with tears. Gently, he patted the thin shoulders and kissed the bruised and bloody face one last time. Into the hand clutching the pouch, he pressed a large glass vial with a stopper. "Spread this when you leave. Use it all—on the bed, floor, and wall, close enough to show it came from one person. It will protect you. God bless you and keep you, dear child." He left the cell, pulling the door closed behind him.

CHAPTER 2

A FULL MOON ROLLED SLOWLY above the blockhouse, spreading its light. In the small cell, a figure moved unsteadily and struggled to rise from the wooden pallet. Remnants of the torn and bloodied shirt and breeches had been carefully removed. Wincing with the pain that any movement caused, this skeletal form—a young woman named Jilliand—glanced at the closed door with fear. She loosened her hair, and the long red matted knots tumbled out, framing her face and spilling down her back. The only child of the lord stood naked in the middle of the cell where her father kept her imprisoned.

Jilliand crawled beneath the board that served as her bed to retrieve the package Silas had promised. Tied together were trousers, worn boots, woolen leggings, and a heavy shirt. She dressed and tried unsuccessfully to smooth her hair down, biting her lip to keep from moaning. For the moment, the salve kept the wounds from drying and cracking. Those conditions would come later. She stood—thin and beaten—but straight. Despite the grime, Jilliand made a striking picture in the moonlight that came flooding onto the floor from a large high window. Not visible in the moonlight, her emerald eyes flashed with hatred—and fear.

Jilliand quickly surveyed the tiny cell. She wished she had a weapon, but there was nothing she could use as one. Remembering the vial the old man had given her, she removed the stopper: It was filled with blood. She poured some of the liquid over the wooden slab where it slowly spread. She splattered more on the floor and threw the remainder against one wall. "God, please watch over Silas and Myla. If not for their care, I would be dead."

As an afterthought, Jilliand picked up the old clothes she had worn and wrapped them around the vial. "'Tis little enough, but I'll not leave anything behind." Holding her breath, she gently pulled on the door. Unlatched, it opened freely. As usual, no one was at her cell door yet. In the distance, she caught the sounds of the guards, joking and talking, settling in for another night of eating and drinking.

I must find the waterway. She crept out and then carefully pulled the door closed behind her. Flattened against the outside of the building that housed her cell, she slid away, fading into the shadows. Jilliand knew the old woman was right. If Jilliand stayed one more night, she would die. *It ends tonight,* she promised herself. *One way or another, it ends tonight.*

Over the years, guards and soldiers had grown lax. The one post they all hoped for was standing watch over the lord's daughter. Once on duty, the men assigned to her could drink, talk, joke, and sleep. This evening after they finished eating, two guards, already a little drunk, stumbled toward the closed door of the now vacant cell. They slouched against the wall and were soon asleep. The younger one woke himself up snoring. He stood and stretched, kicking the foot of his partner to wake him. "One day soon, I will help myself to the vixen. The lord will never know. She is afraid of him, and she would never tell." He wiped his nose on his arm and eyed the cell door, a hungry glint in his eye.

"I think not. Some of the men among us carry sympathy for her. Best to visit the willing whores at the inn," responded his partner-at-guard. Pulling at the door to be certain it was secure, he leaned against the wall again. In truth, he sympathized with the lass. *Yet, what could I do for her?* he asked himself. *I'm just one man. I have my own problems.* It was a weak excuse, he knew. He shook his head to clear it, remembering well the girl's beautiful mother. This child, Jilliand, resembled her. *Pity.*

Men talk when their bellies are filled with food and wine, and in the silence of night, voices carry. Jilliand was due to wed soon. With this match, her father stood to make a small fortune. Her betrothed was a dying old man. Rumor suggested the old man would die the day after the wedding with a little help. Talk late at night indicated Jilliand would not be allowed to live after the wedding either.

Talk like that had meant little to Jilliand. She hated her existence. Death felt not so fearsome. Her entire remembered life—every night and most days—had been spent in that small guarded cell. Jilliand's only visitors were the teachers her father sent in and the older couple. The teachers her father chose had traveled widely, going throughout the land educating the Christian children. They were well aware their continued employment depended upon discretion. Not one word was spoken about Jilliand's plight to anyone beyond the burg walls. However, whenever they were with Jilliand, they treated her with every kindness. Such was the sympathy the teachers felt for Jilliand that they had continued her education beyond what most girls not of noble birth would receive.

The older couple loved Jilliand, treating her with a gentleness she knew only through them. Whenever possible, Myla made certain Jilliand knew everything that Myla knew about her mother. Jilliand knew that her mother had come from a faraway place, that she had lived in a real palace and had been kind and gentle. Myla tried her best to keep the memory of Jilliand's mother alive.

For his part, Silas talked of the world around them and of God. In his humble manner, he tried to teach Jilliand about her mother's faith. Many a night, Jilliand felt God must have forgotten about her. But the couple would not hear of it. They tried always to encourage Jilliand, refusing to let her give up.

Over time, it occurred to the lord that his only child might be given in marriage in exchange for a handsome sum. She was beautiful—just like the mother who died trying to give birth to her. The lord hated Jilliand. Always had. He had wanted a son. In the beginning, with his twisted mind, he had refused to believe she was not a son. He saw to it that she was well educated and insisted she be well trained in defense. He frequently beat her viciously for any mistake. None could fault him if she should die fighting. He could be rewarded handsomely if she died defending a king. As she grew older, though, the lord was forced to recognize that Jilliand was not a son. *Instead,* he thought, *perhaps she would be given in marriage to someone with money.* For her part, Jilliand had grown up praying that one day her life would change or that her father would love her. It never had, and he never did. Her world was ugly. She was allowed outside only when summoned by the lord for training or when he and his men went on what he called night rides. During the times the lord was away, she was allowed to visit the old couple's hut. They had provided her only touch of kindness. She loved them deeply and listened to every word about God, her mother, and a place away from her father.

Jilliand had listened to stories of a world beyond the closed cell door and the rotting logs that made up the walls of the fortress. But more often, there were long nights with silence as her sole companion. Tonight, however, with the first stirrings of hope, she would flee to that world, each step bringing her closer to freedom. Desperate to escape her life and all its horrors, Jilliand gave no thought to what she would do outside the walls. Remembering the old couple again, she prayed. "Please God, take the ones that aided me, before he gets to them."

Slowly, carefully, Jilliand crept along the fortress wall, staying out of the moonlit areas. It seemed time stood still, and every sound was magnified as she inched her way toward an unknown freedom. The entrance gate cast a great shadow onto the grounds. Jilliand easily faded through that shadow. At this point, she could hear the water—and smell it. Stepping hesitantly down the bank, she quickly undressed and stepped into the vile liquid that would soon carry all manner of the day's waste beyond the walls and into the moat. At the point where the water flowed under the wall, Jilliand realized she could never get through, even crouching. Taking a deep breath to keep the stench at bay, she knelt, then crawled. Struggling to keep her clothes out of the water and her back dry, progress was slow. Tears filled her eyes when her torn back scraped against one of the spikes. She bit her lip to keep from crying out with the pain and kept moving. Jilliand finally passed the wall, climbed out of the water, and hurriedly dressed, resisting the urge to run. Instead, she scrambled up to the top of the berm, slipped into the fortress's shadow, and carefully made her way around the wooden walls, away from the gate. Once out, she crouched and crawled down the mound of earth surrounding the walls. Again, she stripped before slipping into the cold water of the moat. Here, the water was nearly clear. Jilliand easily reached the outer bank. Dressed again, she climbed over the mound and onto level ground. She stood up, breathing deeply. The air was clean, without a hint of human excrement, smoke, or decaying food scraps that were the odors that usually permeated her cell. Taking one last look at the walls surrounding her prison, she turned away.

"Even if it must be by my own hand, I will die before I return to this place."

Jilliand gave a fleeting thought to the man she ran from. *Father wished me dead. I wished the same many times.* Her mind had cataloged the abuses. Being beaten, thrown and left to drown in a lake, the isolation—they went on and on. She never understood how to deal with the pain, rejection, and loneliness: She always believed death would be her ultimate release. "But tonight—*this*! Mother, can you *see* this? I'm free, Mother, I'm free!" she whispered into the silence, pushing thoughts of her father aside and away.

Captain Avila stood alone atop the wall surveying the grounds. He watched as the frail old man struggled to carry his bundle. Avila recalled the sadness in Silas's eyes when that very morning they had decided their plan would begin that night. When Silas reached his destination, he paused, glancing up at Avila. Nodding with satisfaction, Avila kept his post for several more hours before he left the wall and walked unhurriedly to the stables. He—like many of the men who fought for hire—had brought his own horses. Unless they were lucky enough to enlist in the service of a rich lord or king, horses and weapons were the soldiers' responsibility. Avila owned two horses, and he had been planning for a night like this.

Captain Avila had been in the service of the lord for many years. Too many. Avila's charge would soon be gone. He would leave too—taking only what he brought. No more, no less. Over the years, he had made it a habit to ride around the outside of the fortress in the pretense of securing it from the time the drawbridge remained lowered until late into the night. This made it easier for late visits by his men to the whores outside the moat. The old soldier cared nothing about these things. It was always with this night in mind that he rode. In the beginning, the lord questioned him. But eventually, the lord, like everyone else, paid him little mind.

The lord's worthless rocky lands, climbing to the southern edge of the English coast between South Seaxe and West Seaxe, were nearly uninhabitable, but they were all the lord had left of his family's wealth. Taxes levied against the few people under his power allowed only a meager subsistence for his men. Many families and soldiers fled before they starved. But the soldiers remaining were happy with the lazy life they lived. They ate and were paid. Paid very little, but what did a man need money for, if shelter and food were provided? The pittance in their pockets found its way into the purses of the women hanging around the grounds and the fortress. Everyone was happy . . . and careless.

Avila waited a respectable time before departing, making certain he was seen leaving alone to make his rounds, as always. Outside the farthest gate, hidden from sight, he had his second horse. Retrieving it, he rode away. The captain touched the locket he always wore around his neck. *I have done my best. One last job.*

Jilliand stumbled along in the dark shivering. The air was cold. Darkness separated her from everything around her, and she had no idea where she should go. The knowledge that her father would order her death caused her little concern, so deep was the hatred she felt for him.

"You must live for your mother." Myla's comment offered little encouragement now. Jilliand only knew she was alone, lost, and freezing. Silas had instructed her to go north and travel beyond her father's lands. *How far north?* she wondered. To keep the cold tolerable, she walked as fast as the black night would allow. The darkness kept the landscape a secret. Jilliand stumbled over unseen rocks, clumps of vegetation, and dips in the countryside. Slowly, she became more aware of her surroundings. She could make out shapes of bushes and trees, but the uneven ground still caused her to fall several times.

In the distance, Jilliand noticed a swath of land where the dark silhouettes of trees were missing. She headed in that direction. She came to a road. Jilliand's teachers had spoken of the patchwork of this country—pieces like scraps of old cloths sewn together for a blanket, with the remnants of Roman roads running through the whole. Although each piece was held by a different lord or king, ownership changed with the winds as men fought over the lands. Jilliand knew her father's northern boundary met a great parcel of land held by a man more powerful than her father. There, Jilliand prayed she might find safety and shelter. But a seed of worry about how she would live began to grow. She knew nothing of cooking, sewing, or tending to a home. She *could* read and write; perhaps she could find work within a monastery. *I can learn. I will be safe. Father would never challenge the monks of a monastery.* She need only find one. Early dawn found her several miles away from her father's fortress, still heading northward. She anxiously looked behind her; but so far, no one seemed to have followed her.

Her eyes took in the green, rolling hills in the distance and the trees that were gathered near the road and then scattered beyond. Birds called to one another. Flowers struggled up between boulders, splashing their color on the hillsides. Every sight was a thing of new beauty. Jilliand was a prisoner—now freed. The breezes blew her hair from her face. Once more she filled her lungs with clean air. Her mood lightened. The sun watched as the young woman walked into her future.

CHAPTER 3

THE LORD LAY IN HIS bed staring at the ceiling. When he married Jilliand's mother, he took all the wealth the woman was carrying with her. None of the men accompanying her knew exactly where she was bound. The lord had heard talk about the woman and who she was, but no one knew for certain. It had been strange that there were never any attempts to rescue or claim her. The rumor was she belonged to a rich king. But no one knew which one or his name. Even the woman seemed not to know or to care. Maybe it was all just loose talk. He quit worrying about it when she became pregnant. With a son, he would be able to find and go to her intended destination, whatever it had been. But then that old familiar feeling of bitterness washed over him. There had been no son, only the girl . . . and she was worth little.

As the child grew, the lord knew he could only hope to rid himself of her if she appeared to have some worth. To this purpose, he ensured Jilliand was well educated. Without the interfering influence of a woman, he made certain she could handle a sword with skill, and her mastery of a smaller version of a longbow was impressive, even to his jaded eye.

Through the years, he watched coldly, as Jilliand tried all she knew to garner approval from him. Nothing had worked. Her attempts only made him angrier. The truth was, he despised her but could think of no easy way to get rid of her. Too many of his men admired her and a certain quiet strength she seemed to possess. She hung on him, like a great chain around his neck.

Then one night over a year ago, around the tables in his dining hall, everything changed. Gossip told of a very wealthy, widowed lord who owned land south of his. After a year of careful talks, lies, and empty promises, the lord had finally won the old man over, and he had agreed to take Jilliand as his bride. Getting Jilliand married off was all that was left for the lord to do. And that would happen soon enough. Finally, he would rid himself of the shackle! With her marriage, he would take on a fortune.

He rolled over and threw the bedclothes off his gut. "This is the day, at last. 'Tis been long enough coming." Sitting on the edge of the bed, he scratched his chin, rubbed his balding head, and yawned. He reached over and shoved the woman next to him off onto the floor. She stumbled to the door and left. Standing to stretch, he walked to the window, which cast slivers of light on the floor of his chamber. The sun was already straight above. No matter, everything was to take place in the evening. Before the sun set again, he would be wealthy beyond anything he had hoped for. This would be his day.

His thoughts turned to his own wedding, those long years ago. His bride was the most beautiful woman he had ever seen, and it mattered little to him that she had never loved him. He couldn't have cared less; she was his. The night the woman died, he had refused to see the newborn child when he was told it was a girl. His temper was legendary, and the child suffered.

Today, he would take that child, now the picture of her mother, and give her in marriage to the aged neighboring landholder. By the decrepit future groom's own decree, the bride's father would be the guardian of the old man's widow and all the monies that would be left to her. She would be allowed to live out her life in comfort in her husband's castle. He also promised to give a large yearly endowment to the church. However, with careful planning, neither the groom nor the girl would live to see tomorrow. Both dead—perfect plan—all their fortune would be his. The lord smiled as he glanced into his looking glass.

The cruelty of the smile staring back at him made him look away. He felt a slight stab of guilt at the lies it took to get the old man to agree to marry his daughter. The lord shook his head in disgust. The idea that any man in his right state of mind would ever give such wealth to the church was beyond him; but then, most leanings of honest men were beyond his comprehension.

"Bring the girl here. She needs to be dressed," he called down the hall. He turned back to the chamber and grunted with satisfaction. Tonight it would end—finally. From the chest in his room, he pulled out the very gown Jilliand's mother had worn when they wed. The gown had cost him dearly, but at the time, he had cared little. He was to marry a woman far above his station. The lord tossed the gown onto his bed. "Tomorrow I will burn the gown. The last trace of the wretched child."

Over an hour later, a page returned, with anxiety and fear contorting his face as he stopped at the door. At last, summoning his courage and taking a deep breath, he knocked timidly. At the lord's command, he stepped inside.

"She's gone." The man trembled, dreading the outburst he knew would surely come. "There is blood everywhere."

"Who is gone?" the lord asked, frowning. "What blood? What are you talking about?" He towered over the frightened man.

"There is blood on the pallet, the floor, and the wall. Your daughter, m'lord," the page said, his voice trembling. "She's gone . . . there is nothing left in her cell."

"*GONE?! This cannot be!*" For a moment, the lord stood still. *All that wealth gone with her!* He himself had agreed with the intended husband's one stipulation: If for any reason Jilliand did not marry him, all the old man's wealth would go to the church. The lord exploded. A vicious slap knocked the hapless page to the floor. "*I'LL FIND HER MYSELF! SHE WILL WISH SHE WAS DEAD!*" Everyone in the burg scattered at the sound of his screaming pronouncements. Some scattered to search for the girl, but most scattered to avoid contact with the crazed lord.

After two hours of searching, it was clear the girl was truly gone. Nearly all his men had witnessed Silas bring her back to the cell, the same as every other night. They witnessed Silas leave without her and knew neither Silas nor his wife had left their miserable hut. The girl never ate after one of her father's sessions with her, so none had entered the cell. Not one man knew anything of the girl's disappearance. None of the people out and about the evening before had seen her. Nor could any explain the blood splattered about her cell. So much of it—surely the woman was dead.

With a rage he could not control, he had several guards whipped for allowing her to leave. He searched the old couple's hut himself. The couple stood by, the wife trembling with fear. It was clear they knew nothing about the girl's disappearance when he questioned them himself. When Silas was taken to the empty cell, he had collapsed on to the floor, weeping like a baby.

The lord surmised that someone must have raped her and in so doing, killed her. *But who?* The only man missing was Captain Avila. Undoubtedly, it was him. Cursing, crazed with anger, he declared Avila an outlaw and charged him with the kidnapping of his daughter. He had men ride to every nearby landowner carrying his declaration. A reward of gold was offered to the one who brought the captain back alive. The lord had plans for how the worthless captain would die.

As the sun sank beyond rotting wood walls, the lord sat brooding and drinking. To an empty room he admitted aloud, "Would not be Avila . . . he loved the mother. Loved the miserable wench, too. Did he take her with him? But all that blood . . . " He shook his head. Despondent and angry, he launched his goblet at the wall.

He heard the talk already going around the grounds and among his house staff. People believed the girl was killed by the lord himself. *Even when she is gone, she ruins my life! Should have killed her when she was born.* As the days dragged on, the few families that remained on his holdings began moving away. It was well known he was cruel; now it was believed he had murdered his own daughter. People were frightened about such a horrendous and sinister crime.

CHAPTER 4

AS IF SUSPENDED ON A string from the heavens, a slice of moon hovered above the waters. It cast a lonely glow over the rippling blackness lapping at the land's edge. The silhouette of the shoreline was broken by the dark forms of Viking ships. Like so many great birds of prey, they swayed with the gentle waves, pulling at their ropes, eager to take flight.

On the same western shore of Denmark, stood a lone figure. His body was wrapped in a bulky fur cloak, over a heavy woolen shirt and pants. Wool-lined boots covered his feet and legs up to his knees. Waves of thick auburn hair reached his shoulders. His upper lip was covered with hair of the same color. Each breath he exhaled left dense steam in its wake; the air was brittle, and the temperature was dropping. Tonight, as on every night this time of year, he walked alone along the water's edge. This was the season he loved best, and he always felt the familiar restless yearning to be at sea, to feel the ship dance over the swells, and taste the salt spray that stirred his spirit. He was Rurik, a Viking sea king. A man who lived for the fight, lived to die with his sword in his hand. He was Viking.

With the fire of conquest in his breast, he felt neither the biting wind off the sea, nor the cold that was heralding the coming winter. His village was settled and silent for the night. But Rurik's mind refused to rest; instead, he reviewed his supply list, the men he would take, and his route. The English to the south would be gathering in their harvest; that harvest would help sustain Rurik's people. His settlement was growing as were other settlements along the coast. *Perhaps the time comes to find new lands to settle*, he thought. *Lands with more room.*

Great changes were afoot. He could feel it. This would be a different journey. It was time. Skuld, the goddess of the future, nudged him.

He looked out to sea once more before returning to the warmth of the fire in a large house he shared with a few of his men. Surrounded by these men, he relaxed. Many of this crew were related, and all were close friends. All except one . . . Gouldon.

Gouldon was different. He was built like most other Vikings and was a wanderer, but he had an accent like men from Wales. He looked vaguely familiar to Rurik. A long history of fighting existed between their two lands, and Rurik felt certain there must be more to Gouldon's story of a great battle that had stranded him on Rurik's shores. But what? Rurik could discover no tales of a ship lost at sea from the people in the areas around him. There was nothing to confirm the story Gouldon told . . . but nothing to prove otherwise, either. Viking tradition dictated that winter travelers were to be treated well, and Gouldon had come the previous winter. Although he joined in all the activities, including the religious celebrations of normal life in a Viking village, he was brash and confrontational. After nearly a year in Rurik's settlement, Gouldon had formed no friendships among the men. He was sullen much of the time, and the man shone only when they were raiding and killing. Askold, one of Rurik's best friends and an earl—or jarl—to the Vikings, had asked more than once to be the one to call Gouldon out and end his ugly saga in the village; but, as yet, Rurik had not approved such a move. Rurik watched pensively as Gouldon once again stalked from the house after another confrontation with one of the men. Each incident and each outing brought Gouldon closer to a showdown with his sea king.

Anger seethed deep within Gouldon's soul. *He* should be the sea king of his clan from Wales, a clan that had raided these very isles, plundering several settlements, laying waste to all they found. Instead, he now fought *for* that enemy, a fact he found harder and harder to accept. Gouldon remembered everything. Three years earlier, in the breaking light of dawn on his brother's ship, they came upon a Viking settlement far to the south. Scouts told the raiding sea king that nearly every man in the village had gone. The scouts were wrong: His brother and his men were totally unprepared for what met them.

Rurik was visiting that same settlement, having arrived by land bringing his men home after a long raiding expedition. The moment Gouldon's ships were sighted, Rurik sent out the warning, and he led a full force of men to meet the invaders. Rurik's men quickly formed their legendary Viking shield wall. The men stood side by side, with their shields held in front, overlapping in the same direction. Each shield was held in the center by its owner's right arm, while his left forearm pressed tightly against the overlapping shield next to him. Thus, the wall of shields was held firm by two men for each shield. Behind the shield wall, other Viking warriors were armed with various combinations of blades, spears, axes, and swords. As the wall moved quickly against the marauders, Rurik's shield line suddenly knelt. Axes and spears flew from behind the shield wall, with deadly accuracy. Immediately the wall went up again. This combination provided an effective defense against a force that had not been expecting any real resistance. In the hand-to-hand combat that followed, Gouldon, his brother, and most of his brother's men were cut down. When Gouldon regained consciousness, he was unable to move. Dead men—his brother's dead men—lay everywhere. Gouldon watched helplessly as a sword wielded by a great Viking plunged so deep into his brother's chest that its point protruded from his brother's back. Gouldon watched the blood spill out and run down his brother's belly and onto the ground. His brother's lifeless body collapsed. When he last saw his brother's ships and remaining crew, they were headed out to the open sea, leaving behind their fallen. Near death himself, Gouldon thought he would soon leave this life. However, the gods had other plans for him. When he regained consciousness again, the battlefield was deserted and quiet—quiet with the heavy stillness of death. Inch by inch, he crawled to the cover of the brush nearby. From that moment, Gouldon would live to find the man who had killed his brother.

Every time Gouldon fell asleep, he relived the battle. It took months for him to heal. But for the help of a few men—outcasts like himself—he would have died. He no longer struggled to survive; he struggled for revenge. When he recovered enough to begin his search for the man who had killed his brother, he knew the man he was seeking was the Sea King Rurik. Although Rurik apparently did not remember him, Gouldon remembered Rurik. Gouldon swore he would take the man, his people, and his family. Everyone would pay. His thirst for revenge was such that it drove him to kill the entire band that had helped him. He would take no chances that one of them might warn his enemy. It had taken three long years, but he was close—so close it was difficult to restrain his urge to kill Rurik now.

But he waited. On the eastern shores of Northern Ireland, Gouldon had assembled a band of men, who were beginning to gather, awaiting word from him. *We will start with this village leaving no life behind.*

Gouldon looked around the settlement he pretended to be a part of. *There will be nothing left. Nothing alive. The women will watch their children die . . . before they join them.* He knew the men would fight to the death for their people. Their efforts would be useless, but they would still fight. Tonight, his thoughts only fed his anger as he walked back toward the building he shared with the bulk of Rurik's men.

He paused as he passed a smaller home. Greida might make this night worth something. He retraced his steps and knocked quietly on her door. The woman, a striking blonde with deep-blue eyes, opened her door, hesitated, and then smiled seductively at Gouldon. Their night was filled with violence. Nothing about Gouldon was gentle, and Greida would much rather have spent the night with Rurik, but perhaps this encounter with Gouldon would help bring him to her. Rurik had been with Greida frequently, but he still had not spoken of marriage. Only last afternoon, she had teased him, flirting, and invited him to visit her. But, he had not yet come to her.

Before the sun's rays pushed the darkness of night away, Rurik was up. Gouldon's visit to Greida was not a secret for long. The entire settlement knew, and with the message given to him about Greida's visitor, Rurik wanted to see the two of them for himself. He walked slowly to Greida's house and, pushing her door open, stood gripping the frame, fighting the urge to kill them both. He knew he didn't love Greida, but to have her take Gouldon—out of all the men— was the ultimate insult to him. The freezing air suddenly blowing into the room roused Greida. Neither she nor Gouldon was expecting Rurik. She sat up and started to speak. Looking at the woman who had been lying in Gouldon's arms, it was as if a steel door had closed; Rurik made a decision. Gouldon would not be coming back. Without comment, Rurik turned on his heel and left the house without bothering to close the door. Greida called out—to an empty doorway.

Two weeks later, Rurik's command ship along with two additional boats, loaded and manned, sat waiting. Families stood along the shore bidding the men farewell. Anticipation sparked the air in what was a routine part of life's rhythm that had been set long ago. While their men were at sea, the women carried on—raising children, keeping the settlement alive, and caring for each other. Rurik's return would bring gifts, grains, slaves, and other items taken by force or purchase—whichever suited best. On this day, the sea king himself had yet to board. Impatient to be off, some of the men called to him. "Let him be," advised Rurik's steersman. "We need the blessings she gives."

Near the outskirts of Rurik's village sat a small home. Larger structures built between the house and the shore protected it from the cold winds that blew off the ocean. Inside was warm and comfortably furnished. There were two more rooms in the rear of the home, open to the main area. Neither room had a door. Near the fire pit, a large kettle sat simmering, its aromas filling the air with the promise of a good meal. An elderly woman named Olga tenderly touched Rurik's cheek. He had come to bid her farewell, as he always did before sailing. "You will have great changes in your life," Olga said as she held his hand a moment longer. Her eyes held his. "Never forget, you are a sea king, Rurik. Your people have need of you. Fight well. You will return safely. This time, your fight will be different. Skuld plays with you. No matter—your future is settled." With that said, she gently pushed him toward the door.

He smiled as he walked from her house toward the shore and the waiting ship. She told him nearly the same things every time he left. The added tidbit about his "different" fight was intriguing. Skuld may be playing with him, but just as often, Rurik believed, Olga played with him too. His smile widened. He loved her. Perhaps Skuld liked what was in store for him. Who could tell? It was in the *future*, was it not? What he had was *now*. He could feel Verdandi, the goddess of the present—this was her hour. He could sense it. There would be changes. It mattered not what they were. They would be good; Olga had just said so.

Greida watched the ships slip away from the shore. When Rurik found her with Gouldon, she had hoped he would become jealous and possessive. But he only became cold. She had waited in vain while he visited Olga. It was clear to Greida that Rurik thought it was over between them. But the power she wanted was more than just being his wife; more than love. It was an obsession that she would never give up. She had several weeks to plan her move, and this time, she would not fail. Rurik had been her goal for two years now. Too long. Nothing would stop her this time. Nothing.

CHAPTER 5

JILLIAND BECAME ANXIOUS AS THE sun came up. Beyond thinking about making her escape, she hadn't had time to think about what might occur next. And next was suddenly now. The wedding her father arranged was set for today, and surely he had discovered her gone. He would be raging, but still there was no sign anyone was following her. The air was silent but for the sounds of the birds.

The rising sun confirmed for Jilliand that she was traveling northward. *Where do Father's lands end?* In the distance, the road continued into a forest. The hills beyond were much larger than any around her father's burg. She hoped there might be safety within such cover. *If there is a road, there must be people*, she thought.

Her senses sharpened by fear, Jilliand heard the horses even though they were a good distance from her. She slipped into a small clump of brush nearby, crouched, and waited. When Captain Avila rode into view, Jilliand caught her breath. He rode alone leading a second horse, studying the ground as they advanced. When he was abreast of her, he sat straight in the saddle and called, "Come, lass. I watched you leave. I'm leaving also. I would like to go with you, but you will be safer alone. Come out, so I can hand over the horse."

Jilliand peered through the branches. Avila sat still, waiting. He wore full armor with a sword at his side. For several minutes she waited. She finally decided to leave her cover, although reluctantly. "But why do you help me?" she asked cautiously.

The captain sat still, studying the road ahead. He could hear Jilliand moving closer. "I loved your mother, lass." Slowly, as he turned toward her, his kind eyes became sad. His voice softened as he continued, "When her husband lay dying, I promised to protect her. I followed to be near her." His voice broke, and his eyes moved away from her as he gazed into the past.

"Mother was married before Father?" Jilliand frowned. "How did she come to be with Father?" she asked.

"I can tell you only that there was a battle." Avila was quiet again. Jilliand waited. Then he continued. His voice was husky with memories. "Take the horse, child. Truth be faced, you'll never get away on foot. There is dried meat, water, cheese, and bread, with much to spare in the bags behind your saddle; you also have a flint and a blade. The days grow cold. You'll need a fire at night. Strike the flint with the blade over a bit of dried leaves, sticks, and such. Keep at it until the sparks catch. When it begins to smoke, blow gently, the flame will come."

He turned once more to face her. "The horse is mine, but you need it more than I. Go quickly. By day's end, you will be well out of his lands."

"Where do I go?" Jilliand asked, looking at the vast spaces around her. "Where?"

"Do not travel on the road; just keep it in sight as your guide. You must take care not to be seen alone. You would not fare well. You must find someplace where people dwell." He paused again. "This land is filled with lakes and rivers. Stay near the rivers. Look for patches of trees and listen for the sound of water. There you will find people." His voice had become normal again. "The lord won't go onto another's lands. You are free. Go, child." He studied her one more time. To him, her mother was alive again before him. Thankfully, nothing of her father could be seen in her. "You will find water easily. Stay alert. You can defend yourself, Lady Jilliand. God go with you."

Jilliand moved closer, standing at his stirrup. He leaned down and handed the worn reins of the other horse to her. He grasped her hand in his, held it for a moment, and dropped a fine chain and small silver cross in it. From beneath his doublet, he pulled out a short blade and handed it to her. With that, he spun his horse around and galloped away.

When Jilliand could no longer see him, she turned to the horse. Her relief and gratitude for this gift was immense. The animal was a large war horse that watched her with wary eyes. The saddle on his back was old and worn, bearing great gouges from battle. The reins had been spliced many times. Behind the saddle rested an old cloak that was tightly rolled with a sack tied to each end.

For a moment, Jilliand stroked the horse's neck and spoke softly to him. "My friend, you and I have far to go." Jilliand led the animal to a small bank edging the road, steadied the stirrup, and pulled herself up. Her slight build meant they would indeed travel fast. Jilliand steered the horse away from the road until it was only a distant ribbon. By the time evening's fading light sighed its last sigh, Jilliand was confident she was now safely on another's land, and she made her first camp within a small grove of trees. Her horse was nearby. Afraid she might be discovered if she made a fire, Jilliand spent the night huddled on the ground against the trees bundled in the cloak. Exhausted, she slept.

For the next two days, Jilliand rode steadily, stopping occasionally to allow the horse to rest and graze. For the first time in her life, she saw the spray of early fall. Hillsides were covered with the colors of summer's leaves slowly changing while light breezes stirred the foliage. The music of songbirds drifted to her. "If I die tomorrow, it matters little. Look at what I have seen and heard," Jilliand whispered. The landscape beyond her, covered with grasses and flowers, drew Jilliand. As her face turned to the sun, its warmth draped over her. With each step, the mantle of fear and intimidation that she had carried for a lifetime began to disappear. Keeping a close eye on the sun in order to stay northbound and on the road to keep from getting lost, Jilliand allowed the horse to choose easy terrain, and they followed the base of a small mountain.

Time passed so easily that Jilliand relaxed and soon forgot about the dangers around her. Suddenly, she became aware of voices. She reined in the horse and froze. Listening intently, she was shocked at how close they sounded. Unable to actually see anyone, she urged her horse to go in the opposite direction from the sounds drifting toward her. A man yelled, "I see her! Look! She's alone!"

Jilliand's mind raced. She was unable to see them, so she quickly turned her horse deeper into the thickets. The brush and trees were nearly impenetrable for the large horse. The men gave chase, as if she were a deer. They were laughing and challenging one another. *I must hide. I cannot fight them off. How do I hide a horse?* Desperate, her heart pounding, Jilliand stopped the horse under a tall, wide evergreen. She pulled herself off the horse and ran among the low-hanging branches of the tree. She smacked the horse, startling him. He ran a short distance and then stopped. As the sounds of the men yelling and hooves crashing through the brush grew louder, the horse bolted. Jilliand climbed as high as she could, and then, clinging to the branches, she waited. Below her, four men sped by—plowing through brush and branches. She heard one of the men call out, "Come, Sir John! We're closing in on her! We can hear the horse. 'Tis not far ahead."

Jilliand froze, barely breathing. A man rode into sight beneath her, looking up and down. He scoured the brush beneath the trees, and then slowly, he began to look up. Jilliand's heart dropped. His eyes met hers, He studied her for an endless moment, and then he nodded slightly and rode away in the direction of his companions. Jilliand sat motionless for a long time after he had gone from sight, trying to think what he might do next. Silence surrounded her. From her place high in the tree, she realized she could see the countryside far and wide around her. She could see no sign of the other riders. Cautiously, she climbed down.

She walked a distance, moving up the mountain, and then climbed yet another tree. Still, she saw nothing. Worried she had lost sight of the road, she began to come down off the mountainside. She stopped several times, but saw no trace of the horse. She had lost her horse and all he carried. This was a serious setback. After hours of walking and searching for the road, she admitted that she, too, was lost. The sun was directly overhead. She tried to stay headed northward. Dusk found her wandering aimlessly, unable to tell in what direction she was traveling because of the thick forest surrounding her. She sank to the ground and leaning against a tree, she closed her eyes. "What do I do now? I've lost my horse and haven't found people or water. What will happen to me?" she asked desperately of the growing darkness.

From someplace within the forest, a man's voice quietly answered, "You keep moving on to wherever you were headed." Jilliand scrambled to her feet and turned toward the sound of the voice, her hand on the blade at her waist. It was the same man who had seen her perched in the tree. He rode closer, with Jilliand's horse in tow. He was of medium height, muscular, and well dressed, and his horse and gear were better than any Jilliand had ever seen. He dismounted and walked toward her. Jilliand backed away. "Your horse is here, as are your provisions, such as they are. I'll build a fire for you, see you safe this night, and then I must move on." Jilliand hesitantly took the reins he handed her. "I do not know how it is you come to be alone and in such a state, but my sense is that you will never give up. Nor should you." He set about making a fire.

"Why do you help me?" Jilliand asked suspiciously, eyeing the man's back.

He straightened up and stood silently, staring ahead for a long while. When he turned to her, he studied Jilliand, her green eyes framed by dark eyelashes. "I had a wife once, who was a beautiful girl, inside and out. She was with child. While I was away fighting, my lands were overtaken, and she tried to escape. Men found her. When they finished with her, both she and the child within her were dead. I would not wish that for anyone."

He shared what he carried to eat with Jilliand. Neither spoke. Still not speaking, the man unsaddled both horses, rubbed them down, and prepared a sleeping place for Jilliand near the fire. Far from her, he spread a blanket and lay down. His easy, even breathing told Jilliand he was asleep. She finally lay down to sleep.

In the morning, both horses were saddled and ready to leave when Jilliand awoke. The man gave her what was left of his supplies. Lifting her onto the horse, he rested his hand on the horse's neck. "Where do you ride, lady?"

"North," Jilliand answered.

"Why?" he asked, watching her closely.

"I . . . I have to go north," Jilliand insisted.

"But why?" he asked again. His head turned slightly, and his eyes narrowed. "Why north?"

In a voice barely audible, Jilliand answered him. "Because I must leave unspeakable horror behind me." She paused. "I do not know where his lands end. I only know I must go north."

"How long have you been running?" The man's voice was gentle.

"Three days."

"Then you are beyond whatever boundary you sought to leave behind. You are in West Seaxe. The lord over this land is a kind man. The road is below you there." He pointed. "It leads north. If you keep in this direction," he nodded toward the mountain base, "you will meet it. But you will be riding through thick forest without protection. Until such time as it is retaken, it is a road frequented by thieves. Not a safe place, certainly not for a woman alone." He patted Jilliand's horse. "However, if you travel more northwest, that way," and again he pointed, "you will leave the mountains and come to a river called Test. It's a safer route for you. Follow it and find people. God go with you, m'lady." Without another word, he mounted his horse.

As he rode away, Jilliand called after him, "And with you, sir. Thank you." He waved at her without looking back. Soon he was lost in the trees. Jilliand rode northwest.

That evening, as she searched the sky for the fading sun, Jilliand noticed an abandoned bird's nest. It was falling apart, barely clinging to a dead limb. From atop her horse, she was able to reach it. *Tonight, I'll have a fire.* A short distance farther, she came to a tiny clearing sheltered by trees and brush. She took care of her horse and then set about making camp. She struck the flint repeatedly, sending sparks into the nest. At last, smoke wafted upward hesitantly. Gently blowing, coaxing it, she finally had flames. Gathering all she could find to burn, her stack of firewood grew. The fire blazed and cast a warm glow around the area. Jilliand lay close to the fire and said out loud, "I'm lost and alone, but I am free. Mother, can you see me? I will live. In spite of Father, I will live." Listening to the sounds of night, Jilliand began to drift off to sleep.

"I am a woman in body only," Jilliand whispered drowsily. "Of what use is a soldier's training to a woman?" Time spent with the old couple at her father's burg made Jilliand keenly aware that she knew nothing of those things she imagined a woman must do. "I cannot cook or sew. What will people think of one such as me?"

"Even so," she heard the night breeze reply, "your father cannot get to you. That is what is most important."

Jilliand's eye caught the old soldier's eye, and he nodded. "I too am alone now. For your sake, I kept a promise I made to your mother so very long ago." As he spoke, a woman's form moved closer, surrounded by mist.

Gasping, Jilliand sprang straight up. *Was that a dream? Was that my mother?* She looked around, and all was just as she arranged it. Clinging to the silver cross hanging from the chain around her neck, she lay back down. The memory of a mother only known through stories would keep her moving, despite the uncertainty that lay ahead. The young woman closed her eyes and, once again, sleep found her.

The next morning, as the sun playfully tossed its full rays through the trees, Jilliand was already on the move. By forenoon, she came to a rapidly flowing creek. It gathered strength as it roared alongside the mountain to eventually plunge over immense boulders and crash into a small lake below. Following the river running from that lake, in due course Jilliand left the mountains behind. Horse and rider pushed onward until they were overcome by darkness. And so it went for several more days.

Many nights, as she settled near the fire, her cloak wrapped tightly around her shoulders, she tried to envision an end to her trek. Her life's experiences were meager. She was raised as a son, and she was well educated. That much she knew. Would that help her? The nights were long, and Jilliand slept little. She sat hugging her knees, staring at her fire. Images of her life swam around her. *What have I ever done that will amount to anything or that would make me valued?* She squeezed her eyes shut as tears filled them. *How am I going to be able to live? I only know how to fight.* Disheartened and alone, Jilliand began to wonder if she would have been better off dying. But when she at last lay down, she saw beautiful stars that filled a dark sky. Listening to the sounds of night creatures around her, her heart began to soften. "No. Better to live," she said softly. "Better to

make him the fool. I live, Father. Despite all that you have done to me, I live."
The small flame of survival, planted by Silas on the fateful night she escaped,
began to grow.

CHAPTER 6

JILLIAND'S GROWLING BELLY AWOKE HER. The bags hanging from her saddle were nearly empty. "They tell me my blood is royal, but even the royal must eat," she noted wryly as she broke camp. That afternoon, she reached a point where the stream she followed joined another, forming a tributary that slashed a wide gash through the land. Two boys were playing on the opposite bank. They stood to watch her.

Riding a short distance downstream, Jilliand found a place where the embankment sloped gently to meet the rushing water. She urged her horse into the river. The animal was tentatively stepping forward when the bank suddenly disappeared. The horse went under, struggled to break the surface, and began to swim. Floundering to stay on the horse, Jilliand lost her grip on the reins and saddle and fell into the icy river. Instinctively, she clawed at the stirrup but was not able to hold fast. Thrashing about, she managed to grab the animal's tail, and with all the strength she had, she clung on.

When Jilliand and the horse reached the other side, the two boys stood frozen, staring at her. Coughing and gasping for air, Jilliand staggered upright and stood to catch her breath. Her horse was breathing heavily but was unharmed. Jilliand looked at the two boys, who were curious about her. She forced a smile and moved toward them. They looked as ragged as she did. Two pairs of great round eyes followed her movements. The larger child stepped closer and spoke, "Who would you be?" Neither he nor his small companion made any motion either to help her or to leave.

"I am alone. I have nowhere to go." Jilliand held her breath, ignoring the question.

Finally, the older lad nodded knowingly. "Come with us. There be others like you." With that, the three left the waterway and walked toward a small hamlet, Jilliand's horse in tow. People nearby barely took notice of them.

The community was much like most of those scattered around England in the 800s. The inhabitants were poor, barely scratching out a living from the land. The huts showed evidence of repeated repairs and makeshift additions. Every face bore the strain of life. The women could look forward to a wrenching childbirth that saw many infants and more than half of the mothers perish. Of the children who lived, few survived past the second year of life. All members of every family worked hard to maintain a meager existence.

Jilliand had no way of knowing how desperate the lives around her were. She only prayed she would be allowed to stay. Entering one of the huts, the younger boy returned with a sympathetic-looking woman. After a quick survey of Jilliand and her horse, the woman nodded. "These two are my boys. This 'n is Kemp. He's the older. Norvin is the littl'n." Smiling kindly, she invited Jilliand into their home. Jilliand handed her horse off to the boys. "I'm called Avril," the woman said.

"My name is Jilliand," Jilliand replied, as she followed Avril into the house. The house was a simple one-room rectangular structure. A pit for cooking and heat was dug into the earth near the center. Smoke drifted up through the flimsy roof. There were two small sleeping mats to one side, and the back part of the room was set apart by a cloth hung on a cord strung across the hut. The cloth was pushed to one side, exposing a larger sleeping mat. Cooking and eating utensils were hung and stacked near the entrance. The floor was earthen. Having been swept many times, it was smooth and hard. Compared to the cell that had been her home, the room was grand. Jilliand hovered near the fire, until she slowly warmed up and stopped shivering. She watched as the woman went about preparing a meal.

When the woman's husband came in, he took one look at Jilliand and thought she must be another straggler left from raids on shoreside villages to the south. "They've started early this year. I'm sorry about your loss. Your horse is in the pen." Jilliand nodded politely. She could see he was not necessarily pleased to see her. Though he spoke softly, Jilliand overheard him ask his wife, "Another mouth to feed, woman?" The wife simply touched the man's shoulder and nodded. The man shook his head but did not respond.

Dry and much warmer, Jilliand offered to help. "May I help, m'lady? Perhaps there is something I might do for you." The woman watched her pitiful efforts to assist. *She speaks well; not like us. She knows nothing about what to do. Where did she come from? I wonder if this lady may have been waited on by the likes of me. She doesn't belong here among us, that's for sure.* Avril was moved to pity and prayed Jilliand could earn her keep. She knew her husband was right. Jilliand was another mouth to feed for a family barely staying alive.

"Come," the woman gently urged her. "There be enough for everyone." Gratefully, Jilliand ate the bread and fish that was offered. The two boys chattered away, as if Jilliand had always been with them. Relieved for the diversion, Jilliand sat listening. Cautiously, she began to relax.

"Days will be shorter soon. The cold comes early. There will be little food for the animals this year," the man predicted, glancing at his wife. "'Twill be a hard winter," he warned. "Should start stacking wood . . . " His voice trailed off. "Nothing to feed the animals . . . " He stared toward the door. With a start, Jilliand realized she could possibly lose her horse.

"Still, we be luckier than most," the woman noted quietly, watching her children. "We still fish. We will be fine, husband." The woman smiled at her husband, squeezing his arm. The family had nothing extra to share, and Jilliand accepted the fact that she could not stay long. *I will ride on as soon as I rest.*

When the meal was finished, the family sat gathered around the fire. The children laughed and teased each other, unaware of life's problems. Jilliand felt a wary sense of comfort. She hugged her knees and watched the flames dance. *Surely there are boats coming through here. Perhaps I can barter work to get passage for my horse and myself to someplace where there are more people. These people are barely existing. I was taught there are larger places. I must find these places.*

"My husband is Calder," Avril told Jilliand, as she cleared some space. Using blankets, Jilliand's cloak, and some dry straw, she made room for Jilliand to sleep next to the boys. For the first time in her memory, she slept on a soft mat. The boys giggled and talked in the dark. Jilliand could hear the man and his wife speaking softly, the wife laughing. *Sounds of life,* Jilliand thought. *Is this what a family is supposed to be?*

Farther south of Jilliand's temporary home, a band of Vikings was about to strike a village without warning. As still as the death they brought, their ship rolled up the river Test under cover of a thick early morning fog. Men fishing along the river never heard the raptors from the north. The warriors were nearly at the first of the huts before they were seen. "This will be a dead run, I fear," Dir, Askold's brother and Rurik's second jarl, noted. "These pitiful people are barely surviving. There will be nothing of value here."

"They might have a harvest. And women, certainly," Rurik replied. "Besides, I am most interested in moving farther up this coastline. Not one village will be skipped. Move quickly." Leading his men, the Sea King Rurik gave a great cry. The men fishing were quickly cut down. "When will the English learn? They can never defend this land with men who cannot fight. This will not even be a challenge," Rurik muttered.

The man who saw the first hut go up in flames ran yelling, "They come! The Vikings have landed!" Mayhem broke out. Most of the men grabbed whatever they had close at hand and bravely stood to defend the women and children trying to scurry away. The invaders killed every man they came upon and rounded up the women and children who were unable to escape. The women who fought back were beaten, raped, and eventually killed. In less than three hours, it was over. There was little harvest and nothing of value. Looking over the children huddled together near the shore, Rurik shook his head. "We will have a long winter if we do not do better than this." He gave the order, and the captives were loaded onto the boat. The boat headed out to sea.

In a day, he met up with his *knarr*—a large cargo ship with a wide hull capable of carrying may tons of cargo. The human cargo they had stolen and a small stash of grain were easily transferred to the vessel. By early evening, Rurik was headed back to the coast. Standing near the bow, he spoke to the two men he trusted most, Askold and Dir. "I think we should keep going upriver. When we were much younger, we took that river once. It flows easily from farther north."

"There are settlements along the way?" asked Dir, frowning. "I do not remember what is beyond."

"There is a monastery farther up. Not large, but enough for us. Just beyond yesterday's landing," Rurik noted. "If we find it soon, we take it; if not, we turn back and go south. There are many places for us to play along English shores." Smiling, he walked back toward the stern of his ship. This was only the beginning of his raids. There would be plenty of time, but the fire of conquest burned in him nevertheless.

Before the sun rose, Rurik's ship was already moving away from the remains of their last stop. There was no sign of life. They moved farther up the river without finding any sign of people. In the afternoon, Rurik's men hid the ship. His crew split into four groups. Each was to scout a different area. If the men returned without finding the monastery, Rurik decided to turn back. Around the fire that night, the men talked. Their report was not a good one: Only one village was found and no monastery. The men left the decision to Rurik. He had always done well by them before, and the raids had only just begun for the winter. Time was on their side. Gouldon, as usual, argued. "We should never have come this way. We have nothing to show for this stop. Why do we stay? We want gold or something of value!"

Exasperated, Rurik challenged him, his voice low and menacing. "If you can tell me of a better idea, please do so. If you do nothing but pick apart my ideas, then be silent. There is no monastery. There is only one settlement. This will be our last stop before we turn and move farther to the south."

At the sound of his voice, a hush fell over the men. Rurik's voice was warning enough. Gouldon ducked his head, mumbled, and walked away from the group. "He needs to leave this life he finds so miserable," Dir noted with disgust. Rurik did not respond, though he was of the same frame of mind for many reasons. Rurik remembered the look on Greida's face: It had been one of panic, instead of her usual expression of cunning. Gouldon's expression held triumph.

In silence, Rurik returned to the ship. A thick layer of clouds set in during the night. By early morning, it began to rain hard, and by midday, the ground was soaked. The downpour dragged on most of the next day. The men were unwilling to fight mud and rain, so Rurik's ship remained anchored and hidden. Lookouts posted around the area kept watch while other men collected rainwater. The fresh water would replace the soured milk they had nearly finished. The rains stopped, but Rurik still waited. Wet huts would not easily burn. Even hunting was forbidden. He knew his men were getting hungry, but hunting required fires to cook the meat, and that was a step he would not take. Surprise was one of his many weapons, and smoke from a cooking fire would ruin that weapon.

CHAPTER 7

AFTER ONLY A FEW DAYS, her acceptance by the people in the settlement gave Jilliand a sense of comfort. Perhaps if she did her share, she would be permitted to stay—at least through the cold time, the time when people would struggle, and a time that Jilliand dreaded. Menfolk preparing for winter were busy cutting and stacking wood, bundling dried grasses to feed the stock, and bringing what few animals they had closer to the settlement. The older boys in the village were working the fields, harvesting what they could of the dying crops. The young ones who were left behind began to follow Jilliand around the settlement. Everyone assumed she had been orphaned in a Viking raid, and she was never questioned about her past.

Determined to earn her keep, Jilliand tried to learn about cooking, making bread, and smoking fish. It was in catching fish that Jilliand proved she could contribute. When a boat stopped by their village, the men were able to barter fish for other goods. Eventually, Jilliand let the boys sell her horse. She stood out of sight and witnessed the last piece of her past disappear. When the boys brought her the money, Jilliand handed it to their father.

With each day, she became more certain this was where she should be and that she would stay and make her place with these people. She began to feel a sense of belonging. One evening, when the family was outside, Jilliand dug a hole beneath her sleeping spot, laid her mother's pouch inside, and covered it with her mat. Her fear was ebbing. She started to feel she had a family.

Kemp and Norvin became her constant companions. Avril treated Jilliand like a sister and patiently taught her how to cook and clean. She taught her how to dry and use the plants they gathered to treat illnesses. The days passed, and life began to have a comforting rhythm. She loved roaming the gentle hills nearby nearly every morning.

One morning just after dawn, Jilliand saw it. Her throat tightened at the sight of a broad expanse of smoke coming from someplace in the distance. Jilliand watched the thick black curls turn to grey as they dissipated in the early morning sky. She quickly ran back to the village. Not wanting to frighten anyone, she hurried to catch Calder. But before Jilliand could speak to him, she saw him pulling his wife aside. "Make ready. Smoke comes. We'll be next," he warned. Avril nodded and hastily began to pack a basket. With a stab of fear, Jilliand watched the boys playing outside with the other children. *I must protect them. Somehow, I must protect them*, she thought.

The next morning an unexpected quick storm swept through. Jilliand stood in the rain, letting it fall over her. With her face turned upward and her eyes closed, she cried, and her tears ran with the raindrops. She was filled with fear of what must surely be coming to her newfound family.

During the following several days, the worry about the Viking raids seemed to be forgotten. Everyone was working to bring their few cattle in. The harvest had gone better than anticipated, and the village continued preparing for winter. The mood in the village seemed as if this was just a routine change of season, but the light chatter around her felt out of place. The couple smiled at Jilliand during the evening meal, as the boys discussed who would be the first up to go fishing with Jilliand. That night, she tried to forget the fear of raids, rolled over, and finally fell asleep to the sounds of her new family.

The next evening, Jilliand sensed something was wrong. She and Avril were hauling wood for the family's fire when Jilliand said, "Is the winter so cold? I feel something more than the coming snow might be upon us."

"Aye, lass . . ." Avril answered. Her voice trailed off when one of her sons ran to meet her.

As they reached the hut, Calder hurled himself toward them, shouting, "They come! Quickly! We leave now!" Grabbing what they could carry, he pushed them all out. Some of the men were arming themselves with laths, or sticks, or whatever else they could find. Other families, like Jilliand's, were simply running into the surrounding hills as fast as they could.

At first, Jilliand desperately ran with them, holding on to the boys to make sure they were keeping up. But then she stopped and turned back. *These people are not soldiers. They have no weapons. They will lose. I must try to help, somehow.* "Leave!" she shouted. "Go quickly! If I survive, I will come to you. Seek shelter with the lord of these lands." Both boys were crying as Avril and Calder wrenched them away from Jilliand. Jilliand had seen what would be left after such raids when her father forced her to witness the remnants of such an attack. No one was left alive. Jilliand ran back toward the village. What she saw filled her with horror.

The raiding party came down upon the village with deadly precision. The weapons and shields the Vikings used were unlike any Jilliand had ever seen. She realized her short blade was of little use. *I must do something.* She ran toward the huts that had not been set on fire and tried to help the remaining women and children get away, yelling at them to keep moving up into the hills She returned repeatedly to pull villagers from their huts and get them away from the fighting. The battle was spreading, and the village was in chaos. The farmers' futile attempts to defend themselves and the lack of real weapons spelled doom for this settlement, like it had for so many before.

She rounded one of the huts that was still standing and scanned the disaster surrounding her. Clearly, it would all be over soon. She was struck by a thought that stunned her: *Mother's pouch!* She ran back toward the hut where she had hidden it. She ducked inside.

Sounds outside the hut were quickly changing. The initial battle cries faded. Jilliand knew the main fight was over; the real horror, at least for the women and children, had begun. Now, the fight's aftermath gave voice to the dead and dying. Wounded men moaned in agony, begging to leave their hell. Women, many already dying, screamed as they were handed the fate of the vanquished. Children wept and screamed as they were dragged from their lifeless mothers. They would not be held hostage and ransomed. Their parents were poor. Their lord was poor. Their pitiful lives were worth little to the marauders. Jilliand felt a sudden stab of fear as a realization hit her. *Maybe some of the children will be spared. But not me; not this time. There is no way out for me.*

Her heart pounding, Jilliand crouched against the wall of the hut as far from the entrance as possible. She forgot about the pouch hidden away. She had not moved fast enough. In trying to help everyone she could, she now found herself trapped. When they came for her, she would force them to kill her before she would be taken. She waited, listening to the awful din. The sounds of humanity dying on all sides rose and fell.

Jilliand's face was covered with soot and blood, her clothes were torn and ragged; she looked like every other wretched soul trying to survive. A strange calm came over her. She refused to stand still and wait for death. The will to survive rose in her chest. Jilliand had to move now if she were to have any chance at getting away. Standing up, she crept slowly to the entrance, trying to determine how close the invaders had gotten.

One by one, each hut was being torched. *Before long they will be at this one.* Her head felt scrambled, and she could not think clearly. Jilliand could hear men talking as they went about the business of destruction. Angry at how little gold or silver was to be had, the victors would be in no mood for mercy. They never were.

As Jilliand slipped out through the opening of the hut and slid along the side, her movement caught the eye of a lone Viking. He stood waiting, his eyes following the dark figure. *Strange this one only comes out now. Perhaps he hides something.* Loath to miss the opportunity of finding anything of value, he watched intently.

Jilliand had stopped and, flattened against the wall, she waited while several men passed. The sun caught her long wild hair, lighting it like a flame. Filthy and ragged, she looked worse than a street urchin. She did not move like one, though. She did not move like she belonged in this village. She was lithe and graceful, athletic, strangely calm, even calculating. Surprised, the man watched her, studied her. *Dressed like a man, this one is, but this one is not a man. She must have thought to fool me.* Scorn shone in his expression as his eyes followed her. He waited. Would she duck back inside the hut—or run?

Jilliand intended to slide around the side of the hut, but when she turned to be certain she was not followed, a man stood only a few feet from her. He saw the line of her face, her mouth, and her full lips. Her eyes caught his. The green of her eyes was like the jewels on the hilt of his sword or the green of the first spring grasses. Jilliand froze, and her eyes locked onto his. He studied her with a new interest. A slight nod from him indicated that she was to come toward him. Hesitating for a heartbeat, she walked out, her head high, her hand on the handle of the blade hidden beneath her shirt. *No, she will not run,* he thought. *She looks unafraid, ready to fight.* He made a quick decision. *She goes with us.*

Jilliand knew there was no one to help her. She glanced at the dead lying everywhere. The huts were nearly all gone. Her eyes turned back to the man. He was tall, lean, and muscular—just like all the rest of the invaders. His auburn hair, wet with perspiration, clung to his head and curled under his helmet. A thick mustache covered his upper lip and dropped just beyond the edges of his mouth. This one looked to be the leader. Gold and silver rings adorned both arms. Around his neck hung a heavy silver amulet in the shape of a hammer suspended by its handle. His mail was splattered with blood. From his waist hung a long sword. In one hand, he held a shorter blade, and in the other hand a large round shield. He stood contemplating her, his eyes narrowing.

Jilliand absorbed the images of the carnage. Three women lying nearby were barely conscious. They were lying naked, beaten, and blood soaked. Jilliand studied the man watching her, and her eyes moved back to the women. *Would that be her fate?* As if he had heard what she was thinking, he walked over to the three and, as she watched, quickly slit their throats. After which, he wiped the blood of his weapon on the belly of the last. Jilliand stepped back, horrified, nearly falling. Pointing to Jilliand with the same blade, he signaled to one of the men, instructing, "Take her on board and see she is not touched."

Although she could not understand him, she knew she was taken. Her eyes darted back to the hut. The man turned and walked away.

When one of the men approached her, she pulled her own blade, but he was quicker. His sword was at her throat, and he gestured toward her blade. Reluctantly, she let her weapon drop. He jerked his head in the direction the rest of the captives were going. Jilliand looked once more at the pitiful remnants of the village, then at the Viking standing before her who was waiting for her to move. Jilliand stepped over the smoldering remains of huts, and dead and dying bodies, to join the line of children filing ahead of her toward the raiders' ship.

CHAPTER 8

MOST OF THE INHABITANTS OF Jilliand's village were either killed or taken as slaves. Some who had run in the beginning like those Jilliand helped may have survived. The pillagers seemed more intent on leaving than chasing anyone once they realized there was little of value to be had. The Vikings held one boy aside and dragged him throughout the village to witness the destruction. He would be released to take the tale to his lord, and word would spread. Fear was a great weapon that the Vikings understood well.

What little grain the village had gathered in was soon piled onto the ship. Jilliand was taken to the bow and left there while the rest of the captives were loaded. She trembled as she looked out and took in the horror these brutal people had left behind. Twice she had tried to help the little ones being shoved onto the deck, and both times, she had been pushed down and a sword put to her throat. She stayed seated and silent after that.

When the ship was loaded, it finally moved away from the shore. From her place on the deck, Jilliand studied the men at work on the boat. They were all tall, athletic, and agile. When they began to row, their oars dipped into the water in perfect rhythm. The ship's operation was precise and smooth. She saw the man who had found her. He was standing at the bow of the ship talking to his steersman and the man who had put the sword to her throat. The three men laughed and turned to look at her. She glared back at them defiantly.

From his place at the ship's bow, Viking Sea King Rurik was barely aware of his ship's movement over the water. He thought only about transferring these captives and heading back out quickly. Winter would come soon, and his own people would need whatever he could bring back. This raid had netted very little, only a few children for slaves. *Oh, and the girl.* He turned to look for her again. Askold had told Rurik about Jilliand's repeated efforts to help the other captives. Rurik knew she was not part of the village. Her clothes, though dirty and torn, were of a finer material than the villagers wore. The blade Askold took from her was well made. Rurik's eyes moved over her figure. Frowning, he studied her. He could imagine what she might look like if she dressed as a woman or maybe was not dressed at all. Now smiling to himself, he turned away.

With the crew steadily rowing, the shoreline was fading behind them. As the ship rode the waves, Jilliand felt her stomach begin to churn; her mouth filled with bile. She pulled herself up and leaned over the side. The nausea and vomiting came in bouts that surged over her. Eventually, the feeling began to ebb. Clinging to the boat's side, Jilliand glanced behind her to see that most of the children were also ill. The crew was busy and took no notice of them or Jilliand.

Nightfall brought with it an uneasy calm for the captured passengers. Except for the low voices of the crew and an occasional child crying, an eerie silence settled over the vessel. Jilliand scrutinized what little she could see of the ship in the darkness. The middle portion of the ship had low sides. *Not a barrier to anyone trying to leave,* Jilliand noted. Oars protruded from holes lining both sides of the ship at precisely the same height and distance from each other. The oars moved in perfect rhythm, rapidly pushing the ship farther and farther from the shore. The ship's carved stern rose high above the sides of the vessel, making a great seaward arch and coming to an elegant point, as did the bow. The bow was higher than the stern, and at the top of the bow's point, a figurehead rose. Jilliand noticed its face had a carved, fierce grimace.

With the cargo, weapons, and captives, the boat was completely packed. Jilliand studied the weapons again. The blades the men carried were longer and larger than any Jilliand had ever seen. The round shields were also much larger. A man would have to be strong to carry and use such weapons. With a critical eye, she studied the crew. They were indeed strong, and most were taller than the men Jilliand had seen. She was an eyewitness to how they easily dispensed with the few protectors of her pillaged settlement. *How would these men do against a* real *soldier?* She had yet to see that confrontation.

Jilliand's gaze drifted off beyond the crew and ship, to the ocean surrounding them. She had never been near the sea, let alone on it. A great expanse of nothing rolled out before her. Jilliand watched as the boat moved across the water. The sea was at once frightening and gentle. It was a quiet night without so much as a puff of air.

Several men began to work the riggings, and soon, a huge sail was unfurled. Jilliand watched in amazement as the giant cloth billowed with the breeze she could not feel. Looking over the side again, she caught her breath. She was surprised at how the vessel moved with such grace and ease. The boat flew on top of the sea as they rode the waves. Forgetting for a second that she was a captive, she looked to the sky. "How is this possible? I have become part of this thing. We move like the clouds," she gasped.

As the wind picked up, so did the boat's speed. Jilliand faced the wind, closed her eyes, and let it blow. Her long hair flew behind her. So caught up in the experience of being, Jilliand failed to notice the men at the bow and several others who were watching her intently. She breathed deeply. The air was clean. Jilliand had been held captive for so long, every new experience was a taste of freedom. Opening her eyes, her shoulders slumped. She would have to find a way off this boat and away from these men. Vikings were not known for their kind ways with the English, especially those for whom a ransom would never be paid—like Jilliand. *Where do these men go? How can I get off?* While these thoughts flashed through her head, she remembered old Myla's words: "You are of noble birth, Jilliand. Remember who you are." Unconsciously, she straightened her back.

She knew one thing for certain and thought, *When I get away, I will never stay with another helpless village. I will find a court somewhere. Someplace that is protected by soldiers.* Right now, it was useless to think about her past or future. She leaned on the boat's side, staring out at a darkened world. Her current situation was daunting. Once again, as with her father, her life was not hers to govern.

When the sun began its ascent, the ship dropped its sail again. The vessel moved slowly toward the coast, hugging the shoreline. Rurik walked to where she stood, watching the sea. Jilliand quickly turned when he came close. She had no weapon, but her body movements were instinctive and defensive. He wondered if she hid another knife at her waist. Purposefully, he quickly moved to her left. With practiced agility, she stepped away, turned, and faced him. He pulled his sword out.

"You would strike down an unarmed woman?" Jilliand admonished him. "But of course you would. I know what you left behind." Her tone was sarcastic. He may not understand her words, but he would know their meaning.

His narrowed eyes never left her face. Removing his smaller weapon, Rurik tossed it to her. "Now you're armed. What can you do?" Though his language was beyond her, his intention was clear. Like a flash of lightning, she caught the sword, held it squarely, and half crouching, began to move around him.

"I see you have been trained. But can you fight?" Rurik noted, as he swiftly moved in on her. Jilliand easily stepped to one side and moved behind him.

"You think to tire me? Good." He studied her. *I would know who taught you.*

There was no mistaking his intentions. For the first few moments, he toyed with her; she moved with confidence, never coming too close, yet not avoiding the fight. Jilliand moved in and away, as she pulled him closer to the side of the ship. The thought came to her that if she could get close enough to the side, she could easily jump over. The shoreline was near enough. Distracted, and concentrating on possible escape, Jilliand tried to step around him again, but this time he was ready. As if he read her mind, she found her chest against the tip of his sword. Rurik nodded toward the deck. Locked on his piercing blue eyes, she struggled to understand. Again, he spoke and nodded to the deck. Not certain what else to do, Jilliand tossed the sword in the direction he nodded.

Rurik's eyes never left Jilliand, and she could hear the men chuckle who were watching. Her chin raised, Jilliand placed her hands on her hips and stood defiant. "You've lost," Rurik noted. Now the men laughed out loud. Rurik studied her a moment longer, shook his head, lowered his sword, and retrieved the smaller blade from where it lay. Jilliand stood glaring at Rurik.

Rurik turned his back on her and walked away. Jilliand had to bite her tongue to keep from shouting at him. *Of what use would it be for me to taunt him? He understands naught,* she reminded herself. One of the Vikings stood aside, watching the exchange with a cold smile on his face. He had no use for the woman, and even less for Rurik. It was clear to him that the sea king fancied the woman. Gouldon's mind began plotting.

Jilliand soon found she was free to wander about the ship, in what little room she could find. No notice was taken of her; it was as if she were a ghost. Yet at times, she felt she was being watched, and she caught different men looking her way. For the most part, their glances seemed to be just curious ones. While she didn't feel frightened for herself, her heart ached for the little children sitting numbly along the deck. She tried several times to speak with or comfort them but was pulled away each time by the same man who stopped her before. He shoved the children if they attempted to get close to Jilliand, so she gave up for fear he might hurt them.

Later in the evening, they came upon a *knarr*. The two ships easily maneuvered into position side by side, were tied together, and the transfer began. All the cargo and captives were being loaded onto the larger ship. It was evident to Jilliand that both ships were under the same command.

When the captives began to board the second boat, Jilliand walked in line with them. She was nearly at the exchange point when she felt strong fingers grasp her arm. Rurik was holding her back. He never spoke; he simply held her firmly until the transfer was complete, and the second boat had begun to move away. Releasing her, he returned to his post at the stern.

Once more, Jilliand felt the sharp ache of loss. Her time in the settlement had given her a taste of belonging to a real family. For the first time in her memory, she had begun to sleep without fear and even to laugh. With the Viking raid, all that had changed. She watched the larger boat disappear as if it had never been. Moving as far away from the men at the bow as she could, she sought someplace to sit protected from the damp breeze. She crammed herself against the stern of the vessel with her arms wrapped around herself. Closing her eyes, Jilliand thought about the old couple from the castle, the closest thing to parents she had known. Her mind wandered to the teachers who had been allowed to come to her. They were kind to Jilliand, telling her of all the places they had traveled. As each session ended, they had listened as Jilliand read to them, from whatever books they carried. She smiled, remembering how quickly she learned Latin and French, when she realized the guards could not understand her. For the first time in a long time, she remembered the old priest who came to see her when her father was away. When her father found out the old priest was seeing Jilliand, the priest was killed. Suddenly, her thoughts turned to her father and turned dark. But she refused to allow fear and uncertainty to seep into her mind. Instead, she tried to remember all she knew about her mother.

Time dragged on. She began to shiver, and her eyes flew open when someone roughly grasped her arm. She made a weak effort to pull away, too cold to do more. It was dark now, with heavy clouds hanging so low the air felt thick. She stood before she recognized the man. Gently this time, Rurik nudged her ahead of him. Back at the bow, he pointed downward and pushed her to the deck. Pulling his cloak from his shoulders, he tossed it over her and then walked away. Grateful for the warmth, Jilliand huddled against the ship's side. Exhausted and lulled by the gentle sway of the ship, she slowly drifted off to sleep.

CHAPTER 9

AWAKENED WITH A JOLT, JILLIAND looked around, disoriented for a moment. It was early morning. Men along both sides of the ship were holding their oars motionless. Rurik stood near the steersman at the bow, watching the water. At Rurik's command, the men on one side lowered their oars and pushed. With another shout from Rurik, the opposite side pushed. Jilliand stood up and slipped unheeded to the ship's edge. She was surprised to see the men steering the craft up a narrow inlet in the land where the river Avon ran quietly toward the sea. Rurik glanced at her briefly, and then kept his eye riveted on the waters below and ahead, constantly calling back and forth to the men handling the oars. Slowly but steadily, the ship moved up the passage. After a long while, Rurik stepped back and studied the land on both sides carefully.

Jilliand heard Rurik yell something to his men. Then she watched as the oars were held out of the water and the men sat waiting. It soon became evident why they waited: The tide was dropping. When Rurik called to the men again, everyone jumped from the boat. Jilliand paused only a second, then followed suit, bounding easily over the side.

"The Norns sent her to you!" the steersman shouted. Rurik glanced back at Jilliand without comment. The boat was lifted onto land. In short order, it was hidden beneath bushes and branches. Rurik walked up to Jilliand and pushed her down next to a tree near the boat. To her horror, he bound her to the tree. She could shift slightly and move her limbs, but the rope around her waist held her securely.

Without speaking, Rurik turned and led his men upstream, following the river. There were settlements along this river ripe for Viking harvest. Jilliand watched in disbelief as their voices faded off into the distance. Unable to reach the knot securing the rope, she leaned against the tree. Jilliand could do nothing but wait, surrounded by silence while the anger inside her began to mushroom. She was a captive, tied to a tree, like an animal. The familiar feelings of rage at her father were taking root again.

In the stillness, Jilliand suddenly caught the faint sound of footsteps coming from somewhere behind her. The steps were deliberate, careful, stealthy. Whoever it was did not want to be seen. The sound of the steps grew closer. Tied to the tree, Jilliand would be easy prey for the owner of those footsteps. Time froze. Jilliand took a deep breath and waited. Gouldon stepped suddenly into view. On this day, he planned his revenge. Because Rurik fancied the girl, he decided to take her for himself, knowing he would be gone before the men returned. Jilliand tensed, waiting for him to make his move.

When he first reached for her hair, she easily dodged his hand. He stepped back, a malignant sneer on his face. Squatting down, again he reached for her. This time she could not move away. Grasping her hair, he jerked her toward him, smashing her lips with his mouth. She turned her head to the side, while desperately trying to push him away. Gouldon only laughed. He moved to sit straddling her legs, pinning them beneath him. He pushed her neck against the tree and began to choke her until she became limp. Releasing his grip and quickly dropping his weapons, he loosened his shirt, while Jilliand struggled to regain consciousness. Retrieving his short blade, he easily cut through the ropes binding Jilliand and then tossed the knife aside.

With one movement, he was on her. One hand groped her breast, while the other tried to tear her trousers open. Jilliand fought hard. Twisting side to side, she pushed against him with both hands. Gouldon laughed at her desperate attempts with a cruel glint in his eyes. She realized he was only toying with her. She knew she was no match for his strength. Suddenly, he pulled her away from the tree and slammed her over, face down, onto the ground. Her nose and lips hit the earth and began to bleed, while the clouds of dust gagged her. Gouldon ripped her shirt up and began to jerk her breeches down. She pushed up onto all fours and tried again to claw herself away. The man grabbed her, lifted her slightly, and then threw her back down, her arms flailing and her head slamming into the dirt. Jilliand's outstretched fingers hit the handle of Gouldon's blade, lying where he had tossed it. Gouldon's breathing had become rapid. He was no longer toying; he was wild and intent on taking her. He was on top of her. Gripping the blade handle, Jilliand turned the blade over so her thumb hooked firmly on the end of the handle, giving her better control. With every ounce of her strength, Jilliand swung it around behind her. She caught Gouldon by surprise and plunged the knife deeply into his side. Stunned, he sat up. Before he could move again, Jilliand quickly pushed herself up onto her side. Gouldon was bleeding profusely and weakening now. Twisting around, she wrenched the blade out and stabbed him again. He tried to speak as blood gushed from both wounds and onto Jilliand. He sagged backward. Blood dripped from his mouth and down his chin. He stared at her in disbelief. Jilliand shoved him. He toppled over and lay dying. Working her feet free from beneath him, she used both feet to push him away.

Gasping, she crawled back to the tree. *I have killed one of the Viking's men.* Numb, Jilliand stared at Gouldon's body. "I think I may have called for my own death," she whispered. With her back against the tree, she looked around. What would happen now? The ropes were still lying in the dirt. The knife was deeply embedded in Gouldon's side; blood oozed from both wounds. Bruised, bloody, and barely dressed, she knew it was over. She had no doubt the Vikings would search for her if she tried to run—especially now, with their companion lying dead. It would be dark soon, and she had no idea where she could go or hide. Jilliand knew they would come for her. The Vikings were not likely to let this go—especially it being an attack by a woman. She was defeated. Weak and shaking, she stared at the man's body. *I think tonight I die.*

The mist riding the river enveloped Jilliand. By the time the men began to return, she was trembling with the cold and still huddled against the tree. At this point, Jilliand lacked the will to even try anymore. The Vikings were in a victorious frame of mind, laughing and talking. Some brought grain, others brought gold, and still others brought various weapons. Fear rose in Jilliand's throat at the sounds of the returning crew and her captor's voice.

Rurik walked toward Jilliand, intent on removing the ropes, but when he saw the dark form lying near Jilliand, he stopped in his tracks. He called for a light. When the torch was brought, the men surrounded her. The battle needed no explanation. Blood was splattered over her breeches and what was left of her shirt. Her face was battered and bloody. Gouldon was half naked and dead, the knife still in his side, a second wound below the knife. Blood from both wounds had pooled on the ground under him. Rurik studied the body, then Jilliand. Shaking with the cold and now fear, she sat staring ahead. Rurik looked back at Gouldon again.

Several others of the crew spoke out. The dead man had been seen frequently watching the girl. Dir placed his hand on Rurik's shoulder, and their eyes met. The blade was well used, Dir observed. The girl apparently knew to how to turn the blade and strike between the ribs. Dir looked at Jilliand and at the rest of the crew. The men kept talking. Jilliand could not understand anything and, at this point, did not care. Her life had run its course.

"Hmm," Rurik said as he grasped the torch and turned to Jilliand again. "Was this your first kill?" He spoke in English with his voice quiet. He held the light near, watching her face. Jilliand only nodded, still staring into the darkness. Rurik walked with the torch around the tree and beyond where Gouldon lay. Again, he stood before her, his torch lighting her face. "Why did you not fight when you were first taken?" Rurik asked in his lilting English. *Why*, he wondered, *did she wield the weapon so well now but not use it during the raid on her village?*

It took a moment for Jilliand to understand his question. *He speaks English*, she realized, as her mind began to focus. Turning her large emerald eyes to his face, she replied simply, "My blade was too short." Rurik's brow shot up in surprise. She was correct, and she knew it, *but how?* Rurik handed off the torch and then leaned down. Easily lifting Jilliand, helping her stand, Rurik studied her face, and his eyes moved over her shaking body. Satisfied, he nodded again. It was clear: Gouldon had not gotten what he died trying to get. *But the woman . . . how did she know what to do?* Rurik helped her onto the deck of the ship and then handed her a heavy woolen shirt. The shirt draping over her small frame provided relief from the biting cold.

Rurik took up his post at the bow. Jilliand staggered to the stern. He saw her leave but did not respond. With the night's gentle wind blowing through her damp pants, she began to shake again. The shirt was soon damp, too. Wet, cold, and chilled to the bone, she was no longer numb or afraid; she was angry. *I must get off this boat. I'll freeze while they are out plundering, if one of them does not kill me first.* She felt her anger intensify. Rurik's crew was not concerned in the least. It seemed the incident with Gouldon was over. Was it over for her? How soon before another man tried the same thing? *Am I safe?* Jilliand wondered. At some point, she felt someone near. Rurik did not attempt to move her. He dropped his cloak over her then walked away. Grudgingly, she wrapped the heavy fur close. She needed its warmth.

The ship moved on, hugging the land's edge. Rurik did not speak to her and let her stay as far from him as she could. When the men left the ship the next time, he came to tie her up again, but she sat down before he could. As he leaned over with rope in hand, she said quietly, "I know not why you do this. I will not run from you." To her surprise, he paused, looked at her, and simply dropped the rope. She stayed still. He left her alone, unbound and free to move. *He understands me. Do the rest of these men also speak English?* He had not spoken to her of Gouldon, but Jilliand could feel he was not angry with her. In fact, it was as if the incident had not happened.

When the Vikings returned, Jilliand was standing against the bow, trying to stay warm. As Rurik approached, she moved away without looking back and again moved to the stern. Trying to block the wind, she sat against the side of the boat, her teeth chattering uncontrollably. Too cold to move, she remained still. She felt someone grip her arm, pull her up roughly, and begin walking with her. She stumbled, trying to keep up as she was pulled along. Rurik guided her back to the bow, sat her down hard, near where the three men usually stood, and again draped her with a heavy cloak. "Thank you," she murmured. Rurik gave no indication he heard. Under the warmth of the cover, Jilliand drifted off to sleep.

Rurik stood at the bow, his arms crossed over his chest, staring out to sea. He knew none of his crew had any regard for Gouldon and were not concerned about the method of his departure. In fact, they all were relieved he was gone, such was the effect of his moods on the rest of them. His men knew the woman clearly belonged to Rurik; they would not give her up and would protect her. Whether Gouldon had any kin that might try to avenge him, no one knew.

Rurik turned to look at his men and then turned to look at the small woman sleeping beneath his robe. He did not worry if someone sought Gouldon. He would deal with that problem, if it became one. He watched the waters. He always felt he knew Gouldon from elsewhere but could not remember exactly. Now, it bothered him. Rurik glanced at his friends. *Who among us can tell what the sisters of fate have in mind?* Watching Jilliand sleeping, he wondered aloud in English, knowing the men could not understand him. "How is it the fates bring me a Christian?" With a caustic smile and shaking his head, he added, "A fighting woman, dressed as a man." Rurik looked over at Jilliand's small form. There was no answer.

CHAPTER 10

RURIK AND THE VIKINGS CONTINUED to raid. They stopped, plundered, moved off to sea, and returned to raid the next site. Each time Rurik came to Jilliand, she promised to remain. He left each time without restraining her. This night, they did not hide the boat. When he came to her, Jilliand noted with sarcasm, "Are you not tired of this? You have to know, I'll not run from you."

Rurik reached out to her. Surprised, Jilliand stared at his hand. She hesitantly placed her hand in his. He pulled her up and removed the chain she wore around her neck. "What are you doing!?" Jilliand's hand went to her neck. Rurik's eyes locked onto Jilliand's as he calmly dropped the chain and cross into a small pouch hanging at his side. Around her neck, he hung a chain with a hammer amulet. Stepping back from him, Jilliand tried to remove the chain. Rurik stopped her. He did not speak, but his expression was clear. Slowly, Jilliand dropped her hand. Silently, Rurik gripped her wrist taking her to the side. She looked at him and then at the men who were now bounding over the side of the boat. Gripping the side, Jilliand leapt over. Wading the short distance to the shore, Jilliand waited as the men gathered around. Everyone was talking and laughing. When Rurik joined her at the bank, he took Jilliand's wrist again and walked to the front of his men with her in tow. *What is he doing with me?* The answer hit her. *He thinks to sell me!* Aghast, she glanced around looking desperately for some way to escape. There was none. With her heart in her throat, she walked toward the unknown horrors of life as a slave. Rurik's men continued to talk among themselves, but as usual, Rurik was silent. There was a smattering of huts whose occupants went about their day, disregarding the Vikings.

In a short while, Jilliand could see a settlement ahead. Near the entrance of a great hall, Rurik dropped Jilliand's wrist, draped her with his cloak, and simply walked inside. Jilliand felt the silence in the room when he entered with her walking freely at his side. His cloak, made of a dark hide, was soft and shining, and it set off the deep copper of her hair though her hair was matted and dirty. Calmly, she walked beside him. *I know not what happens here, but I am not chattel. I am my mother's daughter,* Jilliand reminded herself. Her heart beat rapidly with growing fear, but she refused to allow that fear to show. No one could see what she was feeling.

Seated, she glanced at the men filling the room. All looked like her captor save the men in one group who looked to be English. They were seated near Rurik and immediately began to talk among themselves. "She sure looks like the wife. The wife is dead. Must be his daughter. Was she kidnapped?" The comments came to her across the room as it quieted. With a lurch of her heart, Jilliand realized *she* might have been recognized.

Jilliand remained still, even when two of the Englishmen approached her, and one offered to help her get away. Discreetly shaking her head, she resisted the urge to look at Rurik. The man persisted, asking her why she wouldn't try to leave. She only shook her head again. Although Rurik appeared not to notice, halfway through the meal he leaned to Askold, speaking softly. The food was a welcome change, as were the ale and wine. The men from Rurik's ship ate heartily, though they drank very little. When business and pleasure were done, everyone departed. Rurik walked back, with her in tow, to the boat.

He finally spoke, in his strained English, "Why did you not try to leave?"

"I keep my word. My word is all I have left to me," Jilliand replied. He took her hand and gently folded her fingers around the chain and cross that he held out to her. She dropped the chain over her head and kissed the cross. "Thank you." This time, he nodded slightly, as he took the amulet he had given to her and slipped it over his head.

At some time during the night, the sounds of fighting awoke Jilliand. She jumped up. Rurik and most of his men were gone. The rest were looking toward the burg where they had dined. Jilliand could see nothing, and as the sounds faded, the men on the boat relaxed and began to lie down. Jilliand watched the horizon for a while, but could see nothing. It was clear: The men were not worried about anything. She too lay down under a cloak and drifted off to sleep.

At first light, Jilliand was shocked to see only one ship beside theirs remaining in the cove. That ship was burning. The shore was lined with its crew, all hanged. Among the dead were the men who had offered to help her. She turned to Rurik, but he was already taking the boat out to sea. Jilliand watched the shore shrink away in the distance. Her mind was numb, her heart heavy. "They did nothing wrong, nothing to challenge him. What manner of man is this who captured me? He is no better than my father!" she whispered.

The ship had been at sail for three hours when Rurik came and stood next to her. "You were recognized," he said simply. Jilliand studied the deck; she had not thought what being recognized might do to her or what her father might do. For a long moment, he stood with his arms crossed over his chest, looking out to sea. "By whom were you taken captive before?" He spoke quietly to her, his voice even but with authority. Jilliand wanted to move away from him, as she turned seaward. Rurik's assumption could mean Jilliand's value for ransom was nothing. It could mean she was not worth keeping alive if she didn't belong to anyone. She tried to think what she could tell him. "I asked you a question," he prodded firmly.

"I was never taken captive," Jilliand finally answered carefully. He was well spoken, now that she thought on it. *He is well educated,* Jilliand realized, wondering how she missed this about him before. He looked at her, then back out to sea. Jilliand felt he was trying to match what she said with what he must have heard the evening before. Quietly, she added, "I ran away."

Surprised, Rurik frowned. He looked at her for a long time. "A woman should not dress as a man," he finally replied. Disapproval flashed in his eyes and dripped from his voice. Rurik knew a Viking woman would never be dressed in breeches. In Rurik's world, women were expected to dress as women. He could little understand how it could be any different.

"A woman does whatever she must, to survive," Jilliand responded coldly. "Just as a man does." The stillness between them was thick. Jilliand turned and walked away, leaving him standing alone. She could feel the tears well up in her eyes. Years of refusing to cry in front of her father came to her rescue. She quelled the urge. Loneliness blackened her mood again. *Just when I begin to let my guard down, life reminds me where I am.* Jilliand stared into the dark. *I am changing. I feel more comfortable with these people. I am not so afraid most of the time. Though I know not what I feel. I have seen so many cruelties, yet they treat each other with respect. My people do not do that very often. And my people can be terribly cruel, I know only too well. I am not who I once was. Who am I? Who am I becoming? What would Mother think of me?*

Jilliand's mind returned to her captor. *Had he had every man killed to keep word of me from spreading? Does he think he would lose a ransom? Does he think I would bring him a ransom because I am a young female? I have nothing that would show wealth.* Jilliand struggled to understand. The village she was captured in was pitiful. She had no signs of wealth about her. Her blade and the cross she wore were all she had with her when she was taken. Suddenly, with a stab of pain, she remembered her mother's pouch. *There is a reason I forgot it. If he saw the ring with its great stones and the beautiful silken bag with its gold thread, he would certainly know the worth of it. Then for certain he would believe I would fetch a large ransom. What will he do, when he finds out I am worth nothing?* Jilliand could only think she might become a slave for his household. *Could I do that? Do I have a choice?*

At some point she knew, he would surely make his demand for payment. *But from whom? He must not know who my father is.* She belonged to no one, and she was worthless, although the Viking wouldn't know this yet. Until he did, she must live day by day. Was she really as safe as she felt? Why could she not leave when they were off raiding? She owed this man nothing. Despite that, she had given her word. *Of what value is honor to me now?* Jilliand argued with herself. *Why did I ever promise to stay is the greater question?*

Over time, she learned more about his crew, ship, and Rurik himself. Although he had not spoken to her since that one night, she drew comfort in knowing he could understand. Whenever he was not at the bow, she stood near the steersman, trying to see what he saw in the waters. The older man had begun to point, without speaking, to the waters. Jilliand slowly began to pick out the rocks, sandbars, and other markings.

One day she shyly pointed at a dark shape in the water before the steersman had shown her. He smiled at her, nodding. As the afternoons went by, she pointed time and again, as she learned to note the depth of the water, the direction of its flow, and the nearby landmarks. When Rurik came close, she moved away. *There will come a time, when you will not walk away,* Rurik noted to himself softly, watching her leave.

Each time Rurik left the ship, he approached her. He never spoke: He simply nodded, then left. Jilliand was grateful the men seemed not to notice her now. There was an unspoken truce between them, and she was becoming more comfortable. One afternoon, the crew returned with more women and children. Nearly all the children were listless and coughing. The adults behaved much the same. Many were perspiring heavily. Jilliand approached him. "Are you leaving again soon?"

He did not respond, so she continued, "Most of the people you bring this night are very ill. Your men may become ill, too. While at sea, you could lose many of your men. Better to not take these people. Let them go free, and pray you did not bring their illness back with you." When he did not respond, Jilliand walked away. *He's been told. What he does about it is up to him.* She hoped he would send them back to land when he had time to think on it. The entire crew could become ill. At sea, it would mean almost certain death.

Rurik walked among the newly captured slaves. When he was satisfied with what he saw, he gave an order. Shocked, her hand at her mouth, she watched with horror as every last one was thrown overboard. Moving as far away from him as she could, Jilliand crouched on the deck, covering her ears, trembling. The desperate begging of the drowning women and children exploded in her head. Rurik was unmoved. Jilliand rocked back and forth, with her eyes clenched shut. *I've been captured by an animal. Worse than an animal. I have to get away.*

Rurik watched her, frowning. As always, when speaking to his men, Rurik spoke in his mother language, aware Jilliand would not understand. "She saved us, the crew of the *knarr,* and possibly our village. She is angry I removed those infected?"

Askold watched Jilliand for a moment and then replied, "She is angry they all died, I think." Askold casually observed, "She is a strange one, that woman. Like the Old One at home." Rurik looked at his friend sharply, then back at Jilliand. Shaking his head, he turned back to the steersman.

They sailed for three days before they reached another unknown shore. Jilliand continued to move away whenever Rurik came near. His expression gave her the impression he was amused at her reaction. She tried to convince herself she was more determined to escape if she were given the chance—before Rurik discovered if Jilliand had a ransom or not. In truth, Jilliand realized the advantages of living in relative safety aboard the ship—for however short a time that might be—and that was holding her to the promise she had made. A promise she was not certain she could keep.

The sun was just beginning its afternoon descent when they beached again. Rurik walked to where Jilliand sat watching the crew, ignoring him. She had nowhere to turn, with the stern at her back. When he stood so long without speaking, she looked up to see Rurik had a different expression as he studied her. He nodded slightly toward the delicate cross at her neck. Holding her breath, she sat still, unmoving. He stood as if he had turned to stone. Reluctantly, Jilliand removed her cross, holding it tightly. He held the hammer out to her. She refused to take it. Rurik slipped the chain and hammer over her head and held out his hand. Jilliand shook her head, grasping the cross even tighter. He studied her through narrowed eyes. He did not move, but his jaws clenched. "Please," she whispered. He did not move, nor did his eyes waver. Slowly, she gave up the cross. He tucked it into the satchel tied to his waist. Grasping her wrist, he pulled her up. Silently Jilliand prayed that this might be the place she could leave him. Nodding toward the shore, Rurik waited. *I am tired of him not speaking. Even more reason to get out of this,* Jilliand grumbled to herself. Without looking at Rurik or his men, she jumped over the side and climbed up the bank. Rurik followed.

Off the ship and on shore, he walked to the front of the men, glancing in Jilliand's direction. For a short moment, Jilliand thought of not moving. She knew she had to go with them.

The river's edge was close to a moderately sized village. Rurik's entire crew roamed around, obviously comfortable. As occasionally before, they paid for supplies and goods at some stops. The reaction of the people to them proved that the Vikings had been in this place often. No one was frightened, and most were friendly to the crew. Jilliand realized with disappointment that she would not be able to slip away unnoticed at this stop without someone alerting Rurik or his crew. While they traded and walked among the inhabitants of the small hamlet, Rurik behaved as if she were one of his crew. Jilliand knew the Vikings had traded without killing at other settlements too. What made one place good for trade and another for death? Because nothing was left in the villages they plundered, Jilliand knew she could not slip away unnoticed at those places. She had to get further inland. The excursion seemed to be very relaxing for the men as they strolled along visiting with the townsfolk. For the crew, it was a welcome break—for Jilliand, it was discouraging.

Three days later, with the tide pushing the waters higher, the Vikings traveled down yet another river called Stour. The river was wider and longer; its path twisting with sharper turns, as it flowed toward the sea. The Vikings did not hide the boat this time but left it tucked against the bank at one of the deeper bends. Walking past Jilliand to leave, Rurik nodded to her, as usual. Most of the men had already started walking away, headed inland. When the boat was secured and silent, and the last man gone, Jilliand stood watching the water, thinking. Her hair was dirty and stringy. Her face and hands were grimy.

Gouldon's blood still stained her breeches, and the shirt Rurik had given her was filthy. The crew would be gone at least two hours. Time enough . . .

The land rose gradually into a gently rounded hill. Although unable to see beyond the rise, Jilliand could see the shore before and behind the boat. Glancing over her shoulder at the empty and still landscape, Jilliand made a decision and took off the dirty garments. It felt strange to stand naked without fear. Despite her current lot, she was relaxed. Life now was better than it had been in her cell when she was forced to fight and subjected to pain every day. With her clothing in hand, she bounded over the side. Once in the water, she began to wash her shirt, trousers, and leggings. When they were as clean as possible, she wrung them and tossed them up onto the deck. Swimming to the farther bank, she pulled the blooms off a plant growing near the water's edge. Smelling the flowers, Jilliand smiled. For the first time, she would use flowers when she bathed. She then turned her attention to herself. With an unfamiliar sense of freedom, she bathed and washed her hair thoroughly, over and over, rubbing the flowers into her hair each time. Then, impulsively, she played in the water.

Suddenly, Rurik stopped walking and turned back toward the ship. His two companions laughed knowingly and moved on without him.

The boat was moored far upriver, with a long narrow finger of land between it and the sea. Rurik returned for Jilliand. He jumped over the side and onto an empty deck. Rurik made a quick round before his jaws clinched in anger.

Making another round, he noticed a small mound lying on the deck. Picking it up, he held wet pieces of well-worn clothing. He could hear splashing. Crossing the deck toward the sound, he saw Jilliand in the water, and his scowl was slowly replaced by a smile that played about his face. As his eyes reflected his burning desire, Rurik studied her. Totally uninhibited, she swam, splashed, and dove like a young sea creature.

When Jilliand dove deeper and began swimming toward the boat, Rurik moved to the end of the bow, her clothes still in his hands. Amazed, he watched her easily pull herself up and over the side of the boat, using the oar hole for support. She was athletic and graceful. Jilliand shook her hair loose, brushed the water off her body, and suddenly realized her clothes were gone.

Panic set in quickly as Jilliand looked desperately around the deck. Then her eyes caught sight of Rurik, leaning back against the bow, a lazy smile on his face. With a gasp, she whirled around, covering her chest with her crossed arms. He walked slowly toward her. She could hear him coming, step by step. There was little she could do. She stood helpless, humiliated, fearful, waiting.

Rurik reached out, slowly taking her long hair in his hand. He brought it up to his face, smelling the flowers she had used while bathing. Gently, he pulled her hair aside and stopped at the sight before him. He stared and then carefully traced with his fingers the scars on her back. With his hand on her shoulder, he turned her around. Jilliand stood, with her arms still crossed, waiting. She refused to look at him. He moved her arms aside exposing her and catching his breath. She was more beautiful than he had imagined all these past nights. She was slender, yet she had muscular arms and legs. Her small breasts were firm. Her belly flat.

Jilliand could no longer stand the scrutiny. She made a weak attempt to take her clothes from him. He pulled them back. Jilliand wanted to crouch, to hide, but there was nowhere to go. He walked around behind her again, pulling aside all her hair to expose her entire back. "Who?" he asked quietly. Jilliand remained silent. "Who," he demanded again, this time with a ring of authority in his voice.

"My father." She covered herself again with her arms.

Rurik remained silent, studying her scarred back. Softly, Jilliand continued, "He wanted a boy. I was raised as his son." She paused. "In the beginning, things were not so bad, but with time . . . " Forcing herself to look to the horizon, she continued, "Some things are impossible to hide."

He walked around to stand in front of her again. He gently moved her arms aside once more, brushed her hair away from her face and studied her. His eyes were kind and sympathetic. "Yes, some things are." He handed the clothes back to her. She pulled the wet things on clumsily. Slipping the cloak from his shoulders, he placed it around her.

"The name of this man?" he asked, holding her arms firmly.

Jilliand now met his eyes, her own eyes angry. "He is not a man," she answered bitterly. She tried to pull away, but he held her fast. Pointedly, she looked at the hands holding her captive.

"His name?" he persisted. His grip remained firm.

Carefully choosing her words, Jilliand explained, "I ran away because he sold me to an old man who was dying. When that man died, my father would have that man's wealth."

"It would belong to you." He corrected her. "Even the English recognize that, unless your husband owed someone."

"I would be dead," Jilliand replied flatly. "The men were named who were to arrange my death."

Frowning, he continued, "You know this?"

"I do," she confirmed quietly, looking away.

Though his grasp had loosened, he still held her, his eyes filled with passion. He pulled her closer. Gently, he persisted, "You will tell me this man's name."

Unsettled, she looked up at him. After a long moment, she quietly answered, "No! He will not pay you. The man I was to wed no longer lives. I am worth nothing." Her voice dropped. Fearing his response, Jilliand held her breath. It was out: He would now know that what he had captured was worthless.

"To him, perhaps," Rurik responded, his voice low. "To me, there is no prize I would take for you. I will know the name of the man who would strike you." He released her arm.

Stunned, Jilliand could only look at him as he watched her. She could think of nothing to say. Silently, she stood. "I am called Rurik," he finally announced, waiting.

"I am Jilliand," she responded softly. Stillness surrounded them, but this time, it was a comfortable stillness.

"Can I bring you something?" he broke the silence, turning to walk away. It would not do to bring her around where someone might recognize her.

"Yes, a bow." She quickly added, "A small one with shorter arrows."

He turned back, surprised. "You can use it?" he asked frowning.

"A longer blade too." She watched the surprise open his eyes. "I have retained all that I have learned, and I will use that training if I must."

He nodded slowly, remembering the well-placed knife wounds that killed Gouldon. His eyes traveled over her slight figure, now swathed in his cloak. Nodding again, he left. Jilliand sighed. For the first time in her life, she felt no fear about her new life. Somehow, she felt safe. "A pagan, God? You bring me to a pagan?" she asked, her eyes raised to heaven. "My walk will be with a pagan." She gazed at the landscape beyond the water's edge. Peaceful. "Yet, I am safe—for now."

Jilliand felt someone shake her gently. Jumping up, tumbling over the robe now at her feet, she found herself nearly on him. The sun had just risen. A hush still hung over the ship; most of his men were sleeping. Rurik grinned, "You are happy to see me?"

Hoping it was still too dark for him to see, Jilliand could feel the heat in her face. Before she could answer, he thrust a sword into her hand. He ordered her to do something in his mother tongue. Jilliand instinctively felt the weapon for balance and tested the edge. He nodded in approval. He ordered something again. Jilliand hesitated, not certain what to do. His language was still beyond her.

Suddenly, he moved in on Jilliand, his weapon in readiness. She immediately stood in defense, loose but careful, as she moved quickly around him, forcing him to turn to keep with her. She held the sword in both hands, poised and ready. Again and again, she moved around him, only to move quickly back as he advanced. He laughed, staying with her. He began to move on her, and she easily stepped aside. She was more skilled than he had imagined. He quickened the pace, forcing her to move. Jilliand deftly evaded his sword but was not able to avoid his free hand, which easily caught her hair. Slicing at him, she forced him to loosen his hold. "Ah, you do well. We have played enough. Now we end it," and with that, he advanced on her so handily she soon found herself backed against the boat's side. For a short while, she held her own. In the end, he flicked her sword aside. She spread her arms wide, held her chin up, and waited.

By now, most of his men had formed a ring around them, cheering and laughing. He smiled his approval. When he touched her throat with his sword tip, she refused to flinch. Putting his weapon away, he handed her the sword and said something that, again, frustrated Jilliand. When they were alone, he spoke in English. When his men were about, she understood nothing he said.

Rurik walked to the stern, took an old animal's hide, stretched it, and tied it in place. With a piece of charcoal wood, he marked a spot on it. Returning, he handed Jilliand a bow and a quiver of arrows. She smiled with delight. "You remembered." Running her hand over the bow approvingly, she took one of the arrows. Carefully pulling the bow she tested the weight. *A little tight, but this will do fine.* Turning to him, she asked, "From where?"

He looked from her to the hide. He pointed to a spot on the deck. She stood where he pointed but shook her head. His eyes narrowed, and he pointed to the spot again.

"As you wish. It is too close, but . . . " With that, she shot three arrows into the marked spot. Askold retrieved her arrows. Every man on the boat was silently watching the two of them. Jilliand looked at the target, backed up far behind him, and raised the bow. He stepped aside. Again, she placed three arrows in the spot. Suddenly, the Vikings began to cheer her on.

With the next step back, Jilliand knew she would be sorely tested to hit the target. English longbow men were legendary, but their bows were longer and stronger, as were their backs and arms. With brows knitted, concentrating, she notched the arrow. The men erupted in cheers when the third arrow found its spot. Jilliand knew they had accepted her because he had taken her side; but on this day, she swore she would give no man reason to doubt her. Avril and Calder had accepted her because of sympathy for her imagined plight. These men accepted her because of the person she was to them. *I know not where this leads me, God. But I know You are with me.*

Her thoughts turned to the men on the boat, and while she despised the cruelty they had shown their adversaries, she had to admit that the English did much the same with those they captured. The Vikings were the first men, other than Captain Avila and Silas, who now treated her with respect. Never had she seen men so bound to their leader. They willingly followed him wherever he led them. Perhaps she would also . . . perhaps.

At the mouth of a large waterway, Great Ouse, the ship had been anchored waiting for the tide to rise. It now moved silently up the swollen river. When they reached the predetermined spot, the boat was tied securely though not hidden. Jilliand stayed behind. The crew seldom drank water, preferring ale, beer, or soured milk, as water, when available, was often associated with illness. However, one of Jilliand's teachers told of many rivers all over England, fed by fresh water sources from springs. Taking several flasks, Jilliand set out to search for a spring. When she returned, she was laden with fresh drinking water. Once more, she set out. By her third trip, the bird calls near the boat were familiar. Setting the filled flasks down on the deck after her fourth trip, she was acutely aware of the sudden silence. Not one bird sang. An ominous feeling engulfed her.

Whatever quieted the birds was beyond the stern. Staying low, she gathered her bow, arrows, and blade. Bit by bit, she crept around the deck, searching the shoreline.

Their smoke was visible before she saw the line of men. Moving stealthily, the men were coming toward the ship, many carrying cauldrons filled with burning wood. Jilliand stood, held her breath, and aimed an arrow at the first man. He fell. Silence was shattered by yells coming from the attackers. Changing positions, she notched another arrow and felled the second. By this time, the men were sending fire arrows toward the boat. She stood and felled a third. When she stood for the fourth, a flaming arrow just missed her, hitting the deck. She hastily wrapped an arrow with a strip of her shirt. From the deck fire, she lit an arrow of her own. Jilliand fired back toward a large mound of dried undergrowth just beyond the line of men, now running toward her. The flames grew rapidly. She prayed Rurik and his men would see the smoke. Using one of the water buckets, she doused the flames on the boat.

Standing, Jilliand was unable to notch another arrow before she was slammed backward with the impact of a well-placed shaft. Its force was such that it went clean through her, entering her body just below her collarbone, nicking the shoulder blade as it passed. She fell to the deck, stunned but still conscious. "I have to get off the ship," she gasped. Rolling over, clutching her weapons, she crawled, dragging her way across the deck. She slid over the side, putting the boat between her and the oncoming line of men. Her left shoulder was throbbing, and her arm was nearly useless. She was forced to let go of her weapons. "I do not think I can do this," Jilliand gasped. Doggedly, she struggled until she made the distant bank. Only when she had pulled herself onto land did she realize she was bleeding. She was too weak to do more than collapse. Lying on the bank, she saw dark curls of smoke from her fire had risen high into the skies, carried by the breezes. Jilliand could hear the Viking battle cry in the distance as her world went black.

Rurik and his men were loaded down. A very bountiful harvest had just been gathered by a smaller burg and monastery. That harvest now belonged to the Vikings, along with weapons and jewels found inside the burg's keep and gold from the monastery. Each man carried equal shares of grain and gold. Most also carried weapons. They would need the grain and other stores for the long winter ahead. Rurik knew they had more than earned their bounty. He carried several gowns, some robes, and a stack of blankets. He tucked jewels inside each gown and packed everything into salvaged bags. Catching one of the horses from the burg, he tied the bags onto the animal and led him out. This was a good run.

As he reached the last rise above the boat, he saw the smoke. The cry went out. Men dropped what they were carrying and ran to battle. The attackers heard the Vikings and turned their attention from the boat to Rurik's men. A brutal hand-to-hand battle ensued. Vikings were legendary for their ruthless, fearless fighting, a reputation well earned. Both sides fought ferociously, but in the end, the Vikings prevailed. A battle was won, but the boat was damaged. Looking for survivors, Rurik ordered every man found be put to death. They found three men killed with Jilliand's arrows. Jilliand was not on the boat.

Some of the crew returned to where they had dropped their bounty. Others began repairing the ship. Bloodstains on the deck were a foreboding sign to Rurik. He jumped into the water. Unable to find Jilliand in the water, which by now was beginning to rise, Rurik immediately headed toward the distant bank. Wading up the bank, he anxiously scanned the area. Then he saw her. With his heart in his throat, he picked her up and labored with his load through the rising water, back to the boat.

Jilliand remembered nothing of what happened after she crawled onto the bank and faded into darkness. She awoke to the slight motion of the ship and the voices of the Vikings. She tried to sit up but was not able. Her chest was bound tightly. Her arm was bound and immobile. She was now clothed in a soft, thickly woven gown. Cringing, Jilliand wondered how many men had seen her naked. She tried to rise again but this time was gently pushed down from behind. Standing near her was the old steersman. He shook his head and walked back to his post. The mild rocking of the boat lulled Jilliand to sleep again.

When Jilliand next woke, she was able to sit up. Her chest felt as if it were torn from her, and her shoulder ached, but her arm felt better. She struggled to stand up, grasping the side of the ship. She could see Rurik and the steersman at their usual place. Intent on watching the waterway, no one took notice of Jilliand. Grateful for the privacy, she tried walking. Finding she could move normally, if more slowly, she walked the length of the ship, steadying herself. Repeating the process, she swayed against the ship's side. Wobbly but determined, she paced. Finally exhausted, she slid down the side near the stern, leaned back, and closed her eyes. One of the men brought her a small flask. Opening it, he tapped her shoulder and motioned she should drink. Taking a swallow, Jilliand coughed and gasped as the liquid burned its way down her throat. She tried to return the container, but the man shook his head, grinning, and left the flask with her. She took another swig and then another. As the warm liquid flowed down her throat into her empty stomach, Jilliand relaxed. This time when she stood, she was light-headed and strangely happy. The ale proved very effective in relieving the throbbing of her wounds, though not in her ability to walk straight. Jilliand gave up, slid down the side of the boat, and leaning back against the ship's side, she slept again.

The ship moved farther out to sea. With the passing of days, Jilliand's wounds were healing. Days rolled into nights. The men now acknowledged her when she walked past. Rurik watched her but had not spoken since the battle. To Jilliand, it did not matter. She knew she was safe. That was enough. The weight of worry about her father had gone. Rurik knew full well she would bring him no bounty; he didn't care.

It hadn't taken long for Jilliand to discover that her silver cross was gone. *I pray Rurik has it.* Jilliand spent long hours staring at the sea spread out before her. She was treated well, and there were no walls around her. Her life was not charted, and she had no defined rights or privileges, but she had endured. She was alive!

PART TWO

CHAPTER 11

THE MONTHS CLASHED WITH THE weather, while the aged Captain Avila grappled with loneliness. At one time, he was the favorite of the crown prince of Spain and his wife. Honored by the royal couple, he had supreme command over her guard and was frequently chosen to carry out special assignments. The prince on his deathbed had summoned him again, asking one last favor from his captain. He asked Avila to keep his wife, the English princess, safe. Avila had done his best to honor that command; though as fate would have it, it would not be long for the wife. Avila would end up caring for her daughter. As the princess lay dying, while she gave her daughter one last breath, she made the same request of the soldier. These days, all of that felt like a lost dream. Life makes no promises, nor does it smooth the road for its travelers. Once honored and loved, he now fought for anyone who offered shelter and food. The schemes of men meant little to him. His own purpose had been of the highest calling. For that cause, Avila paid the greatest price. He had lost the family he loved and served, had lost his honor among men, and had no home.

At night, Avila often lay awake. He could still see the princess's red hair and emerald eyes. The memory of her soft laughter brought a rare smile to his scarred lips. Her daughter looked just like her. So much so, it had soothed his heart when finally he left her that day, knowing she would one day be free. He would have stayed after she had gone for the pleasure of putting an end to Jilliand's father, but he knew Jilliand would not survive without the horse. He had carried out his last royal command as well as he possibly could.

A tale was carried far, whispered around fires, and shared soldier to soldier, as it spread throughout the land. Everyone heard of how the lord had gone mad with anger when he found Jilliand missing, her cell bloodied, and his foul plan destroyed. When it was discovered Captain Avila had gone the same night, the lord declared Avila an outlaw. The lord sent word to every landowner that his daughter had been killed by Avila, and a reward was offered for the capture and return of that soldier.

Although none believed the lord's story, finding a benefactor had been hard for Avila. No one cared to lose more men because they employed a declared outlaw. Consequently, Avila became a lone mercenary. But another rumor grew and was soon taken as fact that the lord himself had killed Jilliand in one of his well-known fits of rage.

On this night, Avila lay fully dressed, surrounded by others of his ilk. Old injuries along with old dreams made sleep near impossible. He clasped the locket resting over his heart, beneath his tunic. *How I miss you, sweet Lady. Surely, some day soon, I will join you and his Highness, and be peaceful, again.*

Avila forced his mind to pull out the memories again. Memories of a time when life held so much promise. So reluctant was he to keep living that Avila had developed a reputation for putting himself in danger by his ferocity in battle, and his daring with his weapons. None would have guessed that he hoped to be the vanquished, to be rid, once and for all, of the burden life had given him.

Just as he began to drift off to sleep, Avila heard the sound. He lay holding his breath, the better to hear. Perhaps it was his dreams that awakened him as usual. The sound seemed to hesitate before it burst over the encampment. This was no dream. The battle cries of the Viking were well known. There would be a fight. Captain Avila threw his covers aside and rushed to meet fate.

This night wrapped itself with a thick fog. Damp, cold fingers moved through Jilliand's clothing. *Why do they not seek land and build a fire? Surely nothing more will fit on this ship.* The cold made her wounds feel fresh again. A thick robe was among the other items of clothing Rurik had brought her. Jilliand pulled it from the stack and wrapped it around herself. It helped, but she continued to shiver.

To keep warm, she began pacing the ship's length. As she walked, a few of the men spoke to her. Smiling, they nodded to encourage her to keep moving. Grateful for the camaraderie she now felt, Jilliand smiled back. *Really no reason to stop, I suppose. They seem content . . . and warm.* Jilliand was also warming up. *Perhaps 'tis not just the weather that makes a soul cold.*

Jilliand never spoke to Rurik about her injuries, nor how she wound up in a gown. She was grateful for the clothes. More so for the heavy cloak. Fearing they would spend the winter farther north, she tried not to use the cloak so as not to become accustomed to its warmth. Whatever else winter brought, cold was certain to be on the list. Dressed in the gowns, although they were too large for her small frame, she sensed unfamiliar feelings sweeping through her. She liked the feel of the gowns, the rustle as she walked, and the approval evident on every man's face as she passed. This gown was better than what she had worn in her old life. Perhaps the days would be better also.

In due time, Rurik's ship met up with his *knarr*. When the cargo was loaded, the *knarr* headed out to the open seas. Unloaded and lighter, Rurik's ship quickly made the trip back to the coast where they met three other vessels. They were to make at least one more run. The ships moved up a river like they had so many times before. In short order, each ship was moved onto a finger of land, between the coast and ocean and then hidden. Every man was dressed for battle.

Rurik stood looking at Jilliand for a long time. Jilliand waited, watching the man she knew controlled her destiny. "She goes with us," he stated after much thought. Motioning to Jilliand, he spoke to her in English, "Get your weapons."

"I have none. I lost them when I swam after I was wounded." Secretly, she was glad. Surely, wearing a gown would make the weapons feel out of place.

Rurik nodded and spoke to Askold. Askold brought her a different blade and scabbard. This blade was a length Jilliand was more accustomed to wielding. She slipped the scabbard under her belt, surprised it felt familiar and comforting.

Armed and ready to fight, the crew's movement was quiet and deliberate. *Pray they do not attack another village, for truth, I would not help with what they do.* Given little choice at this moment, she walked along. "Had I known this was our intent, I would have found breeches," she softly noted. Rurik glanced at her but kept moving. Suddenly, Rurik halted everyone. Silently the men behind her moved off to either side.

Jilliand shivered. *This night is black as the devil's heart. Surely, no good will come this night.* She tried in vain to see where they were headed. Stepping around a knot of brush, she saw it. Below her, at the foot of a gently sloping hill, was a small company of English soldiers. The fires gave the figures an eerie glow as they wandered around camp. Jilliand stared, her mind racing. *I cannot fight my countrymen. I will not do this!*

Jilliand stood frozen in horror even as she was bumped along by the men behind her. Rurik, the ship, and everything else was forgotten, except images from the day she was taken. Occupants of the tents below were not farmers. They were soldiers. Though unprepared for any battle—relaxed, laughing, and talking—they would fight. This would be ugly.

"I have to warn them," Jilliand whispered. She scrambled down the small hill and toward the fires. Suddenly, a man stepped into the full light of a huge bonfire near his tent. The guards from her father's burg had talked about the man. His holdings were full of poor peasants, barely able to survive. Still he taxed them heavily and hung them quickly. He treated everyone with sick cruelty, just like her father had. He was her father's only friend. Both were evil, taking a sick delight in the pain they inflicted on everyone in their path. In times past, this man had made crude suggestions about taking Jilliand. The man was too poor for Jilliand's father, and the talk never went any further. Now, unwilling to be seen by a man she despised, she stopped running and crept down the hillside to crouch out of sight. The fighting had begun. Jilliand sank to the ground, riveted to the scene unfolding below her. The slaughter was punctuated by yells and cursing. It seemed to go on for hours before the sounds began to die down.

At last, Jilliand walked to the edge of the destroyed camp, when a group of fighting men burst into view. She gasped when she saw Captain Avila in their midst. Mindless of anything around her, she ran headlong toward him. The captain stood alone in the center, sorely wounded, though he still held his sword. "No!" she shouted at the Vikings surrounding him. "No!" She forced her way through the ring of men to stand at his side. The assault on him paused as the Vikings waited, uncertain what to do next. Jilliand belonged to their sea king.

"Jilliand, child, I'm dying. Let me die with dignity." Avila's face was cut and bleeding, his helmet missing, and his armor splattered with blood. He never looked at her after she burst into the circle. His shield arm oozed blood as did a deep wound in his side. He was staggering, barely able to stand.

The men watched the old soldier and Jilliand. "Why are you here?" she asked him. "Let me help you. Please stop!" she yelled at the men around them.

"I came seeking refuge for the night. I had no place to stay. Leave me, child. I go to your mother. She awaits me." Avila gently shoved Jilliand away.

"No!" she cried. But Avila had already moved into the circle of Viking men, forcing their hand, and was quickly struck down. Crying, she ran to him. Cradling his head, she sobbed. With anger, she surveyed the men around her. One of the Vikings moved toward her. She leaned over Avila's body. "STOP!" she screamed in defiance. The man stepped past her, picked up the old soldier's sword, and with respect, placed it into his hand. The wounded man grasped the handle as he died. The Vikings moved away and left Jilliand alone weeping, lying across him.

Jilliand refused to leave Avila's side. At last, she was grasped by one of the men, who tried to move her away. Wrestling free, she ran back to the fallen captain. She removed the smaller weapon and belts he carried, strapping on both. Kneeling, she kissed Avila's face. The man who had pulled her away came for her again. She jerked her arm away, threw the sword she had been given by Rurik at his feet, and started sobbing again as she stumbled away toward the ships. By the time she arrived, the ships were no longer hidden, but floating in an inlet now swollen with the high tide. Swimming in her gown made movement sluggish and difficult. Dragging herself up, Jilliand climbed aboard the lead boat that was carrying Rurik and his crew. The ship slipped easily away and was soon flying over the water.

Jilliand stood at the stern, looking over the edge, numb. Her heart was shattered. The last link to her mother was dead. As the tears washed down her face, the wind increased. It felt hard and cold. *Just like my heart.* She wept, unaware Rurik had wrapped his cloak around her.

A storm soon found the ship and gripped it without mercy. Jilliand clung to the side, fighting against the wind blowing against her and in her heart. Her old friend's words filled her mind. As the gale blew, Jilliand prayed. So lost in her thoughts was she that she barely noticed the rain pelting her. Lately, she had recovered her will to survive, but that drive was waning.

As she clung to the stern, her tears gradually ceased. *Perhaps instead, I shall stay. I know my mother and Captain Avila are watching over me.* As she talked to herself, Jilliand glanced at the men nearest her. *Yet, how do I live between worlds? Theirs and mine . . . ?* She was cold.

The storm eventually moved away, and the ship stopped rocking. Jilliand hardly noticed. As her emotions settled, she became aware of the stillness around her. Night had come again. She stepped away from the side of the boat, and her eyes took in the crew, most of whom now slept. She was unaware of Rurik standing midship watching her. Rurik didn't understand how she and the old soldier were connected. His men had reported Jilliand's action with the old man but could not understand what they said in English. *He was so old, he must be her father. Perhaps. No. Clearly, she loved the old man. She hated her father. Her lover? No.* He shook his head, refusing to consider such a thing. *No matter; it has ended for the old man. He died with honor and his weapon in hand.*

He found it odd that she had chosen to keep the old man's weapon but not the medallion around his neck. Strange medallion, unlike any he had ever seen.

He turned away once he knew she had recovered and assumed his post near the steersman. The steersman spoke quietly and told Rurik to sleep for they would arrive at their destination in the morning. Clasping the man's shoulder, Rurik turned and walked away. He saw Jilliand as she sat with her eyes closed leaning against the side farthest from him.

She didn't move when he walked by, but he knew she was still awake. Leaning over her, Rurik dropped the medallion onto her lap and walked on. Jilliand jerked upright when the medal fell. In the dark, she could see Rurik walking away. She felt the chain and medallion. Unable to tell what it was, she stood and walked into the moonlight. In her hand, she held the heavy piece she remembered seeing on Avila, beneath his blood-spattered and torn shirt. Examining the medallion, she discovered it was a locket. She knew whose face must be painted inside. Grateful, she looked to heaven. "Thank you, Mother. I have to survive. I will survive. For you. Whatever I have to do." Jilliand spoke softly. Slipping the locket around her neck, she sat back down and slept.

Rurik's ship sailed into the night. A crescent moon rested high in the sky, surrounded by stars . . . stars that would take the sea king home. Rurik gazed at the familiar twinkling beacons he used to navigate the waters. The vessel was silent but for the occasional cough or murmur from the men. Half of the crew slept. Rurik regarded the men manning the boat. Everyone was weary of soured milk. What little food they crammed onto the vessel was nearly gone. *Soon, we stop where we can buy more supplies and hunt game.*

His eyes wandered back toward Jilliand. *She is a strange one.* She helped when she could, had become comfortable with the crew, and never complained. The memory of the scars covering her back brought a flush of anger. He would find out who had done that to her one way or another. Rurik spoke briefly to his steersman, made one last round of the ship, then lay down next to Dir and Askold. Sleep came quickly.

The morning's light found the crew up and about. Jilliand assumed they were leaving to raid. Rurik caught her eye as he left and shook his head. "Just as well. I care not to go," she murmured. As if he knew she needed time, he had not spoken to her since that awful night. The men stood listening to Rurik.

A group of men, weapons in hand, left with Rurik. Quickly to take advantage of the full tide, the remaining men rowed the boat farther upstream where they stopped to tie the boat. A second group, gathering weapons, but without shields or swords, left the ship. The remaining men began maintenance repairs on the boat, sails, and ropes. They also made a clearing, hauled in wood, dug a pit, and started a fire. Early in the afternoon, the hunting party returned. At the edge of the clearing, hung a deer already skinned and gutted. Game birds and fish were being set out. Large strips of venison and more birds were skewered and set over the fire to cook. The fish were hung to smoke. Several hours later, Rurik and the rest of the men arrived heavily laden with grain. The ship was loaded before all sat down to eat. The men ate eagerly, laughing and talking while Jilliand sat apart, making meaningless marks in the dirt at her feet. Every time she thought a conflict within her heart was settled, something happened to stir up doubts again. Could she stay with the Vikings? Could she live with people so different and so violent? Jilliand knew well how violent the English could become, even to their own. Listening to the sounds of the men talking and laughing, Jilliand realized the overpowering issue was safety. She felt safe and accepted; neither feeling had ever been a part of her life before.

CHAPTER 12

BY THE TIME RURIK WAS ready to go ashore again, Jilliand had made a troubled peace with her feelings. Rurik decided to take her with him. When Rurik came to her, he held her hand, not her wrist. His touch was easy. As usual, he led her to the side of the boat, and Jilliand slipped over, gathering her gown around herself to keep it dry. She still felt awkward in a gown.

Jilliand's wavy hair had grown longer and shone red and gold like the setting sun. She had found a pair of breeches in some of the booty and wore them every day, for added warmth and freedom of movement, under the gowns she now wore. Though made of wool, the gowns offered little protection from the weather, as Jilliand had no under-tunics or other garments.

As they walked away from the boat, Rurik informed Jilliand they were to be guests in someone's court. Someone, he added smiling, who would pay him well. He explained that he had been to this burg several times before, in peace. The burg was larger and had signs of greater wealth and more people. He added that this visit would be a good visit, for his men, and for Jilliand, also. Alarmed, Jilliand pulled away from him. She had never pulled loose from him before, and he quickly lost his grip. She ran to the river's edge where she stood, her heart pounding. He walked up behind her. She whirled around and firmly stated, "I cannot go. Are you not a Viking king? If so, you would not drag a slave with you. And what if someone recognizes me? Will you kill everyone again?"

She was not a slave to him; although, he knew he had never made such a declaration to her. Rurik cared little what the English thought of him. "We are too far north now, for anyone to have seen you before." He shrugged, frowning at her. "There is nothing to do about what you look like to them—slave or not."

Jilliand's mind raced wildly, when an idea came to her. Taking the heavy chain from around her neck, she wove it under and up into her hair with the medallion hanging slightly down on her forehead, and then she pulled her hair up. She pointed to a leather strap he had hanging from his belt. Still frowning, he handed it to her. Gathering her hair, twisting it and wrapping it around her fingers, she used the strap to tie the hair in place. Shortly, she had her hair piled up on her head. Rurik slipped his dark sable robe around her shoulders.

She turned and faced Rurik. He stared, his mind working. *She must be of noble birth. I would have the rest of her story.* He commented dryly under his breath, "You're going to be hot. I do not care what the English think, nor should you." He reached for her again. *Perhaps she is right; it is not such a good idea to bring her with me. But it is too late now.*

Taking his hand, she walked with him into a huge hall. The walls were lined with candles that cast a soft light on the room. Tables were arranged end to end, with benches providing seating on the wall side. At even intervals, candles had been placed and lit on every table. In the middle of the room, one large table faced the head table on the diagonal. The head table was elegantly set. The plates were patterned clay instead of metal, and elegantly hammered goblets held wine. The settings on every other table were common metal plates, mugs, and utensils. Jilliand secretly wondered if her father had a place like this. If he did, she certainly had never been privileged enough to enter. She had cared little how she dressed before, dressed as she was like a man in the most ragged of clothing; now she felt like a woman. When she walked into the room, the hall went silent, every person was looking at the tall, muscular Viking, his woman, and his men.

The lord and his lady began graciously seating everyone. Jilliand could feel many eyes upon her. When the meal was served, everyone waited for the lord to begin eating before they began. Jilliand waited for Rurik to begin. Straightaway, the room became silent but for the sound of people eating. In due course, the lord began speaking to Rurik in Rurik's native tongue. He spoke quietly, and Rurik replied in like manner. Both men spoke carefully, as if they were navigating a river frozen with thin ice.

Confident none of the Vikings could speak English, the lady of the castle began speaking aloud, noting how refined Jilliand appeared. However, as the meal progressed, and the wine flowed, she began to mock Jilliand and her clothes to the other ladies. The ladies laughed, making fun of Jilliand and Rurik's men. Jilliand sat silent, never looking up. The lord's wife then discussed her husband's plan to wait until everyone was drunk and then sink or burn Rurik's ship. "The Vikings will all be killed, and the woman," she told them, "will be sold to the highest bidder"—adding she intended to bid on Jilliand herself. Jilliand sat silent as long as she could. Then, leaning to Rurik she spoke so softly that he could barely hear, "They're setting a trap for you."

He nodded at her very seriously. He then spoke to the lord and both men laughed. After a moment, Jilliand leaned over to Rurik again, saying, "His wife looks like an ox. Her mind is more likened to an ass." A smile played about Rurik's mouth. The night wore on. In time, most of the lord's men were drunk or asleep. Jilliand noticed that the Vikings drank from their own flasks; none were drunk. Most of Rurik's men had wandered away, slowly but surely, until only a few were left in the hall.

At last, Rurik calmly rose to his feet and spoke, "We will accept payment in grain, gold, and silver. My queen never asks for payment. I ask for her. She will choose some beautiful gowns such as those seen in this room."

At his words, the stunned lord dropped his cup. A quick survey told the story. The Vikings were gone from the hall; they most certainly had infiltrated the castle, likely wandering at will outside and were, the lord knew, not drunk. The only drunk men were his. He was outmanned and outsmarted. "I pay no fee!" he bellowed and shot up as his chair clattered backward. The hall became quiet as a tomb.

Rurik answered smoothly, "We can live as partners, you and I. I'll keep your shores safe, and you pay me; or you die an adversary, your shores raided until only blackened land and burned-out huts remain. You know I can and will do as I say." With his words, the lord went ashen. Rurik stood waiting.

The lord's wife watched anxiously. Her eyes never left Jilliand's slight, quiet form.

The Englishman stood in silence, staring at Rurik. Sharply, he turned to his wife, "Send one of your ladies. Bring several gowns out for the Viking woman to choose from."

The wife bristled. "I will not! Look at her. She is but a street whore!" She spat the words out in disgust.

Speaking quickly, ignoring her, he turned to his steward, "Bring five gowns, cloaks, and other wraps here. Let the woman choose."

His wife screeched and flew after the poor steward. Jilliand touched Rurik's arm. He leaned down to listen to her, still watching the lord. She said, "Your thought is kind, but we both could fit into one of her gowns."

Solemnly, Rurik nodded in agreement, although he did not change his request. The hall was silent again. The lord stood staring, trying to think. Finally, in defeat, the lord ordered his grain and food stores opened. When the steward returned, he was still being followed by the lord's wife, who was beating him about his head, cursing. He brought the bundle to Jilliand. She looked with feigned amazement at the forced generosity. In the stack of clothes the poor man had grabbed, Jilliand found two simple gowns and carefully laid each piece out. She took a heavy deep-brown cloak, adding it to the pile with the two dresses. Leaning toward Rurik, she softly asked, "May I speak out?" He nodded.

She rose from the table and walked to the now weeping and wailing wife. In a gentle voice, speaking perfect English, she noted, "Lady, your gowns are elegant. The neckline and sleeves are beautiful. Your gowns would be prized in the finest court. My hair color prevents me from wearing some of these beautiful colors. While your most generous gift is deeply appreciated, I would only take these three items." Curtseying respectfully, Jilliand draped the items on her arm. Bowing to the lord, she added, "Thank you for your kind hospitality, sir." She nodded to Rurik and gracefully walked from the hall, her head held high. In truth, she knew nothing about women's style and clothing. Perhaps no one could tell. With pride, Rurik watched her receding figure.

The lady was painfully aware that Jilliand must have understood every word spoken about Jilliand's dress and person. Recovering her dignity, the lady rose and asked her husband, "I would speak with her again. Call her back. Ask the

Viking to call her back." Her husband had no intention of doing such a thing and sent his wife from the room. He could not complete his business with Rurik quickly enough.

One of Rurik's men escorted Jilliand from the hall. Once outside, they did not return to the boat the same way they had come. Jilliand was not surprised to see the boat had been moved. Setting her bundle on the deck near the bow, she removed Rurik's cloak and folded it. Without speaking, she helped load the grain. The men accepted her assistance without notice. The steersman smiled, watching this slender woman with an unexpected toughness about her. *This woman was surely sent to help the Old One who lives with our people.*

When Rurik came aboard, he brought with him gold and silver, which he divided with his crew. Walking to Jilliand, he took her hand, and in it, he placed her cross, along with three heavy silver-and-gold hair pieces, each inset with precious stones. Each was nearly three inches in length with holes at either end. Through the holes a pick, slightly pointed at one end and knobbed with a large red stone at the other, slid neatly in place. He also draped an additional cloak over her arm. He nodded and simply turned away.

Jilliand was moved. She looked at what he had given her. Never before had anyone given her a gift—even a small one. Jilliand kissed the cross before placing it around her neck. She began to take her hair down, but a hand on her arm stopped her. Several of the men, pale and shaking, seemed to be asking for help. Startled, Jilliand could see they were very ill. She felt the heat in one man's touch. He took Jilliand's hand and placed it on his abdomen. She tried to think and recalled a time when she had been ill as a child, Myla had given her a tea made from plants, which the old woman said grew near water. Jilliand remembered seeing the plants on the old couple's table. Jilliand motioned for the men to lie down and pointed to the shore. She would need the plant, hot water, and time. Jilliand quickly left the ship and climbed the bank.

A bonfire was built to spread needed light across the shore so that the supplies they took could be loaded. Taking advantage of whatever time she might have before the ship was ready to sail, Jilliand grabbed a cauldron, set it near the flames, and slipped away. When she returned to the fire with a bladder full of water, Rurik was looking for her. Irritated that she would simply leave without asking him, he approached with displeasure in his walk and on his face. Jilliand dumped the water into the cauldron and then stood to face Rurik.

Jilliand spoke quickly, before Rurik could. Forgetting their differences in station, she thought only of the young men lying on the deck of Rurik's ship. "Some of your men are ill. Perhaps I can help." Without waiting for approval, she turned to leave, praying she could find what she needed and figure out how to use it. Rurik caught her arm, calling to one of his men. Armed with a thick limb tipped with a rag soaked in oil, the man set the rag on fire. With the burning limb lighting the way, Jilliand started to leave. Rurik stopped her and commented, "Low tide comes soon." Jilliand knew she must return before the tide lowered making it impossible for the ship to sail back out to sea. Moving quickly, Jilliand and the man began to search. Swiftly the two moved from plant to plant. If only she could find it. Their search ended. "Please, God, let this be the right one," she whispered.

Jilliand and her escort returned to the shore, where a loaded ship and an impatient Sea King Rurik waited. Kneeling on the ground, Jilliand hastily ground the leaves on a rock and added them to the water in the cauldron, now boiling. Slowly the mixture began to thicken. Lifting the cauldron from the fire, Jilliand handed it off to one of the men standing nearby. "I need a cup," she called to Rurik as she climbed on board his ship.

Some of the men were now rolling from side to side, moaning. Moving from man to man, she made them drink the hot fluid. Jilliand prayed, knowing her life might be forfeited if any of the men died.

Rurik ordered the vessel homeward, to Denmark, just as the tide began to recede. Jilliand sat near the ill men. Eventually, they slept. Sometime deep into the night, Jilliand also fell asleep. When the last man awoke, his stirrings woke Jilliand. He was weak but without pain or fever. The rest of the men were also much better. Walking the stiffness from her legs, Jilliand felt the acceptance from the men as she passed. *I will prove to them I am more than a slave.* Her thoughts turned to Rurik. She was drawn to him, for reasons she could not understand. *I miss having a mother. Someone to answer the questions that fill my head.*

She leaned against the stern, staring at the horizon—without seeing anything. She was no longer afraid, angry, or without hope. Instead, an unfamiliar feeling stirred within her. For hours, her mind grappled with her feelings, trying to comprehend all she had learned of the Vikings, the very men she once believed were devils on earth and void of any compassion or honor. Glancing around, she knew such beliefs no longer defined these men. She desperately wanted to understand the Vikings—and Rurik—as she stood at the stern, alone, a captive on a Viking raiding ship.

As evening fell on their third day at sea, Rurik's vessel moved nearer the shoreline. A smaller warship slid in next to his. Rurik met with the man commanding the other warship for several hours. An English ship had been noticed following Rurik, almost beyond sight. "I listened to the commander of that ship, at the last town, when we docked to take on supplies. He knows of you and your reputation. He has it in his mind to lure you out farther to sea, cutting you off from the shore, and then engage you in battle. He is eager to prove he can slow the Viking raids."

"Why would he talk where you could hear?" Rurik asked, frowning.

"We were not docked near him. We were tied farther up the shoreline. He was too busy boasting to look around. Several merchants heard him. We do not raid that town. The merchants were eager to keep things that way. They shared the information. At any rate, we waited until he left before we sailed. There are two other Viking ships headed this way."

"I think we lead them farther north, before we engage them. Stay close enough for them to see, but not close enough to fire upon us." The other Viking nodded, and Rurik returned to his own vessel.

An air of anticipation gripped Rurik's crew. When Rurik returned to his ship, the announcement was simple. "We will soon fight," Rurik told his men. He stood quietly for a moment, surveying his warriors. "The Englishmen sail toward our homeland. They think to run between our ships and land, to isolate us, as if that would provide them with some advantage. We will lead them to waters they have never sailed. Make ready." Rurik was visibly angry. That the English would challenge them at sea was an insult. The Vikings knew the English could easily be outmaneuvered and any hand-to-hand fighting heavily favored the Vikings.

Jilliand did not understand what Rurik said, but what the men were doing was plain enough: They were preparing for battle, putting on armor, readying weapons, and clearing the ship's floor. When Rurik spoke to her, she was stunned to hear his command. "I am having you taken ashore. You should not have need of protection at this place. You will have food and flint. Take warm clothing." He paused, thinking, as if confirming in his own mind that she had enough supplies. "I will come for you," he added, turning to leave.

Fear rose unexpectedly inside her stomach. What if he failed to come back for her? Without thinking, she answered, "No. I will stay with you." Surprised she would think to dispute him, he turned back, scowling. Recognizing Rurik had no intentions of changing his mind, Jilliand's anxiety quickly became anger.

"You take me when it's easy for you? If you think I am trouble, you set me ashore? Why?" She now stood toe to toe with him, her fists at her side. "I know how to fight." She would not admit to him that she was fearful he would set her ashore alone and for good.

Slowly, Rurik began to smile at her. The broader his smile, the angrier she became, passing the edge of reason as her voice rose. Startled by her aggression, he picked her up and walked to the ship's side. Before Jilliand could struggle, he simply tossed her overboard. *Her temper matches her fiery hair. Perhaps a spell in the cold water will cool that temper.* He already told her what he expected of her.

She had no place in the fighting he knew was coming to this ship. With other things to tend to, he calmly continued preparations for battle.

When Jilliand hit the water, she floundered for a moment, clinging to the blade she wore at her waist. Coming up for air, she could see the side of the ship lined with the men, who were all laughing. Fury and indignation churned inside her. Diving, she swam under the boat. Coming up on the other side, she swam the short distance to the shore. "Viking!" she shouted after she climbed onto the bank. Rurik heard her. Looking around, it took him a moment to locate her. Her arm was raised, with the blade in hand. "Viking! You threw me away," she yelled. "I am free, Viking! Free! I belong to no man!" With that, she sheathed her knife, turned, and simply walked away. When she thought she was out of sight, she ran.

By turns Rurik was angry and amused. "She cannot survive alone. When the English are beaten, I'll come for her. She will be sorry she took it upon herself to leave."

"You *did* throw her away," Askold casually noted, in passing. Frowning, he added, "How will you find her?"

"You jest, Askold. Do you not think people will remember her wherever she goes?"

"Perhaps. Still she will not be safe alone," Askold said quietly. He knew Rurik loved the woman. "You best find a way to handle her if you would keep her," Askold muttered under his breath.

Midnight found a brooding Viking sea king standing at the bow of his warship. Rurik's thoughts were not on the coming battle. That would be simple enough. This kind of fight was one Vikings rarely lost. Rurik had never lost a battle at sea. Instead, his thoughts were on the Englishwoman. She clearly had no idea how to do the things women usually did, but she knew about weapons. She was well educated but unaware of how life worked around her. She was so unlike any woman he had ever known. She had taken him by surprise, this captive of his. He wanted her. This is what the old woman had promised before he left, had she not? He *could* just take her. Suddenly the English ship's silhouette came into view again, and one of his men called out. All thoughts of Jilliand left his mind.

CHAPTER 13

THE ENGLISH VESSEL CHASED THE Viking warship for two days. They moved closer or fell behind, at the choosing of the Vikings. Rurik was careful to stay close enough for the English to see them and continue the chase. Meanwhile, the Vikings skillfully led the English vessel onward toward the Viking homeland and familiar waters. *Let them follow. Closer to shore, their ship will be grounded. That ship belongs to us.* Rurik smiled with satisfaction. His very soul was filled with the coming clash. This was what he loved most. The possibility of death held no fear for him. Warriors who died fighting had the honor of feasting with all the great warriors of the past. He was Viking. His gods fought, his forefathers fought, his men fought. He would do as had been done for centuries before him.

Not a single man with him faltered. Their ferocity and willingness to die was what the English feared most. He told Dir that one man must survive; he wanted the tale told.

Dir nodded. They were loaded, heavier than he would have liked, since Rurik brought along all he could from their last foray. No matter, the old woman had read the runes: There would be a battle, Rurik would win, and he would return with supplies. Simple.

Rurik never doubted he would win. The sisters of fate had played with him, letting him see Jilliand, perhaps fall in love with her, and then lose her. If it were to be, Skuld, the sister of the future, would bring Jilliand back. Now, Rurik asked the Valkyries to carry the upcoming battle. He often wondered if Valkyries ever chose from the vanquished. Surely, he had known men worthy of Valhalla. Valkyries chose those worthy to go to Valhalla, the great hall of Odin. There to feast until Ragnarök—the final doom. Rurik believed the old captain Jilliand had loved should be there. There had been others before him. Warriors fierce and . . . a call from one of his men interrupted Rurik's musings.

Rurik watched the English ship move closer. It became evident the big ship was slowing. Eventually she gave a great shudder, her bow pointing toward Rurik's ship came to a stop, grounded—her crew scrambling to defend themselves from an inevitable boarding by the Vikings. The English captain ordered trunks and anything else of weight thrown overboard trying to lighten his ship and enable her to pull away from the oncoming Viking fleet. They had little time. Rurik's ship, joined by two more, swiftly turned back toward the English vessel. A great roar swelled from the Viking ships. The cry was known as the death call to the English. *God, have mercy on these men I lead,* the English captain prayed. There would be no mercy from the Vikings.

With cries that struck fear into the hearts of the English, the Vikings were upon them. Easily sending spears across the ever-shortening distance, the Vikings peppered the English sailors from all sides. The English valiantly tried to defend themselves, but their spears fell short of the Viking ships By this time, the ships were close enough for the Vikings to send the deadly throwing axes into the English sailors, now scrambling to take cover. Rurik and his men boarded the English ship, fighting hand to hand. The English fell, one after another against the Vikings' skilled use of their longer swords. The fire of battle raged within Rurik, his passion for this activity clear. When the last English sailor was down, Dir brought a young man to Rurik as Rurik had ordered. Rurik looked at the English sailor, then shaking his head, motioned for the man to be killed. The young man was dragged away. Rurik turned back to business, examining the weapons now piled on the deck of the English vessel. Many of the English swords were Frankish. They were of the best steel, kept their edge, and were the most balanced. All of them would be kept. Anything else of value was added to the pile. Ordering the pile to be divided between the three Viking ships, Rurik had his share loaded. Finally, the great English ship was set afire.

As the second and third warships left for home, Rurik stood at his post. Dir and Askold had been with Rurik since childhood. Both men knew they would go in search of the woman before going home. Rurik had never committed to any woman before, but it was clear his time had come.

Rurik turned to his crew. "Dir and Askold will go ashore with me when the sun comes up. There is a cave north along the coast. If we are not there by the end of the fourth day, sail home without us."

As the sun tossed its first rays to awaken the land, Rurik and his two jarls swam ashore, with Rurik's one thought to find Jilliand. She had nearly four days' jump on them.

Dir led them to a small village less than a day's walk upriver. Fearing these men were but a scouting party, horses the Vikings offered to buy were given to Rurik and his men in exchange for the safety of the hamlet. Unable to make the villagers understand, Rurik left a small bag of coins for the animals in the hands of a young boy.

The three Vikings began their search following the river. If Jilliand were to survive, she must find people. People lived near water. Jilliand would be near water.

Jilliand could run no longer. Her legs trembled and ached. Every breath felt like a fire in her chest. Gasping and holding her sides, she leaned over to vomit. Surveying the land around her, the reality of what she had just done quickly cooled her anger at Rurik. Jilliand had struggled before, and that time she had a horse. She knew well what could happen. She had no idea where she was or what people, if any, lived here. *What do I do now?* Her hand moved to the locket hanging from her neck.

By early afternoon, she sensed the rawness of uncertainty; a sensation that had not touched her for some time. For weeks she had felt safe with the Viking. Though the feeling of safety was unfamiliar, it had slowly become comfortable.

Now, today, she was no longer safe. A woman alone was prey, easy prey to many. In her haste to answer her temper, she was ill prepared for the cold or travel or anything else, it seemed. With no other choice, she walked northward praying for any sign of other people.

Eventually Jilliand's clothing dried, but without a cloak or Rurik to provide one, movement would be the only thing she knew that might hold the cold at bay. The land, lacking any indication of either people or roads, toyed with her poor sense of direction. She pushed on, stumbling over rocks and stumps hiding in the shadows. God took pity on her and gently brushed the clouds aside, allowing the moon to shine, full and bright.

At the awakening of the moon, Jilliand shivered with the bone chill of night. When morning's light found her, she was still walking, shivering, and brooding over her situation. She was tired and hungry. She needed a cloak, and she needed a horse. Yet another day and miserable night passed. She drank from small streams and struggled on. The sun was directly overhead on the third day when she came to a trail bearing signs of use.

At the sound of approaching horses, Jilliand hid among the trees just beyond the edge of the path. Several men rode by, headed south. Jilliand could see they carried weapons, though none were dressed to fight nor were they dressed to travel any distance. "They must have spent the night sheltered close by," she reasoned. "I would find that place."

Following the road, Jilliand found herself at the top of a small hill. Relieved, she looked down upon a large settlement. On the outskirts, snuggled close to the small mountain's base, sat a large monastery. The burg Jilliand had grown up in was run down and falling apart, but it had soldiers. The family she had lived with when she was taken captive was ragged and poor. *Little need for protection for them*, she had thought at the time. Circumstances taught her how wrong she was. The settlement before her had no walls that she could see, nor did there seem to be any soldiers for protection, although the activity, animals, and buildings told a tale of stable living. She decided the Vikings had never come this far upriver. Crossing a tiny meadow just south of the town enabled her to skirt the settlement and head toward the monastery.

At the door of the priory, Jilliand spoke to an elderly monk. His eyes were kind, but he informed her that women were not allowed inside. As she turned away, she could hear the door being barred. She walked back toward streets lined with structures. *There must be someone who has need of help,* she reasoned. Men, women, and horses moved about. To her relief, little notice was taken of a lone woman who looked to be a maid from one of the houses.

On one side of the street, several stalls were bunched together. They each displayed various goods for sale. Residents of the settlement could purchase cheeses, chickens, breads, and fish, both smoked and fresh. Farther down the street was what looked like an inn. A sign posted on the door frame warned patrons to stable their horses elsewhere. It looked as if the establishment was busy. Jilliand saw an older lady sweeping off the area in front of the building. Swallowing hard, she took a breath and approached the lady. The kindly woman listened sympathetically but could not use Jilliand. After seeing disappointment shade Jilliand's face, the lady asked her to wait a moment. Disappearing into the house, the woman returned with a small bundle that she handed to Jilliand. When Jilliand took the package, the older woman squeezed her hand. "God go with you, child."

By this time, night was quickly approaching. Searching for a safe place to stay, Jilliand found an open shed. Unseen, she snuck into a corner. She opened the bundle to find cheese and bread. She ate before crawling under a pile of straw; warm and dry, she slept.

The next morning, Jilliand brushed the dust and weeds from her hair and gown, confident she would find some way to earn her keep. She came upon another open market where she traded one of her jeweled hair pieces for a heavy woolen cloak. Jilliand approached several different innkeepers, offering to work for food. Each looked her over. Her hair was uncombed. Her gown was dirty and worn. Yet, the young woman seemed as if she belonged in a carriage, not serving tables. She walked and spoke too well for the likes of their usual customers. She wore no jewels, not even a ring, still one could not be too cautious these days. Fearful of what their husbands would say, every innkeeper refused her.

As the hours passed, Jilliand became increasingly anxious. She was repeatedly turned down. Perhaps to survive, she would need to find some place where stragglers from Viking raids gathered. There she would more easily blend in.

A young man leaning against the stable doors watched Jilliand approaching. He liked what he saw. When she stepped inside at his bidding, she hoped to trade for a horse and saddle. He hoped to bargain for a night of pleasure. He got far more than he bargained for. When Jilliand realized what he wanted, she drew on him. He was shocked at her speed. It was clear she knew how to use the blade.

Backing away, he stuttered, "I meant no harm, m'lady. Just lonely. Take any horse you see. Saddle comes with it. Do not tell the owner about this. I have a family, I do. Cannot lose this work. Please."

He sounded so desperate that Jilliand took pity on him. "Are you certain every horse is for sale?"

He hesitated. "No. In truth, only the red one. 'Tis new to us. Came with a saddle. Too large an animal for you, though."

"Let me see," she demanded. Dutifully, he led her to the back corral. Of the horses penned, the roan was indeed the larger. Jilliand had no idea what he might be worth, and she only had two hair pieces left. Taking the smaller of the two, she handed it to the young man just as the owner joined them.

He studied Jilliand carefully, turning the hair piece given him by the stable hand over and over. "What need do you have for a horse such as that?" He knew nearly every person in the town. He did not know this lady.

Jilliand studied him, also. "I think my need is my own, sir. Are you willing to part with the animal and a saddle?"

"What more can you pay?" he asked. She did not look to him like she had money, at least not now. She used to, though, he'd wager. The one piece he held in his hand was worth what the horse would bring. He wanted more, if she had it. Business had been slow.

She handed over the last of the two jeweled pieces. The man examined it closely. The stones alone would bring a good sum. He looked back at her. "I'll take these for the animal and the gear. I'll throw in the bags left with the horse. Best you leave tonight, though. I will tell any who ask, I sold the horse," his eyes narrowed. "Would not tell them it was to a woman."

She nodded. While the lad saddled the horse, Jilliand followed the man back into the barn where he handed her two heavy bags. Tied together, Jilliand rolled the bags up behind the saddle. With the cloak around her, she mounted. Turning, horse and rider left. Jilliand planned to travel only until she felt the distance from the town was sufficient for her to make camp. However, the horse proved very fit. They traveled easily through the night, following a well-worn trail away from the settlement.

CHAPTER 14

FOLLOWING THE RIVER, RURIK AND his companions rode northward. They saw no other traveler. In their native language Askold said, "I remember this, Rurik. There is a settlement further. We were here several years ago." He constantly scanned the land around them, as well as the horizon, watching for any movement. Vikings would not be a welcome sight. Three alone would tempt a confrontation that could very well go badly.

"I do remember. I made peace with their town. With little protection, they welcomed us." Rurik grinned at his men. "We only needed to repair our sails. The stable hand gave us whatever we wanted."

Dir laughed aloud. "Ah, Rurik . . . whatever *you* wanted."

Askold shook his head. "The Norns looked out for you that day, Rurik. With a ship of men gone many weeks from home, you finally decided against taking the women offered you on board. Wise. Do you think to try that place again?"

"I do." Rurik hoped talk of the recent Viking raids had not reached the town. One more time, he would seek out the same man he met before at the monastery. If Verdandi, the goddess of the present, was still with him, all would go well. He thought of the red-headed woman. *She is not here, but she has been. I can feel it.* Three Vikings rode boldly down the center of the street.

The young lad from the stables watched the three men approach, then scurried out a side door, running toward the monastery. Banging on the heavy wooden door outside the building, he nervously hopped from one foot to the other, looking over his shoulder repeatedly. An old monk finally came to the door. "You bring news of importance, I am certain," the monk said. He eyed the lad, then looked around him to the bustling street just below the monastery. "Why have you come?"

"The Vikings, they are here!" The boy looked back.

The monk's face blanched. He looked beyond the lad once more. The street was busy with horses, people, carts, and dogs. No Vikings. "Are you sure? I see nothing." At that moment, Rurik and his jarls came into view as they rounded the corner of a building at the street's end. The old man squinted at Rurik for a long time. Slowly, he nodded. "Go home, son. We are safe this night." Patting his shoulder, the monk gently pushed the lad away. Not waiting for a second command, the young man was off and running.

The monk stood at the door, waiting for Rurik and his men. As they approached, he called to someone behind him, requesting the horses be cared for. As they dismounted, the monk opened the door wider, allowing the three Vikings to enter. The rooms were sparsely furnished and cold, lacking a fire or any coverings for the walls or floors. Other monks, all dressed in thick robes, were working at tables, lit with only one candle. Rurik glanced around the area. It was just as he remembered. He removed a pouch of coins from his side and handed it to the old monk.

"I have no need for this," the man responded quietly.

"No, but you surely know someone who does." Rurik stood watching him. This old monk and Rurik had spent a long time talking the last time Rurik was here. Unarmed and unafraid, he had welcomed Rurik and his men. The monastery had no golden statues, coins, or other treasures. They lived simply, writing and caring for those living in the surrounding homes. The townspeople were petrified of the Vikings, but the old monk seemed to know something about Rurik that Rurik himself didn't know. They had spoken of Rurik's gods and the monk's God, parting that time, as equals. The monk wondered if there would be a price to pay for Rurik's coins, today.

"How might I be of service to you, Viking Sea King?" The man's gaze was steady and unafraid.

"I come seeking a woman. She might have come here not long ago—maybe two days."

"Are you angry with the woman?" the monk asked, his eyes narrowing. He knew Jilliand had come to his door before she passed through the town, knew how the Vikings treated captured women, and knew Jilliand wore a cross. She was not from the area—the only person he did not know. The monk would not willingly place her in danger.

"I am not angry." Rurik was not aware his voice had softened. The monk was.

"She has red hair and wears one of your symbols. I will not harm her. When did she leave and to where does she travel?"

The old monk acknowledged, "She did come here. She bought a horse and rode toward the river. Yesterday, late." Turning, he opened the heavy door, "Go in peace, Viking." When the three men were out, the door closed behind them. They could hear the sound of a bar being dropped into place across the door. A younger monk walked to Rurik, leading the three horses. The Vikings rode hard, all through the night.

In the clear light of early morning, Rurik found the tracks he hoped for. A single rider, probably light, had come this same way, recently. Following the sign, the three men rode on. Suddenly, Rurik's hand shot up. Everyone froze. Jilliand's voice drifted to them, strong and clear.

Guiding the horses carefully, the men rode to the edge of a small glen. Rurik inhaled sharply. Naked and unabashed, Jilliand moved around to close her camp. She shook her dress, hung close to the fire to dry, then turned to the horse. Rurik's heart beat faster, watching Jilliand work with her horse. *Fate has been kind. The Norns have brought her here, to this place, to me.*

In the early afternoon, tired of riding, Jilliand found a river to follow. When darkness threatened, she began searching for a safe place to stop. She rode into an area where the river widened to meet the sea. Witness to this meeting was a small meadow surrounded by trees and brush. It looked to be a safe place for the two of them. There were no tracks around the area—nor at the bank. There

CLARE GUTIERREZ

were no signs of life; and the air was still and quiet but for the sounds of night birds of prey. Near the forest edge, Jilliand chose a place close to the sea where the shore formed a small cove. Once more, she was on her own. *I can do this again.* It felt less frightening this time. This time, Jilliand knew what she could do. She had a good horse, a weapon, and confidence. *It's a start.*

Dismounting, she began the business of making camp. After unrolling the cloak, she opened both sacks. Inside the first she found a small knife, hard bread, a block of salt, molded cheese, and a large, well-used chunk of flint. This night she would be warm. When she opened the second sack, her horse snorted, walked close to her, nuzzling for the sack. *Tonight you get a treat, my new friend.* Jilliand rubbed the horse's nose before looping the sack handles over the horse's head. Cutting the mold off the cheese, Jilliand ate. Lying next to the fire, under her cloak and covered with stars above, Jilliand felt a sense of exhilaration, only slightly dampened by reality.

Morning opened a new day. The sun brought with it promise. *If I am to find work, I must not look like a whore.* Jilliand was already up and had bathed and hung her dress near the fire to dry. She stood naked, becoming better acquainted with her horse. She walked away from him, whistled, and rewarded him with grain from the sack when he came. She called him over and over, spoke to him when he came, and petted him. He learned quickly. Satisfied he would stay with her, she finished packing, dressed, and mounted. Riding toward a thicket, she leaned down to pet his neck. "We must become close friends, you and I. I wish I knew by what name you were called. No matter. I shall call you—"

"Erik 'tis a good strong name," Rurik's powerful voice interrupted her.

Jilliand straightened in the saddle to face Rurik, Dir, and Askold at the glen's edge. Before anyone could move, she turned her horse and kicked him; he responded immediately. She clung tightly, trying desperately to leave Rurik behind her. For a while, it seemed she would outrun him. She would soon learn he was a far better rider than she was. When he overtook her, he pulled her onto his horse, while Askold caught her animal. Jilliand struggled mightily, but she was no match for the man who held her.

"I told you I would come for you," he calmly reminded her, as she struggled to free herself.

Resigned to the fact she was captive again, she stopped fighting him. "You tossed me aside, remember?" Jilliand shot back, glaring ahead. Rurik held her tightly against his chest, without answering. His arm easily encircled her small frame; she was made immobile. He liked the feeling of this woman against him. He could feel her heart beating rapidly. Too bad the cove was so close; he could have ridden a long way with her held near to his own heart.

When they arrived at the cove, he finally spoke again. "Well planned. You chose to meet my ship here?" For the first time, she could hear teasing in his voice. Realizing he was not angry with her, Jilliand attempted to wriggle away, hoping he would let her go. When she glanced up at him, he was still smiling down at her, though he shook his head.

"What are you saying? There is no ship here." Jilliand looked around. The waters were very calm, with small white-capped waves gently washing onto the sandy shore and slipping back to the ocean. Just a peaceful cove. Angry at his mocking tone, she began to struggle again.

"We were to leave in two days. Since you are already here, we leave sooner." His voice was still teasing. "Stop fighting me. You have been caught, fairly. Twice now." Rurik resisted the urge to kiss the lips so near to his.

Jilliand was furious. He laughed as he set her down, sliding down himself. While their horses were being cared for, he grasped her arm. Leading her along, he walked into the trees surrounding the cove. "Are you staying or must I tie you?" The question was asked evenly, without a trace of anger. He stood watching her, waiting for her answer.

She fought back the tears of frustration. *In truth what else can I do? Already I feel safer.* "I am staying," she answered under her breath.

"I cannot hear you. Look at me," he calmly ordered. She knew better. He wanted her to repeat it and see her face to know.

Turning to him, her chin up, she yelled at him, "I'm staying!"

"Good. Play with your horse while we hunt. It is possible the ship will be here this evening. Best you hope it is. It may be a long night for you, if it is not." Without waiting for a reply, he called to his men as he mounted. They rode out.

Jilliand toyed with the idea of leaving. Was it her word that kept her? "Truly my word *is* all I have. I cannot leave," she argued aloud with herself. "Or is it because . . . ?" The question hung unfinished. She could not know how fleeting the feeling of safety would be.

She busied herself, gathering wood and starting a fire, keeping a wary eye on the surrounding forest. With the fire burning steadily, she formed a smoking rack out of some nearby tree branches. When Rurik and his men rode into the clearing, they brought back a gutted deer. It took little time for them to skin and cut it up. Several chunks of the meat were placed over the fire, while the rest was draped over the branch above the fire, to smoke.

Looking out over the cove, Jilliand smiled to herself. *He came for me, just as he said he would. And he is not angry.* The realization that he actually wanted her gave her an unfamiliar feeling, not the usual knot in her stomach she had grown so accustomed to.

When the men had eaten their fill, Jilliand stirred the embers and turned the remainder of the venison to continue smoking, like she had seen Rurik's men do before. She walked to the shore, where she stood staring out at the black waters beyond. Rurik came to stand behind her. Gently, he pulled her back against him. She stood still. Fear of the unknown made her shiver. "Go get your cloak," he spoke kindly. Turning, he watched as she walked away. She returned bundled in the warm cloak.

"Please . . . " Jilliand began. Not certain what to say, she felt she was not ready for something she feared was coming, something unknown to her. When no words came, Jilliand fell silent.

Rurik stood watching the sea as waves, stirred by a stronger wind, crashed against the inlet. Just when Jilliand decided he had not heard her, he began to speak. Pointing, he talked about where they were in relation to the sky. He talked about the land they were standing on, as well as the land they would sail for, the great mountains, trees, and waterways in his homeland. He spoke of his men, his home, and his life. He described the ties that bound his people together. As he talked, he pulled Jilliand close. She relaxed, leaned against him, and listened.

After a long comfortable moment, Rurik turned her around. He placed the chain with the amulet around her neck and removed her cross, slipping it into the pouch he kept on his belt. "Keep this on; do not remove it. You *must* do this. It will protect you. I do not speak of your god, nor mine." When he finished talking, he stood motionless, holding Jilliand closely. *The Norns play with me.* Shaking his head, Rurik turned Jilliand toward the fire. "Go. You should sleep. We leave at first light." Without waiting for a reply, he walked along the shore alone.

At the fireside, Askold nodded to Jilliand and resumed turning the venison. Jilliand did as Rurik bade her, grateful she would be sleeping alone. She touched the amulet. It felt heavy and unwelcome. Yet, he had not forbidden her God to her, nor demanded she learn of his gods. *Pray he never does.*

The next morning, as mist shrouded the cove and sea beyond, Jilliand knelt near the edge of the water, washing her face. Rurik walked up and stood watching her. Pretending she was not aware of his presence, she finished cleaning up. Standing, she turned to him. He walked closer to her. Reaching out, he pulled several twigs from her hair. "Come eat," he invited, turning away.

"I am not hungry," Jilliand answered, watching him walk away from her. He gave no indication he heard her. She listened to the three men as they made ready to leave the cove. She could not understand her place with him. He did not treat her like a slave, nor like a whore. He treated her as an equal, or maybe a friend . . . or maybe more. He said he would take nothing for her. *What does that mean?*

"Rurik," Jilliand spoke carefully, "what of my horse? I care not to leave him alone here." Rurik looked from the horses to Jilliand then back at the animals grazing peacefully.

"They will stay together and will return to where they belong. Just like people." He watched the horses for a moment, adding, "Your horse will go with the others." Jilliand prayed Rurik was right.

When the Viking ship finally sailed to the shore, everyone boarded with a great deal of bantering among the men. Jilliand did not understand them but guessed they teased Rurik because of her. He didn't seem to mind. Jilliand felt comfortable with herself and these men. Her short time away from them, however, reassured her. Jilliand knew she could take care of herself, if need be. She was learning that her strength came from within. *I am not certain where life will take me, but I know I can manage.* She walked the starboard of the ship, watching the oars dip to push the water aside while the vessel moved away from the shore and out to sea. An English lady and Viking warriors . . .

On the second morning, excitement pervaded the crew as the warship sailed ever closer to home. Standing near the ship's bow, Jilliand watched the distant shoreline expand. Great snowcapped peaks rose in the background. Smaller ones huddled close to the base of the mountains seeking shelter beneath those towering above them. Evergreen trees crowded the mountainsides, while leafy varieties spilled over onto the valleys and plateaus at the mountain bases. Still dressed in the restful greens of summer, vegetation had begun to try on warm fall colors, casting speckles of color about.

Several Viking ships were tethered to the shore, swaying gracefully with the rolling waves. Structures along the seaboard grew as Rurik's ship sailed closer. The settlement appeared more orderly than anything Jilliand had seen in England. Smoke curled up from chimneys, animals grazed, and people moved about. While not surrounded by thick wooden walls like her father's burg, the Viking buildings appeared more permanent. There were smaller buildings made of timber, and many were covered with grasses growing on the sides, on the roofs, and around the structures. At one edge of the common grounds, other larger rectangular buildings sat. They had large doors facing the common grounds. From two of these, men could be seen leaving. A figure standing near the water was the first to spot the returning ship. One shout brought women and children, followed by men, running to the land's edge, calling out to the vessel's crew. With growing anxiety, Jilliand hung back.

Rurik and his men got off the ship and were immediately surrounded by a crowd that was laughing, hugging, and talking. Jilliand moved near the stern of the ship out of the way, watching the women. Nothing looked like she imagined, not the land, not the homes, and certainly not the women. Most of the women in the pitiful settlements Jilliand had seen in England were dirty, their clothes worn to rags and defeat displayed on their tired faces. Clearly, these women were different. Many were short with darker hair, maybe captives like Jilliand. They wore plain loose shifts with sleeves that reached their forearms. Over the shifts they wore colored panels of cloth that reached from the neckline to nearly the hem of the shift. The panels were held in place at the shoulders with thick braided material. Their hair was tucked under simple head coverings. Other women wore similar clothes, but much richer in detail. The panels worn over their shifts were deeper in color, displayed detailed designs sewn along the neckline and hem, and were attached at the shoulders with a jeweled bar pin. Their hair was worn up, but uncovered, and they wore an abundance of jewelry, rings, bracelets, and neck chains. These women were tall and light skinned, just like Rurik and his crew. Though the clothing and hairstyle spoke to a higher station, all the women worked equally hard side by side. When Jilliand finally stepped off the boat, the modestly dressed women greeted her. Animated, speaking in both English and French, the women confirmed they were indeed all servants or slaves. From the way they behaved, Jilliand surmised they must have been treated well, for none were frightened. They spoke excitedly to each other and to Jilliand, as she was herded along with them.

"We'll show you where you can sleep. Come. Do not be afraid. We are treated well here—some of us better than by our husbands at home. 'Tis not a bad place," a matronly woman said, as she kindly took Jilliand's hand. From a distance, Rurik looked around for Jilliand. He stood alone, watching her being led away. Nearby, Greida watched both the Sea King Rurik and Jilliand. Her eyes narrowed with jealousy.

Details of his raids were expected, so Rurik resisted the impulse to go after Jilliand. Instead, he dropped by another home. The home of the old woman, his mother, Olga. After a short greeting, he left Olga inside. As Rurik walked away, Olga came to the door of her home and watched the chattering cluster with Jilliand. Her eyes scanned the people milling around, until she found Greida, who was clearly angry, watching Jilliand. Rurik had not spoken to Greida, nor had he acknowledged her. He had forgotten about her. *Bad times come, I fear,* Olga thought as she stepped back into her home.

The womenfolk led Jilliand to one of the larger huts. Inside was an open space, housing looms, basket workings, and several children. An iron frame held a kettle over a large fire pit just inside the door. Built all along the sides, were sleeping platforms covered with mats and blankets. Just as Jilliand was shown an available platform, a child came to the door and spoke, but Jilliand could not understand what was said. However, she could tell the mood changed at his announcement. A hush fell over the room.

"Is it bad? What does he say?" Jilliand asked, her eyes on the young lad. The women exchanged glances.

"You are to go with him. It will be fine. Just go with him." One of the older women walked with her to the door.

"Where does he take me?" Jilliand hesitated, looking at the faces regarding her.

"You belong to someone," the woman said softly. Closing the door after Jilliand, the women felt sorry for her. Jilliand's time in this settlement could end very badly. Several of the ladies spoke of one woman's reaction—Greida's.

Looking back at the door as it closed behind her, Jilliand's heart fell. *I think on this day, I become what he intended—a slave.* The child led Jilliand to a different house. It was much smaller, housing a place for sleeping, a great fire pit that provided the only light, a chair, and little else. Jilliand walked around looking for signs that other women might live there. Nothing indicated that anyone lived there. Sighing, she set her few belongings on the sleeping slat, folded her cloaks, and began to carry wood pieces from near the door to the fire.

Rurik entered without a sound as she sat near the fire. She only heard his steps when he stood right behind her. "Are you sad, Jilliand?" he asked softly.

"No. Just alone. What am I to do now? It would seem this place is not used often." She turned to him. He could see her beautiful eyes in the light from the fire. Those eyes haunted him every night. *Soon,* he thought. He took her hand. "Come. We visit my brother, Olav, and his family this night. You will like Astrid, his wife."

She hesitated a moment. *Perhaps not a slave after all.*

To Jilliand's surprise, she did like his sister-in-law—a great deal. Olav's home was a long structure with a great fire pit near the front end. The pit itself was surrounded by large, flat rocks set on end. Over the pit, suspended by a chain from a huge center beam in the ceiling, hung a large pot. The pot's contents boiled, sending an aroma into the home that made Jilliand's mouth water. In the middle of the space were several chairs, a table, and a rack from which hung other cooking utensils and different kinds of meat. Beyond the rack, Jilliand could see shelves with plates, bowls, cups, and eating utensils. The far end of the space was dark, but Jilliand could make out several sleeping platforms. The room and its contents made the area feel like a home. Jilliand felt an unexpected wave of relief. Astrid motioned to Jilliand to join her near the fire while she kept an eye on the pot. She handed Jilliand a cup of warm mead. It was apparent everyone was happy to see Rurik, and she felt like the conversation most certainly included her, as several times Olav looked her way and nodded or laughed. Jilliand could not speak the language, but with hand motions and nods, they communicated nonetheless. When it was time to leave, Jilliand was handed a stack of thick, soft blankets. Rurik walked with her back to the house. He stepped inside, added wood to the fire, stood for a moment looking at her, and then walked out without speaking. He knew their time would come but not on this night. It was enough that she was with his people and was welcome. When she could no longer hear his footsteps, Jilliand pulled at the door. It swung into the room easily and was unguarded outside. For the first time, she was in a room alone but not restrained or locked up. Jilliand was grateful to be left alone, though she was haunted by her ill-defined relationship with Rurik.

When the morning sun blessed the village with warmth, Jilliand left her house in search of the women she met when she had arrived. She could hear the sounds of a stream behind her house, and several women walked past her carrying cauldrons of water. Others carried children. Still others walked, laughing and talking, across the compound toward pens where cattle and sheep stood expectantly. She saw men in small groups leaving the settlement carrying axes and other tools. The sound of cattle, sheep, and horses mixed with the laughter of children. People paid her little mind. She obviously belonged to Rurik. He had not restricted her, nor would they. Jilliand smiled to herself. *So unlike father's home, this place.*

Jilliand quickly fell into a routine. Each day she joined the women, where she began learning to weave, cook, dry hides, and make ceramic pots. The women were kind, and with much laughter and jesting, they passed their days. The life was hard, but not harsh. None of these women were afraid. Children ran in and out, taunting, teasing, and playing. Jilliand had never spent time in such an environment. She began to feel more at ease.

From the way some of the women watched Rurik when he walked through the settlement, Jilliand knew they had spent time with him. One woman in particular repeatedly tried to engage the sea king in coy conversation, but he would not respond. He brushed the woman aside. Jilliand soon learned the woman's name was Greida. Though none spoke of it, Jilliand could tell that Greida hated her. Jilliand felt that Greida's loathing was because of Rurik. That knowledge made Jilliand's heart ache if she allowed herself to think about it. Jilliand resolved to push Rurik from her thinking and concentrated on staying busy learning the things these women knew. She would not come between Rurik and Greida. After all, Greida belonged here, Jilliand did not.

One morning, an old woman came to walk with Jilliand as Jilliand carried a cauldron of water to the communal house. Jilliand had often seen her around the compound speaking to everyone, walking slowly, hunched over, usually clutching a basket with her twisted arthritic fingers. Walking in step with Jilliand, she talked nonstop. Unable to understand a word the woman said, Jilliand still felt at ease with her. The woman did not appear to belong to anyone in particular. She lived alone in a house near the edge of the settlement. When she was around, every woman in the village, both Viking and slave, treated her with reverence. Jilliand's morning walks with her became a daily ritual because the old woman sought her out every day. Jilliand did not realize the old woman was Olga, Rurik's mother. In the beginning, Greida had only watched Jilliand, but twice Jilliand had met her within the common area, and both times, Greida bumped Jilliand viciously, nearly knocking her to the ground, and then smiled cruelly as she walked past. To Jilliand's relief, when the old woman was with her, Greida kept her distance.

In the early hours of the morning one day, the old woman came to Jilliand's home, knocking urgently on her door. The words were foreign; the urgency in her voice was not. Jilliand threw on a cloak and ran after the old woman. They scurried across the grounds to one of the family houses. Jilliand could feel the relief in the room when the old woman entered the home. *I think this woman is a healer.*

Jilliand was relieved to see Greida was not present. Children had been herded out to other homes while the husband stood near watching a pregnant woman who squatted, grasping the edges of a sleeping pallet. The mother's moans became louder as the women around her seemed to be encouraging her. Suddenly, water gushed from the moaning woman, and her labor intensified. Jilliand stood out of the way, eyes fixed on the scene. When the baby's head protruded, the old woman knelt, holding a soft blanket to catch the newborn. The mother and babe were cleaned. One of the women handed the babe to the husband. He laid the child on his knee and sprinkled the infant boy with water, showing he accepted and acknowledged the child. The child was put to the mother's breast as the final act of taking the child into the family and giving him all inherited rights. Jilliand remembered Gouldon's attack on her. If he had been successful, she could have been heavy with his child. *I cannot even bear to think on it,* she shuddered.

The people of the settlement were not what Jilliand would have imagined a Viking people to be. Many of those captured had become free members by the second generation. Children were frequently adopted and raised as Viking, without prejudice. Captives were expected to learn the language and customs, as well as adopt the religion. Jilliand could understand and talk with the captive women, but the Viking language was difficult. Still, she tried to learn and was careful to keep her conversations clear of religion. As yet, only Greida had challenged her, and Greida's behavior was rapidly becoming bolder.

Greida made it her business to denigrate Jilliand whenever she could, while keeping a wary eye out for the old woman and the men. Greida's actions and verbal abuse made Jilliand's life increasingly unpleasant. Greida insisted Jilliand carry water and wood to her house, and clean it, while trying to keep Jilliand away from the house Rurik kept for Jilliand. Greida was never pleased with Jilliand's work and made certain the other women knew Jilliand's failures. Rurik seemed unaware of Greida's treatment of Jilliand, and Jilliand was loath to tell him, since she was still unable to understand her relationship with him. For his part, Rurik carefully watched the friendship growing between Jilliand and Olga. Rurik was gone most of the time until evening, when he made it a point to come see Jilliand. She looked forward to his coming and felt a pang of sadness each time he left her. Rurik slept someplace else, and in her heart, Jilliand believed he went to Greida.

During his evening visits to Jilliand, Rurik sat watching her as she learned to work the loom. Sometimes he talked of the traditions of his people, how travelers were to be cared for in the winter, because of winter's deadly harshness. He spoke of the importance of children, explaining how children would ensure the lives of his people long after he and the others were dead. He spoke of their gods and talked about the honor and privilege that came to any Viking who died fighting. He explained that most of the men in the settlement were cousins, brothers, or best friends, all bound by love and a deep sense of loyalty to Rurik and each other. As Jilliand listened, she studied this strange man—this man who did not try to hurt her, was never harsh with her, and who seemed comfortable with her. He seemed so different from the man she had watched kill women, children, and men with equal ease. She observed the reaction of the people to each other, to Rurik, and to her. They *were* all bound together. One evening, during his visit, she observed aloud, "Maybe we, your people and mine, are not so different."

Rurik studied her for a long moment. "There are differences, Jilliand," he replied, quietly. She was not certain how to respond, so she did not. He sat with her longer that evening—seldom speaking, only watching her and dozing by the fire. Jilliand felt comfortable and at peace with him near.

Jilliand proved a quick study at sewing, cooking, and tanning hides. She took her turn feeding the animals and caring for children. Through it all, though, she could feel a growing distance between her and the other captured women. Not a hard one but still a distance. As long as Rurik continued to visit her each evening, she thought little about her station in this place. It was enough that she was made to feel welcome by most of the people.

As for Greida, Jilliand dealt with every confrontation calmly, while avoiding the woman as much as possible. Greida could not have known that cruelty was not new to Jilliand. *At some point, I will be forced to carry a weapon around Greida. I pray I am not forced to use it.* Although none of the women spoke aloud about Greida's behavior, Jilliand could feel they were uncomfortable watching Greida. Jilliand prayed Greida would not make her live as an outcast in the settlement.

CHAPTER 15

THE CHILDREN BECAME JILLIAND'S BEST teachers. Timidly, she tried out the Norse language with the small ones. Each day, Jilliand slipped away to be with them. They explored the entire area, sat on the banks of the river running nearby, and watched the sea. She listened to their stories, laughed at their pranks, and encouraged them as they happily enjoyed each day. For their part, they took great pride in her increasing vocabulary, trying to teach her new words each time they were together. Except for Greida, Jilliand's days were passing easily.

One evening, as Jilliand was weaving alone in her house, a slave came to her. "You are to come," he said. Frowning, Jilliand hesitated, praying it was not Greida who sent him. When Jilliand did not immediately answer, the young man assumed she did not understand him and gestured urgently.

Jilliand set aside her loom, pulled her hair back, donned her cloak, and followed him. Dressed in a simple black shift that reached the ground, she wore no jewelry except the one hair comb she had found tucked within the gowns Rurik had taken for her, the locket Rurik had taken from the old captain, and the amulet Rurik had insisted she wear hidden underneath her shift.

Jilliand was led to the great hall reserved for men. Jilliand had never been inside the hall before and hesitated now. The slave opened the door and stood expectantly. Jilliand stepped through the doorway. A quick survey proved Jilliand was the only woman inside, and there were visitors. She stood still, not sure what was expected of her. Greida watched Jilliand walk into the men's building with jealousy near the erupting point.

Rurik sat at the head of the table in the front of the room. When their eyes met, he nodded toward her bow and arrows, which were lying at the foot of his table. The room was silent as all eyes watched her move with grace and elegance to the front. When she reached the table, she heard him tell the visitors that she could shoot better than any man he knew. Her heart leapt to her throat. *I am to be the entertainment? Surely he jests!* Anxiety tinged with anger began to tighten her stomach. *What if I miss this time?*

Jilliand glanced at the circle of men as she knelt to pick up the bow. Her expression changed suddenly when her eyes met a man sitting near Rurik. He was just as surprised to see her. Fighting to control her emotions, Jilliand gradually straightened. Her eyes were filled with loathing as she glared at him.

In English, she spoke to him, her voice dripping with disdain, "Do these people know who you are?"

"Do they know about *you*, is more the question," he countered. His eyes moved over her, halting at her fist gripping the bow. "I should have known it would be you. No other girl can shoot like a man. Though you have become a woman, I see. You could fetch a small fortune, now."

"No one would pay for me," Jilliand corrected him. "The man with the money is now dead. As for me, my father cares not; you should know, you stood by while he whipped me, coward that you are."

"I believed you dead," he shrugged, draining his goblet.

"In truth? After he left me lying on the ground, you tried to rape me. But you could not. As sorely wounded as I was, you could not take me. Surely, you still carry the scar on your chest. You screamed like a woman. I, on the other hand, never made a sound. Not even when he beat me again," Jilliand ended with contempt. She stood rigid, her hate of this man evident. As Rurik took in every word, his expression changed, unnoticed by either the English or Jilliand. He felt his anger grow. Both his jarls were aware of the change in him. They watched the exchange between Jilliand and the Englishman, waiting for a signal from Rurik.

The Englishman now responded angrily, his voice low and cruel, "I will buy you, and we shall see who screams. This time you *will* die after I am through with you."

"Does he know what kind of man you are? That you would burn his warships while he sleeps? Does he know you would steal his stores and take his women—those you do not kill?" Jilliand continued. Not once did she look at Rurik.

"He doesn't speak English. I care little what he thinks. My time has come. You, I'll take tomorrow, and I'll see you beg for mercy!" Unnoticed by Jilliand or the Englishman, Rurik nodded to one of the slaves near him, then toward Jilliand. Jilliand was to be taken back immediately. The slave trotted toward Jilliand.

"Beg for mercy from you? I would die first." In a flash, Jilliand notched an arrow. She had already drawn the string back on the bow when she glanced at Rurik. His head shook, barely perceptible, but it was clearly *do not*. For a second, Jilliand hesitated. The urge to run the man through with one clean shot was overpowering. The man's face blanched when he saw the arrow set. Slowly, Jilliand regained control. Taking a breath, she turned and left the room without looking at anyone.

Standing, Rurik noted to the men gathered, "It seems they might know each other." A humorless smile played upon his face. "I think we do not need a woman for entertainment after all."

Askold could see Rurik's eyes were dark with rage. "Enough," Rurik said as he turned to the man. "Tell us how you find the coast. Is it good?" Slowly, deliberately seating himself, Rurik picked up a tankard of ale, thus ending the drama. Dir nodded to Askold.

The men began to relax and talk. Askold wandered around the hall, speaking to men, tasting food, and laughing. Meanwhile, Dir ducked out a back door. Walking to the shore, he settled in to wait and watch. His patience paid, for he caught five Englishmen trying to set fire to several Viking ships. Viking culture taught that visitors were to be treated with kindness and assistance in this unforgiving land. That law did not apply to men such as these, Dir reasoned.

The sounds of fighting came to Jilliand, loud and clear. Calmly, she moved to the back of her quarters, with her bow and blade, to wait. Bit by bit, the fighting sounds grew less, until all became silent, but for the low voices of men. Every fiber in her body was alert, and she caught the sound of someone entering. Setting an arrow, she waited. Whoever it was moved with familiarity of her place. Jilliand began to relax. It must be Rurik.

"Why is it you sit in the dark?" Rurik's voice came to her from the blackness.

"I knew not who would enter," Jilliand replied, laying her weapons aside. She stood up and waited. Rurik started a fire and set wood near. He walked to Jilliand and stopped, standing over her. With a gentle touch, he brushed her hair back.

"You knew that man," Rurik observed.

"Once I was afraid of him . . . and of my father. I am not afraid now." Jilliand looked at Rurik, standing so close. She could feel her heart beating as if she had been running.

"You are not afraid?" He watched her closely.

"Not of you. Of this life? Perhaps . . . " she admitted softly.

"Are you not treated kindly?" he quickly asked frowning.

"Yes, I am." She paused; this was not the time to talk of Greida. Looking at him curiously, she asked, "What *are* you to these people?"

He laughed softly. "In time, Jilliand," he said, as he ran his hand over her hair again. "In time." Without speaking further, he turned and walked out.

Jilliand sat down by the fire brooding. She could still feel his touch. "What am I to him, should be my question," she admitted. "I fear my heart goes into forbidden lands. He belongs to Greida. He is not for me." The night was nearly gone before she found sleep.

The next morning, Greida was not about yet. Jilliand went in search of the group of women who had become her friends. The great room became silent when she walked in. Not certain what to say, she simply stood waiting. Olga was sitting with them this morning and spoke up first. "I came to find you. Good of you to join us. We thought you might have left in the night. Tell us what happened in the great hall."

Jilliand had to smile. *The healer speaks English*, she thought as she pulled her cloak off and sat closer to the fire. She told them the story, ending with the fight. The story of the incident at the hands of her father's friend, she did not tell. Let the Vikings tell what they would of that. By early afternoon, anxious to avoid Greida, she left the women's company to look for the children.

From the children, she learned that the Englishman and his men had been to the settlement three times before, trading the Vikings woolen goods for weapons. This was unusual for any but a Viking. The children were excited and could talk of nothing but the fight. Jilliand shuddered at the sight of the hanged men. The captain was not among them. It was useless to get the young boys to talk of anything else, so she left in search of Olga who by now had most certainly left the women's house.

As she rounded the great hall, she ran into Rurik, nearly falling. He smiled at her stumbling, catching her easily. Gathering her wits, she spoke quietly, "Pray tell me he did not get away."

"Why would you think that?" he asked, his eyes narrowing as he studied her.

"I did not see, well . . . he's not . . . there is no sign . . . " Sighing, she admitted, "I did not see him among the hanged men. I looked." She ducked her head.

Gently, he raised her chin. "He did not escape. And he did have a scar on his chest." He smiled and walked past her, without looking back.

Jilliand watched him leave. *I am beginning to care for him. This cannot be a good thing.* She continued on her way to Olga. Finding her at home, Jilliand was soon seated at her feet, helping her pull yarn.

"Jilliand, I am called Olga," the old woman began. "You are troubled, Jilliand?" Neither spoke for a while. Jilliand liked the sound of her name in their tongue. She would miss being here.

"Yes, I am. I fear I have come to love Rurik. This cannot be. I should leave this place." She turned her sad eyes on the old woman. To her surprise, Olga was smiling.

"You cannot leave, Jilliand. This is your home. Perhaps he loves you, too," Olga suggested, watching her young friend. Jilliand was stunned. *Perhaps Greida was not what Greida would have me believe. No matter. Rurik could not be for me.*

"No, he cannot," Jilliand whispered sadly. "I cannot let that happen."

The woman shrugged. "You cannot change fate, Jilliand. The gods will have their way."

Despite Olga's comment, Jilliand became obsessed with getting away. Her promise to Rurik was long forgotten. She had to leave soon, or she would never want to leave. She already felt as if these people were her people, her family, and this was her place. But this pagan could not be for her. She must leave before it was too late. Jilliand would never give up her faith. She knew Rurik would not give his up either. If these people tried to coerce her into participation in the pagan rituals, Jilliand knew she would be forced to challenge them. Greida's behavior and comments made it clear; that time would come soon. Such an event could mean she would be banished from the settlement or killed. Better to leave while she was still accepted—and alive. For the next several weeks, Jilliand studied everyone she had interactions with, trying to understand what was done to survive in this inhospitable land. She studied and planned. Greida planned, too.

CHAPTER 16

ONE AFTERNOON, THE SETTLEMENT HELD a great celebration. The hall was filled to overflowing with people eating, laughing, and singing. Most of the houses were also occupied with people celebrating. From his brother's house, Rurik sent a maid to fetch Jilliand. Finding Jilliand's house empty, the maid knew where to look, and Greida reluctantly released Jilliand from her chores. Jilliand entered the main room at Olav's house and found it filled with adults caught up in the festivities honoring one of their gods. She didn't understand the reason for the gathering, but she did understand Rurik's slight swagger. He was drunk.

"Maybe it's time to see if you also *think* like a man," he challenged with a slur that made his Norse accent more difficult to understand.

"Men who are drunk are mean," Jilliand observed calmly, answering him in his own language and deftly avoiding his grasp.

"Women who are drunk are easy. Come drink with me," he grinned.

"Are you not man enough to take me whether I am drunk or not?" Jilliand spoke defiantly, without thinking.

Rurik's face darkened ominously. The house grew silent. Sensing perhaps she had gone too far, she had to say something to cover her insult.

"I said," she continued indignantly, her mind racing. She attempted to speak in his native tongue, purposefully confusing the words. "You take me to drunk . . . men take drink to . . . " Pretending she was flustered, she stamped her foot. By this time, everyone was trying to interpret what she was saying. Rurik leaned forward, concentrating, struggling to comprehend.

As if greatly frustrated by her own lack of expression, she tried again, her chin high, hands on her hips, while the hushed crowd strained to understand her, "You dog's ear . . . you . . . you cow foot, you . . . Oh!" In a show of anger and frustration, she stamped her foot again.

"What is this you say?" Rurik asked, frowning. His brother had begun to laugh. Soon everyone was laughing. Rurik failed to see the humor of the exchange as he continued to regard Jilliand.

"Perhaps she is too well bred to curse you, Rurik," Dir noted between gasps for air. The house was now rocking with laughter.

Jilliand stomped through the door, slamming it behind her. As she left, she heard Askold yell, "She's a fit queen for you, Rurik, if you can tame her temper."

Rurik rose from his seat and slowly followed her out, pausing briefly to pick up his cloak. He leisurely walked behind her, watching her run to the village edge. From there, she darted into the surrounding woodland.

Following, he found her sitting on the ground, sobbing. He had never known her to cry. The tears, from one he knew to be strong and determined, moved him, but he could not make sense of her outburst. Wordlessly, he pulled her up and wrapped her in his cloak, and then walked her back to her house. "Do not challenge me again, Jilliand. You would not like the answer," he spoke softly. Opening the door for her, he turned and walked back to his brother's house. Jilliand sank onto her bed, her eyes filled with tears that spilled over and dropped unheeded from her chin. For a long while she sat just that way, as the tears fell. Leaving this man would be hard indeed.

The next morning, as was now her habit, Jilliand walked to the women's house. Joining them in their chores, she was indifferent to the gossip. The chatter faded into the background, while she planned her departure. Greida had not been seen.

Later in the afternoon, Jilliand sat with her old friend. "You make a mistake, Jilliand," Olga casually noted.

"You know what I think?" Jilliand asked startled. "Does my face speak for me so plainly?" If the healer knew, maybe everyone knew.

"No one knows, child," the woman gently corrected Jilliand. "Your heart is troubled." For a moment, the room was silent while Jilliand wrestled with her decision. "Perhaps we are not so different from you? Perhaps you worry in vain. No matter—the Norns play with you oftentimes." She continued to weave, her bent and crippled hands still making the looms sing.

"Norns?" asked Jilliand.

"Yes, the three sisters of fate. Urd of the past, Verdandi of the present, and Skuld of the future. I think Skuld plays with you the most. You cannot change what will be, Jilliand." Olga looked kindly at her young friend. Thoughtfully, she continued, "Tell me of your god."

Jilliand hesitated. "Speak, child. I am old. No one bothers about me now. I do what I please. Some day you will also—I see that for you. Now talk with me. We are friends, you and I, Jilliand." Olga smiled at her.

Jilliand talked of God's power of forgiveness, His love for all creatures, His great sacrifice, His mother, and His strength for the weakest of His people. Olga listened intently.

"Your god is like a great king, then, like every king should be," she noted thoughtfully. "Jilliand, you will do what you must, but you should know that this is now your home. You cannot simply walk away. Too many have come to know and care for you. Still, you will do what you must. Go in peace my child. Come to me when you can." With that, she picked up her things and stepped into a back room, closing the door behind her. Jilliand knew the time to leave had come.

The walk back to her house made her sad. Jilliand tried to capture every detail of her surroundings. "I must remember this—all of it. I will never find another place like this." She surveyed the area while the wind swirled around her, its cold hand grasping her heart. "I am losing my family."

Greida watched Jilliand walk homeward. *Soon Rurik will leave, and then I will rid this place of her forever.* Greida's dislike had grown into hate; her jealousy filled her heart with venom. Now it would be Greida's chance to turn the settlement against Jilliand and then have her slain according to their law.

Rurik frequently took his men on short raids. It had become a habit for him to see Jilliand and let her know he would be gone. This day, he felt a sadness encircling her. After they parted, Rurik stopped to look back at her closed door. This was not the time to speak of how he felt. His mind must focus on other things. As he walked away from her house, he felt a stirring in his heart. *When I return, the waiting will end.* Satisfied, his mind set on the venture ahead, he set sail.

As soon as the village returned to everyday activities with the men gone, Greida began her plan. Calling everyone to gather in the middle of the settlement early one morning, Greida found Jilliand. Greida was nearly six feet tall and muscular. Her long blonde hair was always worn in a tight braid, wound around her head. She stomped when she walked, her voice was loud, and her face had grown hard. Rurik had been her conquest since she first came to the settlement. So far, besides spending several nights with her, he had shown little interest in making their relationship anything permanent. Greida intended to change that, today, now. Grasping Jilliand's arm, she forced Jilliand to the center of the assembled people. Unaware Jilliand could understand her, Greida spoke. "See the Christian? She is not one of us, nor could she ever be one of us. She thinks to take Rurik? He is our sea king. This one is not fit to clean his floor. Look at her." Greida pushed Jilliand hard. Jilliand stumbled but did not fall. Greida was at her side immediately.

Greida viciously grasped Jilliand's hair and jerked her around. "Rurik belongs to me. He would never take *this.*" Greida's voice was filled with contempt. Jilliand pulled away from Greida. She had no weapon, nor was she certain the rest of the settlement would stand behind her if she injured Greida. The inhabitants stared at Greida and Jilliand, not certain what to do. The silence was overwhelming. Jilliand tried to think. Before she had a chance to do anything to defend herself, Greida ripped at her shift. "See, she even wears her symbol. Look!" The shift tore from Jilliand's neck. A gasp escaped Greida.

The women and children crowded closer and then began to murmur. Clearly exposed was the amulet hanging from its chain. Someone shouted, "That's Rurik's!" The cry went up. "That's Rurik's" was repeated louder.

Quickly, Jilliand, her own voice loud and clear, replied. "Yes, it is a gift from Rurik. I have worn it since he placed it on me." She turned to Greida. "You have made your case. You claim you belong to Rurik. I do not challenge that. Only he can decide."

"It will not matter," Greida sputtered, desperately trying to recapture the moment. "You are banished! Go! Get out! Leave this place!" She shoved Jilliand hard. "You are not welcome here any longer." Greida was taller than Jilliand, and her anger gave her added strength. Jilliand flew backward and fell to the ground. She got up immediately. The crowd had again become silent, stunned by what they saw. *It was true,* they thought. Rurik did favor Greida at one time. Clearly, he did no longer. But all were reluctant to interfere with Greida. She was a dangerous adversary.

Greida came at Jilliand again. This time, Jilliand was ready and stood her ground, easily dodging the hand raised to slap her. Greida became more enraged. Jilliand realized there would be no good ending. Jilliand would be forced to defend herself, and Jilliand knew she may have to kill Greida. Greida was much larger, but she was clumsy and did not know how to fight. Jilliand turned and pushed her way through the people now beginning to talk among themselves. Jilliand ran to her house. From the sounds outside, the people were coming too. Jilliand quickly left without looking back, carrying only what she had brought with her and the flint Rurik had given her.

Olga, awakened by the commotion outside, slowly made her way through the throng of people. Jilliand was already gone. "What happens here?" she asked. Silence greeted her, and most refused to look at her.

Greida stepped up close, sneering, "Jilliand is gone. I have banished her."

Olga was clearly shocked. "On whose authority do you do this?"

Greida refused to answer. She only turned away, ignoring Olga. "Now, our people can return to the way we were."

"The way *you* were?" Olga pointedly asked. No one answered. *Stay safe child. Rurik comes home soon*, Olga thought. She looked around once more, to be certain her young friend was indeed gone. Olga knew she was in no shape to look for Jilliand, but Rurik was. *He will come home and find you, Jilliand.*

Taking now familiar trails, Jilliand headed deep into the forest. The afternoon temperature was dropping, but her cloak and the walk kept her warm. She kept moving. When the trail became unfamiliar, she was forced to walk more slowly, but she could not stop. Only movement would keep the cold at bay.

When the sun's rays broke through the darkness the next day, Jilliand was farther from Rurik's village than she had ever been. With daylight filtering through the treetops, Jilliand could see she would need to change direction to reach the shoreline. From there, she would swim out to an island just beyond the shore. She had planned to leave Rurik, anyway. Greida's confrontation made it all easier. From the children, she had learned that ships frequently sailed along the island's far shore, and the Vikings never, never went to the island. The chunk of land looked to be large, was certain to have game, and was not a place either Rurik or Greida would look to. It was said to be where one of the Viking gods, Frey, instructed his emissary, Skirnir, to hide magic apples—apples that kept the gods young. *I could use a magic apple or two*, Jilliand noted. *It will be a safe place to stay alone until I can board a ship.*

In a short while, Jilliand had reached the water's edge. Undressing hurriedly and bundling her clothes tightly, she ran into the sea. She was not prepared for the cold that sucked the breath from her. It would be impossible to swim; she was barely able to move. She turned around. Back on shore, dressed, and wrapped in the cloak, she shook uncontrollably. Never had she felt such cold. "I must find another place to go," she sputtered through chattering teeth. "No wonder their gods hide things out there." Jilliand trotted along the shore, trying to warm up. *I must do better than this.* After several hours, she was forced to veer further inland, to escape the cold wind now coming off the water.

It was mid-afternoon when she first saw the smoke. Somewhere to the north a settlement was burning. There would be people banded together if anyone survived. Perhaps she could travel with them. *But . . . who would burn a Viking village?* Late in the afternoon, she came upon a small group comprised of a few frightened women and many children, at a loss as to where to go. Everyone crowded around Jilliand, talking at once. They needed someone to help them; Jilliand was the only one around.

Some of the women and most of the older children wanted to return to their village. They hoped there were survivors. Others believed they were being followed. If they were being tracked, it would only be a matter of time. Others in the band insisted on retracing their steps, although none carried weapons. There had not been time. The men of the village had run to fight while the women had hustled the children away from the violence. "There is great danger in going back without weapons and in the gathering darkness," Jilliand warned. "Even with daylight, your travel will be slow because of the children."

An uneasy silence fell over them, and then the arguments began. Eventually, Jilliand's attempts to at least have the very youngest stay behind won out. It was agreed the older boys and Jilliand would return to look for survivors. The women and remaining children would stay in the glen, hidden among the evergreen trees and low growing brush still clinging to the last of its leaves. Everyone helped build makeshift lean-to shelters of fallen tree branches and brush.

With first light, Jilliand and the older boys began walking. The boys were already well trained. Like spirits, they slid silently through the thick forest. When the sun filled the valley with light, Jilliand looked on what remained of a community not unlike the settlement Rurik ruled. They climbed over burned remnants of homes and pens. Bodies were everywhere. None were left alive, not even the infants. Looking at the carnage before her, Jilliand slowly realized that both sides in this conflict were Vikings.

"Come, tell me which man is of this place and which is an enemy. I cannot tell. They look the same." Jilliand looked around for anyone who could speak to the bodies lying around. One young boy stood beside a burned-out shell. The eyes he turned to her were filled with deep sadness. When he spoke, it was with bitterness.

"They were brothers. Neither was foe, until neither was friend. They are both dead. We are all that's left. Let us be gone from this place." He turned back toward his companions. The knowledge that the Vikings did this to their own kind was unsettling. It was not just a horror visited upon the English. Without speaking, Jilliand began to gather any weapons, blankets, and food-stuffs she could find. The boys tried to help. It was a daunting task for these very young men. Before long, night crept around them. The small band of survivors left the remnants of their homes. Each held swords and shields, and what they could find of blankets and cloaks along with several pots packed with food.

When they made it back to the glen, the tale was told. The women with the troupe simply moved about to make fires and began putting foodstuffs together. After the group had quieted down, one of the boys who looked to be older than the rest approached Jilliand where she sat on a log. After watching Jilliand's reaction to the battle site, listening to her knowledge of the best weapons to gather, and listening to her speak, he sat beside her and spoke to her. "I am Helgi. We have heard stories about you. You are the woman who fights like a man. Will you help us now?"

Jilliand glanced at the young man. He was bitter, young, and bent on revenge—a combination she knew well. "What is it you would have me do?" She studied his earnest face, waiting for his answer.

"I would go to his place. Do to his people what he did to mine. I would kill his sons, enslave his women. Destroy his holdings!" As he spoke, his anger hardened his words.

"Then you would make innocent children, babies, and mothers suffer as yours have done? Suffer for something they took no part in?" Jilliand stood and pulled the boy up to walk. When the boy did not answer, she added, "I see no justice in what you would do. The one you would punish is dead, along with his brother. Their quarrel brought both places to a bitter end. Think you his place can survive without their men? They will be taken over by someone but not likely someone who loves or cares for them."

Another young man had joined them, listening intently. "I am Sloveig, friend of Helgi. I think we should go to them and be the ones to take over. To care for them and bring an end to this," the second boy stated firmly.

Surprised, Jilliand studied the speaker. He looked to be more comfortable with everything. He was very sad but not bitter or angry. "What is your place in all this? Are you the son of either man?" Jilliand asked.

Sloveig shook his head. "I am a brother to both. I lived in both places." He paused as if thinking. "I think we bring families to us. To be one with us. We can do that." He jostled the other boy. "We, you and I, can be the sea kings of both peoples. We can do this. You are my friend, Helgi. I will follow you." As if the matter were settled, the speaker stood straighter and walked with confidence.

Helgi frowned and then studied the ground before him. He kept glancing at the speaker. At last, he stopped walking. "Your plan is better. I agree. We can do this." With that, he grasped the arm of his friend. All three returned to the group, now waiting expectantly.

Helgi raised his long blade. "I am the one to lead. All stay who are with me. Any who wish to leave, keep moving. I return to the place this began. We will be the ones to end this. We will make our homes there. We will take the peoples of that place to us. Who stays with me?"

The group stood around looking at one another. None spoke nor moved. "Helgi," Jilliand stepped up. "Most of the women and the few men who might be waiting for you at the standing settlement are probably slaves. What would you offer them? The very young children are much too small to understand what you ask. But the older ones, they could understand. Speak to them, all of them. Why should they join you? Tell them."

Helgi listened intently to Jilliand. He knew what Jilliand told him was true, and he realized what he could offer those sitting near him. Turning, he again spoke out. "All that would come with me will be given freedom this night, to serve, to live, and to fight by my side. Together, we forge a new settlement. Ours. Not to be torn by brother against brother. Who comes with me?"

This time, all the adults and young men old enough to comprehend even parts of what he said raised their hands, shields, and blades to him. "Helgi, Helgi . . . " the chant began. Helgi turned back to Jilliand and spoke, his voice strong, "And you, Lady. Who do you stand by?"

Jilliand felt the eyes of the entire party on her. They could not have known she was but a captive. Worse, she was banished, forced out of the community. She had to think of something. "I would go with you until you reach your place. Then I leave you. I am English. If I stay, I bring danger to you. I stand alone."

Helgi nodded. Without further comment, he turned and was soon surrounded by the group. When the grey light of the short day was gone, the band settled. Fires were fed, food was eaten, and shelters made stronger, to shield them from the cold and wind sure to come with darkness. Jilliand paced around and around the perimeter of the encampment during the long night, trying to ignore the gut-wrenching pain in her heart. "Mother, what am I supposed to do now? I am lost, more than these people. I cannot go back. I cannot stay with these children. Can I leave them to their own fates?" She stood with her face turned upward, toward heaven, quietly praying, "God, if I am supposed to help these children, please let me know how." She heard the crunch of frozen plants being crushed against the icy ground as someone walked toward her. It was Helgi.

Helgi was beginning to worry about the commitment he had made. He had watched Jilliand pacing. Eventually, he walked in step with her. "This will not be easy, this thing I do," he ventured. A heavy, wet snow that clung to all it touched began to fall. The large flakes plummeting to the ground were so thick even the campfires were barely visible. The temperature had settled, and the winds died down. Enormous evergreens appeared to open their boughs to the snow, as if they welcomed the cover of the coming winter. Other trees were nearly all bare. They stood out, each a solitary guardian of the thick forested hillside.

"No, it will not. But if you have support from the families of both places, you can do what you've set yourself to do." Jilliand looked at the dark form of the boy walking with her. He was so young, and while Jilliand realized Helgi had already begun training to fight, he would not have had any training to be a leader. Unless . . . "Was one of the brothers your father, Helgi?" The air was silent, and for a moment Jilliand thought he had not heard her.

"Yes." His answer was sharp and angry. "I loved them both." He added bitterly, "Now I have nothing."

"That is wrong, Helgi," Jilliand quickly responded. "You have far more than nothing. You have the blood of both men flowing in you, together as one. You must take the best of both and make that knowledge yours." She waited for some reaction.

"I can do that," he replied with quiet resolve. The night was silent around them. Helgi started to walk away but paused. "How does an Englishwoman come to a Viking land?"

"By losing the fight, Helgi." Jilliand's voice was soft. "By losing the fight." Helgi stood still, watching Jilliand. Then he turned away. With a wave of his hand, he walked back to the fires.

Jilliand watched him until he moved from her sight. She continued to walk, now moving higher into the forest, where the evergreens grew closer together. Morning found her high above the small band. With no solution to her own dilemma in mind, sorrow in her heart, and the reality of what these children faced weighing her down, Jilliand had not slept. Distant clouds were now gathering in force, to crush what was left of fall. *How I have changed. From a thing beaten, to a woman. Is this what women do? Are we sent to help people when we have no answers for our own problems? How can I tell Helgi the one who could help him the most is the one I must leave behind?*

Jilliand never felt the cold of the passing night nor the bite of early morning, so lost was she in her own thoughts. How could she stay? Greida would always be an obstacle, but not the only one. Rurik was a pagan, his gods were not hers, nor would she ever take them. Her time with his people had been ample proof of the two demands Vikings made of those they captured and chose to allow to live. Language and religion. Language she was mastering. Jilliand had taken care to keep out of any discussions of their gods. She could tell more than one of the women living in the communal building still secretly clung to their Christian faith. Although Jilliand now understood how the amulet she wore protected her, she did not believe Rurik would allow her the privilege of clinging to her faith. An impossible obstacle.

Jilliand's thoughts again drifted to the group of refugees camped below her. She knew Helgi could become a sea king, but not if someone didn't teach him. If help did not come, someone else would take over the rule of Helgi's people.

CHAPTER 17

LEAPING FROM THE BOAT TO the shore, Rurik suddenly felt a great burden. Something he could not name pulled at his heart. The women looked down when his eyes met theirs. The children clung together, wide-eyed, and watched. Something was wrong. As he walked toward Jilliand's house, he knew she had gone. He could feel it. With each step, his pain and anger grew. He found Jilliand's house cold and empty. She had taken only what she came with and was gone. Now worry seethed within. *She dares to leave now? She'll not leave again!* he promised himself.

Stepping from Jilliand's house, he was met by Askold's wife. "You must speak with Greida. She banished Jilliand. There was a confrontation. I think Greida was lucky Jilliand was unarmed. Jilliand left that afternoon."

Rurik's eyes bore into the woman's. "Not one of you spoke for Jilliand?"

"No," she answered softly. "It happened quickly. We know Jilliand belongs to you, Rurik, but you have not made it clear to Greida. She has been set aside. Nor, it would seem, have you made it clear to Jilliand where she stands with you. We would follow where you lead, but you have yet to tell your people how you feel."

"To Jilliand, I have not made my intentions clear. Greida knows exactly where she stands with me. She has known well she has no place with me after I found her sharing her bed with Gouldon. Where is Greida? Bring her here." Rurik's voice was hard.

When Greida was found, she was taken to the meeting building. Word spread that all were to attend and witness what would take place.

Greida was shaking with fear. She had seen that look on Rurik's face once before, when he caught her with Gouldon. Only then, he was preparing to leave and chose not to act on his anger. There would be no reprieve this time.

"Who among you can speak to the conflict between Greida and Jilliand?" Rurik stood before his people, his eyes moving over the crowd. It began slowly, but soon more of the women, slaves, and children came forward. Rurik was taken aback by what he heard. He knew much of what Jilliand had endured was because he had not made her place with him known to all. Greida, however, knew exactly what her own place was.

"You, Greida, what do you have to say?" He turned to the woman.

"I belong with you . . ." she began. Her voice, high pitched with fear, broke.

"You lie, Greida. When I last saw you, I finished it. You know this well, do you not? I found you in bed with Gouldon. Do you deny this?" Rurik challenged her. Greida only shook her head.

"Travelers or visitors are to be treated with respect and kindness when they come to us with the cold. You failed to do this. You acted without authority in a way that endangers Jilliand. It could never be your place to banish anyone. It is time I made it clear to all here. You are dead to us. You are no more. You chose your path when you lay with Gouldon. I should have made this decision that night." Greida began to wail and beg. "Take her from my sight. Finish it tonight. Now." Several men grasped Greida and dragged her from the building. Silence filled the hall. Never had Rurik been so angry. At first only a few went, but soon nearly all the people left the hall and followed the men dragging Greida. At a small clearing outside the main settlement, Greida was quickly beheaded. The crowd was a silent witness. With the truth out, Greida's fate was accepted without protest.

Rurik gathered some of his men. Not one questioned what they knew would be a quest to find Jilliand. Olga came to him as he readied to leave. "You will not hurt Jilliand." She looked at him directly. Rurik refused to reply. "I ask you for little, but this I ask." Her voice softened. "She is my friend, Rurik. She has become a part of me. You will not hurt her. Find her, bring her home. She belongs with us." With eyes that matched his own, she held his gaze. "You know well, our fate is not ours to decide."

The morning offered little light during winter, but it did hold the silence well. That silence was broken by movement far below her. Jilliand heard the approach of the men long before she saw them. She thought of the sleeping bodies below. If it were Rurik, and he were not stopped, it was possible he might take his anger at Jilliand out on the band. She remembered well his order that she never leave. *I know Greida will spin the tale against me. Will he listen to me?* She began to run down toward the group, weaving in and out of the trees. The steep mountainside with fallen trees covered in snow made progress hazardous. Jilliand fell several times, hurting her ankle when she stumbled over a loose rock. Ignoring the pain, she hobbled toward the clearing and burst into it at the same time Rurik and his men stepped into the little glen.

They were not expecting the huddled mass of children and smattering of adults that met them. Olav and his jarls spread along the perimeter, routing everyone out. Helgi stood with sword poised, ready to take on any of the men with Rurik. Helgi realized he was no match for them, but still he refused to lower his sword. Jilliand knew she may have lost favor with Rurik, but she had to speak for the people who were now startled and confused.

Limping to Rurik, she faced him. "Please do not hurt these people," she begged. He had not yet spoken nor looked at her. She could not hesitate, for fear everyone would be put to death. "Please," she touched his arm.

"I think you would worry that I will hurt you," he responded coldly, his voice tight. Still not looking at her, he watched as his men rounded up the refugees.

"I can do nothing about that, but I can ask for mercy for these people and children. They did not help me; I came upon them. The place where they lived was burned by your people." Jilliand spoke calmly and forcefully.

Caught by her words, Rurik scowled at her. *What else happened while I was away?* He knew it should not be possible, but he also knew the woman pleading with him would never lie.

Jilliand continued, "Not the people from where you live, but your people—men from this place." She waved her hand indicating the land they both stood upon. "You should be well pleased, because the women were working away from the houses when they were attacked. Their first thought was for the children of their masters. They saved many of the young people sent to them when the alarm first went out. Yes, I do ask for mercy for them and the children of the people killed by their own kind. They have agreed to follow Helgi, the son of one man. He will need support, Rurik. He would bring both families together." Jilliand's eyes searched Rurik's face. "Please, he will need help to become a Viking leader. You can help him better than any man."

Rurik turned to Dir and Askold. "Take them all back. The smaller children should stay with the people who cared for them, at least now. The older males will stay in our house. The younger women will stay . . . "

At this moment, Helgi stepped up and spoke out, "We have done no wrong. Let us return to the houses that still stand. Let us take the place of the men that led both sides to death, brother against brother. I will unite them. I can do this thing." His confidence and sheer determination moved Rurik. He stood a long moment, regarding the young man before him.

"Dir, you and Askold go with them. Take them all. If it is as he says, begin their training. They must set aside the anger held by both places. Take our men with you. I'll see you in the morn." With that order, he grasped Jilliand's wrist and stalked away. Jilliand could barely keep up with him. Her ankle, swollen and stiff, could not bear her weight, and she staggered. He stopped abruptly and stood still. Neither spoke, until the glen was empty.

"Why did you leave? You gave your word," he said as he pulled her around to face him. His voice was stern, cold, and angry. In truth, he was sorely angry with himself. He had let Greida get out of hand.

Jilliand frowned, rubbed her hands together, looked down at the ground, and finally looked at him. He waited in silence. In vain she tried to think what she could say that would not offend him. She could not return and live with Greida's hatred. "I was banished by your woman. I cannot go back." Softly, gently, she added, "There is more. I must not return because I am falling in love with you, Rurik. That cannot be." She hesitated. "I am a Christian. You are a . . . "

"I am a pagan. That is your word for me, is it not?" he finished her sentence sarcastically. He walked away from her slowly. Jilliand watched him, trying to think what she could say. At last, he returned to lean against a tree near her, his arms crossed, watching her closely. She had spoken of her feelings for him so softly; he wanted to hold her, yet his anger was still not cooled. Mostly, he knew, because of himself. He never would have believed he could love a Christian.

"I do not know what a pagan is," she admitted quietly, looking beyond the glen, a somber shadow over her eyes.

"So you would run to not love a pagan?" he continued, ignoring her comment, still watching her.

"No, I chose not to spend my life with one who could not love me, so I left," she finally responded, turning to him. "I know all I care to know about such an arrangement."

He stood looking at her for a long moment, studying her. "You have much to learn," he observed at length.

"About what?" Jilliand retorted, defensively. How could he begin to know what was in her heart?

"This country," he looked around them, "the weather," he looked to the sky, "the language, and . . . me." He stood watching her watch him. Walking to her, he held her face with his hand, not harshly, but firmly. "Do not run from me again . . . "

Jilliand interrupted him, "I did not run, Rurik. I crept, walked, stumbled, swam, sort of, that was horrible—but I never ran . . . " her voice trailed off. *This is not going well.*

Frowning, releasing her face, he repeated, "You swam?" He looked at her, surprised, as he took her arm. "Where? Why?"

"Apparently, I was not thinking clearly. These waters are freezing," she noted humbly. "I thought to swim to the island beyond. To live alone."

For a brief time, Rurik was silent, watching her. He had to struggle not to laugh at this independent English lady. Then he continued, "This belongs to you, Jilliand. It is safe for you to wear, now, but you must not speak of it." With that, he removed his amulet and replaced it with her cross. "From this time forward, you answer to me, no one else."

Jilliand gasped. She touched the cross, her eyes filling with tears. "I cannot return, Rurik," she whispered sadly. "I cannot. Not with Greida. I think she loves you very much. She is one of your people. I will not be party to this mess."

"Greida does not live with my people anymore. She never loved me nor belonged to me." He spoke carefully, watching Jilliand. "She was with Gouldon most recently. You took care of that," he grinned. He could see the question in Jilliand's eyes. "She lives no more, Jilliand." Jilliand's mouth opened, then shut. She started to speak, but he stopped her. "Greida broke important laws of my people. More than one, in fact. She knew the chance she took, when she started. It's over." He watched her digest the information. He could see the question settling in her eyes. "It's over," he repeated. "No one will challenge you again. My people are your people." His voice was softer. Jilliand searched his face, then looked around the glen. By returning her cross, he was allowing her to keep her religion. She looked back at him, nodded, and turned. Without Greida to push her around, life would be much better.

"Now walk," he instructed, pointing the way—again fighting the impulse to laugh. Her spirit pleased him, and her admission of her feelings for him pleased him even more. He felt an unexpected lift of his own spirit. His anger was gone.

Jilliand assumed Rurik, having found her, marched her in front because she was his captive again. In truth, he noted how she favored her left foot and would see why. As she moved ahead, determined to appear confident, she struggled with each step. Pain brought a flush to her face and tears to her eyes.

"Stop," he commanded. Sitting her down on a fallen log, he noticed the tears. "Crying will not make it any better." With that, he began to gently examine her ankle, by now swollen and purple. He stood up, thinking. "We go on," he decided, helping her up. "Darkness comes quickly." *Time to see what the English are made of.* He walked ahead, setting a much slower pace. *If she stays in front, we will wind up lost.* Rurik smiled to himself.

Darkness grew, as they continued their trek. "How beautiful the moon. See the stars?" she blurted. Rurik turned back to watch her stumble, trying to look at the sky while limping along. Smiling, he walked to her, shaking his head.

"Stars can take you home." Rurik spoke softly, as he wrapped his cloak around Jilliand. She frowned, looking at the sky, trying to see what he saw. Rurik watched her, now bundled in his cloak, the moon shining on her face. Suddenly, he pulled her to him, pushed the hood off, turned her face up, and kissed her lips. The kiss was long, gentle, and soft.

Jilliand was breathless as Rurik ended the kiss. "I do not think the stars will bring me home." Her voice was hushed as she gave in, "I think you will."

He gently traced her mouth with his finger. "Does this mean you will love a pagan?"

"No, it means I *do* love a pagan," Jilliand replied, looking at him squarely. She knew the conflict within her heart was over.

Rurik stood in front of her, pulled the hood up again, and noted softly, "You are learning."

They moved along the trail, now walking side by side, his arm around her, helping her hobble along. He continued to point out stars and talk of the weather. He was relaxed and happy. This felt good. For her part, Jilliand had given way to the feelings growing inside her heart. *God brought me here; He will see I am safe.*

Rurik made certain he and Jilliand spent time together each day. They walked along the river, throughout the settlement, and along the trails surrounding his home. Rurik spoke of his life and the Viking people; Jilliand listened. Rurik did not treat her like a slave but as an equal. Rurik was gentle, respectful, and kind to her. With him she felt safe, and more, she felt content, and for the first time in her life, she felt what she believed must be love.

Jilliand's observations and interactions with the people around her, and the history Rurik shared with her, were so different from the tales about the Vikings she had heard. She knew there were innumerable days like the day she was taken, when people suffered unspeakable abuses, were killed, or taken captive. She came to understand that fighting was a deeply held ideology for all Viking. From the earliest age, every free male child was carefully trained to fight; consequently, every man was a skilled warrior. It was well known that Vikings had no equal on the seas. She loved Rurik, more than she would have thought it possible to love any man.

One afternoon, as they walked together, Jilliand asked about the young man Helgi and his people. "Does Helgi do well? Has his anger cooled?"

"Yes, to both. He will be a great sea king. He learns quickly. There were older men in the place he took. They help him. His friend," Rurik chuckled, "his friend Sloveig is the perfect friend. Always near, helping and keeping Helgi's head out of the sky."

Rurik stopped walking. "Your father. I would know his name, Jilliand. I will not ask again." He spoke quietly, but with authority.

Jilliand walked a bit further. "You would have me tell you, you would kill him, and I would bear the guilt for a lifetime. Is that what you would have for me?"

"How can you feel guilty for something I do? I would end the life of the man that brought you such pain." He walked up to her, his hands behind his back, watching her.

"Rurik, if he had not done what he did, I would not be here with you. Because he hated me so, he gave you a gift, sir. I am grateful for you, each day." She smiled at him. "Are you not grateful to him?"

"How is it you turn my thoughts so easily?" He studied the English lady beside him and said, "I do not think your father hated you. I believe you must have looked like your mother. I believe he loved her. You took her away from him. He was not man enough to care for you. No matter, he should pay for what he did to you," Rurik persisted.

"Oh yes. He should be punished for giving me to one such as you. One I love. How awful of him," Jilliand added with mock gravity.

"I see you still will not tell me. I will find out what I need to know. I always do," he smiled back at her. "Here, this belongs to you." Into her hand, he placed the soft satchel she had hidden in the hut from where she was taken captive. Jilliand believed it long lost. Just the feel of it brought tears to her eyes.

"You saved this for me?" Jilliand asked. Impulsively, she threw her arms around his neck. "You cannot know what this means to me. This and the cross are nearly all I have of my mother."

He returned the embrace, holding her firmly. "Perhaps, I should just keep you. Like this."

Blushing, Jilliand squirmed away. Glancing up at him, she saw his slow smile. "I believe we should get back. You might be missed," she teased him, as she turned to wander slowly back.

He walked with her, saying little, just watching her walk. She was busy talking about the plants, the land, and generally babbling. He smiled again as he realized Jilliand was flustered. *Good. Soon enough she will come to realize what this is we both feel.*

Days sneaked by. Most of the men were busy constructing a new house and two new ships. When night draped the village with darkness, Jilliand wandered through the new house. She liked the smell of the wood and the changes each day brought as the house came to life. Sometimes she walked around the area to look at the ships. Jilliand loved roaming the village at night. She still felt awed by the fact that she could stroll about, without fear. Jilliand felt safer in this place without Greida.

Each night, Olga had watched Jilliand as she roamed around the new house and ships. *I think I will walk with her. My time may be short; I have much to tell.* The sight of Olga hobbling toward her so late at night surprised Jilliand. "You are still awake?" Olga only smiled, but from that night on, she and Jilliand walked together. Olga kept the fiery visions that lately so often disrupted her sleep to herself. *Fate will have its way.* As the two friends strolled throughout the settlement, Jilliand learned a great deal more about these people she now called her own. Her home.

The living quarters went up slowly as the wood had to cure. The vessels, however, went together quickly because the ship's wood was utilized while still green, allowing pliable plats of wood to be bent in the unique shape of the ships. She watched as the Viking sea predators took shape. Any spaces between plats that might allow water to seep into the vessel were plugged with moss and tar. She saw both men and women helping to sew the huge sails. She took notice of the care taken to measure and cut every oar the exact same length, ensuring each oar would enter the water at the same time, thus increasing the speed of the boat. It occurred to her again and again that the idea her countrymen had of the Vikings was so wrong. Clearly, Viking families loved each other and cared for one another.

Signs of the coming winter were all around. The land had long ago lost its fall colors and donned the more somber dress of the long frigid season on its way. It gave Jilliand reason to worry; she dreaded the cold. So far, even the wet snows melted. Soon, they would stay. Adding to her uneasiness, everyone was helping prepare for the winter except her. No one seemed to notice, but her attempts at weaving, cooking, and sewing were still slow, though improving. Fear of stepping outside what seemed to be the women's role kept her from hunting. The small children were Jilliand's salvation. They came for her nearly every day, and together, they learned more and more about each other.

CHAPTER 18

RURIK'S HOMESITE WAS A SMALL collection of houses surrounded by cleared land and dotted with sheep and cattle. Pens for horses completed the picture. The forest grew thick around the area. Buildings were close to the shore, where the ships were built. From the gossip with the women, Jilliand knew similar settlements were scattered along the shoreline of this country. The women told Jilliand that Rurik was well known along the coast. It was clear his decisions affected everyone in this community, as well as others. Major meetings were attended by men from different settlements. The women did not participate in making laws, battle plans, and such, but they kept the communities together. To Jilliand, it appeared the women were well treated and respected.

The one piece of their culture she never asked about was their religion. In her heart, she felt God would care for these people who looked after their children, each other, and travelers with kindness and fairness. The slaves they captured were treated no worse than those of the English. Viking women were treated as well as the women of England. At times, it was easy to forget how cruel Vikings could be. Jilliand knew only too well how cruel Englishmen could be.

One afternoon, with winter heavy in the air, Rurik came looking for Jilliand. The children stopped him. "She's gone again," one small girl somberly announced, shaking her little head. Rurik turned immediately and headed for

Jilliand's house. His eyes searched the house. Indeed, she was gone. Her cloak and the cloak he gave her were gone too. A search of the settlement proved she was nowhere to be found. Anger boiled inside him, with no thought to reason. *Again? Now what?!*

Rurik stormed out. He found the young girl again. "Where, child?" She only offered a shrug, but her little bright blue eyes darted toward a trail leading from the clearing. Rurik found Jilliand quickly. She was kneeling down picking plants. Her cloak was spread out and filled. The cloak Rurik had given her was spread about the ground where she knelt. He could hear her singing softly as she plucked different leaves. Rurik stood watching her for a moment, then walked to a nearby tree, where he sat down, still watching her.

Jilliand heard someone. She smiled seeing it was Rurik. Delighted, she waved her hand over the area. "Look at all I have found! By myself! I have learned so much from Olga." She smiled at him, her eyes bright. "I am helping to get ready for the winter, too. I still cannot weave very well, nor cook so well." Her voice dropped, then lifted again. "There are other things I can do."

Rurik patted the ground next to him, "Come sit." She stopped what she was doing to sit next to him. "What are they for?" he asked, picking up some twigs and studying them.

Jilliand could tell he wanted to speak of something else. "You are angry with me?" she asked frowning, leaning away from him.

"No," he answered simply. He watched her, wondering how she would react to what he came to say.

Still frowning, Jilliand prodded him. "You trust me not," she scolded him softly. "You thought I left?" He caught the sad note in her voice.

"I was wrong," he admitted. After a moment, he continued, "I watch you with my people. I see that the children love you. Everyone loves you, Jilliand," he said as he reached to brush back her hair. He was quiet for a moment. Looking at her, he announced, "They have finished the house."

"Does that mean someone will now stay in that house?" Jilliand asked. She heard the talk that the house was for Rurik. Perhaps he would take another into the house. Her heart caught.

"Yes," he replied quietly, "someone will."

"Will you still come to visit me?" She looked away. He pulled her hair aside so he could see her cheek, as she studied her hands.

Ignoring the question, he noted, "We celebrate the new house tonight."

He does not answer me, Jilliand observed. *I think that means no.* Anxious to change the subject, Jilliand asked, "What can I do?"

"Do you like Astrid?" Rurik asked, watching her closely.

"Yes, very much." Jilliand frowned. "Why do you ask?"

"She can tell you what you can do." He paused. "I am sorry your mother is no longer in this world."

Gently, Jilliand touched his face. "Do not be. If she were still alive, I would not be with you."

"Do you like it here?" he asked quietly, watching her eyes.

"Yes, I do," Jilliand assured him.

"The hard snows come soon. I will leave then." Rurik's voice was low.

"Am I going with you?" Jilliand quickly asked.

"Not yet." Rurik stood, pulling her up. He waited while she gathered the cloaks and plants. "We must return. There is much to be done tonight." Walking back, his hand closed around hers.

"Not yet," he says—*that's not "no." Perhaps I still have a place with him.* Jilliand's heart was hopeful.

Determined to make whatever celebration was coming a success, Jilliand refused to think about what Rurik might soon do. *After all, I am English.* Instead, when he left her to walk toward the meeting hall, she took her plants home and then walked to the house of Rurik's brother, Olav. It was overflowing with women and children. Many stood outside laughing and talking. Nodding to Jilliand, one of the children opened the door for her. Olga came to her, muttering about storms, visions of a great fire, and times gone by.

Jilliand shared with her the bounty of plants she had gathered. The old woman laughed at her young friend. "Soon enough, we can work these. Now we work you."

Puzzled, Jilliand watched as her friend limped past. When she asked how she could help, the room became quiet. "When the air around me is still, I know I have said or done something I should not have said or done. Which is it?"

Turid, Askold's wife, smiled. "Come, Jilliand. We should talk." She, Astrid, and Dir's wife Helga gathered around her. "See the gown? It is new. The robe is also. A gift from Rurik. Your new house has a chair, new blankets, a thick sleeping pad on a carved bed, pots for cooking, and mats for the floor. There is plenty of wood for a fire. No need to venture outside. It is time. You will be bathed and made ready," she finished gently.

Jilliand's smile slowly faded as the realization sunk in. "No, I do not think so. I must speak with Rurik. This is not my celebration. We celebrate because his house is finished." Her rising panic made her voice higher. The women looked at her and each other.

Olga noted dryly, "Just like a man. They speak not when they should; only when they should hold their tongue. It is as Turid tells you, Jilliand. Do not be afraid. You know him well enough."

"Apparently not," Jilliand retorted, turning to dash from the house, leaving the women staring after her.

Rurik was surrounded by his men—his brother, his jarls, his warriors, all friends and, most, family. He had never thought about this day much. That is until he first saw Jilliand. From that time onward, it seemed he thought of little else. The men sitting around teased him. With pride, he knew more than one man was envious; his woman was beautiful. Suddenly, the room fell silent, as the door opened and she stood there.

In broken words, mixing both languages, she asked to speak to him. He frowned. *This is not the way it should be. She comes much too early. And alone . . .*

Switching to English, she looked at him, "I would speak with you."

The men began to laugh, as several called out to him, "She changed her mind!"

Calmly, he stood and walked to her. Taking her elbow, he led her outside, closing the door to the laughter following them. "Turid tells me we are to be . . . " She hesitated. " . . . married, I think. Is that true?" Jilliand's face was strained with anxiety.

"Yes," he answered simply.

"You did not ask me," Jilliand said.

Rurik frowned down at her. "Did you not say you loved me?"

"Yes, I do, but women like me are married off for money, not love. You will not get money for me." She paused, struggling to get to the real issue.

"I know that," Rurik replied, studying her face. He could see that her eyes were filled with fear, her face laced with shame. "What is it, Jilliand?" His mind rushed to find the reason for her discomfort. *Could it be she had been with another?* At the thought, he felt jealousy and anger.

"I have no one to ask . . . I . . . " she paused, struggling to finish.

"Yes?" he quietly urged her.

"I have no idea what to do. I have never been with a man before," she finished softly, looking down at the ground, wishing it would swallow her.

He lifted her chin to look into her eyes. "I have never been with a man before either," he responded seriously.

"You are mocking me," Jilliand replied under her breath.

"Jilliand, I know what to do, and you will know also. You will be fine. We will be fine. I love you, and you love me. We should be together," he finished, still watching her face. She nodded and turned away. Rurik reached for her hand, pulling her back. "Do not be afraid of me. I would never harm you," he whispered in her ear. Gently, he kissed her face, then turned back to the hall. He was elated. He would be the first to let her taste love and all it had to offer.

Jilliand was filled with anxiety. *Can I be what a woman is supposed to be? Do I even know what a woman should be?* She began the slow walk to the people waiting for her. For the second time since coming to her new home, she began to weep. Children, excited with the coming festivities, were running and playing. When one young girl noticed her crying, she ran to Olga's house and called for her mother. Jilliand was met by the women and children. "Come, Jilliand. Women help women. It is our way," Turid said as she smiled.

For the next several hours, Jilliand slowly began to accept what was coming. She was a woman raised without a mother, a woman whose own father had despised her and raised her as a boy, a woman captured by the terror of the English shores. She, Jilliand, would be the wife of a man who loved her. A man she had grown to love. Once bathed, she was dressed in a soft beautiful gown given to her by Rurik. Over the gown, a white robe was placed around her shoulders. Her hair was woven with flowers. Jilliand could scarcely believe this time had come to her.

Olga explained the ceremony to her. Rurik had made two payments for her: one for guardianship of her, and the other for guarantee of her virginity. Because she had no family, the payments would be kept for Jilliand. He would give her the keys to their house. Jilliand now had a home, which belonged to her. Olga also explained the sword he would give her, in the belief he would soon have a son. She added that normally, the father of the bride would pay a dowry to Rurik. This was forgiven by Rurik. "Do you have a ring to give him?" Her eyes were as gentle as her voice. Jilliand paused.

"I do. It's at my house." She and Turid walked quickly to her little house, where Jilliand removed the lid from a jeweled box. Inside, she opened the blue silken bag given her by Silas. From the items that fell out, she picked up a ring that had belonged to her mother's father. The large emerald was embedded in a gold band. "The ring is very special to me."

Turid gave her a quick hug. "You are very special to Rurik. Come, they wait for us." She and Jilliand joined the women waiting outside. The women escorted her with the children running alongside them.

Rurik sat waiting in the great hall. Decorations changed it from a meeting place to a place of celebration. *Jilliand, today we wed, because this day is a sacred day for Freya, the goddess of fertility. Soon we will have sons.* His eyes were fixed on the door. When she was brought in, a hush fell over the room. Even the children were quiet as everyone strained to see the woman who would soon be the wife of their sea king.

Jilliand stood at the door, uncertain what to do. She could not see him, so she waited. Rurik slowly stood up, stunned. "She is beautiful. If her mother looked like her, her father must have died when the mother did. No matter, he should have cherished this child." His voice was hoarse with emotion. Jilliand was still looking for him, her head held high, proud. Then, drawn by something felt deep in her heart, Jilliand's eyes locked onto his. He smiled at her, encouraging her, as she began to walk toward him. Her movements were graceful, serene, regal. Every inch a queen, slowly, she came to him.

Jilliand heard nothing and saw nothing of the people. Her eyes were for Rurik alone. From the crowd of guests, an older Viking sea king gasped, "'Tis her. Just as I first saw her. The daughter is the mother again. Rurik must hear the story. He truly takes a queen."

As Jilliand neared Rurik, she became aware of the murmurings in the crowd, "He takes a wife. The Sea King Rurik takes a queen." Olga stood near Rurik. As Jilliand came closer, Rurik extended his hand. Jilliand felt his fingers close around hers, firmly, gently. He pulled her closer, then turned to face the old healer. Jilliand could barely understand what was being said. It happened quickly. Rurik handed a fine Frankish sword to Jilliand. The hilt was laden with jewels, the blade long and heavy. Then, taking her hand in his, Rurik slid a beautiful gold ring, set with emeralds and rubies, onto her finger. Jilliand opened her other hand. Clutched in it lay the ring she slid onto his finger. Jilliand softly whispered, "My mother's father . . . my grandfather."

Olga observed happily, "Now I might see grandchildren of my own. This is a good day, Jilliand." Jilliand suddenly realized that Olga was Rurik's mother.

Rurik slid two arm rings, one in gold and one in silver, both with intricate designs inset with small precious stones, on her right arm, and then he turned around with his wife, facing the vast room full of his people. "I give you a queen today: Jilliand, my wife." Great cheers went up, women came to hug her, men clapped Rurik on the shoulder, and many jokes were passed between the men. At last, Rurik led her back to the front of the room. "Let us eat our first meal as husband and wife." He watched her tenderly. "Are you frightened, Jilliand?"

"No, Rurik. In truth, I am not," she murmured. "I am in love with you."

Grinning, he held her face and kissed her, long and hard. The room filled with cheers. "We eat! And we celebrate!" At that, mayhem broke out. Food was passed along the great tables, children ran in and out, and people talked and laughed. Rurik shared a tankard of mead with his new wife. The sweet taste of honey matched her thoughts.

Many a Viking warrior approached the table to congratulate Rurik. Finally, their leader had taken a wife. An older man approached Rurik. "Might I speak?"

"Of course, my friend. What is on your mind?" Rurik asked with respect in his voice.

The man turned to Jilliand. "Your mother was a great woman. Brave. You would be much like her, I trust. Good for Rurik and his people. May the gods smile on you always, Rurik and Jilliand." He bowed and slowly left the hall, followed by Olga.

"Olga is your mother," Jilliand noted aloud, watching the couple leave. "She is a kind and wise woman. I am blessed she is my friend."

"You have no idea," Rurik laughed. "You have no idea."

"I would learn from the old man, more of my mother. Would I be permitted to talk with him?" she asked.

"Yes, love. I will see that you know where to find him." It would be a visit Jilliand would always remember. "He longs to sail again. I think he sails with us this time." Rurik watched his wife. Pride filled him.

"Is he not too old to go off sailing?" Thoughtfully, Jilliand looked back to where the old man had gone. "He can hardly walk."

"Jilliand, it is not a good thing for a Viking to grow old. He would rather die young, fighting. Fate had him win too many fights. He grew old." Rurik spoke gently.

Jilliand flinched. Her eyes found Rurik's. "Do you believe that too?" Jilliand could not hide the alarm in her voice.

"I am a Viking," he answered simply. Reading her alarm, he held her hand. "Jilliand, do not think on tomorrow. Today is what you have and," he smiled, "tonight."

Neither could know how his statement would haunt them both.

The rest of the evening passed quickly. Jilliand was nervously awaiting that moment when they would leave and she would be alone with Rurik. At last, he stood, pulling her up with him. He could feel her hand tremble. "Do not be afraid, Jilliand. Remember, my love for you is deep and grows more each day. One does not fear love." His voice was gentle, soothing. He placed her robe around her as he handed her off to Turid. The women slipped out the back with her.

Opening the door to the couple's new home, the women stepped into an area already warmed by a glowing fire. Candles were lit near their bed, a raised platform with a beautifully carved headboard. On the bed was a thick, soft pallet, covered with thick blankets and pillows. Slowly, they removed her cloak. She stepped out of her dress, letting it fall at her feet. A soft sleeping gown was slipped over her head. The flowers were removed from her hair. Jilliand lay down on the bed, while the women hung her clothing and stepped away. *I am frightened. What happens now?*

Rurik was escorted in by his brother and jarls. He too was changed to a bed shirt and then led to Jilliand. The men gathered the women and quietly walked out. Rurik lay down and reached for her. He ran his fingers through her hair. It was soft and smelled of flowers. Jilliand lay still as if frozen. He lightly brushed the wavy strands back from her face, running his finger along her jaw, turning her head so that he could look into her green eyes. He could see the uncertainty in them.

Without rushing, deliberately, Rurik slipped his hand down the gown and grasped her breast, gently and firmly. At his touch, he heard her sharp intake of breath. He could feel her heart pounding. His hand traveled up, following her breastbone, until he was at the neckline of her gown. He began to remove it, and Jilliand began to tremble. Feelings she had never known existed flooded her mind and body. She longed to reach for him, but did not, for fear the moment would end. When she lay before him naked, he smiled.

Rurik's hand moved over her body, exploring every curve, with a slow, gentle touch. He had lain with women before. He had violently taken women before. Nothing he had ever done in the past had been like this. He felt like he was touching something fragile, yet strong, innocent, trusting; someone he loved, someone he would protect. At first, Jilliand could not take her eyes from him. As his hand moved downward, she closed her eyes and let herself be taken. At some point, she was not even aware of exactly when, she clung to him as he took her with him. They spent the night in a passion of discovery and love. Jilliand could never have imagined a touch so tender, so gentle. He knew just what to do. Jilliand responded eagerly. *Rurik was right. We are fine.*

The two were lost in time. He reached for her again, kissing her lips, her face, and her neck. Jilliand leaned back as his mouth warmed her neck and then her breast. His hand moved down her flat belly. Jilliand gasped with the pleasure he gave and reached for him. When they at last lay spent, she slept, nestled in his arm, her head on his chest. A day came and went before they rose. "I am hungry, come let us find something to eat. Surely mother will have food." Rurik smiled lazily at her. Jilliand could hardly believe how her life had turned. From a beaten, despised child to a woman loved.

Her hair fell about her head in a wild mess when she stood to dress. Rurik lay watching her, smiling. He often thought of the first time he had seen her naked, her fiery hair wet and plastered to her body after she had bathed. "The gods have smiled on me," he whispered. When he, too, had dressed, he opened the door and stepped out. Pulling her cloak about her, Jilliand followed him.

Everyday routines had continued, as if nothing had changed. The wedding celebration went on for a month: People came to visit, children came in and out of the house, and life became a wonderful place.

Jilliand and Rurik fell into their own pattern. He spent most of his days hunting, planning, and overseeing the new ships being built. Jilliand was busy drying foodstuffs and learning to make clothes and blankets. Nights belonged to them. He took her beyond her imagination, beyond feeling, and just when she thought she could stand no more, he gently moved her again. Time touched them with an easy grace. She was happier than she had ever been. Without warning, a storm moved in.

Arising early one morning, she opened the door to a wonderland of snow covering everything. Jilliand caught her breath. "It is beautiful, Rurik. Come see!" she turned to him. He rolled, yawning, onto his side, smiling at her.

"You have not seen this before? It must have snowed where you came from," Rurik teased her.

"Of course," she replied, pertly, "but the world looks quite different now."

"You know what the snow means, Jilliand," Rurik commented, watching her face.

"Cold weather?" Her answer was light, happy.

"It means it is time for us to leave. Now is when the people we raid are bundled in; no one is ready for a fight. Now is when we can take the most in the quickest time. Our ships are fast. By the time they know we are there, we have already gone. Now is the time for fighting." As he spoke, he grew excited. He loved the fight, the clash of steel, the victory, the sea, the wind—he loved it all. This was his time.

Quietly, Jilliand watched him. She knew her love alone would never keep him from the sea and the battle. He was a Viking sea king. "How long will you be gone?" she asked, trying hard not to sound broken.

He turned to her, dressing quickly, "Not too long the first time. When we next go out, perhaps I'll take you with me." He studied her. She was looking at him with sadness in her green eyes, though she smiled.

"I would go this time, if you asked," Jilliand replied softly.

Rurik walked to her, lifted her face, and kissed the lips that he had grown to love. "I know, but you cannot go this time. I will return soon. I will bring you gifts," he added, his face buried in her hair.

"I only want you. You are my gift," she answered, gently turning him toward the door. "Go, I'm sure you have much to do before you leave." *God go with you, my love*, Jilliand prayed.

Two days later, Jilliand stood with the rest of the village at the shore, waving them off. Four warships left that day. Each with sixty men. They were to meet with another fleet of ships, then another, bringing the total number of ships to twelve, with over seven hundred men. The men were anxious to be off. Unlike the armies Jilliand was familiar with, the Viking warriors were all friends and/or relatives. They were bound by honor, kinship, and a deep sense of unity. Each man—agile, strong, and healthy—was built for the task at hand. Jilliand shook her head, a little sadly. *The English will have little chance.*

CHAPTER 19

RURIK HAD ONE DESTINATION IN mind for his warships on this voyage. Once out of sight of his lands, he broke from the convoy and led his ships along the southern English shoreline, though still far enough out to avoid notice. After several days, he directed the ships toward land. Silently, they crept up the river Test, unloaded, and hid the ships. "We seek one particular man for the blood eagle. This is not a raid for bounty." The order was firm. Ten men were left to watch over the boats; the rest followed Rurik.

After three days' travel over land, they came to a run-down burg settling down for night. The lord of the burg once had a plan to fill his coffers. The plan had failed miserably when his daughter went missing. Since that time, he took little interest in his own land or men. His cruelty had driven nearly all the people around his castle away. Times were hard enough without the weight the lord's anger forced upon them. The land was untended, crops were poor, livestock dying, houses left barely standing, with scarcely any signs of life. It was a dismal time. The boundaries of holdings throughout England were continually shifting as lords fought to take control of larger parcels. This lord had such a pitiful place that it had been overlooked. The few men left with him were careless and lazy, preferring to spend the night with any willing female and refusing to stand guard. There was little left to guard anyway. Surely no one cared to overrun this dilapidated burg.

On this night, as every night, the gate of the burg was only partially closed. Several of the men left the castle and walked to one of the few squalid houses left outside the wall. There they took turns with the two women inside the brothel. What little the women were paid was just enough to purchase fish and a few other items for their huts that sat on the outermost edge of what had been a settlement around the burg. Their families could ill afford to anger the men who were now lying near the dying fire of the brothel.

The Vikings struck with speed and precision. Rurik knew what he wanted and that it would be easy prey. Rurik and his men silently slipped around the huts, quickly killing the few men they found close to the main gate. The Vikings were inside the burg before the soldiers within the walls even knew there were Vikings about. The burg was quickly overrun. Rurik's men swept into the great room in the center of the keep, below the lord's living quarters. The lord, roused by the noise coming from below his room and fuming over being awoken, strapped on his sword and grabbed his whip.

As the lord entered, the sound of the heavy wooden doors slamming against the wall stilled the large room. At the sight before him, the lord blanched. His castle was crawling with Vikings. Most of his soldiers were captive, and several were dead. One Viking, obviously the leader, advanced across the room. The lord tried to fend the man off with his whip and then tried to run him through with his sword—but failed at both.

The Vikings encircled the two men. "This is the man." Rurik's voice was filled with authority and resolution. At his announcement, several men moved toward the lord. The lord knew—for the first time in his life—a fear beyond reckoning. He struggled mightily but in vain. His shirt was ripped from him. His screams of agony filled the room as his back was sliced open and his ribs were cut away from his spine and spread wide. His exposed lungs were then removed and left lying on the man's back. Rurik offered the bloody scene and the lungs he had removed to his god, Odin, thanking him for success in this battle and in those to come. The few men left alive were unable to stand after witnessing the sacrifice. Rurik paid them no mind. He had taken what he came for. He quickly found the lord's chamber, searched it, called his men together, and left. When the sun shone upon the burg, it revealed a deserted fortress. Every man, woman, and child had fled. The lord remained as the Vikings left him—sprawled facedown in a pool of blood.

Rurik's ships were long gone by daylight, joining the larger fleet, and continuing along the coast, taking whatever they wanted. The episode they had witnessed filled the hearts of his men. They were anxious to put their weapons to even greater use. Before he returned to his homeland, Rurik and his men would find and destroy several monasteries, taking anything they could use or trade.

Snow had come to stay. Strong wind blew giant drifts over the ground, while the cold worked its way into every corner. Bundled, Jilliand trudged to the house of Rurik's mother. Knocking quietly, Jilliand waited. It was a comfortable place. The main room had a fire pit with several chairs, a loom, and a bench. The chair closest to the fire pit had blankets on one side, as if waiting for company. Two rooms were beyond this area. One room had a long table filled with plants. An oil lamp sat on the table. There were plants hanging upside down to dry and baskets of plants in every space. Inside the smaller second area stood a large bed with an ornately carved headboard, thick sleeping pads and thick blankets, another small table, a lamp, and a chair.

Olga's face lit up when she saw Jilliand at her door. "Come in, daughter, come in. Come sit by the fire. We can weave and visit. Things we do well, you and I." She pulled Jilliand into the warmth of the room.

For a few moments, they talked of the weather while the old woman finished baking fresh bread. Then Olga grew silent. She watched this small thing her son had seen fit to bring into their fold. The girl was strong in ways not usual for a girl. Still she needed a friend. More than that, she needed a mother. She had much to learn and little time to learn all about being a woman.

"Tell me what you think, sitting there so still, Jilliand." Her voice was kind and soft.

Jilliand just looked at her, trying to find the words.

"You are with child, are you not?" the woman observed. "It is to be expected. You took a husband. One of the things they do best . . . make us mothers. Not a bad thing, I think. But difficult. Are you afraid?"

"How do you know?" Jilliand sat back in the chair, surprise on her face.

"I know many things, little one. You are with child. That is good. Now, tell me, are you frightened?" she pushed.

"No . . . well, perhaps a little. I know not enough to be frightened. But if I am with child, Rurik will not take me with him. I would be with him. I miss him. I miss the sea. Perhaps I am not such a good Viking wife." She leaned her head back on the chair, staring at the ceiling. "Do you think I carry a son? Who really knows? Does it matter? It must: When we married, he gave me a sword for his son."

The old woman chuckled. "Of course. They take a great deal for granted, these men of ours. Jilliand, do you still pray to your god?" Olga watched her carefully.

Without hesitation, Jilliand answered, "Every day. He is as important to me as yours are to you, except I have one God. He must be all things. I fear I keep Him quite busy," she smiled ruefully.

"You must not tell people you pray like that, but do pray." Olga's eyes pierced Jilliand's—not unkindly, but seriously. Then she sighed and moved on. "I have lived a long time and have traveled many places. I, too, traveled with my husband when he left to fight. We were a good team, he and I," she said as she smiled to herself. Her eyes softened at the sight of the young woman before her. "I have seen things. I believe your god has power, too. I believe he is right for you, though we are not of the same beliefs. Just know I love you like a daughter. I believe your god will take care of you. Now, we must be certain that you stay healthy for that child growing within you. Have you broken your fast this morning?"

Jilliand tucked Olga's advice away. It was good to have a mother here on earth. "No, I am not able to eat in the morning. I spend every morning leaning against trees, while my stomach empties onto the ground. Hunger only comes later," she admitted, laughing a little.

"Try dried bread. Let it get hard. Eat on it before you arise. It helps." She pulled a boiling pot sitting near the fire off to the side. "You should come here every day to learn what I know. Someday I will be gone. You have little experience, and you have a great deal to learn, in a short time. We start tomorrow. Today, you and I visit an old friend of mine." The woman handed Jilliand a bowl of soup. To her surprise, Jilliand enjoyed the meal, and she felt like it would stay down. When they had finished and cleaned the little area, Olga walked to the door. "Come along." She slipped a cloak off the hook near the door. Peeking out the door, she added another before stepping out. "'Tis good to move about, even in the cold."

Jilliand was just learning to use the snowshoes everyone wore. The flat, broad woven paddles allowed them to walk quickly through the heavy snow. The shuffling gait was easier than tramping through, but either way was extremely tiring. Jilliand marveled at her mother-in-law. *She must be more than fifty, yet she puts me to shame. I am dying! If I do not hurry, I will be lost behind.* Struggling to move faster, she concentrated on each step.

Jilliand was so busy trying to keep up, she had no idea where they were. When she caught up at one point, she was gulping for air. She gasped, "Is this where we stop? I can only hope!" Looking around, Jilliand could see this settlement was much like Rurik's, though not quite as large.

"Yes. We have come to visit the man who knew your mother," Olga announced. Suddenly Jilliand was alert, looking around for the man. With snowshoes removed, both women moved at an easier pace. She and Jilliand made their way to the largest house of the group. People, out and about, shouted greetings and waved to them. The door opened as Olga raised her hand to knock. An old man stood smiling at the two women. Jilliand recognized the man who had spoken to Rurik at their wedding. "This is Asger, my friend of many years." Olga introduced him. "And this is Jilliand, wife of Rurik."

"You will get limber fast with this one," Asger said, affectionately smiling at Olga.

Jilliand was still breathless, but now with anticipation. She could only nod her head in agreement. When both women were inside and seated beside the fire, he served them a warm ale of sorts. Jilliand was afraid she would leave it on his floor if she drank it down. "None for her, she carries my first grand-child," Olga informed him motioning toward Jilliand fondly. "She still feels the sickness each morning."

"Ah, so that's the way it is. You move carefully, eh?" Asger nodded his head knowingly.

Jilliand's smile was weak, at best. "Yes . . . and slowly too. Mother moves as if she has wings on her feet. I cannot keep up." Asger laughed, patting Olga's hand.

For a while, the two old people talked of common friends. Jilliand waited patiently for the time when she could speak. At last, Asger turned to her, "I am pleased you have come to visit but believe you come with purpose. Is that true?"

"Yes, it is true," Jilliand acknowledged. "I understood you knew my mother. How could that be?"

"I know who you are because you look just like your mother. She was taken during a raid on English soil. We landed two days after her ship had landed. We had been following them, but I do not believe they ever saw us until we attacked. When we took your mother, I thought I would later be paid a great ransom. But, instead, one of her soldiers came forward and traded all the group's arms, horses, and supplies for her. I took what he offered, and he took the woman. I heard, but do not know if it is true, that they were overtaken by another lord. Would have been easy enough, since they were unarmed. I also heard your mother married that lord, in exchange for the freedom of the few soldiers left. It is said her father was a brother to the king of Northumbria." His voice softened, "So you now know, you *are* of royal blood. A fitting queen for Rurik." He patted her hand, kindly.

This was the same story provided by Myla and Silas in her father's burg. Listening to the Viking gave Jilliand a little more information about her mother;

she clung to every bit she learned, especially now. "I wish I could return the kindness you have shown me." The old Viking smiled. He only wanted to die fighting. To go to Valhalla, to feast with other Viking heroes, until Ragnarök, the final battle of his gods. The Englishwoman would not understand.

When their visit was finished, Jilliand and Olga took another route. This short trail led directly to Olga's house. Olga grinned, just like Rurik. "This path is convenient for two old friends to see each other. Nights can be very dark and long here. But they need not be cold and lonely."

Jilliand kissed Olga gently. "Be careful, now that you are a grandmother. We share a child, you and I. Your grandchild will have need of one such as you. Still, live your life well; you have earned that right."

Lying in her bed alone that night, Jilliand thought of the differences between Rurik and herself. Jilliand's God was kind, just, and forever. Rurik's gods were fighters, tricksters, and were all waiting for some final battle of the worlds. It was little wonder the Vikings were so fierce. She wondered how the English ever won a battle with these Viking men. As always, Jilliand's thoughts turned to Rurik. She remembered how Myla and Silas had been with each other. The family she stayed with near the river had love and respect for each other. *I believe these are feelings that many couples must share. How does a woman who is in a marriage for other reasons grow to love the man she must live with? Did my mother ever love my father?* Sighing, she turned over and let her mind bring Rurik to her once more. *Come home soon, Rurik. I grow lonely here.*

Rurik would come home. Jilliand felt his coming. Late one afternoon, she hurried to Olga's house. "He comes, I feel it. I cannot explain, but he comes." The old woman smiled, bobbing her head with understanding.

"Here, take this. It is a good thing to drink, warmed, on a cold night. He will be hungry, too. And surprised to see you. You have grown." Olga smiled and handed Jilliand a crock of stew and a jug of honey mead.

"I cannot think of Rurik being gone again. Rurik intends to take Asger along the next time he leaves. Will it make you sad to see him go?" Jilliand asked. Olga stood looking into the flames dancing in her pit. "No. I will be proud for him. I will be lonely, but soon I go too, child. It would be better if he goes before me."

Impulsively, Jilliand hugged the old woman. "You have been very kind to me. I have learned much from you. How can I repay you?"

"You already have," Olga softly replied, placing her hand on Jilliand's small but growing belly.

Returning to the house she shared with Rurik, Jilliand made certain there was enough wood, put a kettle over the fire to heat the mead Olga had sent, placed the stew pot close to the fire, and baked fresh bread. She set a large tub further to the back, and then put several round rocks near the fire. As a final touch, she brought in four large jugs of water to warm near the fire. Bundled in a soft blanket, she sat in her chair, watching the door.

When the door opened, she sat still, waiting to see his face in the light from the fire. Then, slowly, she stood. Her heart pounded, her eyes misted over, and she could hardly breathe, such was her joy in seeing him again. The door closed quietly, and then he stepped into the light. He dropped his weapons where he stood. The distance between them was breached in two steps, as he swept her off her feet, holding her in his arms, kissing her hair, her face, her neck, and her face again.

Jilliand felt desire rise in her, as she felt his breath hot on her skin. "I am no longer complete if you are not with me, Rurik." Her voice was husky with emotion.

He carried her to the chair and sat with her in his lap. Looking at her face and running his hands through her hair, he gently followed the curve of her jaw with his finger; then the line of her lips, and the hollow at her neck. He bent to kiss her again, tenderly. Soft lips caressed hers. With his eyes locked on her, he moved his hand, slowly, gently down. When he felt her breast, his brow shot up. He moved to the other one. Jilliand smiled up at him, "They match, husband."

"Hmm . . . and grow?" He looked at her through narrowed eyes as his hand loosened the ties on her dress and opened the front. Carefully, his hand explored further. "A son?" he smiled broadly at her. "You already are giving me a child? Lucky for me, you are not further along, wife. I have been gone too long." With that, he carried her to their bed.

When at last, they both lay drained, Jilliand turned to him, laughing. "I thought you would be hungry."

"I was," he answered, smiling and relaxed with his eyes closed, "For you. Now, I would like food. And tell me how you spent your time. I will tell you how I spent mine. I think I had more fun. I want you with me, when next I sail," Rurik said. "If the child is born then, so be it. If not, so be it. You come with me."

Jilliand was well pleased. She didn't care where they would go, only that she would be with him. To be with him when he sailed may not be usual, but nothing about her life had been usual.

As Rurik finished his meal, he eyed the tub. "You think to get me in there? Why?"

Jilliand simply smiled. One of the things she found most pleasing was the Viking attention to cleanliness, which was contrary to stories she had heard her whole life. She began to fill the tub, placing heated rocks in the water to ensure it would stay warm longer. Then, gently pulling his hand, she led him to the tub. He scowled, but allowed her to pull him. His manhood demanded attention.

"Hmm . . . we'll see," his wife said as she smiled sweetly. When he was seated, leaning back, and she began to scrub him, he smiled.

"This is not so bad. Do I get to bathe you?" He lay there, with his eyes closed. As she rinsed him off and added more hot water, she could tell he was falling asleep. Dry and lying on the bed, he hardly knew when she covered him and cleaned up the house. He slept. Ever so gently, Jilliand lay down beside him. He didn't wake up, though he reached for her and pulled her closer.

Rurik's return meant a celebration was under way. The great hall was filling with people. Other warriors and their families were filing in. It was a time reminiscent of Christmas for Jilliand. After the celebration, they would begin to repair the boats for his next expedition. Rurik's fleet alone would consist of eight ships. He would take families with him this time. Jilliand never asked where they were preparing to go. She was going too; that's all that mattered.

Jilliand stood in her house, finishing up with the sweets she had baked. She softly sang songs that she believed were long since forgotten. *From where did I hear such music?* She could only vaguely remember the sounds of voices coming to her in her old cell. She shuddered at the memory of that place. Rurik opened the door to the smell of sweet breads, pine needles in the fire, and the sound of Jilliand's voice, soft and clear. He had with him Dir and Askold, and their children and wives. Jilliand did not hear the door open. Everyone stood quietly, listening. Finally, she felt the draft and turned, shocked to see the small crowd. She held her breath, unsure how they would take her songs.

Everyone's eyes were on her, except the children. They had heard her sing before. Their only mission was to discover what smelled so good. Running to her, giving her hugs and quick kisses, they began searching the room, looking for the treats.

"Just like they tell you." Askold pointed to her. "She sings all the time. It is true, Rurik."

Jilliand felt a certain fear for the first time since she had come to this place. Before Rurik could answer, she asked, "And of what do they say I sing, Askold?" She wanted to say she meant no harm, but she had a feeling that would not matter if someone perceived she sang to her God.

"They only say you sing and that your songs bring much joy. The gods are pleased to hear you sing, Jilliand, and they smile on us. Even warriors like the sounds coming from your mouth. She sings for us tonight?" he asked Rurik.

Jilliand could see the disapproval on Rurik's face. He answered carefully, "Of what would you sing, wife?"

"I want the bug song!" Dir's youngest daughter chimed in. Surprised, Rurik glanced at her.

"No, the bird one. It's the best," insisted Askold's youngest son.

God love these children. They have saved me again, Jilliand thought. "I would sing for the children first. Then, for the older ones, I sing of the Viking ships. If that would be allowed."

It was agreed she would sing. Everyone decided to taste the sweets before they left. The children crowded around Jilliand. She laughed at them, scolded them, and hugged them. Even the tough older boys were relaxed with her. When it was decided everyone should move to the hall, Rurik stayed behind to speak with his wife.

He stood looking at her sternly. "I have allowed you to speak to your god and wear your symbol. Do not take those privileges lightly, Jilliand. You will not sing to our children of your god. You could lose this." He touched her beloved silver cross. His tone allowed no room for discussion, but Jilliand was not known for letting that stop her.

"I will sing to our children of my God, just as you will tell them of your gods, teach the boys your skills, and love the girls for their smiles. Do you know so much? You think my God does not speak to yours? I love you, Rurik. I come to your bed of my own will. I would die for you and your people. I will keep my God in my heart. I sing to the children of things they must know. You will see." With a pert movement jutting her chin out, she turned to leave. Rurik smacked her bottom, hard. She froze, took a deep breath, and whirled, ready to do battle, but he quickly covered her mouth with his, kissing her long and gently, smiling, his eyes filled with mischief.

At the hall, Jilliand was happily moving through the crowd. By this time, she knew nearly everyone there. She was seen as a member of this great family. She was a friend, a teacher, and now, with Olga's help, a quiet leader.

As promised by Rurik, Jilliand finally stood to sing. The children yelled out subjects of songs, and she began to sing. First, she sang a lullaby and then moved up the age groups. When she felt she must stop, she noted, "I have one more. This is for the young warriors among us." Her song ended with, "The sea opens her arms. With the sea's waves, Viking ships disappear into the mist."

When she finished, she sat down. "Jilliand, from where do you get such ideas?" one of the men asked.

She glanced at Rurik, "I make them up from what I know."

A small voice came to her, "Did your mother sing those songs?"

"I never knew my mother," Jilliand smiled, a little sadly. "There was no one to sing to me."

"How is it you know such things? You have told our young men stories of battles. You talk of things only men know. How do *you* know these things?" another man asked.

"I have been in battles, many battles," Jilliand explained quietly, "My father wanted a boy. When my mother died during childbirth, he made the decision to raise his only child as a boy. And so he did, until time went on and it was no longer possible to hide what I am."

"Is that when Rurik saved you?" a child's voice asked.

Jilliand smiled, "No, not yet. He took a little while to get around to me. I had to outride other men and struggle for many months before he came for me."

"Did you run from him too?" the same child asked.

"Who prompts this child?" Jilliand asked, and the people laughed. "No. I did not run. It is impossible to outrun a Viking." Before any more questions could be asked of her, she looked down.

Rurik immediately stood. "She was beaten by her father until she escaped from him. For that, we sailed last time. That score is settled." Jilliand gasped. Her eyes sought Rurik's. His eyes locked onto hers, without wavering. "It is done, Jilliand, as I said it would be." He would not tell Jilliand that her father had been the sacrificial offering to Odin in the rite of the blood eagle. He turned back to the hall. "We celebrate!" At his words, the hall erupted into gaiety. Jilliand sat still. She could hardly imagine not worrying about her father finding her somehow. Rurik placed his hand on her shoulder. "You are not to be sad, Jilliand," he ordered. "Your last tie to England is gone."

Jilliand turned to him. "I am not sad, Rurik. I feel as though a great weight is taken from me."

"You feel what is expected. Now is a time for celebration." He took her hand, and together they walked among their people.

Back at their house after the celebration, Rurik pulled Jilliand to him. "I have something for you. Come see." He led her to the chair by the fire and handed her a small pouch. He sat cross-legged on the floor, watching her.

Jilliand smiled at him. He was like a child. Slowly, she opened the pouch. Pulling the first things out, she found more combs for her hair—beautiful silver combs, with jewels in them. Pulling out more items, she found gold bracelets and several gold chains. At the bottom, she fished out a small bag. She opened the bag and brought out a small pendant and a ring that matched the ring she had given Rurik on the day they were married. At first, she was puzzled. "Where have I seen these before?"

Then it hit her. She jumped up so quickly that everything in her lap went flying to the floor. She sought out the locket she had kept from her old friend, the captain, and opened it. There it was: the painting of her mother wearing the same pendant and the ring. Her eyes filled with tears. "But, how?"

"It matters not how. I got them." He was standing by this time, carefully fastening the chain around her neck and slipping the ring onto her right hand. Touching them, she looked at him, her eyes brimming. She wrapped her arms around his neck and buried her face on his shoulder.

"Enough—this is a time for celebration, not crying, woman." He smiled at her, wiping her tears away.

"Sometimes women cry for joy," she whispered.

CHAPTER 20

IN THE MONTHS THAT FOLLOWED, the settlement was charged with a sense of anticipation. Jilliand knew Rurik must be planning for something greater than the usual trips he had taken before. Rurik was building up his fleet. Men were coming to talk, commonly staying until late at night. She was happy he frequently chose to meet in his home. She simply laid out plenty of food and drink for them and then walked to Olga's house.

Her thoughts constantly turned to the upcoming voyage. Just the thought of leaving with Rurik made her heart lighter. *What will it be like on the ship this time? I must bring practical clothes for me and something for our child, in case he comes early.* Jilliand's mind made list after list.

As the days grew shorter, Jilliand grew larger. She had no experience with being pregnant. The changes in her body were not comfortable. She was a small woman. Rurik was a large man. This baby would be a large boy. At first, she refused to think about it. As the time to leave came closer, she could no longer ignore the impact of the weight she carried. By the end of the day, her ankles were swollen, and her appetite began to shrink.

This morning, Rurik had rolled over in bed, pulled her to him, and began exploring her changing body. He loved to rest his hand on her swollen belly and feel their son move. "Tonight, we gather to make an accurate accounting of the supplies we take with us. I will be late this night. We leave in one day's time." He was slowly arousing her and himself. She returned the favor, smiling in satisfaction when he lay quietly, next to her.

With the passing days, Jilliand had already come to accept what Rurik was now saying. "You must stay here, Jilliand. Your time is coming soon. 'Tis not a good thing for you or my son to be with me now, though I want you with me. Other families are going this time. You cannot." He held her gently, tenderly. "I will return before your last month. I will hold him and be certain all know he is my rightful heir." For a long moment, he was silent. "Ah, Jilliand, as I love to be with you, I love the coming fight as much. I am Viking."

"No, Rurik," Jilliand softly corrected him. "You love the fight more. I know that and can accept that. You are Viking. I love you deeper for it."

Jilliand accepted she would not be leaving with him. She would not endanger his child. She never could have imagined how cumbersome the pregnancy would be, nor could she imagine how she could ever manage alone on a ship filled with men should the child come before they returned. Even the thought of the women on other of Rurik's ships did little to lessen her apprehension. Since her arrival at Rurik's settlement, Jilliand had witnessed several births. To her, it did not seem something the men should watch. It would be hard enough to have Rurik see her then. She was not certain she could get through the coming ordeal as well as the women around her seemed to have done—with stoicism. *Truth be told, I now dread what is coming.*

The time came for Rurik to leave. The ships were being loaded with weapons, foodstuffs, and other supplies. Jilliand felt a surge of pride watching him. She waved to the steersman, remembering his kindness when first she met him.

Olga lay her hand on Jilliand's arm. "I'll not see my son again, child. One never knows, but I feel you carry a girl. Ask Rurik to name her for me. I have had a rich life, Jilliand. You made my last year one of great joy." It saddened Jilliand to think Rurik might not see his mother again, but Jilliand knew the old woman was probably right. In the last several months, Olga had begun to move much more slowly, ate little, and was distant when the women were all together. Jilliand was the only person she wanted around her.

Turning again to the ordered chaos from ship to shore, Jilliand watched the men. Asger was on Rurik's ship. He proudly helped everyone wherever he could. He stood at the side and waved to Olga. His eyes held Olga's eyes for a long time. Neither was sad. The love between them was evident. Jilliand envied them. She had to struggle to hide her sadness from Rurik. It seemed unbearable to be without him. Her hands went to her growing belly. *Thank you, God, for this child. The time will pass quickly until his father returns to welcome him.* Her silent prayer was carried on the winds beginning to build.

As Jilliand watched the preparations with sadness in her heart, Rurik came ashore to speak with her before he had to leave. Holding her close, he kissed her. "You have made me proud, Jilliand. You belong where you are now, with me. You must stay home this time. You are not to risk yourself nor my first child." He smiled at her affectionately. "Come, let me feel the child once more. And let me touch the lips I love. I will come for you before the child is born."

Jilliand kissed him again as he held her tightly. "Fight well, Rurik. Return in two months to greet our child. I will always love you. Remember, Viking, I will wait for you."

He nodded, touched her face, kissed her lips once more, and left. Jilliand waited until they were long out of sight before she wept. A dark sense of foreboding crept into her heart and took up residence.

PART THREE

CHAPTER 21

RURIK HAD ONLY BEEN GONE one month, but already Jilliand felt a cold emptiness in her heart. *Can I live for these endless months without him around me? Why do I feel so heavy? I have his child within me, and his family is now my family. Why do I feel such darkness?* Jilliand could not shake the feeling. It woke her in the morning and followed her during the day. It was the last thought she had at night. She prayed for the quick return of her husband to keep her aching heart quiet.

This day, like every day now, the air was crisp and cold. The mornings were grey and dreary, with temperatures hanging near freezing. Only when the sun was directly above did its rays scatter the darkness, though the temperatures rose very little. Darkness would come again in the afternoons. The land seemed to pull within itself. Very few animals stayed out. Wolves could be heard in the distance. The cattle, sheep, and horses were kept in pens inside sheds providing shelter. On some days, the settlement was so quiet, with the only lights coming from lamps, candles, and fireplaces, that one could imagine it deserted.

Jilliand had already walked far behind the settlement and up a hill, as was her habit each morning. Her every thought was about Rurik. Somehow, she had to find a way to put him aside and concentrate on the coming birth. Her vomiting was so severe, it was embarrassing. She wondered why it continued. Climbing the hill kept her body busy, even if her mind refused to give up its mission, just as her thoughts refused to leave the man she loved. She stopped to rest below an outcropping of large boulders. She came here frequently, having discovered she could watch her village go about its life from here. The beauty of the soft lights coming from below was comforting to her. In the dim sunlight, in the distance she could see waves foam as they touched the land. Someday, she knew she would see the sails from Rurik's ship upon the horizon.

Quietly at first, a sound broke through her fog. She turned from the sight of the waves, tipped her head, and stood, listening. The sound was so soft that Jilliand was uncertain it was real. *There it is again.* She began to move farther up the hill, looking around. A rumble, getting louder and louder came to her. Horses—lots of horses, she was sure of it. At the hilltop, she climbed upon the rocky point, looking for the source of the sound. Heads appeared first, bobbing up and down. Over one hundred men on horseback plowed toward the houses now left with few men to defend them. The riders cried out as they swept into the hamlet. Jilliand shuddered as she recognized the sound. Like a great army of locusts, the invaders began killing everything around them.

The slaughter going on below stunned her for a moment. The cries of the women and children jerked her to action. "Olga!" Jilliand tried to scramble off the boulders and down the hillside through the thick brush and trees. Awkward with child, and struggling through the snow and over rocks, she fell several times. As she came closer to the scene, she stopped. It was already nearly over. Sinking into the brush, Jilliand covered her ears, trying to block out all the sounds of a one-sided, swift assault. Only burned-out shells of houses were left. Bodies of the men, women, children, and animals were strewn about.

The raiders were Vikings, but their yells to each other were in a language Jilliand had never heard. Jilliand's own village now looked like the ones she had seen burned those many months earlier. Jilliand watched, stunned, while the men below crowded along the shore, climbing into boats that now waited at the cove—boats she knew had not been there earlier. When the last ship had sailed away, Jilliand stumbled out of the forest edge and made her way across the remaining distance to the houses. Seeing the massacred women and children—women and children she knew—lying about sickened her. She moved from body to body sobbing, barely able to walk. No one was left alive. Great plumes of black smoke rose to hover under the cloud mantle.

She ran to Olga's house, where she found the old woman alive but pinned under the rubble from the roof with a fire edging toward her. Struggling, Jilliand was finally able to help Olga crawl from the path of the flames.

She was dazed but did not appear to be badly injured. The two women left the hut and moved slowly around the settlement hoping to find other survivors, but the sound of more riders echoed through the clearing. "This way," Olga urged Jilliand. Well hidden behind the brush and evergreens, the women watched more raiders searching every pile of rubble and looking over every body. Twice the invaders dug through the remains of Rurik's home.

"For what do they search, Olga?" Jilliand whispered.

"For you, Jilliand. They search for the wife of Rurik." Olga reached for Jilliand's hand. "And his child." Hand in hand, the two watched the search. The old woman continued, her voice so low that Jilliand leaned closer to hear. "Many years ago, before Rurik found you, he was visiting the village of his older cousin. That village was set upon by Vikings from another land. Because they believed the men of the settlement were still in English waters, the raiders did not expect to meet any resistance. Instead, they met Rurik, his men, and the men of the settlement who had just returned from raiding in England. Most of the invaders were slain, but I am sure one lived. Several years ago, a man came to us in winter. He was not one of ours, but Rurik honored our laws and made him welcome. This man stayed. In my dreams, I saw he was brother to the sea king who led the raid and who was killed on that day. I spoke with Rurik of my dream. He listened but allowed the man to stay. Perhaps the better to watch him. The man, called Gouldon, did not return with Rurik when he brought you home." Jilliand felt the air rush into her lungs with the story.

"I killed that man," Jilliand whispered. The memory of his attack was still vivid.

"I know," Olga replied.

"This raid is because of me?" Jilliand's heart was in her throat.

"No, Jilliand." Olga turned back to her. "Because of the killing of the invading sea king. To find you now would only add to their victory, it would not change its purpose." Olga pulled Jilliand closer. They huddled motionless and hidden. A cold, heartless silence descended on the smoldering remains of what had been Jilliand's home.

They watched as the men abandoned their search and boarded a lone vessel, which moved quickly toward the open seas. The same seas Rurik had sailed when he left. Jilliand sank to the ground, and tears filled her eyes and ran down her face. In what seemed like an instant, everyone was gone. The houses and corrals were torched. The home she shared with Rurik was burned to the ground. The children were dead. The animals were dead or had run away. Nothing remained alive.

Struggling to see through her tears, Jilliand and Olga stepped out into the open. Olga's face filled with deep sorrow, but she did not cry. Jilliand did, again and again. "Can we not go to Asger's place," Jilliand begged. "I must protect Rurik's son."

"That is not a place for us now, Jilliand. Those men went there first. It exists no longer, I'm certain." Slowly and painfully, the older woman limped along. "Come, we must leave and find shelter. First, we will try to find blankets, cloaks, anything to protect us from the cold." Turning back to the ashes of their village, the two began to search for anything they could use.

Finding a cooking pot, Olga put some smoldering debris inside. She gathered anything that might burn, and she and Jilliand bundled it together. Jilliand found several blankets and heavy cloaks. They found flint and a blade. With a knife, the women cut strips of beef off the dead cattle. Loaded with all they could carry, they moved farther into the forest cover. Travel was difficult for Jilliand's small body. She knew she would not be able to go far.

"This child causes you much pain, Jilliand?" Olga asked. Jilliand, concentrating on putting one foot before another, only nodded.

When they stopped to rest, the old woman placed a hand on Jilliand's belly. "The child comes soon," she worried aloud.

"No . . . not for at least two more months." Jilliand refused to think about how or where a birth could take place. Her son. Rurik's son. She placed a tender hand on her belly.

"Jilliand, the child comes soon," the old woman insisted. "We will stay here. The child will need our help." Not waiting for Jilliand to agree, she began preparations. Jilliand had no idea what to do. She tried to help, but Olga stopped her. "No, you must stay still. Keep the child in you as long as possible." Jilliand sat down and leaned back against a tree. She let the woman take over. Olga went about making a larger fire, creating a place for Jilliand to lie down, and tearing one of the smaller blankets into strips. Olga found branches she could pull to shield them against a wind sure to come.

For several hours, it seemed Olga was possessed. The forest was riddled with waterways, and the old woman found a stream. She had water boiling in the pot and stacked the strips of the blanket nearby. She set pieces of meat near the fire to cook, and hauled as much wood as she could close to the fire. Jilliand had no choice but to let Olga do what she wanted.

When the first pain struck, water gushed from between her legs. Gasping, she struggled to stand. "This is too early. The child comes too early," Jilliand cried. With Olga's help, she moved near the place the old woman had prepared for her. Clinging to the trunk of a tree, Jilliand squatted. Wave after wave of agony rolled over her. The pain was intense, and the contractions came nearly one upon another. Jilliand's total concentration was on each contraction and what must be coming. The pain grew stronger, and still the baby did not move. Time dragged on, hour after hour.

Jilliand was wearing down. At last she felt the urge to push. The child would not come. Again and again, Jilliand pushed. When it seemed she would die with the child still inside, the child turned and was born. Hours of labor were finally over. Exhausted, she fell against the tree, struggling to see her child— the son of Rurik. "More, Jilliand! You must push more. Everything has to come out." With the last bit of strength left in her, Jilliand clung to the tree again and pushed. When it all ended, she crawled onto the blankets, reaching for her child.

Wordlessly, and ever so gently, Olga lay the dusky, lifeless, little girl in Jilliand's arms. Jilliand could not cry. No sound came from her. She looked up at Olga, a confused expression on her face. Olga shook her head. She laid a soft hand on Jilliand's face. Jilliand began to shake her head, "No, no . . . please no." Tenderly, Jilliand traced the small face with her finger, held the tiny hand, and kissed the bloody head and cheek. For many minutes, she held the child to her heart. At last, still holding her tiny daughter to her chest, she clawed at the tree for support and stood. Staggering a short distance, she lay the infant down and, kneeling, tried to dig a grave. Even with Olga's help, they were unable to dig into the frozen earth. Jilliand didn't know what else to do. She was cold, inside and out. She sat back, clutching the babe.

"We must burn the child's body," Olga gently whispered. "We cannot leave her to the animals." Stricken, Jilliand looked at the old woman, and holding her dead child tighter to her heart, she refused. "We cannot leave her alone for the animals, we cannot take her with us, and we cannot stay here. I believe your God waits for this child, Jilliand. Let her go." At last, Jilliand nodded.

Wrapped in her mother's blanket, the body of the sea king's daughter was burned. Olga helped Jilliand pile rocks onto the tiny mound of ashes. Then they burned the afterbirth. Kneeling beside her child's ashes, Jilliand tried to pray. Instead, she began to weep with a pain so sharp she felt she could not breathe. *How could this happen? Rurik's first child dead, and his people all gone.* Her mourning echoed through the forest and returned to her heavy on the wind.

When at last, Jilliand ceased weeping, she raised her head to look for Olga. The old woman, still as stone, was seated on the ground leaning against a tree, her eyes lifeless. "No Olga! No!" Jilliand stood slowly and staggered to Olga's side. She sat down next to the old woman. Gently, she brushed the cheek once so soft and full of life, and now cold in death. After a long time, Jilliand rose.

She built another simple pyre, this time for her husband's mother. It took all her strength to roll the woman onto the brush mound. Lighting a branch from her fire, she set the pyre aflame. When she finished, Jilliand slumped onto the pallet that Olga had prepared. She had no tears left. "Perhaps it is time I die also." As if dead inside, she pulled the blankets and cloaks over her body and closed her eyes.

When she finally awoke, Jilliand was at first confused. *Where am I?* Her night had been filled with ghastly nightmares. But when she looked around, she careened back to the present and knew what she had lived through had been real.

Death may come for me next. Surely I cannot survive months of winter alone. "God, what do I do now? I cannot take any more. Please . . . " she begged aloud. Grasping the silver cross at her neck, she lay staring but not seeing. A ray of sunshine infiltrating a dusky world found the pitiful heap of a lost and broken woman. The light slipped around the evergreens, pushed through the brush, and spread gently around her body. The sun was refusing to let the darkness hold her. Instead, it gave her strength. "If Rurik is to find me, I must live," she murmured in a voice that was tired and unsure.

Jilliand's dress was torn, bloody, and caked with mud. Her engorged breasts ached—a constant reminder of her dead child. Her legs shook when she tried to stand. Clinging to a tree, she steadied herself. She staggered to the next tree, and the next. Jilliand fought against the nagging fear that she truly would die alone. Walking was grueling. She was so weak that she could not go on, and she finally crumpled to the ground. She grasped the locket, praying death would come quickly. Struggling to make her cold, stiff fingers work, she opened the locket. Her mother's face looked back at her.

"I cannot give up, Mother. You never gave up. The man that wore this never gave up." Through tears Jilliand spoke to Captain Avila. "You must help me, my friend. I do not know what to do. Give me some direction. God, You have taken care of me all these years. Please do not abandon me now. I am so lost. Help me, God," she prayed. "Help me. Help me. Please help me."

She remembered the flint and built a fire. Her mind crept into the dark world of exhaustion, where images of her life flickered before her eyes. She shuddered with the memory of her father, tried to recall everything Myla and Silas had told her about her mother, and remembered how freedom had felt for the first time when she had left the cell outside her father's castle. The days aboard Rurik's ship, the kindnesses of his people, and the love his mother gave her warmed her heart. Hesitantly, Jilliand eventually let the memory of Rurik fill her mind. His gentle touch, his kiss, the passion they shared, and the home he had given her made her moan with sorrow. *I must find a way to go on. He will come for me. I'm sure of it. He must. I promised I would wait.*

CHAPTER 22

RURIK LED HIS VIKING FORCE across the Baltic Sea toward a great land known as Rus—that would one day be called Russia. Weather pushed violently against them. The Viking warriors were accustomed to the sea and its many moods. However, this storm forced them to struggle mightily just to stay afloat. Twice they were forced to seek land and repair the ships, but they finally landed along the coast of Rus. Eventually, after over two months, they reached a site near the lands now sunk in battle. The Slavs, settled farther up the coast of Rus, were deadlocked in a battle for control of the land. Rurik intended to step in and rule both sides. It was taking too much time. Rurik was agitated over the delay. He knew Jilliand was near her time, and he had to get back soon. Everything he did now had a new purpose.

At first landing, Rurik met with the sea king of another Viking fleet. Years of fighting together bound the two men as friends. The man was as close to Rurik as Olav was. After customary greetings, the man took Rurik aside to speak quietly in private. "I have sad news to share, my friend. I have news of a great raid and fire. I know it to be true, Rurik. It began at the settlement below yours and then continued up the shore. Your entire homesite and all the families who lived there were killed." The older Viking clasped Rurik's shoulder.

Rurik was stunned. For a moment, he could not speak. "How do you know this is true?" he asked, his voice tight, his eyes narrowed. *How? Everyone?* The anguish was like a sword, piercing his very being, his mind, and his heart. He could not think beyond what he heard. This could not be. The sisters of fate would not play such a joke on him. Not Jilliand and the child. His life. He became aware that his friend was speaking again. With great effort, he listened.

"I went to the house of your mother, Rurik. It was gone. Everything was burned. The house you shared with your queen and the empty homes of Dir and Askold are gone. It is said that followers of a man named Gouldon sailed from the lands of Wales seeking you. They found only women and children. They did what Vikings do, Rurik. I followed that ship. I now give to you the arm rings and sword of that sea king. He and his entire crew are now dead. Their ships were burned, and all they carried destroyed." He clasped Rurik's shoulder again, handing him the sword and rings. "I am sorry, my friend." The silence around them became thick with Rurik's pain.

"In the ashes, I found this." The older Viking held the sword Rurik had given Jilliand for their firstborn son. "It was in the house you shared with your woman." The blackened blade lay cold and ugly in Rurik's hand. In anger, Rurik raised the sword and with a mighty thrust, sank it into the ground. The hilt quivered as Rurik walked away. Standing alone, staring out at the sun sliding beneath the horizon, he saw Jilliand's hair. He wept bitterly for the woman he loved. When his friend left the next morning, Rurik stayed on the beach for hours staring at the sea.

Over the next weeks, Rurik and his ships were repeatedly driven back out to sea by the inhabitants of the new land. Never before had he been forced to retreat. This time, when they were no longer pursued, Rurik stood at the bow, an ache deep in his heart. His jarls cornered him. Askold's voice was hard with anger. "We can defeat these people, Rurik! You must put thoughts of your wife and son out of your head. You are a Viking. Fight like a Viking!"

Dir added, "Your wife and son look down on you. Fight to be with all the warriors you've known. Your men need a Viking sea king. They need you. You cannot give up now." When Rurik would not respond, the men walked away, exasperated. All was silent, but for the sound of the waves as they rolled under the ship. Rurik's sorrow was draped over his vessels like a great black shroud.

For several days, Rurik stood looking out at the sea. Then, ever so softly, it came to him. A silent whisper, as if Jilliand called to him. *Do what you were meant to do. I will always wait for you.* Slowly, the voice grew in strength, until he felt as if

Jilliand were standing at his side. "She lives here," Rurik spoke into the wind, his fist upon his chest.

Rurik called his men together, spoke briefly, and turned the warships around. A great cry rose from his vessel and was picked up by the other ships with them. The king was back. The companion warships were rapidly changing direction. Then suddenly, as one, the ships fell silent, and each man slipped back to what they were born to be—Vikings.

Men on the shore were taken completely by surprise. Having watched the Vikings sail away defeated, they never imagined they would return. The fight was quickly won, as Rurik gained control of the coast. It took longer than planned, but Rurik's people came to stay.

In time, Rurik and his jarls took over Novgorod on the Volkhov River. A fortress was soon completed to house his warriors. Other buildings followed to house the families that had sailed with him. Within three years, he had increased his holdings to an immense area. This new land was known as the land of the Rus. Rurik was now Prince of Rus, a land that would one day be the largest country in the world—Russia. All the while, in solitude, Rurik mourned. *Why did I not bring Jilliand?* The darkness of night sheltered him as he ached and walked in deep sadness. He drove himself and his men hard. He was restless, determined to keep the weight of Jilliand's death at bay. Only at night did he allow his mind to hold her memory.

Rurik never spoke of Jilliand, though he mourned her every day. When they had left their settlement, the families of most of the men, including both Dir and Askold, had sailed in a *knarr* behind Rurik's fleet. Over and over, he asked himself why he had not taken Jilliand with him. Settled in the new land, his brother and jarls tried to pull Rurik out of his darkness, but he lacked the power to climb. He went about his work to settle this land, expand its borders, and bring a people together, doing what he had done all his life. Now, he moved as in some world caught between the living and the dead. Still, Jilliand stayed in his heart.

As if the heavens knew she had borne all she could, the next day was finally as bright and sunny as any for the season. Jilliand forced herself to get up and pushed onward, veering back toward the coast, hoping to find people. For several days she traveled this way.

At last, Jilliand came to a village not unlike where she had lived with Rurik. Walking into the middle of the grounds, she stopped and waited. Jilliand knew she looked frightful. Bloodied, dirty, torn, and ragged, she stood. For a moment, all speaking around her ceased as the inhabitants of the village stared. One Viking finally came to her. He was taller than Rurik, heavier and older, though he still moved with ease. From the reaction of those around him, Jilliand knew he must be their sea king. "Welcome, traveler. From where do you come?" His voice was calm and quiet, but a deep frown creased his forehead, and questioning hazel eyes peered at her through his narrowed lids.

In his tongue, she replied, "From the north shore. I seek passage to England on one of your warships. I can use both sword and bow. I can be another eye for the steersman." Jilliand paused. Looking at the man directly, she added, "Rurik the Viking Sea King is my husband. His place was attacked, and all are dead." Gritting her teeth, fighting tears, she added, "Rurik and his ships were not there. I must go to where he can find me."

She waited while her words sank in. The man's frown relaxed, and he simply nodded. "Come, make yourself warm, eat, and rest. My wife is yonder," he said, pointing toward a large dwelling. "Tell her I sent you." Nodding to Jilliand again, he left her. Jilliand walked toward the place he pointed out. The man's wife was tall and pretty with thick blonde hair braided and piled on her head. Her dress was covered with panels of bright blue fabric interwoven with intricate designs in gold and red threads indicating her high station. The lady graciously welcomed Jilliand into her home.

Inside, she prepared a bath for Jilliand and helped bind her swollen breasts. The woman gave her a clean, thick, heavy gown and worked Jilliand's long hair. When the husband returned, he welcomed her to their evening meal. He noted her arm rings, the rings on her hand, and the small blade she carried with her. He never asked, but Jilliand could tell he would want to know her story. He had given her shelter; he had a right to know.

The woman's eyes filled with tears of sympathy as Jilliand told of losing her child. "You lost your family, your child, and one you considered your mother in one day. The fates have played hard with you; perhaps they have better plans for you now." Her voice was soft and gentle. Jilliand fought to keep from crying at the kindness being shown to her. She was praying this man would be willing to help her move on.

"You say you were taken during a raid on English soil. You wish to return to England? Why?" he asked pointedly. "You could stay here, with us. You are Viking now. You belong to Rurik."

"I must go where I believe my husband will search. He knows I will be waiting for him. I must return to my people until such time as he finds me." Jilliand could not explain how she felt. She had already seen the destructive remnants of Viking vengeance on Rurik's family. "I cannot endanger this place too. Word would spread that I live with you. Perhaps in England, I will be more difficult to find—by Rurik that is true, but more so and more importantly, more difficult to find by his enemies."

The Viking nodded. "You would know best what you have to do. Yes, you may travel with me. My ships leave in the morning. I will put you ashore where we have an agreement with the English." He instructed his wife to find an additional cloak and some shoes for her. Jilliand removed both of her arm rings and offered them to him. "No, Jilliand. You are still a Viking queen. I will look for your Rurik while I am gone." Without another word, he turned and headed to his sleeping quarters, calling, "Come soon, wife. I am cold this night."

The next morning, the sea king's wife held Jilliand closely when she bid her farewell. "Thank you for giving me a moment of peace," Jilliand whispered before she stepped away and boarded the lead ship. Standing at the stern of the vessel, she memorized every detail of the village—a place so like her home.

Watching the shoreline grow smaller, she felt the wound in her soul grow larger. *Perhaps I am not meant to have a family, a place, a home.*

The gentle motion of the boat and the sounds of its crew brought Rurik back to Jilliand. Her chest ached. Fighting to keep her tears at bay, she stared out at the horizon. The sea king's crew accepted her presence without comment, as if she belonged to them all. Respectfully, they made way for her when she began to pace. Memories of her time with Rurik and his ship filled every corner of her mind, nearly breaking her. "I cannot do this," she whispered. And just when Jilliand thought she would perish with the weight of grief, the ships slid into a cove blanketed by thick fog.

Vowing to bring word to Rurik of Jilliand if he could, the Viking sea king stilled his ships, while Jilliand slid over the side and waded ashore. Climbing a dune near the water, she looked down on a small village. The heavy fog hung above the settlement, but Jilliand could see people going about their morning. Sounds of life drifted up to her.

The Viking led his ships further along a waterway and moored them against the bank, still hidden within the fog. Suddenly, the Vikings stormed from the ships and laid waste to the small English hamlet without warning. Stunned, Jilliand stood frozen listening to the chaos. *How does this constitute an "agreement"?* Jilliand ran a short distance toward the village, then stopped, shaking her head in a silent no. Poor farmers and the few men acting as guards were no match for the onslaught. The ensuing fight was tipped heavily in favor of the Vikings. It looked to be a sad and quick end for the poor English.

Suddenly, as if carried by that same fog, English soldiers thundered onto the scene—horses rearing, men with swords and lances, and foot soldiers with great shields and more swords. "I would not be joined with either side. I must not be seen with the Vikings nor with the English," she said, speaking to the wind that carried the battle. Jilliand frantically surveyed the area.

Pulling her gown up above her knees, Jilliand raced down the dune and sprinted around the outskirts of the village. Trying to get farther inland away from the fighting, she ran through the mud and over fallen carts. She scurried past huts and other buildings, many on fire. Men from the village dashed wildly about without direction, trying to escape. Jilliand darted around them. Stopping to catch her breath, she looked back. The fight was turning against the Vikings. There were more than ten English soldiers to each Viking. This English army came to fight—and win. The English pushed the Vikings back. Several Viking boats were already gliding away from the shore, as fire arrows peppered the water around them.

Whirling around, Jilliand bolted past the timbers of a wrecked barn that was barely standing. She slammed right into an Englishman who suddenly grabbed her roughly around the waist. He was young, had the wild look of his first real battle, and the triumphant look of one with his first prize. Jilliand tried to push him away and pull her blade, but he was too strong and quick for her. With a flick of his hand, he knocked her smaller sword away, sending it flying far beyond her reach. Even so, she kneed him as hard as she could in the crotch. He moaned in pain, releasing her as he gasped and sank to the ground vomiting. Jilliand turned to run. She had not gone three steps, when she was again caught. "Stop!" another man ordered her. This man was much taller, older, and obviously a leader with the English. His grasp was like steel, and there was no hesitancy.

Looking in his eyes, Jilliand knew she was taken. The younger man was stumbling toward them by this time, cursing and threatening Jilliand. Jilliand never looked at him; she kept her eyes on the man holding her. He looked her over. When she pushed her hair from her face, the man grabbed her wrist, turning her hand over to examine it. "Leave her be," he ordered the younger man, in a tone that bade no argument. He freed Jilliand's wrist, grasped her arm, and walked away with Jilliand in tow.

"I had her first," the young man muttered under his breath, wiping the contents of his stomach away from his mouth. He staggered toward her with fire in his eyes.

"Did you not even look at her? Look at the clothes and jewelry she wears. Leave her to me," the older man said as he regarded a group of his men now gathered. "No one is to harm this lady. Anyone who does will answer to the king." Pulling her along, he asked gruffly, "Can you ride, lady?"

"Yes." Jilliand nervously glanced over her shoulder at the growing crowd of men watching them. She was easily lifted upon a great fighting horse that displayed his discontent over the passenger. Gripping the reins, it took every ounce of Jilliand's strength to control the animal, but all the while she continued to talk softly to it. Slowly, the horse settled. Jilliand was quickly surrounded by English soldiers. At a command from her captor, who obviously commanded this troupe, the mounted men moved out, and Jilliand had no choice but to go with them.

Jilliand concentrated on the land ahead and never looked back. If the Vikings were being slaughtered, she didn't want to see it. They rode hard through the night without stopping. Jilliand never spoke, nor was she spoken to; she just rode. Every mile took her farther away from Rurik.

In two days' time, they arrived at the largest burg Jilliand had ever seen. Although it was night, the stronghold was ablaze with light that spilled onto surrounding grounds. A deep, wide, water-filled moat surrounded the whole estate. Large flags flew at the entrance. There were great walls of dirt over thirty feet wide, behind which huge fortresses were positioned at each corner. Men on top walked back and forth. A giant gate that became a drawbridge was lowered, and the soldiers escorting Jilliand rode through. Jilliand dared not look around. She was pulled off the horse by the same man who had lifted her up. His treatment of her was neither friendly nor cold.

That man took her through a large building centered in the burg. It rose above the surrounding walls, with encircling walkways atop the structure. Guards were posted all along the walkways at each of the four entrances and, Jilliand noticed, throughout the inside. She was taken down halls and into a vast room, filled with charts, a large table and chairs, knights and servants, and elegantly dressed men. At the head of the table sat a man. Jilliand knew by his dress and the manner in which the men treated him that he must be the king. The hall went silent when the soldier walked in with his prisoners. For the first time, Jilliand was aware that the young man who had accosted her was also a prisoner. He was clearly frightened and trembled as he knelt before the king.

The older soldier gently pushed Jilliand down, as he too knelt. The hall was filled with an air of anticipation as the king apparently had expected their arrival. "I am told this man attacked you," the king said as he gestured to the young man kneeling beside her. "Were you harmed?" Jilliand looked into his dark eyes that bore into hers. His voice was quiet but powerful.

Without looking at the young soldier next to her, she responded, "He pulled me from the fire."

The king frowned. He looked from the older soldier to Jilliand. "I believe you lie. Is it not wrong to lie to your king?" His eyes narrowed and looked deeply into hers.

"Are you my king?" Jilliand asked, her gaze never wavering from the king. She knew her cloak was filthy and her dress was torn and muddy, but she held her head high. "Is it not wrong to punish a soldier for doing what every soldier in your kingdom does to the women of those he has vanquished?" The king shook his head slightly. He walked around her and studied her.

At length, he asked the soldier, "Why do you bring her here, Sir Edward?"

"She wears your ring, Sire—" the older man began.

"No!" Jilliand quickly interrupted, suddenly anxious. "I wear my own rings. I have taken nothing." She turned toward Sir Edward. He remained kneeling on one knee, watching the king. "I have taken nothing," Jilliand insisted again. "I wear what belongs to me, nothing more."

The king raised his brows slightly. Returning to his chair, he glanced at Jilliand as he sat and then commanded Edward, "I would see the ring. Bring the woman closer."

Jilliand was pulled up and pushed the short distance to the king. Wordlessly, he held out his hand. Jilliand slowly extended her left hand for him to see. He took her hand, looked at the ring given to her by Rurik, and then released his grip. Very softly, she murmured, "This is the ring my husband gave when we wed." Still silent, he looked at her again. Jilliand returned his gaze, and he held it.

Finally, taking a deep breath, Jilliand extended her right hand, showing him her mother's ring. The king started, stood up, and grabbed her wrist. He pulled her closer, pushed the hood off her head, the cloak away from her shoulders, and then stepped back with a slight gasp.

"From where did you get this ring, lady?" His voice was still commanding, but softer.

"From my mother," Jilliand replied, as she pulled her wrist away and closed her fingers protectively over the ring.

The king spoke to his page, "Take the lady to the queen's chambers and send several women to assist her."

Jilliand stepped back. "Sire, I have no need of the queen's quarters. I would ask only to be allowed safe passage to . . ." she hesitated. She knew of no place to ask passage to. She only wanted to leave this place safely. "I would have no need of the queen's chambers, Your Majesty," she finished weakly.

"Ah, lady. I beg to differ with you. You have great need of what the queen's quarters can provide, starting with a bath." She could see a slight smile on his face and hear men chuckling in the room.

At first, Jilliand was too startled to think of a reply. Just the thought of being thrust upon an unsuspecting queen forced Jilliand to persist. She muttered, the words stumbling from her mouth, "I cannot go to the queen's chambers, Sire . . . "

The king interrupted again, "Avail yourself of the gowns you will find there, too." He was already returning to his seat.

"Your Majesty . . . " Jilliand began doggedly.

"Yes?" His gaze rested on her, and a strange expression changed his face. It was kind, and a teasing smile grew as he watched her begin to squirm.

"Where is the queen? How is she to feel about this?" Jilliand was horrified. She could not imagine how his wife might react to her uninvited presence. *In the queen's own chambers? And taking her gowns?*

"She is not here. I expect you to join me at court this evening. We dine soon."

She stood frozen. The king tipped his head to the side, his eyes twinkling. "Is there something else, lady? Perhaps your hearing is poor?"

Choosing her words carefully, Jilliand replied haltingly, "Is it possible you do not know the queen well?" Several men coughed to cover their laughter.

"The queen is away. I expect to see you when we dine, lady," he repeated pointedly. Jilliand was certain she could see a smile on his face before he turned to Edward. "Release this man on the lady's word," he ordered. Looking at the young man, he sternly added, "You should thank the lady for your life, boy." Jilliand knew she, too, was now dismissed.

A page waved his hand toward a hallway and door, bowing slightly to Jilliand. Jilliand resigned herself to what promised to be a disastrous evening.

Jilliand was led upstairs and down a long hall. The page spoke briefly to some men standing guard. He stopped, unlocked a heavy door, and pushed it open for Jilliand. She stepped into a place that seemed to have been shut up for a very long time. The rooms were cold, dark, and dusty.

The page lit candles, started a fire in the fireplace, and said, "There will be someone coming to help you soon, lady. If you have need of service, please just speak to one of the men outside the door. Can I do anything else for you?" He studied her and wondered, *Who is this woman that the king takes under his protection? I should care for her well, I think.* He then backed away.

Numbly, Jilliand shook her head. *Would that I could leave too,* she thought. She glanced around the chambers, which were the largest Jilliand had ever seen. Everything was furnished richly, with heavy tapestries hung on the walls to keep out the cold. The large overstuffed mattress on the bed was bare. The bed itself was large with ornate carvings on the headboard. One lone chair sat near the fireplace. A second room had a table, chairs, and empty shelves. The rooms spoke of station but felt void of life.

A knock on the door announced the arrival of the promised lady-in-waiting. "Lady, my name is Becca. I have come to help you." After bowing slightly to Jilliand, Becca continued. "The other ladies are coming with water for your bath. The king asks that you be in court to dine. We must make haste, lady. You should not keep the king waiting." Not capable of speaking, Jilliand simply nodded. Becca moved the chair away from the fireplace to make room for the tub.

"Do not worry yourself about the room, lady. By the time you return from dining, it will look like new." She opened the door to more ladies, all young and serious. A tub was soon filled with warm water, Jilliand was bathed, and her hair washed with a sweet-smelling soap. Next, Becca wrapped her in a blanket while she dried her hair. "Might you be pregnant, lady?" Becca gently asked, noting her swollen breasts and the blood-tinged water.

"Not anymore." Jilliand spoke under her breath and stared into the flames of the fireplace. Becca continued to dry and comb Jilliand's hair, keeping her thoughts to herself, for a moment. Then she carefully asked, "Might I bind your breasts for you? They would be less painful, lady." Gratefully, Jilliand agreed.

"Now, lady, come look. Which gown do you like best?" Becca looked from Jilliand to the gowns in an armoire and back at Jilliand. "They may be a tad large for you, but fear not, we can alter them." Jilliand stood beside Becca looking at the gowns, which were beautiful but much too large for Jilliand.

"The queen is much taller than I," Jilliand offered timidly, wondering how on earth any of these could be fixed quickly. "How long has the queen been gone?" Jilliand asked no one in particular. Silence met her question. "Let me put it another way. How angry will she be if I must cut a gown?" One anonymous giggle burst forth in the room. Taking a deep breath, Jilliand turned to the women. "Please, ladies. Pick something for me that looks well but that will not take too much work. We are quickly running out of time." At that, Jilliand was crowded out. She stepped back, grateful she had help. It took every lady in the room, including Jilliand, to reshape the gown for her. Nonetheless, Jilliand was pleased with the result. Never had she seen or, much less, dressed in a gown like this. Her heart ached to have Rurik see her now. The fabric was a deep russet color, with a low, square neckline that revealed the tops of her tightly bound breasts. The skirt fell in soft gathers from an empire waist to graze the floor. Jilliand removed her arm rings and her mother's pendant. Her locket, silver cross, and her rings were her only adornment. Becca deftly rolled and piled her hair atop her head.

"I think you are finished, lady." Becca walked around Jilliand, admiring the group's efforts.

"This is beautiful." Jilliand could hardly believe it was truly her standing before the looking glass.

CHAPTER 23

BECCA ESCORTED JILLIAND TO THE dining hall. It was alight with candles and several blazing fireplaces. Men and women were wandering about, laughing, talking, slowly moving toward immense tables set with opulent platters and goblets. Staff stood about, patiently waiting to serve. The king sat at the center of a long table on a slightly raised platform at one end of the hall. His men sat on either side of him overlooking the room.

Jilliand and Becca stood quietly, listening. Slowly, Jilliand began to walk through the men and women gathered along the sides of the room. Her shoulders slumped. *I do not belong here.* Then she turned and spoke softly to Becca. "I cannot do this. We must go back now." Without hesitation, Becca turned with her new mistress.

"She's leaving? Stop her," the king commanded, leaning to the man next to him, his best friend and confidant, Sir Alexander. The king fixed his eyes on her. One by one, the occupants of the great hall noticed and followed his gaze.

Before Jilliand could make it out the door, Alexander was at her elbow. "Lady, His Majesty requests your presence at his table." Jilliand looked up into a scarred but handsome face of a man who looked to be about the age of the king. He smiled slightly.

Jilliand felt like a cornered animal. She pursed her lips and, thinking aloud, said, "What if I choose to leave anyway?"

"You will not," Alexander softly assured her.

"You would drag me to his table?!" Her brows shot up.

He continued to look at her without replying. His eyes were kind, but his manner was of one who gives commands that are to be followed.

"There would be little dignity in that," Jilliand noted wryly.

"None," he agreed seriously, shaking his head.

Defeated, she took his offered arm and was escorted to the king's table. By now, the room had become silent, as all eyes followed this newest member of court being escorted to the waiting king. The men watched with interest. The ladies watched with a touch of jealousy. This new lady was beautiful. Whispering soon confirmed that no one knew the young lady's name.

As they wove their way to the front of the hall, Jilliand spied the young man who had recently captured her with the intent of taking his pleasure. He stood against the wall, aghast when it was apparent she was purposely walking toward him. She stopped, speaking discreetly, "Sir, you are one of the king's men?"

The young man was horrified. He could now see she had not just been some wench. For the second time in his brash young life, he felt fear. He had nearly raped an acquaintance of the king. He answered with trepidation, "Yes, m' lady."

Jilliand noted, "You would do well to remember, things are often not what they first seem." She spoke so softly he had to strain to hear her. She smiled and then nodded to him as she walked away. All eyes in the room followed her, wondering what she might have to say to a simple soldier.

"Lady," Alexander whispered, as they neared the king's table, "By what name are you called?"

"Jilliand," she whispered back, "and you?"

He grinned, "Sir Alexander, at your service, lady."

When they reached the king's table, Sir Alexander announced, "Your Majesty, may I present Lady Jilliand."

"Lady Jilliand, welcome to my court. How kind of you to join us. I know you have had a trying day." The king nodded to her.

"You have no idea," Jilliand murmured, as she curtsied. She heard Sir Alexander chuckle and saw the king smile.

"Please, come sit with us," the king continued. "We have need of a lady's influence, I fear."

This time, she clearly heard snickering from the room. It promised to be a long night. "Thank you for escorting me." She smiled at Alexander, ignoring the laughter.

"My pleasure, Lady," he replied softly.

A place was quickly set for her at the king's left. The kitchen staff set wine, utensils, and a platter with bits of roasted duck, venison, cheeses, and bread and fruit before her. When she was seated, the crowd resumed its chatter, but she could not eat. Fearful of drawing more attention, though, she tried to pick at the meat, pushing the food around her dish.

The king leaned toward her. "Tell me if it works, Lady."

Jilliand looked at him, questioningly. "Your Majesty?"

"When you mix it." He pointed at her platter with his fork. "Does that make it taste any better?"

Jilliand blushed, but smiled. "I find your hearing and sight are both excellent, Sire."

He smiled back. The conversation around the table was lively. Jilliand was intentionally drawn into the discussion, no matter how she tried to avoid it. The king turned to her. Although his face was serious, his eyes twinkled, "Tell me, Lady, do you prefer a short or long blade?" His tablemates again went silent. When that happened, the room became silent, and all eyes were on her.

Looking directly at him, Jilliand responded, "A short blade, certainly. I am neither strong enough nor tall enough for a long blade. However, in truth, I prefer the bow, Your Highness." When she finished speaking, she took a sip of wine and turned back to him. He was still looking at her, his brows raised in surprise.

"A bow, Lady?" he repeated, frowning slightly.

"Yes," she repeated, "a bow. Of course, mine was much shorter than any man's bow. Still, I am quite accurate." She watched him for a second and then added, "It is well known that the English bowman is by far the most feared of all opponents."

He looked out to those in the room. "Lady Jilliand says the English bowmen are the best. We agree!" He raised his cup to her, as the men called out and cheered.

Talk drifted to other topics. Jilliand glanced around the room. In a while, she leaned toward the king, "Sire, if I stay any longer, I will be your entertainment. Please allow me . . . "

"You sing, Lady?" His eyes twinkled again.

"Never more than once," she quickly shot back, "but I may snore."

The others at the table laughed with the king. He smiled at her, thinking, *She is who I believe her to be. There is no doubt.* He nodded to Jilliand, drained his goblet, and then informed her, "Of course, Lady. I would speak with you in your chamber shortly." Before she could protest, a man behind her spoke into the king's ear.

The king reached for Jilliand's arm. "Wait, I wish to introduce you to someone."

Jilliand followed his gaze to see another well-dressed, refined gentleman approaching the table.

An announcement was made. "His Majesty, Prince Philippe of France."

"Welcome back to court, Prince," the king greeted him. Standing, he took Jilliand's hand. "May I present Lady Jilliand."

The prince's eyes were afire. He took a second longer to look into Jilliand's eyes and then bowed low to her. "Lady Jilliand, how pleasant to see a beautiful, fresh face at court."

Grateful for the practice she had gotten with the captive Frenchwomen living in Rurik's village, Jilliand took a deep breath before responding in clear French, "You would be wise to not say that again, sir. Your implication could be most unpleasant for the rest of the ladies of this court."

Taken aback, the prince continued. "Your point is well taken. You speak my language?"

Smoothly, Jilliand responded, "And you speak English. Very important in these times, would you not agree?"

He bowed deeply, but before he could respond further, Jilliand added, "I am so pleased to meet you, Your Majesty, though I was just leaving. Please enjoy yourself, Prince Philippe. The king is in a wonderful mood tonight."

Not waiting for anyone to respond, she rose and joined Becca, who was standing nearby. "Get me out of here—quickly," Jilliand whispered to her. "I am not comfortable here."

Back in the queen's chambers, Jilliand was pleasantly surprised to find the room had changed. The study was clean and warm. The sleeping quarters were also warm with a fire splashing light onto the now polished floors. The few candles lit near a freshly made bed cast a soft glow. The chambers felt lived in. Jilliand slowly walked around the room. She brushed her hands over the carving on the bed, felt the wall tapestries, and stopped before the fireplace. The wood crackled, and small cinders floated up the chimney. Suddenly, Jilliand shivered. "I still smell the burning and see the bodies," Jilliand murmured, watching the flames from the fire dance. Becca, standing nearby, heard.

"Then you should bathe again, Lady." She immediately gave orders to the rest of her staff. Becca remembered the blood in the water from Jilliand's first bath. She had seen the scars that covered Jilliand's back. *This lady must have led a hard life. She seems kindly turned, not like the last lady to occupy this room. We must do all we can to keep this lady here with us. She is the king's favorite. No other has been in these rooms since his queen left.*

"Do you think I have time?" Jilliand was already undressing. "The king will be here shortly." Now, more than ever before, Jilliand wished she had proper clothing to wear in this strange court. Clothing that would tell the tale of her station. Clothing she wore as Rurik's queen. *Pray I know how I am to behave for this court. I need the rest a stay here would offer.*

"We'll make time, Lady." Becca poured lavender oil into the water, then cupped it over Jilliand. Becca worked Jilliand's hair into great lathers, with scented soap. "Even the king will wait for a beautiful woman, Lady Jilliand," Becca whispered into Jilliand's ear. Jilliand felt a dart of fear. She had no intention of being the king's lady. Rinsing her lady off, Becca wrapped her in a towel warmed in front of the fireplace. With her wet hair combed into cascading ringlets dancing down her back, Jilliand slipped into a soft green robe. There was no gown.

"It is much too forward to see the king in only a robe, Becca. I would feel better armed, if I were dressed. What do you think is proper? In truth I have never been in a court such as this." Jilliand glanced at Becca. *No matter how I dress, I call attention to myself. Perhaps the ladies and I can sew simple gowns from what is available. I do not wish to be the object of gossip.*

"I believe the king knows you are preparing for night, Lady. He also knows you have brought nothing with you. The robe will be very modest, I assure you." Becca was already looking through the hanging bed gowns. "But we'll find a bed gown for you."

The search proved none of the gowns could be utilized. Jilliand stood thinking aloud. "Would that I had a soft shirt. Maybe tomorrow we can look over what I might do with what we can find." She tried to smile at the ring of young women surrounding her. "My heart is sore. Perhaps, I can begin to heal with your help."

A younger girl suddenly darted out of the room and returned shortly with a long, soft shirt. "Lady, I have this. It is soft. Perhaps it would make a good nightshirt for tonight." She proudly held it out for Jilliand. "It is not one a lady would wear, and it too is large, but not as large as the gowns you have seen thus far. Feel, Lady, it is very soft."

Jilliand felt the material. It was indeed soft and not as voluminous as the rest. "Yes, this is perfect. Thank you so much." She slipped it over her head just as a knock at her door announced the king. "Quickly, take him to the study. I care not to entertain visitors in my sleeping quarters." She hesitantly wrapped the robe over the nightshirt.

I cannot meet with the king dressed in a bed gown. Panicked, Jilliand looked around the room. The dress she had worn was already downstairs, to be washed. There was nothing else to do. Her eyes closed, Jilliand shook her head. "It keeps getting worse," she moaned.

The ladies ushered Jilliand into her study and opened the door for the king.

The king stepped into a room he had not been in for over seven years. He stood motionless, surveying the area. Strange how it now seemed warm and inviting. He had to look away to keep from laughing at Jilliand. She looked like a child trying to dress up in her mother's clothing. Walking to the window, he looked below. "Jilliand, did you know you can see the gardens from this window?" He motioned her to his side. Jilliand walked over and peered out the window.

"The moon reflects on the water, like the flame of a candle," she noted softly.

The king looked at her, put his arm around her, ignoring the stiffening he detected, and walked with her back to the seating area near the fire. Sitting down, he indicated Jilliand should do the same, then he began, "Jilliand, remove the ring on your right hand."

Slowly, with alarm, Jilliand closed her fingers around her ring, watching the king intently. "If you look at the underside of the ring, you will find . . . " he began.

"A lion and a dove," completed Jilliand. She watched the king with a strange sense in her heart. *What is this I feel?*

The king continued softly, "The lion stands for . . . "

Jilliand quietly interrupted him again, "Strength, power, leadership, a king."

"And the dove, Jilliand?"

"Everything he saw in the woman he loved," she whispered. "Kindness, honesty, peace, gentleness . . ." she finished. Jilliand remembered well the stories Silas and his wife had shared with her.

"Do you know what this woman looked like, Jilliand?" the king asked.

Jilliand was no longer aware of anyone in the room. Becca, Sir Alexander, and the king's page stood by silently. They listened to their king and this lady—a lady who had shown up in the king's council chamber, ragged and dirty, now transformed to a thing of beauty.

"I do." Jilliand stood and walked to the fireplace. Her hand slowly moved to the locket around her neck.

"Jilliand," the king's voice was low and gentle, "she had hair that rivaled the sunset and emerald eyes with flecks of gold. Eyes that flashed with passion and anger. She was petite, thin, and graceful. She moved regally. Her husband loved her deeply. She returned that love."

Jilliand stood spellbound. *Does he speak of my mother? It must be my grandmother. I do not believe my father loved my mother.* In a voice, as hushed as the room itself, she asked, "Did you know this woman?"

"I did," he replied. "This woman had a son, who became a king when the woman's father died. That son was the only heir to a particular throne in England, even though the woman was no longer living in England. When her husband, the crown prince of Spain, died unexpectedly, the woman returned to England to be with her son. I am that son. I was eighteen when she and her guard were overrun by a rival trying for my crown. She——"

Jilliand finished telling the story she had heard so many times from Myla and Silas "——agreed to marry that rival, a lord, in exchange for the safe passage of her men. The captain of her guard offered his service for ten years, without fees, to this same lord." She could now add the reason he would do such a thing, "That captain loved the woman. The woman had one child with the lord before she died in childbirth." Finished, Jilliand looked at the king.

"No," he gently corrected her. "The woman was with child when she married the lord. She was with child when she left Spain, Jilliand." He paused, watching her. "I know this because she told me herself. Her wish was to come to me and raise her child with a brother——a king. Mother feared for her life and yours if I tried to claim her or the child, until she could get to me."

Closing her eyes, Jilliand turned away from the king. It was many long moments before she could speak. So many things were rushing into her mind, like leaves in a whirlwind. So many things were beginning to make sense, yet still circled at the edge of reason. "I was raised as a boy in all things, including defense with weapons and education. I can use a blade, sword, and bow. I can ride. I speak English, French, Italian, Spanish." She paused for a heartbeat. She could hear her own voice echo in the room.

"I knew nothing about being a woman. When it was no longer possible to disguise my womanhood, his cruelty was heightened. I still bear the scars." Jilliand opened her eyes, looking into the fireplace. "Perhaps all this explains his anger at me." Turning she looked at the king. "Could he have known I was not his child?"

"I do not believe so. I was the only one other than our mother that knew who your real father was. The lord she married did not know, though he found out she was related to me, the king. I do not believe he knew she was my mother. You are the daughter of a Spanish prince and English princess. You are the sister of a king, Jilliand. Make no mistake, there was nothing noble about that lord's anger." Only the sounds of logs spitting in the fire could be heard in the room. The king's voice softly broke in, "He may have hoped the child would be male, to therefore lay claim to the crown by way of the mother's station, knowing only that she was on her way to my court. He was in fact so certain the child would be a boy that he planned an attempt on my life. His men failed. I chose to let the lord go unpunished, for fear he would kill the child—you—if it was a female and survived. A rumor was carefully circulated by me, that I had a bastard son; a male child to claim the crown. When you were born, it was a well-kept secret by that lord, that you were indeed a female. His people were threatened if word should get out." The king walked around the room. The memories were painful for him, this much was certain.

"When it was certain you were to be married, our plan was to take you before you reached the wedding site. Then we received word you had disappeared. With the captain gone also, I prayed that you and he were together." The king sank back down, and years of a dark secret were ended.

The room was quiet again but for the crackling of the fire. Jilliand stood still staring into the flames. If her brother knew all along the child was a girl, if he knew all he just admitted, would he not also know how that child was treated? Cold fingers of abandonment gripped her stomach. At last she spoke. "How do you know all this?"

"Different messengers were sent, but I felt the messages must have come from a member of the lord's household." The king's eyes were filled with painful regret. "I was never told how you were treated, only that you were held secure. The last message was delivered by an ancient couple. They told the tale of your life and how you escaped. They both died shortly after arriving here."

In relief, Jilliand nodded slowly. The old couple had not been harmed. "What became of the place where I was raised?"

The king was quiet for a long moment. "It was destroyed when the Vikings came. They killed the lord although very few of his men. Strangely, they did not plunder nor burn the huts of his burg. It was as if the only reason they came was to take the lord. He was captured. His body was later found." Jilliand's brother, King Aethewulf, shook his head. "I think he repaid the lord for what he had done to you." Looking at his sister, he softly asked, "Was that Viking the husband you speak of?"

Jilliand looked at the man claiming to be a brother, the ones listening to her tale, and finally, at the flames in the fire. "Yes, he is mine," Jilliand replied, her voice soft and filled with pain. Just the thought of Rurik caused a wave of sadness to wash over her heart. *My nightmare continues.* She looked back at the king. He sat with a frown marring his forehead. He looked at Jilliand intently . . . waiting. Jilliand knew she must tell the whole story. She met her brother's gaze steadily and began.

CHAPTER 24

"MY FATHER'S HATE FOR ME began when I was born, I believe. As for the way he treated me, it must have started when I was but a child. My only memories of my life are filled with pain and loneliness. I was taken to a cell in the soldiers' compound. I was only seven years of age." Jilliand faltered. Taking a deep breath, with a shaking voice, she continued, "Although educated and raised as a son, I was still an outcast. That older couple cared for me. If not for them, I would have been killed." Jilliand told the story of her life—living with a man she had always believed was her father.

Taking another breath, she finished in a voice now normal and in control. "Eventually, I ran away. The captain who agreed to stay with the lord for ten years was still there. He helped me leave. He gave me this cross from my mother and, when he died, a locket he had always worn."

Jilliand paused, her thoughts on her old friend. Turning to look at the king, she murmured, "The couple that cared for me spoke often of my mother. They gave me the earrings in this silken bag." She walked across the room and returned with the bag, handing it to the king. Jilliand opened the locket again, showing it to the king. "My husband brought me the necklace and ring you see on her in this painting. I wear that ring."

In an even voice, the young woman continued, "The scars on my body have healed. Those in my heart and mind have not." Finished, she walked slowly to the window and stood looking down on the lake below. "There are now fresh scars on my heart."

The room remained hushed, as each reflected on the words of the king and Jilliand. "Am I permitted to walk in that garden?" she asked, breaking the silence, without turning from the window.

"Would you like to walk now?" the king asked, rising.

"If it pleases you." Jilliand turned to him.

Offering his arm, everyone stood. "What my sister, Lady Jilliand, speaks of this night is not to be discussed further." He looked squarely at his page and Becca. Without further comment, he opened the door and the party walked.

Silently, they moved around the garden paths, each lost in thoughts of what was revealed. The king's mind worked over how Jilliand's life had turned. With a stab on his conscience, he knew he should have done more to rescue her. Yet, there loomed the reality that the lord could have easily killed the only link he had to his mother.

"Sire," Jilliand's voice was soft, "Do you mean what you say? Are you my brother?"

"Yes, Jilliand. I knew it the moment I saw you, although you were hidden by your hood," he smiled down at her, "and by the dirt."

"Your queen? What of her?" Jilliand asked.

"My first queen died, after she gave me two sons. The second wife cared not for me, my people, nor my country. She left, without consummating our marriage. It was annulled." He laughed. "I laugh now; but at the time, I wanted to skewer her!"

"That cannot be true. You would want to live your life with one who cares not for all you stand as guardian of?" Suddenly, Jilliand's eyes filled with tears. Tears that spilled over and ran down her face. "I fear I am beyond what I can handle. I am lost to a husband, who may believe I am dead. A husband I loved. I buried my first and only child, along with my dearest friend, the child's grandmother. Perhaps I should return to the rooms you have lent me. I believe I have great need of a bed."

"But of course." He immediately turned and began retracing their steps. "However, Jilliand, the chambers are yours for this night only. Beyond mine, are chambers I will give to you. I will see that you and your ladies are moved tomorrow. Make what changes you would." In little time, they returned to the rooms Jilliand occupied.

"Jilliand, you have lost a great deal. Know you have gained a brother and his kingdom. Welcome home, little sister." He kissed both her cheeks, then wrapped her in his powerful embrace. "Please come to me when you have rested. I have yet to hear the story of your husband." He could feel her gasp, trying to hold back the tears. He stepped back and held her shoulders. "Let the tears fall, dear Jilliand. You are safe now."

Struggling to maintain control, Jilliand nodded. Alexander moved closer, raised her hand to his lips, saying, "Lady Jilliand, welcome home. My services are yours, Lady." Bowing, he and the king took their leave.

Once inside the room, Jilliand was readied for bed. She dismissed Becca and curled under the blankets. When she could no longer hear the ladies, Jilliand broke down. For hours, the sobs tore at her very heart. "Rurik, am I never to see you again? Do you even know I live still?" She moaned aloud to the empty, dark room. "My heart is heavy. I want to go home. The place that truly was my home. I want my family back." She sat up, hugging her knees. "I do not belong in this place." Becca and her ladies lay in their sleeping quarters beyond Jilliand's rooms. Hushed, they listened to the mournful sounds coming from the bed chamber.

When Jilliand finally rolled over, slowly waking, the sun was shining through the stained-glass window. She lay still. Her life seemed like a bad dream. She wanted to be grateful for her newfound brother. Yet it was Rurik who occupied her thoughts. He and his small daughter and her tiny head with tufts of red fuzz. "I must stop thinking this way. It will not bring them back to me. Ah, Rurik, you taught me to love. Please come to me now, teach me to live without you, if I must." Jilliand closed her eyes tightly.

Timid knocking at her door told her the ladies were afoot. Rising, she answered them, crossed to the window, and looked out onto the gardens below. The plants were beginning to dress for the coming spring, but the frost clung to them stubbornly refusing to give up. She could see the paths winding their way around the remnants of hedges and flowers. The lake drew her attention again.

"Is it terribly late, Becca? I would walk around the lake when the sun is shining. Come, let us go quickly, before we are missed." Smiling at Becca's wide eyes, Jilliand threw a blanket around her shoulders and opened the door. The hall was already filled with people passing. "Who are these people in the hall?" Jilliand whispered to Becca.

"They are the king's men, running errands for the king. I know another way, Lady. Come with me." Caught up in the excitement of an adventure, Becca led her back down the hall away from the stairs. She carefully opened a plain door, motioned to Jilliand, and took the steep steps down. The ladies came out close to a large pillar, hiding the door from common view.

"You are good," Jilliand complimented her new friend. "Just look at the sky. The lake looks soft now. So still, not one ripple." She walked with Becca, taking in every detail. "Becca, you must be patient with me. I have moments when my sadness weighs heavily upon my mind. In those moments, I cannot stop the tears. It passes. But if it should happen when I am not alone, please help me get back to my rooms."

Becca nodded, "Certainly, Lady." She watched as Jilliand wandered the peaceful gardens, a sad smile on her face. Finally, Becca warned, "Come, we must get you inside. The garden will be filled with gardeners and such. Better they not see you in your nightshirt."

From a window above, King Aethewulf watched his sister. He had often thought about her and how her life might have gone. When he had learned that his mother had died in childbirth, the weight of guilt and grief nearly drove him mad. Now, looking at the young girl below him, he felt an intense sadness. "I should have done more to find this child." Watching her, he smiled to himself. She looked like he remembered his mother, only more so. "I will know what she learned from the Viking. She was dressed as a queen. Her ring looks to be valuable. I would see her with a sword. And a bow. And on a horse. We have much to go over, she and I," he mused.

As Jilliand whirled to come back toward the castle, Aethewulf started.

"Ricart," he called his page, "is that not my nightshirt, the one we could not find last night?"

The young page looked out, his words jumbling over themselves. "I, er . . . it would, that is, I think it might be, Your Majesty. How ever did Lady Jilliand come by it?" As soon as he asked, he bowed, blushed deeply, and again began to stutter.

"Hush, boy. She is my sister. I think perhaps one of her ladies may be the culprit. No matter, looks better on her anyway," he laughed. Watching her from the window, he continued, "How long I have wondered about that child. Where she might be. If her life was safe. Now she is here, I wonder what comes to her next," Aethewulf spoke quietly. The time of Viking raids would be upon them soon enough. Some days, Aethewulf and his men won. Most often, the Vikings still moved without restraint, up and down the coast. Maybe Jilliand would be his answer. If the Viking king still lived and ruled, perhaps Aethewulf might exact an agreement from that Viking to stop the raids, in exchange for his sister. *It is clear she loved the Viking. Maybe . . .*

When King Aethewulf and Alexander met that morning, Aethewulf shared the adventures of his missing nightshirt. While they talked, the king studied his friend. *This friend who has never married, preferring instead to serve his king. Maybe now is the time.* Even as the thought crossed his mind, he was pushing it away. *Jilliand has just come home. I would not ask her to leave yet. Still . . . if the Viking no longer lives . . .* He set the issue aside to think on it later.

That afternoon, he sent for Jilliand. She came into the room where he and his general council were meeting. As soon as she opened the door, she stepped back out. "Jilliand, come here. I wish to speak with you." She looked some better, though sadness clouded her eyes, and the gown she wore revealed that she was even thinner than he had thought. She nodded to the men surrounding the table.

"You sent for me, Majesty?" Her voice was even and quiet, though hesitant to interrupt his business.

"I would know why it is we lose to the Vikings so often. What makes the Vikings such fierce warriors? Can you help me . . . us," he waved his hand to include the room, "to understand?"

Jilliand looked at the men before her. She paused for a moment. It was clear these men would listen to her out of respect for their king. Would they believe her? Perhaps. "What do you do, sir?" she asked quietly, each man in turn. At first, they hesitated to answer. A nod from the king brought their response.

When she had gone around the room, she stood looking at them. "I see the king has bishops, lawyers, accountants, knights, earls, and advisors. This is good for the king. I wish him wise counsel."

"Well?" King Aethewulf pressed her. "What has this to do with anything? Every king has such men. Even the Viking, surely."

Jilliand began, "A Viking king is surrounded by men who are, each and every one, warriors. From childhood, every free male is trained to fight; to ride; and to use a sword, a lance, and an axe. Every man is in excellent physical shape. They are loyal to the king by kinship. The relationship is intertwined like a stout rope. They fight next to kinsmen and friends. They truly would die for the king, without hesitation. Each of them. Dying in battle is how they assure their place of honor in their afterlife."

There was mumbling around the table. "Please, I mean no disrespect. Your lives are different, by necessity." She paused. "You must realize how they think. They and their main gods are warriors. The Vikings' whole religious belief, as near as I could tell, revolved around getting to a place for a great final battle. Each man cared not to live long, he cared only to live well, and die fighting." The men were quiet, but Jilliand could feel their resistance.

Her glance went round the table. "We are not like that. My God is a kind and gentle God. He cares for His people. He would keep us always with Him, when we die." She stopped talking, fearing she may have said too much. What could these men possibly understand? They had never seen anything but violence from Rurik's people. Of greater concern was her fear that the bishop would condemn her. Jilliand could see the look in his eyes.

The bishop watched Jilliand, frowning. Then he asked, "Child, did you pray to their gods?" His face was filled with concern.

"No," Jilliand replied quickly, looking at her brother. "My husband even chose to allow me to wear my cross. I was never witness to their worship."

The bishop interrupted, "I know people they take captive are required to accept their gods. Why would you be treated differently?" His voice bore a ring of discernible challenge.

Jilliand gradually turned to face the bishop squarely. "Because he loves me." The room was silent, though Jilliand was aware that several of the men at the table glanced at one another. "In many ways, they are not that different from us. Their treatment of the people they conquer is not so different from my English people." Her voice softened. "They love their families." At this, her eyes filled with tears she hoped none could see. "They are kind to their wives, and they treat all travelers with respect and care."

Jilliand looked at these men. Many were overweight, slow of foot, and accustomed to easy living. Few of them had actually fought the Viking. Those who had would never forget it. The ones with that experience listened intently and were now studying the men around them.

"They are all pagans. God is *not* with them," declared the bishop firmly. His voice was even, but his look indicated he was chastising her.

"They are pagans, Bishop, but they know it not. To them, we are the ones doomed," Jilliand replied quietly. She was finished speaking. She doubted these men would take to heart anything she said. She was just a woman. No matter. They asked, and she had answered. She turned to leave.

Aethewulf stood. "One thing more. You say this Viking *is* your husband? Does he live still?" The silence in the room was heavy. When Jilliand nodded yes, Aethewulf continued, "Why are you not with him?"

"He believes I am dead," she replied softly. "At times I wish I were," she added.

"Thank you, Lady Jilliand." He stepped to her and lifting her hand kissed it. Jilliand curtsied before she walked out. Watching her leave, Aethewulf had an unsettled feeling.

"We have soldiers; they are loyal because I pay handsomely. That is not the loyalty they might have if they were related to us. Farmers try to help. What do they bring? Sticks, rakes, and no training." He walked around the room. The shield line, the drive, and the disregard for death were all part of the package of a Viking warrior, which included his expertise with weapons. A formidable package.

"The Lady Jilliand needs time and care, to bring her back to God." The old bishop watched his king thoughtfully. "We have God on our side," he reminded King Aethewulf, smugly.

The king nodded. "Yes, and He is the mightiest of allies. Still, the Vikings have wreaked havoc on our lands and with our people for hundreds of years. She brings good information," he noted. "I will meet with Alexander and my men at arms this evening. The weather grows warm now but will soon enough be cold. Vikings will come again. This winter, I will be ready."

"Perhaps this queen may have influence on the Viking king. We may have an ally against the Vikings, if we know who the king is," Alexander noted quietly to Aethewulf as they left the room.

"Or where he is. Time will tell . . ." Aethewulf walked on, deep in thought.

The bishop waited until the room was empty before speaking to his page. "Fetch the Lady Jilliand to my special study, immediately. I would speak with her in private."

Jilliand had not yet entered her rooms when the bishop's page stopped her. "His holiness the bishop wishes to see you, Lady. Come with me." Jilliand glanced around. Only Becca stood near. "You are to come alone, Lady." The page spoke firmly. Bowing slightly, he indicated the way. Jilliand hesitantly walked. Her heart was in her throat, pounding. She had heard stories of what happened to people who were believed to have accepted the pagan gods. Unnoticed by anyone, a lone figure listened to Jilliand and the bishop's page.

What can I say? I can tell he does not believe me. God, please help me say words that would change his mind and heart. You know I am innocent of any pagan worship. You know I love only You. Help me. The sound of Jilliand's steps bounced off the walls of the dimly lit hall. Her steps took her deeper into the bowels of the castle.

Unheard by either Jilliand or the bishop's page, other feet now raced in the opposite direction.

The page opened the door to a room filled with heat coming from a great fire, burning in an open pit. A chair with straps attached sat at one end of the room. A cage-like table with chains, rods, and whips hung from the wall. Jilliand felt her stomach turn. Several men stood, leaning against the walls, watching her. The bishop stood with his back to her, staring at the blaze before him.

"Child, come sit with me and visit." He indicated a small chair placed very near the flames, while he sat opposite her, farther from the oppressive heat. Jilliand sat. She forced herself to look into the bishop's eyes, awaiting his next move.

"I will ask these men to leave so that I may hear your confession, before we begin." He waved his hand, and the men started for the door.

"Wait!" Jilliand commanded firmly, "I have nothing to say that these men cannot hear, as by this setting I must assume they have heard other confessions made to you."

The bishop was taken aback but allowed the men to stay. Without hesitation, Jilliand knelt and began. When she was finished, the bishop prodded her. "Have you nothing to say about the Viking gods, the man you call a husband, and his religion? You must make your confession complete, child."

Jilliand raised her eyes to meet his. "I did not discuss my God with him, nor did he discuss his religion with me. He allowed me to wear my cross. As he was a sea king, none questioned his decisions." She stood up. "Do you not think it sad that you take me to task over something that did not happen but have not one word of comfort for those things that did happen to me, at the hands of a man of our same religious faith? Does the fact that he was of our faith relieve him of any burden for what he did to me and to my mother?"

At that moment, the king flung the door open and entered, followed closely by his guard with Becca trailing them all. "What do you think to do?" King Aethewulf's voice drowned every other sound in the room. The king stood over the bishop, his anger oozing danger. The bishop sat paralyzed. Aethewulf turned to his sister, "Have you been harmed, Jilliand?"

"No, Your Majesty. Only unsettled." Jilliand's relief at the king's arrival nearly buckled her knees.

"You are never to speak ill of, or to, Lady Jilliand. If she is harmed in any way, you are held responsible and will answer to me. Am I clear?" Aethewulf leaned closer to the bishop. "Lady Jilliand is my sister and, as such, is to be protected at all times. Anyone who disregards this order pays with his life. And," he added looking around the room, "'twill not be an easy death." The king looked at each of the people crowded into the room. Taking Jilliand's elbow, he led her away. At the door, he paused. Turning, he looked directly at the bishop. His voice was cold, firm, and even. "God never left Lady Jilliand, nor did she leave Him."

Away from the bishop and his room of horrors, Aethewulf took Jilliand beyond hearing of the people following them. "I am sorry you were subjected to such treatment, Lady. Are you quite well, for certain?"

Jilliand was still trembling slightly. "I am well and will be always grateful for your timely arrival, Majesty. However, I think I have an enemy."

"No, you do not. He was doing what he thought best. I have no doubts, you will win him over with time." The king kissed her hand and left her to her ladies, now gathered around her. *Just in case, I will be certain she has escorts,* Aethewulf noted.

Jilliand watched her brother walk away, followed by his retinue. *I have no desire to win the bishop over. We will both be dead and gone before that could happen.*

CHAPTER 25

TRUE TO HIS WORD, KING Aethewulf moved Jilliand. Her new chambers provided greater privacy without the easy entrance from the king's own chambers. One room had a small fireplace, a bed covered with thick blankets and pillows, a finely carved armoire, several chairs, and a modest trunk. The second room had several chairs placed before a grand fireplace, a small table with chairs, and a compact writing desk. The walls and floors were covered in the usual custom with thick tapestries or rugs, to hold the cold at bay. Candle sconces were placed strategically throughout the area. Tall windows allowed the sun's rays to fill her chambers. Despite that, Jilliand had to force herself to move through each day. The belief that Rurik would find her was her lifeline—a line now thinly stretched.

Several weeks later, restless as always, Jilliand wandered down the passageway out into the gardens. There seemed little she could do in this new life; at her elbow there were people eager to do everything for her. She dared not sew or paint as someone suggested, for fear they would discover how ill prepared she was. Heedless of the retinue following her, she spoke aloud of an idea that had just come into her mind. "I would like to ride." *I'm the king's sister. I can ride if I choose.* "Send a message to the groomsmen, I am on my way." With that, a young lady dashed to the stables. Jilliand walked with renewed energy in the same direction. To be far from the eye of court would be a welcome break.

The stable was in a flurry trying to ready the horses. Everyone knew the king's sister was the newest member of court. Though improper for a woman to ride out alone accompanied only by her ladies as protection, the king's sister refused to allow anyone else to attend her. So far, the king himself had allowed her to do as she chose. The stable master saw Jilliand and several of her ladies off, despite his protests at the possible dangers afoot. Jilliand was in no frame of mind to listen. He gave up.

She is a different sort. Not at all timid nor shy. Best let the king know of this. As soon as the riders were out of sight, a worried stable master hastened to the king's council chambers, but he was stopped at the door by the king's steward. Unwilling to interrupt the king in conference with others of far more importance than a simple stable master, the steward refused to be swayed.

"I will wait," the stable master shrugged. *Lady Jilliand will be long gone by the time I get to His Majesty. It seems she can take care of herself, for a while at least. Perhaps Lady Jilliand needs some time away from all that it means to be the king's sister.*

Four hours later, the stable master was led before the king. Bowing low, he informed the king, "Your sister has left, Your Majesty. She and several of her ladies left alone riding over four hours ago. She rides well, but alone. There were no guards or any other men with her."

"What?!" the king gasped. "You say she left alone? How is that possible? And why man, did it take you four hours or more to bring this news to me!?" His voice reverberated off the walls. Conversation ceased immediately, as all eyes were on the king and the stable master.

"Sire, I was not allowed to enter," the stable master replied quietly. He added, "I would not leave news of your sister being alone with anyone except Your Highness, fearing for her safety."

The king turned on his heel. "Ready my horse. We ride immediately. Alexander!" Pointing at the steward, he added, "You and I will discuss this when I return." He walked rapidly from the room, leaving the worried steward in a now empty room.

King Aethewulf, Alexander, and ten men left, riding the same direction Jilliand had taken. She had nearly four hours' head start on them, but she would not be familiar with the lay of the land. *Perhaps she will be on her way back? Not likely,* her brother thought. *Not if she is anything like her mother.*

"Alexander, where would she go, my wayward sister?" He secretly enjoyed the ride and was amused she would think to leave alone. Not wise nor safe, but it underscored her self-confidence and independence. She was truly her mother's daughter.

"It is quite possible she simply likes to ride, Aethewulf. We could make this a pleasant afternoon, if we should catch them before dark." He grinned at his friend.

For her part, Jilliand had no idea where to go. She simply needed to be free of the restraints that came with living inside a castle, as a member of a king's court. It became clear quickly that everyone expected her to be the lady of the castle. *Just what am I supposed to do? If only Aethewulf would remarry. That would help.*

The ride was proving to be very pleasant. When the first afternoon shadows began to sneak over the land, Jilliand knew she should start back. In the distance, mixed within the chatter and giggles of her ladies, Jilliand thought she caught the sound of horses and riding gear. She listened carefully. There were horses coming toward them, Jilliand was sure. She quickly ushered her small group into a nearby thicket, shushed her ladies, and waited. The curve to the road hid the oncoming riders until they were nearly abreast.

The king and his men rode by the thicket, without pausing. This presented an opportunity Jilliand could not resist. After waiting a short while, she quietly moved her ladies well behind the last rider, planning to eventually encircle Aethewulf's group. Her ladies were enticed into silence, with the promise of surprising the group of young men riding ahead.

Alexander and Aethewulf exchanged puzzled glances. They had been together all their lives, much of it spent in battle. Unable to hear riders other than their own troupe, both felt rather than heard the movement of horses beyond their view. Looking back at the empty road, Aethewulf idly flicked his reins while in thought. Nodding to Alexander, he and Alexander peeled off to the side of the column of riders. As they veered away, Alexander pointed to two of his men who did the same on the opposite side. The eight remaining men continued forward.

Aethewulf saw them first. Pointing, he smiled. With raised brows, he looked to Alexander. Alexander nodded. Joined by the two additional soldiers Alexander had engaged, they waited until Jilliand and her ladies had passed, then slipped in behind the little troupe of women. Jilliand was still signaling her women to be quiet, but they were doing a poor job. Over the noise they made, she could hear little. Yet, the men ahead rode without indication that they suspected anything. She strained to see her brother. He was missing; the troupe had shrunk.

Instantly, she realized they had been outmaneuvered. When Jilliand raised her hand to stop her ladies, Aethewulf whistled, and his men immediately surrounded the ladies. Whirling her horse around, Jilliand rode through the ladies, until she was between her ladies and the king.

"Yield to your king," Aethewulf commanded, in a mocking tone. Jilliand looked at him squarely and shook her head.

"No, I do not yield." Before anyone could respond, she kicked her mount and shot past the surprised soldiers. The horse could feel his rider urging him on. He quickened his gallop, leaving the small crowd behind. Aethewulf and Alexander gave chase. Aethewulf was not yet gaining on her, but she could go no further. Blocked by thickets and fallen trees, she came to a sudden halt. Nearly unseated, Jilliand was able to slide off and pull the small blade she still carried.

Aethewulf had already pulled his horse up, scattering dirt clods and dust as he came to a stop in front of Jilliand. His blade came out also. Drily, he noted, "It seems you have too much time on your hands, Lady. I would see that remedied." Never losing sight of her, he smoothly slid off his horse.

Jilliand laughed. "Come Brother," she taunted, "surely you cannot expect me to yield so easily."

A slow smile spread across the king's face. "Yield, you will, Lady. And the victor will be the first without a weapon." He began to carefully circle Jilliand, still smiling.

"This will be a short affair I am certain, since your sword is thrice the length of mine, Sire. Still, you will have to work for it, Brother." With that, she easily sidestepped him and moved behind a clump of brush.

By this time, the entire troupe of men and women were gathered around watching. One of the ladies called out a wager for Jilliand. Aethewulf called back, "I'll take it, double. I'm certain Lady Jilliand is good for it."

As much as Jilliand wanted to give her brother a worthy opponent, she knew she should not chance embarrassing him before the men and women now clearly taking sides. Moving out with a small shrug, she intended to drop the blade, but Aethewulf would not allow her that choice. He moved in on her so quickly that without thinking she had taken a defensive stance and moved around him. They danced and moved about, slowly coming closer and closer.

Just as Jilliand again tried to drop her weapon and bow out, Aethewulf called to Alexander, "Give Lady Jilliand a real sword, Alexander. I would see how she can use it." He was still smiling, but his eyes were serious.

Frowning, Alexander reluctantly did as his friend bade him. Lowering his own weapon, Aethewulf gave Jilliand time to change swords. Hefting it, she gripped Alexander's sword with both hands and stood ready. *I am of little sense, thinking I could ever match Aethewulf. What began as a game may get much too serious.* Jilliand could feel her pulse quicken. Aethewulf moved toward her with lightning speed. She fended him off the first charge, knowing full well he only tested her reflexes.

Dashing behind the clump, she held her sword with one hand. "Perhaps the match is over, Sire. Neither one of us would draw blood on the other."

"The match is not over, Lady Jilliand. I think you need a lesson in defense," he goaded her.

Provoked, the years spent fending off her father burst unexpectedly into her brain. Suddenly she was again in the corral, surrounded by men watching as her father pushed her beyond her capabilities. She stepped out from the clump and came at him, as quick as the thought hit her. He was startled, but ready. They moved about with each swing becoming more intense. When one of the ladies screamed, as Jilliand narrowly missed Aethewulf's point, Jilliand was shaken back to the present. She stepped back, dropped the sword, and with her head high, announced, "I yield to the king."

She stood still, watching him with her flashing emerald eyes. He lowered his weapon, walked to where she stood, bent to retrieve Alexander's sword, and silently handed it off. Sheathing his own, he turned to study his sister. "We will talk, you and I." The words were spoken quietly, with authority and a sense of finality. He no longer smiled at Jilliand.

Keeping her own counsel, Jilliand walked to her horse. Aethewulf assisted her. With his hand on her stirrup, he spoke softly, "You must let the past leave, Jilliand. He was wrong. But what is done, is done. Because of the man that claimed to be your father, you have skills few women ever gain. I pray you never need them. Now, we ride. I would speak with you tonight. I have enjoyed this day—the day you surrendered to your king and brother." His mood was again light. As he smiled up at her, his eyes were kind. "We will ride more, but you will never ride without armed escort, and you will not go without letting me know when you leave and where you ride." He stood waiting for her acknowledgment.

"Yes, Aethewulf," she agreed. "It is good to be home," she finished softly, as her lashes caught the few tears she could not hide. Turning away she leaned to pet the horse.

The ride back to the castle was not quiet for long. The ladies were happy to keep the soldiers talking, while Aethewulf and Alexander spoke of business. Jilliand rode in her own world. *How I miss him, Mother. I still feel as though a sword has run me through. Will this last for my lifetime?* she asked silently. Rurik lingered in her thoughts.

When they reached the castle, Aethewulf set Jilliand on the ground. Grinning openly, he kissed her cheek. "You are your mother's child, Jilliand. Do you believe you can get these ladies presentable in time for court? I am starved." Taking her hand, he led her down halls and eventually to her chambers. "I did enjoy today, Sister. However," he added, "you would be a tougher adversary, if you were not hampered by your gown. Pray change into breeches the next time we duel." Jilliand smiled back, kissing his hand as she curtsied. She heard him call to Alexander, as he walked away.

Happy chatter filled Jilliand's rooms. After trying unsuccessfully to settle them down, she casually mentioned there would be a new group of men at court, as Alexander had called in additional forces to begin training for the winter raids ahead. "They are rumored to be exceptionally good-looking. I have not seen them, but it might be worth your time to make ready as fast as you can. Surely we should have first pick, don't you agree ladies?"

Amid giggles and coy suggestions, the ladies managed to change Jilliand and clean up themselves. With only moments to spare, they entered the dining hall, and it fell quiet.

As promised, there were scores of new faces, all turning to survey the ladies approaching the king's table. Jilliand could feel Alexander and the king watching her. When she was seated, Aethewulf leaned to her, "Alexander is a very good man, Jilliand. You need a good man. He would treat you like no man here could." He did not wait for her to reply; instead he resumed talking with the men at the table. Jilliand knew what he said to her was true. *But he is not Rurik. Rurik has my heart*, she replied silently.

Unable to eat, she finally sent the plate back. The king was well aware of his sister's preoccupation but chose to let it slide. As the evening wore on, Jilliand begged to be excused. "I tire, Your Majesty. It was a wonderful day. Thank you for taking the time to humor your little sister. I promise I will not expect the same too often, as you do have a kingdom to care for. Now, pray let me slip away to find my chambers."

He nodded, kissing her hand. "We will speak tomorrow, Jilliand. Sleep well." Jilliand spoke quietly to her ladies, asking only two to accompany her and allowing the rest to stay. She promised to send the two back once she was through with their services for the night.

Alexander stood. "I would escort Lady Jilliand to her chambers, if it pleases you."

The king nodded to Alexander, while he watched the slight figure of his sister take her leave. Startled by a hand at her elbow, Jilliand was not so surprised to realize it was Alexander. "I have escorts, Sir Alexander, if you have business you must attend to this night."

"I do have business, but I have something to say to you, Lady Jilliand." He walked along with his hands behind his back for a short distance. Jilliand could feel a lump in her throat.

"I would serve you, Lady Jilliand. King Aethewulf and I have been as brothers all our lives. I would serve you as a friend, a brother, and a knight. I feel your sadness heavy as a rock in your heart, often coming to the surface to cause great ripples in a life I pray is easier for you here with us. When you are free to love again, I will be the first to claim your hand. I can see you are not free. Do not ever hesitate to ask for me. What I can do, I will. What time we can spend together, we will take, without giving cause for gossip."

Taking her hand, he kissed it, and then holding her hand on his arm, he walked the hall to her door. Bowing low, he bid her a goodnight. When he straightened, he saw that her eyes were filled with tears. "Weep not, Lady. I am happy to have your friendship and have great need of a sister. Do not feel sad for me or for us. Only let your heart mend, Lady."

Jilliand watched him walk away. How could she tell him she would never love again? "Oh Rurik, of what do you think, as you go through your day? Do you ever think of your queen?" she whispered. Within the quiet protection of her private chambers, for a long moment, Jilliand stood before the looking glass. *I hardly recognize the woman that looks back at me. I am no longer the beaten girl, nor the contented wife. I am a princess . . . unwilling, but a princess nonetheless. I fear I no longer know myself.*

Becca watched her mistress as she prepared for bed. "M'lady, you are so mournful. Will this feeling never leave? You are too young to have this in your heart."

Jilliand smiled sadly. "Becca, most women of my station marry not for love, but for kingdoms. I was blessed to love and be loved by the king who captured me. I cannot imagine living with another man. It is proving very difficult to go through life as one without a heart. Perhaps all the more difficult because he still lives. I *know* he lives." Her voice was so soft, Becca could hardly hear her. "Sadly, he does not know I, too, live."

When the sun found its way into her sleeping chamber, it found an empty bed. Jilliand was restless again. The feeling was strongest in the early morning hours. Swiftly running over a mental list of things she and her ladies could do, she had everyone scurrying by the time they broke fast. And so each day went by, much too slowly. Jilliand did her best to fill the time. She was becoming skilled with her needles and threads, tended the gardens, and spent time teaching her ladies how to read and write. A task the king found mildly irritating. "What need of such learning do your ladies have?" he had asked her during one of their long walks.

"Do you think they will always be my ladies? What if they should find themselves alone in another's service? How much easier to please their mistress, if they can do these simple things. Surely, you cannot believe any man you consider a fit husband to one of my ladies would be threatened by their learning?" When Aethewulf did not immediately respond, she smiled up at him. "Besides, it keeps my own skills sharp. A good thing, do you not agree, Brother?"

The king never answered only shook his head and laughed. He loved to walk with her, loved teaching as they visited. It gave him someone to talk with, other than his council and Alexander. She proved to be a quick study. Her education had been what could be expected of someone from that man's court, but it had not been sufficient for a princess—the king's sister. So it began. The king taught; Jilliand learned.

CHAPTER 26

ASKOLD, DIR, THEIR FAMILIES, AND other families had sailed with Rurik to the land called Rus. They worked with him, fought alongside him, and watched as he thrust himself headlong into every aspect of creating a safe, permanent settlement in an inhospitable land. He was successful, but no matter what Rurik did, he was not satisfied. Both jarls knew what really drove their sea king. The ache for Jilliand never lessened. Winters were long—however no more brutal than from where he came. But to Rurik, without companionship, they seemed so. He did everything a good leader would, with his usual attention to detail, personnel, and the welfare of the inhabitants. Warmer weather brought with it opportunities for exploration and expansion of his new domain, yet Rurik remained numb. He had not even been to sea since they settled in Rus. His friends worried about their king. With Jilliand dead was it possible Rurik had lost all the qualities he once embodied?

One particular mountain near his village frequently served as a vantage point to survey the land below. At the mountain's summit, Rurik, Askold, and their horses were silhouetted against a setting sun. The peak was skirted by a gently sloping perimeter that slid into an open meadow overlooking a valley. From the dwellings nestled in that valley, smoke meandered skyward. People and animals milled about. The scene spoke of a pause in the struggle to survive that allowed the dwellers to simply live.

"You need a woman, Rurik," Askold noted for the hundredth time. Rurik was silent. Their horses stomped impatiently, with their breath rolling from their nostrils in short grey puffs. Years had passed, and Rurik still sat alone beside his fire at night. Shaking his head, Askold kicked his horse forward gently, and the men rode down the hillside onto the meadow. Spring was moving in; it was a time of renewal and coming warmth. Trees were still bare, rivers only slightly thawed, and grasses still brown. Yet, the sunlit days were longer, and the promise of spring clung to the gentle breezes brushing the landscape.

Askold was startled when he heard Rurik agree. "I do. Perhaps Inga, the overlord's daughter. He took his defeat poorly. I still hear rumblings of rebellion." Rurik tipped his head, allowing the sun to warm his face. It felt good. "Jilliand is dead. It is time I believe the runes. I will take this wife. My son will come from her." Nodding, a decision reached, he glanced at his friend. Askold was still digesting the news, staring silently at Rurik. Rurik marry again? Now that it was spoken, the idea felt strange.

"Inga?" Askold repeated, frowning. "Are you certain, Rurik?" Picturing the woman Rurik spoke of, he began to smile and then chuckle. His laughter bubbled until it exploded, echoing across the meadow, bouncing off the surrounding rocks to return, as if in disbelief also. Inga was well known. She was pleasant enough to look upon, but her disposition was the thing of which legends were written. She gave "sharp" a new meaning. Askold tried to control his mirth, but one look at Rurik, and it would begin again. "Maybe it is not so bad that you are still alone. Or, maybe you can control the woman."

"Enough!" Rurik heeled his horse and crossed the meadow with Askold. With eyes narrowed, Rurik noted, "A marriage would settle Inga's father down, until such time as a son is born."

"Then?" His friend pushed.

"By that time, a son would be undisputed king. If it is a daughter, Oleg will be in line. He is a good man, a good leader, and our people respect him. This would be easier put to rest if you or Dir would step up to take my place if needed. I know you better than you know yourselves, it would seem. Either could rule these lands."

Askold was quiet for a long time. Rurik knew Askold struggled to find words to explain why neither he nor Dir wanted any more responsibility than what they now had.

"It matters not, my friend. My mind stays the same. Inga will be a good wife. I will have heirs, and life will go on." Smiling, he slapped Askold's shoulder. Turning back toward the meadow, his eye caught sight of a red fox dashing along the forest's edge. In that instant, Jilliand's face flashed before him. He felt as if a lance had found its mark. "Would be better," he muttered. Determined to move beyond Jilliand's memory, Rurik turned his horse around. "Askold, you will ask for Inga's hand for me. 'Twill be interesting to see what gifts her father might offer, but it makes no difference. I will have Inga."

"As you wish, Rurik. And may the sisters of fate give you peace, at last." The two men rode back toward Novgorod.

In two months' time, Rurik stood before his bride in their bedchamber. He willed himself to think only of Inga, the woman who was now his wife. He took her hand and led her to their bed. The night was filled with passion. Rurik could not keep Jilliand from his mind, but the union with Inga felt right. By morning, he lay next to his wife, comfortably dozing. It would be good.

As time wore away the excitement of untested waters, Rurik realized his friend Askold was correct. Inga was sharp tongued. Rurik learned quickly that she also had her father's cunning. She and Rurik worked well together as rulers—poorly as lovers, though they did eventually have a child. She only became gentle and kind when she interacted with their son, Igor. Inga simply did not love Rurik. Due in large part, he believed, because she must have felt he loved another. Maybe she did not know for sure, but Rurik did—Jilliand still filled his heart.

He loved a ghost. Even now, she roamed freely in his mind. When Inga again became pregnant, Rurik was slightly surprised. They were seldom together. No matter: He would have a second son. Igor was coming of age, at nearly five years of age. Soon, Rurik would take him from his mother to live and be trained with the men, a day he knew Inga dreaded.

One morning as she lay awaiting her birthing time, Rurik came into the room. He stood near her bed. "I know I have not been easy to live with, Rurik." She turned away. "It will soon be the day you take our son to the house of the men. He already knows much about this country, weapons, and warfare. I am afraid he knows little about ruling and fairness. For that, I take responsibility. I know you will teach him well."

Rurik turned Inga's face so that he could see her, and she could see him. "You have been a good wife, Inga. Our son is strong because of you. You have done your part well. Now it is time to teach him to be a Viking ruler."

At the words "Viking ruler," Inga's face blanched, and her mouth became a bitter line. "He is not a Viking, Rurik. Not while I live and breathe. He is Rus. Only Rus." Angrily she pushed his hand away.

"Then pray you have a daughter, Inga," Rurik quietly answered, as he stepped back from her bed. "Lest you again taste the bitterness of truth. He is Viking. Any son I have is Viking." Before she could answer, he continued, "I pray you deliver our child safely, and you both live. Son or daughter, I will love the child."

"I know not why," she snapped at him. "Why would you love another's child?"

When the words came to him, Rurik froze. For the first time in their marriage, Inga felt fear. Rurik's face became cold, and his eyes seemed not to recognize her. "I pray to the gods for the health of the child, no matter who the father might be. And yours, so we might finish this conversation." Turning on his heel, he stalked from the room, without looking back or closing the door. The ladies attending Inga stepped aside quickly, and an ominous feeling filled the chamber. With Inga's admission, Rurik would not stay to acknowledge the child. That night, as tears ran from Inga's eyes, the initial pain of childbirth struck her.

The daughter Inga carried died trying to enter the world. Inga died the next night. Rurik watched his son struggle to understand what was happening. Igor mourned his mother and hated the tiny dead infant that had taken her from him. Rurik patiently talked with Igor all through that endless night and the next day. As he sat on the bed next to his now sleeping son, Rurik realized he felt little sense of loss over Inga, and his anger at her revelation had been dampened by her death.

Rurik began to feel a growing restlessness, as if he had left something undone. He gave Oleg greater responsibilities, all of which he handled well. But Rurik was increasingly exasperated with his son. Igor responded to Oleg's teaching without question; but with Rurik, heated arguments were frequent. For his part, Igor spent more and more time with Rurik's men, and less and less with his father, believing Rurik was not the one to teach him what he would need to learn. Igor thought he could take his rightful place as the prince of Rus if he listened more closely to Oleg. Rurik did nothing to change Igor's thinking. Rurik's thoughts were the same, every day. *I long to be gone from this place. To where, I know not. I only know I should go.*

One evening, as the sun began its descent beyond the horizon, an older sea king, well known to Rurik, came ashore with his men. They were greeted warmly and escorted to Rurik's home. After a meal, the Viking and Rurik walked alone around Novgorod. The sky became lit by millions of stars. The moon hovered overhead, dashing light upon a snow-covered landscape. The air was sharp, and the men moved briskly to stay warm. "What news do you carry from the south?" Rurik asked. He had not been on an expedition in many years. "Do you still find the English settlements easy prey? And the monasteries—are they still houses of wealth?"

"Why do you ask? Are you of a mind to sail again?" The older man stopped and turned to him, awaiting his reply.

"Truth be told, I tire of my life. I sorely miss the sea, the battle, that life." Rurik searched the skies looking for familiar star formations. When the old man did not answer, Rurik glanced at him. The old Viking sea king met his eyes.

"I have other news, Rurik. This time out, I heard talk of a woman. Her hair red as the sunrise. Her eyes as green as the stone in your ring." Rurik stood motionless, barely daring to breathe, waiting for a name—her name. *Could it be? Could she be alive?* His mind begged; his heart raced. "Go on—where did you hear of this woman?" He dared not believe it could be Jilliand, after all these years. "She lives?"

"That I cannot say. She was seen years ago in a village below where your home once stood. She was believed to be your queen. Can that be true?" The silence held both men prisoner. At last, Rurik nodded, slowly.

"It must be." Now his voice was strong and firm. It had to have been her. His restlessness had a purpose. There was something he was supposed to do. Life again had a reason.

By the time he bid the old Viking goodbye, Rurik had a plan.

CHAPTER 27

JILLIAND LIVED WITH HER BROTHER, the king of Wessex. As the king's sister, she had everything. Yet, time moved slowly for her. She walked at night, rode frequently during the days, and when he allowed, she crossed swords with the king. Yet, even after eight years, Rurik still wandered around her in heart, whispering in her ear, and kissing her lips. She no longer cried during the days; the nights, however, remained unconquered. It was then her tears fell.

The Vikings continued to wreak havoc along the English shorelines. Monasteries were hit with a vengeance, the monks were slain, and their valuables taken. On occasion, the English won. Aethewulf listened for word of Rurik, the man his sister still loved. He now recognized the name and what lands Rurik ruled. Yet, he had heard no word of any raids made by the prince of Rus. Perhaps the man no longer lived. Perhaps Aethewulf's plan to use this man to forge a truce between their peoples was to be fruitless.

One afternoon, the king sent for her. "Majesty, you wished to see me?" Jilliand said and curtsied to her brother. When he stood, his council stood, and at his nod, they left the room. Alexander stayed on for but a moment.

"Lady." Alexander kissed her hand. "Pray tell me, are we going to ride this afternoon?" His voice was teasing. Afternoon rides had become a normal pastime for both.

Glancing toward her brother, who was watching and listening to them, she smiled. "I think not. Perhaps it would be better if I waited, at least a couple of days." She and her ladies had been late to dinner the last two nights, much to her brother's disapproval.

The king held out his hand. "Come with me, Jilliand. I would walk with you." He took her to the gardens she loved. Since that first night long ago, Jilliand had walked these paths so many times she could easily walk them with her eyes closed.

Jilliand feared he intended to speak to her of marriage—again. Best to have it out in the open. She waited quietly. He walked along, as if thinking on his words. "I think I may understand your hesitancy to wed again, Lady. However, it is not proper for a woman to go about without a man to care for her, escort her. You are so young, Jilliand. You could have children, a home." They walked on.

Trying to decide how to explain her thoughts, Jilliand hedged. Turning her face skyward, she watched a flock of geese flying south. The leaves were fully turned and falling. The harvest, what there was of it, had been gathered. The air had a snap to it. Winter was coming again. *I know winter well. It has been in my heart for so long.*

"It's been nearly nine years or more, Sister. Is that not time enough to wait?" he asked kindly, pressing her. "It might be this man no longer lives."

Looking sideways at him, Jilliand pointed out, "I think it is you, Brother, who has a new yearning. You worry because you would not want to leave me alone." Jilliand smiled at him. "Fear not, Majesty. I can care for myself. Although," Jilliand's eyes twinkled with mischief, "you might find it convenient to deed a small hut and bit of land to your sister. I could keep men to guard me, if you thought it wise.

"Aethewulf, I have seen the way you and the dark-haired beauty from Spain look at each other. That is as it should be. I have no desire to be in her way. Surely, you can find someplace I might live, without burdening me with some helpless man." She studied him through emerald eyes, smiling. He loved to see her smile. It had taken so long to happen.

"You are quite astute. I wish to make her my queen. As always, I find I cannot force you into anything. And I will move you, as you have requested. I have the perfect spot. Would you be willing to settle near the coast to the south of here? I will see that you have men, and you can change whatever you deem necessary in the house." As he spoke, he was already making a list of the men he would send with her. At the top of his list was a young man named Nate who had been trained as one of King Aethewulf's personal guards. Aethewulf knew Nate would take good care of his sister. Yes, Nate must go.

To the south, where the Vikings might land! Perhaps I can find Rurik, or at least hear of him, Jilliand thought. "It would be perfect, Brother. I thank you for agreeing to my wishes, although knowing you, I believe the deed has already been done. When will it be ready for me?" She danced at his side. *To be free from court, on my own. I could only dream.*

"It is ready, Lady. I have in mind the men I would send with you. If you see evidence of Viking ships, you are to send someone here, at once. I doubt you will find any, as the raids have seldom been in that area. However, it is good to have a post there." He smiled to himself. It had been many years since the Vikings had landed where he intended to settle Jilliand. He would have his sister close, but the lady that lit the fire in his heart, he would have closer. Best of both worlds. He toyed with the idea of sending Alexander as head of Jilliand's command, but could not think of him being gone from court. He enjoyed Alexander's company too much. "I should have your escort named by tonight when we dine." He looked down at her. "You are like a little vixen, Jilliand. Will you behave if I leave you so far away?"

Jilliand laughed. "Perhaps the king would define behave?"

"The king does not have a need to define it, only to have you agree to it. *And?*" he asked, his brows raised questioning.

She smiled up at her him, the brother she had grown to love. "But of course, Sire. I *always* behave."

"Hmmm." He shook his head, still smiling. They walked along, while he spoke of his desire for the hand of the Spanish princess. "Ride with me in the morn, Jilliand. We will leave quite early, before the court is awake, shortly after sunrise. I'll have a horse for you."

"I would love that. I will see you then." She started to walk away, but he held her back.

"Jilliand, you are planning to dine with me this evening, are you not? And you should think on marriage. Now more than ever. We will speak of it again after you have had some time to make your new castle into your home." He spoke with finality. He had a look in his eyes that Jilliand had come to recognize as a command, not suggestion.

"Of course, I dine with you, Brother. I have not ever missed our evening time together. *Marriage?* That I cannot in good faith promise, but I will think on it." Her eyes were solemn.

"That you will," he noted. "You *will* marry, Jilliand," he added.

Gently, Jilliand responded, "I cannot, Aethewulf. I am already married. My heart is not mine to give."

"And that matters how? He is a pagan if he lives at all." His voice rose. His face flushed with sudden anger and frustration; he stopped and held her back by the elbow. "Jilliand, I *ask* only as a courtesy to you. The choice is not yours. I am the king! I am *your* king. I do not ask this time. My thought is in your best interest."

"My best interest, Your Majesty? Where were your thoughts for my best interests while I was slowly dying at the hands of a man who was not my father? The man who forced my mother and yours into a marriage she never wanted. He was, by all I have been told, very cruel to her." Jilliand had not intended to let these words leave her mouth, but they fled from her mind into the air, suddenly thick between them. She was unable to stop. "I think you cared not so much then. Perhaps you think to use me to secure some holding for you, some loyalty—or for whatever reason kings marry off family. I am my mother's daughter. I am not some golden coin you can pass off at your convenience." Then her voice softened. "If I am in your way, I will leave. I sought shelter when I came to you. I can seek it again, Brother. I would not be a burden to you. Rurik lives, I'm certain. He *will* come for me."

Aethewulf stood looking at her—the replica of the mother he knew so well. His anger dissipated instantly, and he grasped her shoulders, holding them fast. "You are not a burden, Jilliand. I will give you more time. I have carried the guilt over your life for many years now. I would be free of it." His eyes pleaded. "I must see you happy, Sister."

Jilliand reached out to touch his face. "You have done well by me, Aethewulf. There is no reason for guilt. If it brings you comfort, know I forgive you any imagined harm. Forget what I said in anger. God knows what will be—not you nor I." She smiled slowly. "I see you have my temper. Mother is laughing now."

Aethewulf bent to kiss her forehead. Try as he might, he had not been able to convince her to marry. At some point, he would be compelled to force her, since it was inconceivable to leave her alone. If his sons died or were killed, Jilliand would be next in line for the crown, but that could not happen if she were without a suitable husband. She knew little of life, let alone the challenges of ruling a kingdom. If Rurik were to come back for her, this land could become a battleground, unless he vowed to serve Aethewulf.

Back in her chambers, Jilliand gathered her ladies-in-waiting to share the news of her move. "All of you must carefully consider what we are undertaking. Because the king may wed, we will not be coming back. If you feel you have ties here and would work for a queen, please say so now. I do not demand anyone go with me."

The room was silent, and the ladies looked at each other, digesting the news. Becca finally spoke first, "Lady Jilliand, I love the queen I now serve. I would serve no other by choice. I for one, would go where you go." Bowing, she turned to begin preparing Jilliand's evening clothes. The remaining ladies agreed. In the years they had been together they had all grown close. Given a choice, they would not part with her.

Jilliand smiled. "It is done. Shall we get ready for court?"

Jilliand awoke the next morning to the thought, *My own home.* She could hardly believe it. She didn't care what it looked like, or how big it might be. That she was to be left alone, out of the constant glare and focus of court, was the gift. When she met her brother that morning, she could not contain her eagerness.

"One would think you rejoice to be away from your king, Lady. At least pretend you are saddened to be sent away." His eyes twinkled.

"Oh, Aethewulf, you have done so much for me. To place me in my own home is beyond what I could have asked for or expected. I am deeply grateful." Her emerald eyes were alight with anticipation. The king laughed. He had gotten what he wanted, as usual. His Spanish beauty would be with him, and soon he would have another heir; his sister would be near enough to see her whenever he felt the yearning.

Aethewulf rode with Jilliand and her attendants as they made the trek to her new home. By early evening, they were riding through a tiny settlement with many vacant huts scattered outside a large berm that surrounded the burg. Surprised and curious onlookers watched as Aethewulf and his party rode toward the courtyard. The king had come.

A deep moat filled with water surrounded the burg, forming another barrier between the berm and an inner wooden fortress. More huts and other structures were inside the walls. Inside the courtyard, Jilliand was delighted to see she had stables, more living quarters, and several run-down but promising gardens. At the center of the courtyard was a tall, square building—the keep. Aethewulf led Jilliand through the great open door. Within the keep, rooms had been cleaned, fires lit, and windows opened. It was like a dream to Jilliand. *My own place. Look Mother, can you see this? My place. I'll make it a haven for anyone venturing this way.* Impulsively, she whirled and ran to her brother, hugging him tightly.

The king laughed. "I shall miss you, Jilliand. I plan to visit you as often as possible. Unannounced, of course." He stood and watched her dancing around the empty room. Satisfied with the success of his plan, the king was in a jovial mood during dinner and long after. In the early daylight of the next morning, he and his men left, promising to return soon to see the "lady of the castle." Jilliand happily waved them off on their return journey. She surveyed the area, changes flashing through her mind. She would start with the few families who remained. As soon as Aethewulf was out of sight, she walked through the gates and into the settlement beyond, a walk she would take many times in the coming days.

Jilliand now had her own ladies, soldiers, and people to help her run the keep, including kitchen and general staff to keep the place clean and orderly. She also had stable hands and a groomsman to care for the horses Aethewulf had given her. Her people included the few living around her burg. In the first four months, she had taken in fifteen more families. They could work the land in return for a portion of the harvest that would be saved for all so that they could survive the winter months. The gardens within the confines of the burg were cleared out and awaited the spring planting. Fruit trees were trimmed back, and the walkways were cleaned.

Jilliand frequently rode through the little hamlet outside her walls, speaking to the people she saw there. She knew for her to be as safe as possible, the people must want to protect her. They must feel a bond strong enough to give warning should danger come into her new world. Nights, she lay in bed, thinking of Rurik. *If he could see what I have done, he would be pleased.* The business of caring for the people around her and activity of running the burg gave her a greater measure of peace.

In the beginning, few travelers ventured her way. As word spread of her kind heart, more came. For added protection, Jilliand gave orders for the king's colors to be displayed prominently in many places—from the flags over the entrance to the guards' clothes to a large banner hanging against the wall in the grand hall. She prayed that the message she was under the king's protection would keep her safe.

The first months in the burg were difficult for everyone, with all the hard work, but Jilliand's excitement and joy at finding herself unbound slowly spread. Daily, everyone became more comfortable. With the exception of the captain of Jilliand's guard. He was young and ambitious and deeply resented being sent from an exciting life at court. He realized he could never return to service with the king if he left Jilliand, but he felt sure he could talk some of her guard into leaving with him, and they could find service with one of the other lords who held land nearby. It took some time for him to convince the rest of the guard to join him, but early one afternoon, he simply rode away with more than half the regular guard following him out the gates. Jilliand watched them leave and wondered how she would survive left with little protection. She would be forced to provide training for all the men, inside and outside the burg.

Josh was a middle-aged man sent by the king to run Jilliand's stables and tend the stock. He had worked quite happily for the king, and the move to serve Jilliand was not one he relished. He was gruff and made no time for nonsense, so most of the stable hands skirted him. When the guard abandoned Jilliand, Josh hoped she would give up and return to the king, thus allowing Josh to return as well. But Jilliand would hear none of it.

Her fear that Aethewulf would call her back to court clouded Jilliand's reasoning, and she ordered her people to remain silent about the soldiers. Her people were loyal, and not even a whisper of her predicament left the grounds or surrounding huts. What few soldiers remained began working with the young men in and around the burg. Somehow, they would provide protection for Lady Jilliand.

Josh was the last to come to her side, and Jilliand soon found he was much kinder than he let on. Slowly but surely, they forged a tight bond, and she frequently wandered to the stables to visit with him. He became one of her most trusted friends.

One morning, as she stood stomping to stay warm, Jilliand called to him from the door of the stable. Her breath formed clouds of white when it met the cold air. Winter had arrived in earnest. "Josh, will it snow every day the rest of this winter here? I am sorely tired of being cold. Poor animals. They must tire of this also." Despite her heavy clothing, she shivered.

Josh glanced in her direction. "No, Lady. Just as you change to heavier coats, so do they. They be fine, in a covered place." He straightened up, holding his back. "Best you not stay out too long. My back warns of a coming storm. 'Tis not a good omen."

Jilliand laughed, looking skyward. "It is as blue as the iris of spring, Josh. Be sure you have plenty of wood though, sir. Just in case," she teased.

This one is too independent. Some day she is going to pay I fear. Pray tonight is not the night, Josh worried to himself. *Her guard is not about, and she won't wait. Perhaps, Sir Alexander should hear of this. Her guards, those still left, seldom accompany her these days.* As time living on her own passed, Jilliand had become comfortable with the few men she had. Josh shook his head, watching Jilliand and her ladies mounting their horses. *Most busy the guards are, trying to train the young men here. She has need of these young men, true enough. At least they will be men who would stay with her. Still, they be raw and untested.* Josh knew the training these men were getting could not match what they would have received in the king's own camp. It seemed he alone also recognized their numbers were far too few. The troubled stable master watched Jilliand and her ladies ride out of the compound.

For her part, Jilliand knew Josh did not alarm easily and decided this day's ride would be shorter than usual. Despite her resolve, time sneaked away, and fate made ready to take advantage.

When the group finally stopped for a midday meal, Jilliand was alarmed when she noticed the youngest member of her ladies, a girl named Bethy. Jilliand watched in horror as Bethy slowly slid, limp, onto the ground. "Becca!" Jilliand called, as she dismounted and ran toward Bethy. When Jilliand reached her, the woman was already unconscious. She cradled Bethy's head and watched helplessly as life withdrew from the young woman's body. "Who knows about this lady?"

"Bethy is new to us, Lady. Came only one week ago. She said she had no family," Becca replied, kneeling next to Jilliand. Looking at the rest of the party, Becca added, "Can anyone tell more? Was Bethy ill when she came to us?" At her words, every face became grave, and the women withdrew from the girl and from Jilliand.

One of the young men riding with Jilliand spoke up. "No, not ill, Lady. Bethy was with child. She was forced to leave when it was discovered she carried the child of the lord's only son. She swore the son forced her, but she had no family to speak for her good name."

"How sad," Jilliand murmured. Blood pooled around the dead woman. "Come, wrap her in something. We must return." Just then, a cold gust of wind struck them. Glancing skyward, Jilliand was surprised to see dark clouds gathering. "Move quickly. I fear Josh may be right. It looks to storm." The body was rolled into the blanket brought to spread for their meal. No one else spoke, as it was secured across the horse, and the troupe turned back homeward. The group's mood was as somber as the weather.

From a distant hill, two well-armed men watched the scene. The men had been following the party all day. As it left, the two riders turned and rode in the opposite direction.

True to Josh's predictions, Jilliand and her group barely made it back before a vicious storm hit. As many as would fit into the keep crowded inside. The fires popped and danced with the draft that was pushed down the great chimneys by howling winds. The gloom of the storm raging outside only served to further darken the general atmosphere. Even with warmth, food, and wine, the young woman's death reminded everyone how fragile their own lives remained.

Jilliand worked tirelessly to care for the people crowded into her keep. She also made sure that everyone, including those living outside the walls, had plenty of wood to stay warm and enough food to eat for the night, taking the supplies to them herself. When finally alone in her own rooms, Jilliand sank onto her bed, exhausted. *Today was not a good day, I think. How great a price that poor girl paid for what was most probably a rape.* For the first time in years, Jilliand thought back on her life with the man she had believed was her father. Her time in that life and what followed before she came to trust Rurik had taught her well. To survive, one must be steadfast and focused on one purpose: to live. *Life is not easy for most of God's creatures—certainly not for women.*

CHAPTER 28

THREE DAYS AFTER THE STORM, a lone rider entered the gate after requesting a place to stay the night from one of Jilliand's guards. He took meticulous note of all around him with the practiced eye of a soldier. Having spent the morning hours riding and observing the people and the huts surrounding Jilliand's burg, he knew there were no soldiers outside the walls. Inside the walls, he could see that the burg could be taken with little effort. Though a king's banner and colors were clearly visible everywhere, there were no signs of anyone who looked able to take up arms for the lord of the holding. *The one who takes this burg would also fight the king of this place. It is at best, a day's ride to get to the nearest king and his help. By then, one could plunder this place and be gone. Ah, where are the Vikings when you need them?* He continued to survey the area.

The afternoon meal was attended by Jilliand's remaining guards and a few others. Patiently waiting to see what the lord of these holdings looked like, the man stared when Jilliand entered the room. She was alone, with only her ladies in attendance. *This is too easy to pass up,* he thought, his plan forming even while he smiled and greeted those around him.

There are few signs of wealth, although she must be connected, the man reasoned. *Else how does she carry the king's colors?* After the meal, he wandered among the people in the room, until he came near Jilliand's table. Inviting everyone within the burg to the grand room to dine had become something done frequently. It gave Jilliand a chance to connect with the people around her and kept her in their minds. Immediately, she saw the newcomer sitting with several of her groomsmen. He was not known to her, yet seemed vaguely familiar.

"Becca, find out who that man is. I have an uneasy feeling about him." Jilliand watched the ease with which he moved. He looked to be younger than her brother, but older than Rurik. He was well-built, moved with the grace of a swordsman, and his shoulders looked as though he could notch an arrow with ease. His coloring was that of one who spends most of his time outside. His dark hair hung in loose curls that just grazed the collar of his shirt. His tunic was cut well in the longer style favored by nobility at the time. His clothing appeared to have been made from a fine material that had been colored black. The cloak on his shoulder was trimmed in ermine. When Jilliand realized he intended to approach her, she quickly looked away.

"Lady, I would thank you for allowing me the pleasure of the company of your people this night." He bowed. When he stood straight, his green eyes looked into hers. "I would speak to the lord of this holding if possible." Again, Jilliand had the feeling she knew him.

"What business do you have with the lord, sir?" Jilliand asked, smiling. She kept her manner as unconcerned as possible. She believed he must already be aware there was no lord here. She suspected he also knew exactly what little protection she housed. Her stomach began to tighten. When next he spoke, Jilliand recognized him.

For a moment he did not answer. Instead he looked at her and at those seated with her. "My business is my own, to discuss with your lord. If this is not a good time, pray tell me when another might be better." His eyes held hers. Jilliand knew at that instant that he was quite aware she was alone. Prince Philippe of France remembered Jilliand well. She was even more striking than he remembered from their one brief encounter at King Aethewulf's court. The prince had been so taken by her beauty that he could not remember anything King Aethewulf had said. He only remembered the woman now sitting before him.

Standing, Jilliand answered. Her voice was soft and cold. "You should know, Prince, it will not be as easy as you think." The prince acknowledged her comment with a slight bow and a slow smile. With that, Jilliand turned and left the room.

Once out of sight, she pulled Becca close. "You must tell Josh to take my horse and leave immediately. He is to tell His Majesty we are in grave danger. Without help, I fear we may fall. And Nate, send Nate to me. Quickly! I fear we have little time."

In her chambers, she changed into breeches. Tying her hair back, she buckled on the long blade. Slipping the short one into her belt, she grabbed her heaviest cloak, her bow, and a loaded quiver just as Nate knocked on her study door. Jilliand was already headed toward one of the staircases leading out the rear of the keep. Nate ran to catch up.

"Nate, now, while it is still night, bring what animals you can inside the walls. I fear we may soon be under siege." Jilliand was already at the bottom of one of the staircases leading out the rear of the keep.

"Nate," Jilliand's voice carried with it a sense of urgency. "If I were the attacker, I would surround the burg, thereby cutting off any help or escape. We will need men to stand watch. Take care to keep the back gate closed. Just in case . . . "

"We pulled the bridges as soon as he left, Lady." Nate started walking away, and then stopped to study Jilliand. "Lady, who is the man? For whom does he ride?"

"He is a son of the king of France. Why he is here, I do not know for certain. We will find out, soon enough." As Nate turned to leave, Jilliand called to him, "Take care, Nate. This may not end well."

Nate's eyes found Jilliand's. "If it does not, I would tell you this—to have served you has been an honor, Lady Jilliand." In the next instant he was gone.

Word that Jilliand was in danger spread quickly through the burg and beyond. Men and boys began to rush toward the burg, forcing Jilliand to have the gate lowered. With the gate down, Jilliand's people flooded in. The men came to help, the families came for safety. After raising the gate again, two of the soldiers remaining from Jilliand's old guard took charge and begin preparing for a siege. Buckets were filled with water and placed within easy reach of anyone on the walls. Fires were lit throughout the area to fight plummeting temperatures. Every man able to use a bow was stationed on the walls, with every extra arrow available. Two men were placed in each tower to keep watch beyond the moat. Meanwhile, Jilliand hastily prepared for casualties. The great room was cleared. Blankets and other items to care for the wounded were stacked on the head table. At her direction, the kitchen staff had begun to cook large kettles of thick soup and bake breads. Jilliand tried to remember anything she had ever heard about battles. The lord she had believed was her father who held her captive had not fought; he had only plundered after the fighting was over. Her own experiences had been the sudden unexpected raids from the Vikings. Sadly, she had to admit that most of the men with her this night were only slightly better than farmers when it came to fighting.

The animals herded inside the walls were penned in the back, close to the keep. From the crowd of men and women gathered, one man stepped up. "I am not a soldier, m'lady. I never fought. I can fight for you, and for my wee ones. I . . . we . . . would stay and fight with you. The men who would overtake this place are already coming. Tell us what to do."

Jilliand looked at the people. "I have never done this thing before either. Together, we can stand strong. The king will come soon. Until he gets to us, we must hold."

One of the soldiers stepped forward. "Tell me, do we have a weak place—any place someone could overrun us?"

"The towers—what about the towers in back?" one man called out.

"Of what do you speak? Explain!" Jilliand ordered.

The man moved forward. "I helped, when the walls were falling. The back towers are loose and weak; the wood is old." He turned to several men standing around him. "Remember? If they find that place, they can get in." As he spoke, men began to crowd closer.

"Can they find it?" the soldier asked.

For a moment, the room was silent. Jilliand pushed them. "Can it be broken through? Can we block it?" The second soldier shook his head.

"No matter. We will not let them find it. Oil. Do we have oil?"

"Yes, we have many barrels of oil, Lady," another man shouted. "It is stored below the keep. Why?"

"Quickly, roll the barrels out!"

Jilliand called to the tower for an update. "How close are they?"

"Not yet through the huts beyond!" came the response.

Jilliand ordered the oil to be dumped onto the water before the invaders were in sight of the burg. It spread quickly, forming a thick blanket that eventually covered the water in the moat. "Keep the fires going. We will need them." Jilliand looked straightaway at Nate.

Nodding to Jilliand, he continued his rounds, talking to the nervous men waiting for something none had seen before. Nate's own heart beat steady. His devotion to Jilliand gave him a strange calm. *We will hold. For Jilliand, we hold.*

The night brought with it a mass of heavy clouds, and the snow began to fall. With darkness upon them, the invaders had set up camp just past the huts that clung to the land beyond the moat. Their fires made eerie globes of light, a constant reminder of the danger lurking on the far side of the great berm and moat surrounding the burg walls.

All through the night, snowflakes brittle with the dropping temperatures continued to fall. Morning broke clear and bitter cold. Groups of men and boys stood around the fires. Kitchen staff slipped among the men serving hot soup and chunks of bread. Jilliand walked around to every man, speaking with conviction, bringing the message of victory. They would hold until the king came.

"Look! They come!" Standing in one of the towers, a man was wildly pointing. Quickly mounting the steps to stand on the rampart above the gate, Jilliand looked beyond the huts. Like a wave, the men moved steadily toward her. The front lines were on foot, armed with lances and shields. Behind them, more men rode armed with lances. Thinking on how few men and weapons she had, Jilliand's heart dropped.

Under her breath, Jilliand gave words to what her heart felt. "Hurry, Aethewulf, or you will come to my funeral." To the man next to her, she nodded. "They think to overtake us with numbers? They shall see the taking is not for them!" The frightened man looked back at the advancing mass and then at Jilliand. She clasped his shoulder. "They will soon know what English-men can do."

"Are they not English, too, m'lady?" he asked, glancing back nervously at the columns pressing forward.

Shaking her head, Jilliand replied, "*We* are English!" She went to every tower, encouraging the men who defended her. Anyone who could use a bow was placed in areas that offered the most protection but still allowed the greatest view. She sent younger boys around to tell the men that not one arrow was to fly until she gave the word.

When the horde outside her walls reached the berm, an invader on horse-back carrying a white flag rode to the top. "Lady, our prince would offer you a chance to save your people and yourself! Yield! Open the gates; drop the bridge. Every consideration will be given to you." The rider sat waiting for a reply, his white flag whipping about his lance in the cold wind. Sitting in the front line, Jilliand saw Prince Philippe. He wore armor. On his head, he clearly wore a crown.

"Your prince should play another game. He will not win this one. Leave, before I separate you from your horse!" Jilliand yelled back. Standing on the rampart above the gate, Jilliand's hair had come loosened and now fell about her shoulders. Both her hair and black cape caught the winds that were steadily growing in strength. The woman's courage caught the prince's fancy. The messenger below her began to laugh. He raised his lance and stood in his stirrups, as if he intended to respond to her. Before he could speak, Jilliand's arrow pierced his throat. Stunned and gasping, he looked at Jilliand and fell from his horse.

For a moment, every man on both sides was motionless. Then, from the invading horde, there came a cry. "The castle and all in it will be mine!" Philippe yelled. Foot soldiers began running up the mound and dove into the moat, followed by a second wave of men. Jilliand stepped behind a raised pil-lar, waiting. When the first wave of men was halfway across the moat and the second wave of men well into the water, Jilliand yelled, "Now!" A shower of fire arrows fell from the walls, instantly lighting the thick oil on the water in the moat. Men in the water screamed as they were suddenly ablaze. Those still on the banks stumbled against those ahead, trying to stop, and thereby pushing more men into the ring of fire. Men were turning and scrambling back down the berm, only to run into the advancing line below them.

The horses closest to the berm were rearing in fear from the smell of fire, burning flesh, and the chaos around them. Watching the scene below her, Jilliand knew any chance she might have to live was gone if the castle did not hold. She watched for the reaction of the crowned man below her. He and his generals quickly gathered, regrouped, and changed tactics. Wave after wave of arrows sailed over the walls while the oil slowly burned off. The courtyard cleared as everyone sought shelter. When darkness fell, the assault stopped. Younger boys ran throughout the courtyard gathering arrows, hoping to find some unbroken ones that could be used again. Behind her, a great fire burned, providing warmth for the men on the wall, who took turns standing near it. Silhouetted by that fire, Jilliand stood on the rampart, watching the globes of light from the encampment beyond.

Philippe stood leaning against a wagon, looking up at Jilliand. This conquest was not as easy as he had expected. All the women *he* knew were, at this moment, sitting in front of a fireplace—sewing, gossiping, whatever it was those women did. But this woman . . . "Majesty, what do we do now?" said one of his generals, interrupting his thoughts.

"Even beautiful women must eat. Nothing gets in or out alive." Turning, he walked slowly toward his tent.

"Perhaps she is a witch," offered a soldier, glancing at the woman standing on the rampart.

"A witch? No, but before this is done, I will know who she truly is. We will be forced to push tomorrow. Surely, King Aethewulf is on his way. If we cannot take her tomorrow, we leave." Prince Philippe stood staring at the fire that warmed his tent. He remembered well meeting Jilliand at Aethewulf's court, but later that night when Philippe looked for the woman, she had vanished. *Not this time, Lady. You will not walk away this time.*

Prince Philippe was up before dawn. He stood at a large table set with food, wine, and papers, surrounded by key men and studied a drawing of the moat, berm, and wooden structures that made up Jilliand's burg. "Is this drawn correctly?" He glanced around the table. Several of the men studied the drawing more carefully. "Send someone to check it. This may be our answer."

All was quiet until late morning. Then, only sporadic arrows flew toward Jilliand's men. The burg was now loosely encircled. Jilliand paced atop the wall. "I don't understand this. What is happening?"

"Is this a siege, m'lady?" one man asked.

"It does not feel that way. It feels as if he is waiting for something." Jilliand looked out over the distant camp. She could see men walking about but without purpose. *What does he see that I do not?* Her eye caught the prince, standing at the entrance of his tent. He stood looking at her, Jilliand was certain. But he stood as if he had won already. *Could it be Aethewulf is not coming?* Jilliand thought desperately, as she left the rampart. Inside her study, she looked over her burg plans again and then paced around the table, trying to think. Nate and two soldiers came into the room, not certain what they should do next.

"Lady, I do not think we are under siege yet. When that comes, the lines surrounding us will be tighter." The older of the soldiers watched Jilliand.

"Just the same, we need to watch our supplies carefully," Jilliand said and sent a page to tell Becca. "There must be something about this place I do not see—Nate, what does he know that I do not?"

"Perhaps your brother does not come, Lady," Nate offered softly.

"He would not leave us. Josh got through—he must have. He left before this man even had time to return to wherever it is he came from." Jilliand stood still. "Do we know where he came from?"

"This we know," Nate answered. "One of his pages stopped at the home of your blacksmith, pretending he was in need of food. He told of his prince, a man that has defeated two lords below King Aethewulf's lands. The prince declared himself king and now moves forward."

"Why would he say such a thing so openly? These lands belong to Aethewulf, if we can but hold. Nate, you must try to get to the king." Her voice dropped. Quietly, she spoke to Nate. "I begin to fear Josh may not have gotten through." Nate immediately left the room, dashed down the back stairs from Jilland's study and ran to the stables.

Jilliand stood before the plans trying to think. Leaning forward, she studied the back moat. "Can this be correct?" Puzzled, Jilliand pointed to the plans of the rear berm. "It is not even half the width of the rest. The moat also looks narrow here. If they find that—" At that moment, she heard cries from the yard below. From her window, she could clearly see men crowding the court-yard, with swords drawn, fighting the farmers, who had now begun to back away. "Drop the bridge!" Jilliand commanded, as she ran from the room.

"You open for them, Lady?" one of the soldiers, running with her, questioned.

"Yes. I would not trap my people. They cannot fight these men. Open the gates!"

Bursting from the entrance of the keep, Jilliand immediately took on the first man she saw. Not expecting a woman to wield such a weapon, she easily ran her shorter blade into the man's stomach. She quickly pulled her sword out and moved on. The battle was short but bloody. Jilliand had long forgotten she was the lady of these holdings. She fought with a fury born of desperation and anger. As she moved with agility from one opponent to another, she eventually found herself backed into a corner. With no escape for the lady, everyone stood motion-less. The prince walked through the circle, his eyes flashing. "You are defeated, Lady." The words were spoken with a finality that took Jilliand's breath.

"Please, let my people go. They are only farmers, not soldiers. I yield to you. You have won. Let these people go. A king rules all he conquers. They are now your people. Protect them." Jilliand let her sword fall from her bloodied hand.

"They fought me, Lady," the man answered, his eyes locked onto Jilliand's.

Jilliand's voice softened. "At my command."

"All in command who oppose me will hang," he noted, looking at the slight lady before him. He had not expected to fight a woman for these lands, but given what she had, she fought well. He stood still, looking into her green eyes.

"So be it," Jilliand acknowledged. "I was in command. My lands and all on them now belong to you." With that, Jilliand removed the smaller blade from her belt.

"Your army?" He pushed her.

Shaking her head, a sad smile broke out on her face splattered with blood and dirt. "There is no army, Prince. Only one lady." Her arms dropped at her sides, yet her back was straight and her chin was up. The area was deadly quiet. While he was loath to hang a woman, certainly one who fought like this one . . . this beautiful one . . . he knew it would send a very clear message to all who opposed him. He had a decision to make.

"If there is a dungeon in this place, lock the lady up." As he turned to leave, he caught sight of her eyes again. Her voice may have softened, but her eyes reflected fire. She simply bowed to him.

"Majesty," the man following him spoke urgently, "we should move on. Surely King Aethewulf will be here soon. The lady carries his colors."

"King Aethewulf will not come. At least not until word reaches him." *This fighting woman did not behave like a mistress . . . I know he has not remarried . . . Now that I think on it, she looks just like Aethewulf himself.* "His sister! She looks like Aethewulf. It's his sister! I have his sister in my dungeon!" As soon as he spoke the words, he turned to the man. A broad smile filled his face. His decision regarding the fate of Jilliand was still not clear; however, the stakes rose in his favor. She could be ransomed or taken back to France. A pawn for France. "His sister, what a gift, is it not? Confine everyone within the burg walls. None are to be harmed." Prince Philippe needed to plan carefully before Aethewulf and his men descended upon his newest acquisition.

JILLIAND

The first rooms Philippe visited were Jilliand's chambers. He hoped to find greater understanding of the lady now languishing in the dungeon below. She was the sister of a king—a very wealthy king, who held control over the greatest parcels of land of any monarch. Because he was known to be a very Christian king who had no taste for fighting, the prince had reason to believe everything would end very well indeed. Aethewulf had already given one of his sons part of his kingdom rather than fight over it. His first wife reportedly had died, and the second had left the king—an action that had cost the woman's family dearly. *Time to visit the lady below.* First, though, Philippe had business to take care of inside the burg.

Jilliand had been taken to a cell in the dungeon, a place she had only been to once. It was cold, damp, and dark. Now she could only pray Nate would get through. She began to pace.

CHAPTER 29

A DARK SHAPE CLUNG TO a horse in full gallop that was racing toward King Aethewulf's royal residence. The horse pushed against winds that plowed into beast and rider. When he was at least half a day's ride from his destination, it began to snow hard. Barely able to see the road ahead, the rider was forced to slow the horse. The snow thickened. Still the rider pushed onward. The horse struggled forward at times barely moving. The wind howled. When it seemed all might be lost, the light from the king's burg shone forth. Sensing an end to the run, both horse and rider found reserve strength. The powerful animal took his rider home.

Alexander was just leaving the stables for the king's hall, when Nate flew through the gates.

"Sir Alexander, they are taken!" Nate called out. "I fear for Lady Jilliand's life! She would not leave and stayed to fight with us!" The young man jumped from his horse as he shouted over the roar of the storm, calling for a fresh mount. "You must come quickly. They cannot fall! I ride with you, sir."

Alexander grasped Nate to slow him down. "Stop, boy." Alexander looked around for his second; Riley was a well-seasoned soldier who had been with Sir Alexander many years. "What do you see for this storm, Riley? How much worse?"

Riley had been watching the skies all afternoon. He had never been wrong when it came to his weather predictions. "It will get much worse, sir. Would not do to leave tonight. Just *who* has attacked Lady Jilliand?"

"I am about to find out. Gather men. Make plans to leave at first light. It is dark already and will only get darker." He left Riley. Turning his attention to Nate, he pressed him. "Who attacked Jilliand's castle? Who, lad?"

"I do not know, but I think he is a king . . "

"Go on," Alexander ordered.

"The man attended Lady Jilliand's court one night ago. She sent Josh to get help from King Aethewulf that night. Then she and the few soldiers still in her service made ready to defend the castle as well as they could. Lady Jilliand has already stopped two or three advances. We should go quickly, or she may not survive. The invaders have surely gained entrance by now!" He was clearly afraid for his mistress. "She killed the first man. She put an arrow through his throat. I fear the invader will not deal well with her. You must help her, sir," Nate finished, anxiety filling his eyes.

"Believe me, that I will. As soon as I can get to her," Alexander responded grimly. "Who does the Lady Jilliand have with her?"

"She has a few soldiers, her usual ladies, and four pages. All the farmers came to fight, and she fought too." Nate was clearly exhausted, but Alexander knew he would have to see Aethewulf. He pulled Nate along with him as they ran for the king's chambers.

"Does she not have the captain and his men?" *Jilliand is too independent. This escapade could cost dearly.* Alexander shook his head. He was angry—at the storm and the lack of protection for Jilliand—but more at her carelessness. Yet, he knew she would not change. Her thoughts were not like any other woman he knew. *She never worries about the things that could happen . . .* He realized that Nate was now talking about the captain.

The lad had stopped mid-sentence, looking squarely at Alexander. Alexander was stunned at what he heard. "No, sir. He felt being the captain of Lady Jilliand's guard was beneath him. He left long ago. Only a few soldiers remain. We all fought." It took a moment for Alexander to digest what he heard. He cringed at what this information meant for Jilliand.

After hearing Nate's story, Aethewulf snarled, "It takes more than a crown to make a king, boy. Tell me how many men he has and are they well armed?"

"He has less than when he started, Your Majesty." Nate told both men about Jilliand's battle tactics. Aethewulf's thoughts formed quickly. He knew Jilliand would fight, but based on Nate's information, that fight would be useless. *She could be killed.* His heart sank at the thought. More likely, she would be taken captive. *Though if she is taken, what might it take to free her?* Even as he asked, Aethewulf knew he would not give up his throne—not even for his sister.

As if he read the king's mind, Alexander stated, "We'll take her back and hang this would-be king." Aethewulf didn't respond.

By dawn the next morning, Aethewulf and Alexander were riding with three hundred men and Nate. They rode four abreast. Travel was slow but steady. Alexander had ridden through every kind of storm, but he hated snowstorms the most. As the snow deepened, the horses were hard pressed to keep moving. The winds blew the snow into great drifts. The company of men rode all day and into the night struggling forward against the bitter cold.

It took little time for Prince Philippe and his men to secure Jilliand's burg. The people within the walls were ordered to clean up the courtyard and take care of his men. When all the wounded were cared for, and Philippe's men were fed, Jilliand's people were allowed to return to their homes. Philippe's men were sitting in groups talking and eyeing the young women nearby. They had been given strict orders to leave the married women alone. That order mattered little to them as there were plenty of single women as well. For his part, the prince intended to visit the prisoner being held in the dungeon.

At the sound of keys rattling at the door, Jilliand looked up from where she sat on the floor. The door opened, allowing the light from a flaming torch to flood the cell. Jilliand closed her eyes for a moment against the light. Prince Philippe stepped past the guard and stood just inside the door. When she opened her eyes again, she sat motionless, waiting. "Do you not stand before your king?" His voice was even, calm.

"Who are you?" Jilliand asked, hoping to discover if he represented France or was doing all this on his own. If he did indeed ride for France, there surely would be more French soldiers coming. If he rode for himself, at least Aethewulf stood a better chance. She remained sitting. The man walked to her, extending his hand. Jilliand took his hand and allowed him to pull her up. He led her from the cell.

"I, Lady, am the man who holds you and all your lands. Your people are well and unharmed." He stopped speaking as they passed the guard.

"Thank you," Jilliand hesitated, "Your Highness." She moved up the steps. Since he gave no indication where he intended to go, she led him to her study. He followed, willing to see where she would take him. Inside the room, she looked around.

"Do you think something might be missing, Lady?" he asked sarcastically.

"I am not certain when I might see this room again," Jilliand responded quietly. She turned and faced him. He watched her look him over. His eyes were a green-blue, his hair dark brown. He stood over six feet tall and was broad shouldered and muscular. His expression showed he was pleased with himself.

He sat down and leaned back in a chair, watching Jilliand. "Your room is comfortable?"

"You are being sarcastic again, Your Majesty." Jilliand was suddenly very tired. She longed to sleep and then awaken to a normal world again.

"Explain how you know to use a weapon so well," he ordered. Waving his hand, he indicated she was to sit. Jilliand sat down, grateful for the soft cushions.

"My mother married a man who wanted a son. I was well educated, trained to use a sword and bow, and know something of fighting." Her voice was strained as she thought of how much she did *not* know about fighting.

"I should have you put to death." Even as he said the words, he knew he would not. She was bloody and dirty, but still a beauty. Her spirit had been visible from his first meeting with her. She would live. A crown might not come to him through this prisoner, but money surely would.

"For defending my people?" Jilliand could see he was unsure of himself. She realized if Nate or Josh had gotten through, she would become a pawn in this game of kings.

"You personally killed at least one of my men," he noted, watching her eyes. Her eyes were striking, filled with every thought in her head.

Jilliand laughed dryly. "I killed several of your men. I think we are even in that regard. The men you killed were but farmers, stable hands, and other groundskeeper. The men I killed were trained soldiers. It would seem you bear the greater burden."

His brows shot up, and he laughed aloud. Her audacity was unexpected. She intrigued him more with each word she spoke. "I agree. I think I will leave this place to your king, who is, I believe, your brother. Instead, I will take you."

Jilliand's heart lurched. She had no desire to leave this place, nor to be this man's toy. *How would Rurik ever find her? Would he even look?* "I would be a burden. I am certain you must be accustomed to scouting a place out, moving in, taking what you want, and then quickly leaving. What on earth would you do with *me*?"

He looked at her, surprised she could not think of all he could do with her. Then, he smiled, slowly, with satisfaction. He would take her with him. Now. Tonight. Suddenly, he stood up. "I know you are tired. I also know you can ride. While I do not like to cause you undo discomfort, Lady, we will leave tonight. If you would like to take anything special with you, anything you can carry on horseback, please get it now." He stood and waited.

Now Jilliand was stunned. She couldn't believe what was happening. Just by looking at him, she could see he would not be patient. Glancing around her study, she moved into her sleeping quarters. He followed her. She took the heaviest cloak, the combs Rurik had given her, and the silken bag from her mother. She still wore the rings from her mother and Rurik. She slipped the locket over her head and put the earrings on. Looking around the room once more, she added another cloak, and then walked away.

"Do you have a favorite steed, Lady?" he asked, as he walked with her to the stables. His men were gathering their things together. Having spent several months with this man, they were no stranger to quick departures.

Jilliand thought of the horse she had sent Josh away on. "I did. My horse Lancer, but he is not here any longer." By this time, they were near the stables. When she stepped into the barn, she froze. It was Lancer. "How did he get here?" Jilliand looked around, expecting to see Josh.

"The horse came back on his own—riderless," the prince noted casually. Jilliand's heart ached at the news. Philippe continued walking along the stalls. He ordered Lancer saddled and chose another horse for himself. His men had already taken their horses outside and were ready to ride. Jilliand moved away from Philippe whenever he walked near her. If he noticed, he did not react. Before anyone could assist her, Jilliand was on Lancer.

They rode all night. The snow had stopped falling, and the sky was clear. Stars filled the abyss above them, and the moon was full, reflecting off the snow giving light, as if God Himself wished to help them escape. Lacking a blanket of clouds to hold the cold at bay, the air bit into both horses and riders. Thankful for the warmth of her cloaks, Jilliand rode on, her mind on Josh, who certainly had been killed while trying to bring help. *Nate's horse is not back. Perhaps he made it.* In one fateful evening, her life had turned again.

As daylight broke, Jilliand began to ride more slowly until she was behind several of the men in the party. Moving to the outside edge of the group, she suddenly urged Lancer forward. Responsive to every move and touch of his mistress, Lancer shot out. The unanticipated run caused a moment of confusion. "Get her!" She heard Philippe's voice break through the clamor of men and horses. Lancer easily stayed ahead of the pursuers. As he pulled farther ahead, Jilliand heard the same voice yelling, "If you do not stop, the horse dies." Immediately, Jilliand pulled up on the reins, slowing Lancer. At the same time, she threw her arm up. Turning the horse around, she quickly slid off and stood aside, waiting.

With his face dark with anger and his voice cold, Philippe rode up, nearly atop Jilliand. She stood firm. In a clear, scornful voice, he observed, "You care more for the life of your horse than your own?"

"He has no choice in what I ask of him."

"You play a dangerous game, Lady." He looked at the small woman standing before him, unafraid, defiant.

"Let me go. I am of no use to you. My father is dead. I have not seen my husband in years, and my brother has no desire to barter his kingdom for a sister he barely knows. We—you and I—lost good men for nothing."

He looked at her, deliberating. "I think to keep you," he decided aloud. "I believe I shall see you are well kept, in a cell, for the rest of your life," he finished coldly.

If his intention was to frighten Jilliand, he failed. "I will not do that," she announced flatly. "I have years of experience with being kept in a cell by one who did not love me. I will not do that again."

Philippe got off his horse and, with purpose, walked the few steps to Jilliand. Towering over her, he softly informed her, "If you try to leave again, I will kill the horse." He then turned her around and lifted her onto Lancer. His men were grouped together, watching the exchange between their leader and the one who played havoc with all in her path. Their admiration for Jilliand was growing.

Without speaking, Philippe moved them out. When Jilliand did not immediately move up near him, he glanced back, caught her eye, and pointed to the ground next to him before facing forward. Jilliand brought Lancer up next to him. She rode silently, without looking at the man who now seemed destined to claim her.

As the horses battled with the snow, Jilliand struggled to remain awake and in the saddle. Two nights without sleep began to take their toll. Philippe watched the lady riding as far from him as she was allowed. Several times he thought she would certainly fall off the horse. "Lady Jilliand!" he sharply called. Jilliand was startled, alert, looking around. "Come closer," he commanded. Hesitating a moment, she urged her horse closer to him. "Closer," he ordered.

"Am I to run you over?" Jilliand asked sweetly.

A wry smile broke out upon his face. "Now you are mocking me. I want your horse against mine." When Jilliand had maneuvered her horse as close as she could, he quickly reached over and pulled her onto his horse in front of him. Jilliand stiffened, trying desperately to push back, but the bulk of her cloaks hindered her movement. With a shooting pain in her heart, Jilliand remembered when Rurik had held her the same way. "Stay still, Lady. If I allow you to continue, you will soon be lying in the snow. While that might cool your temperament, it will also slow us down. Just lean back. Sleep." There was little Jilliand could do; exhaustion quickly took control. She slept.

She awoke when Philippe gently shook her. The sun was already well on its journey to midday. "We are stopping so the horses can rest. You will feel better if you walk around. There will be something to eat shortly." As he spoke, he slid her down off his horse. Jilliand stumbled a few steps before she regained her footing. Her body felt stiff, and the nap had only served to heighten the weariness dragging her down. She walked among the men now busy setting up camp. A second fire was soon blazing. Jilliand walked toward the farther fire, trying to stay away from Philippe. Watching the men, she noticed one young soldier visibly shivering. Jilliand stepped over to him and slipped her outer cloak around his thin shoulders.

"No, m'lady. I cannot," he said, quickly rejecting the offering. Jilliand removed the smaller cloak she had worn beneath the outer cloak and exchanged it with him. "No, I cannot take this." He tried to hand it back.

"Take it. I have little need for two and will probably have no need for the one I keep. You are freezing, lad." She placed it around him. This time he kept it. Gratefully, he nodded to her, thanking her under his breath in Norse.

Without thinking, Jilliand answered him in his native tongue. As soon as the words were out of her mouth, she knew she had made a terrible mistake. She and the lad stood looking at one another. She felt the silence grow heavy around her. Nodding slightly, she walked away, her heart in her throat.

CHAPTER 30

MANY THOUGHTS WERE RUNNING THROUGH Alexander's head during the long trek to Jilliand's burg. Taking her back to the king's court was not one of them. The king had a new wife and was already expecting their second child. The new queen was very proud of her position with the king and made certain every man, woman, and child in the court knew it. No, Jilliand wouldn't go back with the king. However, it was possible Alexander would stay with Jilliand. *Does she still love the Viking? That is the question. Moreover, does it matter?* His mind roamed over familiar ground.

Aethewulf, too, rode in silence. If Jilliand and her guard were not able to hold, he would be faced with the prospect of refusing to pay ransom for her. He loved his sister, but he would not jeopardize his kingdom for her—or any woman for that matter. He glanced at Alexander. His friend was staring ahead, thinking, no doubt, of the woman they rode to save.

What manner of man wants a woman just to use? Perhaps most, but not any man I respect. Alexander remembered his last conversation with Jilliand. When her great emerald eyes had looked at him that night, he knew she was sad—and still in love with the Viking. Under his breath, he cursed. Aethewulf would not barter for Jilliand. Alexander understood that about his king and friend. When the invaders discovered she was worthless, they would probably kill her. He knew in his heart such would be her fate. Worse, he was certain she would not die quickly. He could hardly think on it. Somehow, he would kill Jilliand himself and save her from what seemed inevitable.

The king and his men rode over the berm, crossed the moat, and entered the gate where the drawbridge lay open, unguarded. Silence hung over the courtyard. The darkness was unbroken—no candles, no fires, no move-ment. Life in the keep and its yard had vanished. Aethewulf and Alexander scanned the area. Horses stomped, riding gear clinked, occasionally someone coughed—nothing else could be heard. The stillness was finally broken by King Aethewulf's voice. "We know not who came, where they went, nor what they may have taken." Ignoring the knot in his gut, he ordered that anyone found in the area be brought to the great room in Jilliand's keep.

In two hours, the keep was alight with fires and candles. A clamor of voices echoed off walls and found its way down every hall. When the king entered, a hush fell over the entire populace. He took a moment to scrutinize the faces turned to him. "Lady Jilliand has cared for each of you. She is not here. Can anyone tell me how that is possible? How could she simply disappear?" The people in the room remained still. "Am I to believe she flew away? Disap-peared like the smoke from a burning log?" His voice rocketed off the walls, as its volume rose with his anger.

"Majesty," one older man stepped forward. "We do not know the men who took Lady Jilliand. She did not flee; she stayed and fought with us."

Several women began to quietly sob. The fear in the room was palpable. "I think they are afraid of you, Your Majesty." Alexander looked from the crowd to his king.

Aethewulf nodded and sat down. Alexander questioned how the fight began, how many people were with the mysterious man, and what was done to defend the burg and Jilliand. With the answers to his queries, Aethewulf realized his worst fears were indeed true. Jilliand had been taken hostage. He left the room, choosing to plan his move in the room he knew best: Jilliand's study. Inside, with a fire blazing and a cup of wine, he paced. Eventually, he slumped into a chair. Alexander and several men stood waiting.

"I cannot risk all these men and my throne over one woman." His voice gave away the decision he had already made. Alexander turned on his heel and left the room. Aethewulf dismissed the remaining men. He sat alone, brooding for a long time. The fire died down, and Alexander did not return. Aethewulf found his friend outside walking the grounds.

"You know I speak the truth, Alex," Aethewulf softly noted to the one man he trusted over all others.

"The issue is, Majesty," Alexander replied through clenched teeth, "I can find another lady-in-waiting, another page, or another soldier. I cannot replace Jilliand." He walked away, his boots crunching into the crusted snow.

"No matter," Aethewulf shot back, "I have made my decision." If he heard, Alexander gave no sign.

Throughout the long night, Aethewulf struggled with his decision. He would follow his sister's captors, with the sole purpose of identifying them only. He would not fight or pay for her. He could not. She meant nothing to the security of the throne. His third son lay in his mother's arms, healthy and fit. When at last the sun pushed back the darkness, he sat alone before a dying fire.

It took little time before Aethewulf and his men were ready to leave. They knew which direction Jilliand had been taken, but the question as to where the invaders had come from remained unanswered. Nothing had been destroyed in the burg or in the surrounding huts, and anyone not killed during the fight was left unharmed by the victor. Time had been taken to clean up after the assault ended. Clearly, Jilliand had been the object of the battle. The king and his men set off.

Alexander rode next to his king. For the first time in memory, a deep chasm lay between them. Alexander admitted he wouldn't be determined to rescue Jilliand either—except that he had fallen in love with her. Aethewulf was correct. At stake was one of the largest holdings in England. The king's dream had always been to unite the kingdoms, moving toward one great country. His sons could carry on after his death. One of those sons had already claimed a section. Alexander knew Aethewulf had two more sons. Jilliand would not be ransomed. The man who now had Jilliand was from another country—but what country? What might be the price for her?

"Alexander." Aethewulf was determined to break the silence between them. "You are like a brother to me. I know you care for Jilliand, but unless she were queen and the mother of a male heir, she would not be considered a pawn to maintain hold over this kingdom." Alexander rode on in silence.

"I know, Aethewulf," Alexander eventually acknowledged. "I am aware of the changing boundaries that surround every kingdom. In this case, however," he looked squarely at Aethewulf, "there is the great chance that once it is known she is not worth any ransom, she will be killed—after she is raped, of course."

The king had no answer. He stared at Alexander and then faced forward. He truly had not thought of that small detail. Alexander was right. Such would most likely be the fate of Jilliand. She, who had already faced so many trials. Turning, he looked back at Alexander. "I had not thought of that, Alexander." He turned to look at the force behind him. Riding was miserable. The wind bit at them, and the thawing roads became wet and sloppy as the horses sloshed onward. The identity of Jilliand's captor remained unknown. Watching his friend, Aethewulf knew Alexander would ask to be allowed the chance to free Jilliand. Aethewulf also knew he would grant that request.

When darkness began to take possession of the land again, Alexander sent a rider to a small knot of lights in the distance. When the man returned, he had secured an area for their camp. Of more interest, he had news about the unit of men that had taken the king's sister. Alexander pulled away from the company to speak with the man. When he rejoined Aethewulf, he shared the news regarding their campsite. But the information regarding who had taken Jilliand, Alexander kept to himself.

The king's men soon had tents up and food ready to be served. When Aethewulf sent for Alexander, he was told Alexander had ridden into the town, seeking information about Jilliand. For hours, Aethewulf sat alone in his tent. The longer he brooded, the more determined he was to let his sister go. No woman would cost him his kingdom—not even the sister who looked like the mother he had adored.

A cold, grey sky greeted Aethewulf when he emerged from his tent. All night long he had waited for Alexander to return. With no word from his friend,

Aethewulf ordered camp broken. Sitting atop the knoll looking down toward the hamlet below him, Aethewulf felt deep regret pierce his heart for the first time in his life. At what price did he keep his kingdom?

The king and most of his men returned to Jilliand's burg. The remaining men waited for Alexander's return.

Rurik studied a Rus winter landscape stretching as far as the eye could see. This land had never felt like home to him, no matter how hard he tried. White, silent, and cold, nothing more. He could hear Oleg talking with the men— Oleg's men now. Oleg was a good friend and would be a good leader. The time had come. When Inga had died after delivering a dying infant, he had felt sadness for their son, Igor, to be left without a mother. Rurik also felt relief at the passing of a woman whose love and infant belonged to another man. With the help of the clan, Rurik had raised Igor, and he was now a young man. The young man had his mother's temperament, and he and Rurik clashed more frequently these days. Rurik did not hesitate to leave. It truly was time.

The deed was done: The lands Rurik ruled were passed to Oleg. Oleg had agreed to take Igor in as his own. When Oleg's time came to step down, Igor would take over as the ruler. Rurik knew Oleg would teach Igor well. It was meant to be. Carefully, Rurik slipped the ring given him by Jilliand onto his finger once more.

The Rus was a great country. Rurik believed it would become even greater. The sisters of fate had smiled on him after all. He had successfully taken the land and its peoples with little fighting. For years now, their fighting had become less and less a pastime. Ships moved goods around, trade grew, and the people were satisfied. His job was done.

Saying goodbye, Igor had held his father close, grateful for the chance to be with Oleg and mindful of the responsibility his father gave to Oleg. "Is father sad, Oleg?" Igor asked, watching the receding figure of his father and horse.

"No, he is alive again," Oleg noted with satisfaction. "Rurik lives again."

As Rurik rode away, his heart felt light. For the first time in years, he felt young. He was a Viking again. He was free.

He would search for Jilliand, if she still lived. If she did not, he would find another place to live out his days. There were still fights to be fought. His journey was not yet over. Perhaps the fates played with him. Or perhaps, as Dir predicted, they were guiding him to her. He smiled at the thought of the hair and eyes like no other's.

It took Rurik months to make the journey from Rus to Norway. He stopped at each settlement, taking his time to come ever closer to the land of Jilliand's birth. He stayed longer in Norway, while the weather wrestled with itself, struggling to give up winter's cold. Before spring could reach the land, Rurik was aboard ship again. Warships still ran the waves, along with merchant ships. The ship he was on was a warship, much like his ships of old. The crew was eager for adventure, to capture slaves, plunder villages, and search for gold that was becoming scarce.

Their first stop was the coast of Denmark, at Rurik's request. He jumped over the side, and waded ashore. Turning back, Rurik raised a hand to the boat as she slid away from the shore, heading back to sea. Its sea king answered his salute. Rurik turned, surveying the land. Vegetation had reclaimed the area where once Rurik's own settlement thrived. Homesites were overtaken by trees. Their branches still bare from winter's freeze, reached skyward, ghostly skeletal arms clawing in search of the sun. The earth remained frozen beneath layers of snow.

Rurik shivered. Not from cold, rather from the gloom that seemed to permeate the area. He was drawn to the home he had built for and shared with Jilliand. His heart ached. When he reached the spot, now marked only by a few standing poles, he paused, remembering the love this place once held.

Suddenly alert, he stiffened. The stillness of the air seemed broken, yet Rurik could hear nothing. There . . . again . . . like a soft whisper. He whirled around. Snow lay around him, broken only by his own footprints. Closing his eyes, he begged, "Again, come again. I listen." He felt the sigh surround him again. "She lives. I know she lives!" The boat was long gone. For a moment, the Viking stood, thinking. Nodding with determination, his mind clear, he began walking; climbing up the hillside, away from the shore.

For several days, Rurik walked. At some point, he began to veer toward the water again. He knew Jilliand would not have walked along the water at the beginning for fear of the raiders. She most certainly would have moved inland. She knew the land well. Later, she must have looked to the waterways, searching for people.

Eventually, he came to a settlement not unlike his own, except this village bustled with life. As he walked toward the larger of the structures, he was approached by several men. After a brief conversation, he was escorted to the leader.

Rurik spoke of his journey. The man, much older, shook his head with disbelief. "I remember. I know of this woman, Rurik. She was your queen?"

"Yes." Rurik leaned toward the man. "What can you tell me?"

"She was here, years ago. She fled your home during the raid you speak of. She spent the night with my family, in my house," the man told Rurik.

"And the child she carried?" Rurik asked, his voice hoarse with emotion.

"She lost the child and the child's grandmother after the raid. The child was born too early. The grandmother died when they tried to move on." The man continued quietly, "We sailed the next morning, with her on board. I left her on English shores."

"English shores? Why?" Rurik frowned, trying to understand. "*Why?*" he repeated.

"She requested it. I tried to convince her to stay with us, but she would not hear of it, for fear she would bring an attack to this place too. There was a battle when we landed. I saw her taken captive by an English soldier. I believed her story was over." He paused, watching Rurik closely. "Perhaps I was wrong."

"I do not know where she is, but she lives. Of that I'm certain." Rurik looked at the older Viking. "She lives." He spoke quietly.

"Rurik, we still raid. I leave in five days. My ships will sail to shores we have not yet walked. Come with us. When you know it is time to leave, you are free to leave." He placed a hand on Rurik's shoulder. "I always need good men. You are one. If you wish, I would give you a ship. You could sail for me?"

"I could," Rurik answered, "but I will not. Not this time, friend. I sail with you only as far as England."

The older Viking nodded. "It is settled."

As the older Viking promised, in five days they sailed. The ship made shore along the southern coast of England, near Dorset, a place known for the people's willingness to trade with the Vikings. Along with the rest of the men, Rurik left the ship. Standing on the shore, he surveyed the landscape. *If I stay on, I would be expected to join the raids. This time, I am not raiding. I am hunting.* He walked with the Viking crew to the township. When the men began to barter for supplies, Rurik left them. He had other business. Rurik looked for the stables.

Leaning on the gate to the stable corral, he studied the horses there. A stable hand approached him cautiously. "Lookin' to buy, are you, sir?" His eyes ran over the jewels in Rurik's sword, the gold rings on his arm, and the size of his frame.

"I am." Rurik continued to watch the horses.

"There be a better one I know of," the man informed him. "He eats more than all the rest together." As soon as the words left his mouth, he grimaced. The Viking before him looked to have money, but often those were the stingiest.

"Show me," Rurik ordered. He followed the stable hand to the back of the stables. In the corral beyond, alone, stood a Viking Norwegian Fjord Horse that was unusually tall for its breed, about fifteen hands high. It was a yellow-tan color with a mixed light and dark tail and mane, typical of its breed. Known for its strength, calm disposition, and great stamina, the animal watched the men looking at him. Both men entered the pen. Rurik ran his hand over the animal's neck and withers. He could feel the muscles. He checked the animal's legs and hooves. "I will take him," Rurik told the stable hand. "After all, he is a Viking horse, is he not?"

The man felt his throat tighten. Vikings had not raided in many years, preferring instead to trade, but the stable hand's memory was much longer than many years. "Yes, 'tis." The man breathed a heavy sigh of relief when Rurik walked away.

"I will come for him shortly. Have him saddled and ready." Rurik turned back and tossed several gold coins to the man. "I'll pay the rest and more when I return. Just see the horse is ready." The stable hand nodded eagerly to Rurik. "I expect the gear you saddle him with will match the value of such a fine horse," Rurik added casually.

The stable hand nodded again. He knew the asking price of this horse was small. Not many English cared to own a Viking horse. If he played his cards correctly, he stood to make a nice stack of coins this day.

Rurik walked to a nearby inn to eat. An older man watched him enter and studied the Viking closely from the back of the room, hidden as he was by the shadows. Rurik felt he was being watched before he found the man. Taking up his tankard, Rurik walked over to the man's table and sat down. "Do you have something to say to me?" Rurik challenged him.

"Not often one sees a Viking alone and without a ship," the older man calmly observed. "You are searching for something?" The man's weathered face spoke of years in the sun. The sparse hair on his head was as white as his beard. His back was bowed, and his hands gnarled with age. His blue eyes were clear and steady. Nothing about the old man was threatening; nor was he intimidated by Rurik. The two men sat and talked. By the time evening unfolded, each was comfortable with the other.

"If you are so moved, you could ride with me. I will provide the horse." Rurik at last stood to leave.

But the old man stood up slowly and, seemingly in pain, moved toward Rurik. "I will walk with you, my friend. I have never seen the one you seek but understand your drive to find her." Holding on to his walking stick, he led the way out of the tavern. "You must not give up, Rurik, Viking King." He mumbled a bit and then added, "I knew such a love once. I let matters of the world interfere. Our time on this earth—however you see it—is short. Make every sunrise count." By this time, they were at the stable door. "Go with God, Rurik. He watches you too." He clasped Rurik's shoulder. Swaying as he walked, he left Rurik to gaze after his crooked frame as it disappeared.

"I remember well the time when the sight of a Viking would fill men's hearts with fear," Rurik mused. "Perhaps Jilliand's god does see me. Perhaps her god leads me to her. She believed our gods, hers and mine, know each other. Maybe they do."

Concluding his business with the stable hand, he rode out of the village in search of the one woman he loved over all others. She haunted his dreams, interrupted his thoughts, and drew him ever closer. That night he slept under the stars, his horse near, with his mind at peace. He felt a strange comfort in this England.

As morning broke, Rurik was already riding. Rain clouds clung over the land, refusing to move on, while the sun struggled to force its way through. Rurik passed several meadows and the woodlands that surrounded them. The ride was pleasant enough, though he paid little attention to the area, now that he knew with certainty his course lay before him. His mind drifted to Jilliand and his dead child. *Did I lose a son? What would a son borne by Jilliand look like? Not like Igor, for certain. Igor was large boned and thick like his mother. No, Jilliand's child would have been . . .* Suddenly alert, he reined in the horse. The sounds of battle were faint, coming from deep within the woods. Rurik advanced.

The din of conflict became louder. Rurik rode to the top of a hill on the far edge of a forested area. Smoke drifted over the battlefield before being carried upward by a breeze. Viking ships were moving away from the shoreline. *Perhaps the English have defended themselves well,* Rurik thought. Below him, Rurik could see horses and men littering the ground. A large encampment flying the English lord's colors stood to his right. Rurik's eyes took in every detail. The Vikings had withdrawn, but although the English had been badly injured, they had not been bested. Judging by the size of the Viking ships, the English far outnumbered the Vikings. As Rurik studied the scene before him, a man came from the larger of the tents. He walked as one defeated. The men that walked behind him were quiet and subdued. Rurik realized the English must have paid the Vikings to leave. It was probable the Vikings took with them one of great prominence as hostage. Most likely it was the defeated man's son. This would assure the English kept their part of whatever bargain was struck. Rurik felt his pulse quicken with the old fire. Vikings still roamed the seas and fought. Vikings still won.

Rurik watched until the wagons laden with the bodies of those of importance were loaded and rolling away. The battleground itself was still strewn with the bodies of both English and Vikings—an ugly testament to the true spoils of war. Rurik rode from the scene. His search for Jilliand would not be easy.

Through that summer and deep into the fall, Rurik roamed the coast, seeking information that might lead him to Jilliand. In one of the larger villages, he spent time walking the streets talking to people. His persistence paid off. A woman so old she could barely stand and claiming to know of Jilliand stopped him as he walked toward an inn. Her speech was as slow as her movements. But when the woman spoke of Jilliand, her eyes lit up. "I knew a lady, such as you talk of, sir. She has been long gone. I believed she was dead. But I hear tell she has returned to England. Talk says she stays with King Aethewulf." The woman paused. "How do you know of her?" The woman's eyes were watery, but she looked up at the Viking without hesitation. Rurik thought of his own mother, gone these long years. He reached out and touched her shoulder.

"I took her as my wife. I believed she was killed but have heard that she may still live. Your words give me hope, woman." Rurik pressed several coins into the old lady's hand, nodding respectfully, as he turned away. *I must find this king*

Jilliand lives, I feel it. If she loves another, I will not stay. I only need to see her once more, and I will walk with fate to the Valkyries.

By now, the snows had begun. A white shroud covered most of the lands. Temperatures dropped quickly at night. Rurik hoped to find shelter soon. Across a wide valley, a smaller hill ran along its northern boundary. Silhouetted against a darkening sky sat a great wall whose wooden logs defined the expanse of the settlement within. A bustling town lay sprawled outside the main gates. From his vantage point, Rurik could see the burg and grounds were larger than any he had seen on English soil. *This would be the king I have heard about. Stories tell of a king's fierce fight against the Viking raids. Tales of a king who defeated the Vikings more than once. A king who would not be a friend of mine.* Rurik had heard all the talk, seen several burned villages, and even watched a battle where Vikings barely defeated men wearing the same colors that were flying at the corners and over the drawbridge of the burg. More importantly, Rurik heard the rumors of a lady with red hair who lived with the king. *Jilliand—could it be Jilliand?*

The people living around the burg looked well cared for. The homes and animal shelters were suitably tended. *Maybe this will be the place.* Rurik urged his horse onward. With self-confidence, he rode through the great entrance. Boldly moving across the moat and through the gates, Rurik was challenged. "I have business with King Aethewulf. I am Rurik, from the Rus. I come seeking information." Rurik was neither threatened nor intimidated by the number of soldiers around him. More than one man's eyes followed the lone rider. One man slipped around a corner and ran to alert the captain of the guard.

The captain of the guard stepped to a doorway to watch Rurik. The Viking was unafraid and clearly knew what it was to be king. Although older, Rurik still cut a striking figure. He was slender, muscular, and taller than nearly all the men around him. At his side, he carried a great sword whose hilt was laden with priceless jewels. A smaller blade hung at his other side. Around his arms were rings of gold and silver. He wore a heavy golden ring on his right hand. On his left, he wore a ring like the ring worn by the king. From a thick silver chain, the amulet of Thor hung on his chest. Over his shoulders, he wore a heavy cloak of the darkest sable.

It had been years since Rurik felt the need to survey his surroundings with a warrior's eye. Without thinking, he began to do so again. Taking note of the exits, where his horse might be kept, and the placement of the king's guard, he entered the courtyard. He walked and spoke like one with authority and power.

Rurik could see the signs of wealth, manpower, and wellbeing of the people around and inside the burg. Would Jilliand give this up for him? He was no longer a sea king, no longer the prince of Rus. He was only Viking.

When he dismounted, one of the court guards started to take Rurik's weapons, only to have the sword drawn on him. Quickly stepping between the two men, the captain ordered the Viking be allowed to enter the keep with his weapons. "He wears the king's ring."

Rurik gave no hint of surprise at this information. *It is the ring from Jilliand. I wear it again. Does she wear mine still?* His thoughts were always on her. He remembered the day she had given him the ring. *If she does not wish to . . . no, I cannot think on it. She will come. She must come. I draw comfort from this information. She must be here.*

The captain spoke quietly. "The king is not here, Viking. He is at Lady Jilliand's." His eyes pierced Rurik's. "The lady's burg lies one day's ride south, near the water. You can see the keep from the road." He turned to walk with Rurik. "If you wish to stay the night, I will see you have a place to sleep." The weather had settled, but the bitter cold lingered.

"No. I leave tonight," Rurik replied.

"Eat with us, then." He led Rurik on to the barracks.

The men sat at a long table, with others of the king's guard. The men talked in subdued tones, often glancing at Rurik. Rurik wondered how several Viking men at the table came to be with King Aethewulf. This was not the time to ask. The talk among the men indicated Aethewulf had left with a full regiment. "Does the king fight for Lady Jilliand?" Rurik casually asked, as he finished his meal.

The captain looked at Rurik for a moment, before answering. "No. He has fighting men with him but will not lose his kingdom over a woman, even his sister." His tablemates became quiet. "The lady rides alone."

"I would give up my kingdom for Lady Jilliand," Rurik quietly noted, swirling the wine in his goblet.

"That is easy to say if you do not have a kingdom to lose," the captain noted, watching Rurik. The table was silent, as the men waited for the Viking to respond.

For a long moment, Rurik sat quietly, staring at his wine. Rurik looked across the table at the captain. "I gave up my kingdom for this lady. I am Rurik, Prince of Rus." His voice was quiet and even. "Lady Jilliand does not ride alone."

The captain studied the man before him. Then, nodding, he began, "There is one who rides for Lady Jilliand. His name is Alexander. The king will give him men, and Alexander will ride for the lady." He stopped to refill his goblet. "We believe the man who invaded is one of the sons of the king of France. Most likely, Prince Philippe. He looks to take land for France."

"This Alexander, does he know Lady Jilliand well?" Rurik asked.

"He does. He loves the lady, but she does not love Sir Alexander." Then the captain smiled. "She loves a Viking." The men around the table relaxed. "Come, there are men here who will ride with you. I tell you also—we now know more than a third of Prince Philippe's men are Viking. They ride with him, but they are not of his thinking, I would say."

"Viking?" Rurik frowned. "How do you know this?"

"Some of Lady Jilliand's wounded men were brought back here." Standing up, the captain ordered supplies and heavier clothing for Rurik. "I do not know how the Viking men came to ride with the Frenchman. Some Vikings ride for King Aethewulf." The captain nodded toward the men who were sitting and watching Rurik and the captain.

Rurik also stood up. "Any that would ride with the prince of Rus, come with me." Seven men stood. Among those standing were several Vikings. Rurik nodded, pleased.

Temperatures plummeted as darkness fell. Both riders and horses were bundled as Rurik and his men rode south. Something about the soldiers' manner gave warning to Rurik. What were the gods telling him? Clearly, these men rode for Jilliand. No matter. They would fight well for her, he would see to that.

Of greater interest was the information that many of Prince Philippe's men were Viking. They might also fight for Rurik.

At early morn, a soft glow in the distance grew. Rurik led the men around the settlement, ordering them to be silent and ride slowly. "Does the Viking ever rest?" one of the Englishmen whispered. The few Vikings with them only laughed. Thoughts of the coming battle, hunger, and fatigue weighed on most of the men. Still, some remembered Jilliand warmly, and others believed in Rurik. They would all follow the Viking. When Rurik had led them well beyond the burg and its surrounding huts, he finally stopped. Rurik's Fjord had greater stamina than the rest of the horses, but even he was slowing.

"We will rest here. Feed the men and horses." Rurik turned his horse over to one of the men. *What are the gods telling me? I see Jilliand, cold and frightened.* Rurik began pacing. Camp was quickly set up. Eventually, Rurik sat down to wait, his thoughts on the coming fight, the man he pursued, and the woman he loved. *Surely, the gods would not lead me to her, only to have her taken again.*

"For certain, any Vikings riding with the man we pursue will join you." One of Aethewulf's guards stretched out next to Rurik. Rurik looked at the young man. The guard was anxious—not afraid, but ready to get into the battle.

"That will be determined by the reason they ride with the Frenchman." Rurik also stretched out. "If the French hold hostages, the Vikings will not leave the Frenchman. If the Frenchman promised to pay for sailing or fighting, yes, then they will come with us."

"Why do we wait?" the young man asked, his impatience unchecked.

"I wait for information," Rurik replied, as he closed his eyes. "Do you know of Lady Jilliand?"

"I do. Lady Jilliand saved my life once. I was very young, very foolish, and filled with the fire of conquest. She spoke out for me." The young man lay staring at the sky nearly hidden by the forest. "She lied for me, actually." The guard smiled at the memory. Just as he dozed off, hoof sounds of a rider split the air.

Rurik jolted up immediately. A horse burst into the camp. The rider, an older man with the manner and confidence of an experienced fighter, rode directly to Rurik.

"The Frenchman who took the lady has nearly two hundred men. They were moving south." The man dismounted. "Sir Alexander should catch up with them around midday. He and his men intend to fight the French, but he has only half the men the Frenchman has, if that many."

"How far away?" Rurik asked.

"Nearly a day's ride," the man replied, shaking his head. "If we are to be any help to Sir Alexander, we must move."

"Ride!" Rurik ordered. In only moments, the glen was vacant. The men rode hard, steadily gaining on their quarry.

CHAPTER 31

BEGINNING WITH FIRST LIGHT, PHILIPPE pushed his men hard. The prince had no desire to fight, certainly not when he was on the run himself. Alexander's troops hit Philippe's men just as Philippe stopped to rest the horses at midday. The hand-to-hand battle was vicious. At the first cry from his rear guard, Philippe shouted at two of his men, and with Jilliand in tow, rode deep into the nearby forest. There, while the men hastily set up a tent, he dragged Jilliand off her horse and shoved her hard into the tent where she fell on the ground. "Your shoes, Lady," he demanded, hovering over her with his hand outstretched.

"Your Highness?" Jilliand asked. Surely she had misunderstood.

"Your shoes! Now! Or I take them off myself." He leaned toward her, danger in his voice. "You cannot run from me if you are barefoot. The snow lies heavy on the ground, and the cold is deadly." Jilliand's heart fell when she understood his intent.

Removing both shoes, she handed them over. "Leggings, too," Philippe instructed. "I want to see bare feet. Make haste, Lady! I don't have much time."

Jilliand handed him her leggings and sat down on a makeshift bed. Tossing several heavy covers and another cloak onto the bed, Philippe left. When she was certain he had gone, she stepped to the flap, peering outside. A thick blanket of snow covered the ground as far as she could see. There was no guard at her tent, but it didn't matter. She was captive, as surely as if he had chained her to a wall. Huddled under the covers, she waited.

Alexander was horribly outnumbered, but his men fought hard. The thought of Jilliand on his mind pushed Alexander to battle with ferocity. Still, the fight was turning for Philippe. Alexander hoped to get to the French prince. If the prince were killed, the battle would belong to Alexander. Taking a desperate chance, he fought his way into the middle of Philippe's men, his one thought to save Jilliand. Too late, he realized the prince had already slipped away. Men closed in around Alexander. As he went down, he heard the thunder of horses and yells above the din of the ground battle

Philippe rode back toward the fighting. He could not see Alexander but was stunned to see Alexander's men were being aided by another force. He could not tell where the additional men came from, nor who they rode for. Desperate, Philippe turned his horse and rode hard, back to Jilliand. A few of his men followed.

Jilliand listened to the distant sounds of battle. The noise of riders coming toward her tent grew louder. Jilliand prayed it would not be the prince who came for her. It was. He ripped the tent flap open. "You were not expecting me, I can tell. No matter. I am here. Get your shoes on—now!" He tossed her shoes and leggings back. "Your rescue was in vain. No wonder—too few men. It matters not. The king's sister. What might I do with you?" His eyes moved over her hungrily, causing Jilliand to cringe

As soon as her shoes were on, Philippe grasped her arm and yanked her up, shoving her toward her horse. *I have no value now. Perhaps this is my time to die. My heart is tired.* Jilliand glanced at the few mounted men waiting for her. Her thoughts were interrupted when one of the prince's men rode near to report that many of his men had left before the fighting began.

"Left? To where?" Philippe demanded, angrily. "Are you certain they are not among the dead?"

"I am certain. They were gone before any real fighting began," the man noted grimly. "I thought those types liked to fight."

"No matter. We do not need them now." Prince Philippe would come to court a hero. Perhaps his father could still get something for this lady he had kidnapped. He looked at her again. She was a thing of beauty, even if she did have an air about her. He would tame her. Although he tried to disguise it, Jilliand could feel a sense of urgency in him, worse than before. That same feeling hovered about his men. Philippe rode as fast as he could push the horses.

With unseeing eyes, Jilliand stared at the road. The land was dead with winter's frigid temperatures, white with snow, and empty of all life. *Bitter as my soul, Rurik. How I wish you had run me through. To have loved one such as you and then lose you seems not fair.* Exhaustion made her vulnerable to the sadness waiting to claim her heart once more.

Philippe studied Jilliand. She never requested anything to be made easier for her. She refused to be beaten. Philippe had not planned on taking anyone hostage. As soon as he saw Jilliand, he had recognized her. She had changed little since the time he had first seen her.

For weeks now, Philippe's band of men had moved along the coast ravaging everything in their path. It was luck that he found the Viking men. It took a lie told by Philippe, a French prince, to get the Vikings to fight for him. In exchange for the lives of Vikings held by France from last year's raids, the Vikings had agreed to stay with him for one year. There were no prisoners being held by France. All the Vikings taken had been killed. These men would not have known that little detail. Now, they rode and fought for Philippe. They were fearless fighters. In truth, they tolerated the travel and weather much better than his own men. *Strange that they gave way so easily. They never had shied from the fight before.* Philippe looked back at his men again. Only two Vikings remained. *No matter. We travel more quickly now.*

The taking of Jilliand changed Philippe's plans. Without Jilliand there would have been no delay in leaving after laying waste to her burg. Now, it seemed probable King Aethewulf would try to take her again. Better to make it to sea quickly. He watched Jilliand, who gave no indication that he was even present. *That will change.* Philippe looked around, wondering just how long it might take to reach his ship. *Do I have enough men left to man a ship?* He glanced behind him, once more.

"To where do we ride, Prince Philippe?" she asked, without looking at the man she grew to despise more each day.

"Does it matter?" His answer was curt.

Jilliand did not answer. She merely glanced at him and then looked away, her heart sick at the glint in his eyes. To even think of Philippe touching her made her ill. Lancer could easily outrun any horse, but she would not risk him. She leaned down and gently patted his neck. She heard Philippe give an order for them to stop. Pulling Lancer up, she gratefully slid off to the ground. Quickly putting the horse between her and Philippe, Jilliand was thankful when one of the men took Philippe aside to speak with him.

Suddenly, they were riding again. Jilliand caught the look of anger on Philippe's face. Turning away, she pretended not to notice nor hear his con-versation. She gathered that several more men were no longer riding with them. A persistent feeling of anxiety charged the air around them. Alert, Jilliand glanced at her captor. He was counting the men behind him. Jil-liand glanced back. Every man was warily scanning the land around him.

Philippe looked beyond the riders again. "Your brother follows us, Lady. Seems you do not know him so well." His tone was cold. Jilliand was surprised to see that Philippe was actually frightened.

"'Tis not my brother," Jilliand replied, watching Philippe. "He is a king. He would not sneak around. These are his lands." Jilliand could not think what might have caused the men to leave Philippe. She looked quickly at the men behind them. The young Norseman still rode with them. He returned Jilliand's gaze. Her mind working, she turned back.

"Why would you think you are followed?" Jilliand asked, trying to sound unconcerned. "Did you not withstand the fight?"

"Do you think my men would just ride away? They have no place here." He looked back once again. "They do not even speak the language. They belong in France." He rode in silence for a distance. "If not your brother, then who?" His voice was flat.

Jilliand looked at the quiet forest and fields and then at Philippe. "I only know my brother. My people would not follow you, and they have no horses. Perhaps your men quit."

Philippe snarled, "Frenchmen do not quit, Lady. You best think of something else to cheer me with."

"I would not cheer you, Highness," Jilliand answered coldly. "You know your men. I have nothing to say on the matter." She prayed someone would come for her.

The noise of the horses and the riding gear were the only sounds she heard No one spoke. The group rode in silence for several miles. Jilliand found herself looking around—for what, she could not say. Suddenly, she gasped. Ahead of them, to her left, she saw it: a man hanging, his body swaying slightly in the wind. She saw him kick weakly. With no thought as to who he might be or why he had been hanged, she touched Lancer. Horse and rider bolted away from the party to the left and sped toward the man.

Philippe had been surveying the forest to his right. When Jilliand rode away, it took him off guard, and he could not understand what she was yelling. He only knew she was getting away. With lightning speed, he notched an arrow.

Jilliand glanced back toward Philippe, calling, "He still lives! Quickly, we must cut him down!" She saw Philippe release the arrow. Stunned, she cried out, "No! Look!" Frantically, she pointed toward the hanged man. Lancer was still loping toward the trees when the arrow found its mark. He jolted, then began to trip. Jarred, Jilliand was able to jump off. She hit the ground that was soft with several feet of snow. Horrified, she ran to her horse. Lancer made low noises as he tried to raise his head. Blood was flowing freely, staining the snow as it cascaded down his side. Crying, Jilliand knelt to lean over him. "Quiet, Lancer. It is over now. Quiet my friend," she spoke between sobs.

As the great horse died, Jilliand turned toward Philippe, who by now was dismounting near her. "Your man dies, and you kill my horse for helping him?" Jilliand was shaking. Until that moment, Philippe had not seen the man. Now he did. The man was already dead. "I hate you, do you hear me?" Jilliand screamed. "I hate you! I will never be with you!" Jilliand turned and ran blindly into the woods.

"Yes, you will," he called after her, grimly. "If I have to shackle you to the bed, you will be with me." Philippe turned to the men behind him. "I want the woman—alive and unharmed. She will be mine." Determined, he mounted and rode after Jilliand.

Jilliand raced through the trees, choosing the thickest woods. Philippe would have great difficulty following her, unless he got off the horse and ran after her. Instinctively, she knew he would not do that. He was a prince, and so he would try to run her down.

Without warning, a man stepped from behind a tree to grasp her arm. "Keep running, Lady." Jilliand was startled to hear him speak in Norse. "Go as deep as you can. We will find you when it is over." He lifted Jilliand's hand to his lips then disappeared. Jilliand ran without looking back. The sounds of Philippe's charging horse grew more distant. Unable to run his horse through the dense vegetation, he stopped, frustrated. Still Jilliand ran. Darting between the trees growing closely together, she pushed ever deeper into the forest. Behind her, she could no longer hear Philippe. The faint sounds of fighting came to her. She kept running, intent on putting even greater distance between herself, Philippe, . . . and whatever else was happening.

Then the sounds of battle shattered the silence around her. Vaguely, she was aware of an echoing yell. There it was again. "What is that?" she whispered. "Who *are* these men chasing Philippe?" Jilliand stopped to catch her breath. The light was beginning to fade. Piercing the air was a scream unlike any other she had ever heard. Shuddering, she stood as if paralyzed. Again, the agonizing scream faded into the evening breeze. "Whoever that was, his death did not come easy. What will Philippe do to me?" Jilliand felt fingers of fear and despair grip her.

It was beginning to snow again with great, heavy wet flakes. Her shoes were wet, her feet were getting colder, her hands were numb, and her face ached. One lone tear rolled down her cheek. Quickly, she brushed it off. "Mother, I fear this time I will die. I have not the will to live. I have nothing left. I have no place to go." Her throat tightened. "I will freeze this night. I am through."

She half-heartedly searched in the fading light for a brush thicket, a rock pile, anything to crawl under. There was nothing. Standing under an old evergreen with long, drooping branches, she whispered, "Oh, Rurik, tell me what to do."

Philippe rode hard after Jilliand until the vegetation became too thick. To catch her, he would be forced to send men on foot. He knew she could not go far, but she could freeze to death. The sound of fighting pierced through his determination. Reining in his horse, he listened. Whirling the horse around, he headed back toward the sounds. He would have to fight to keep Jilliand. *You do not know Aethewulf as well as you think, Lady. He does come for you.* Philippe broke into the clearing where fighting had begun again. With a leap, he cleared his horse and joined what had quickly become hand-to-hand combat. The men fighting Philippe's men were clearly winning. *This fight is over. We are not going to win. Jilliand . . . I must get to Jilliand.*

Philippe called to any of his men near, as he ran after his horse. If Philippe caught Jilliand quickly, he could still get away. Mounting, he sped toward the wooded area where he last saw Jilliand running. A great cry reached him, while the sounds of running horses spread around him. He was being chased. Philippe was cut off and forced back toward his men, who by now were prisoners. A large group of men who wore Aethewulf's colors and Vikings who wore Philippe's colors surrounded the battleground. Philippe was taken to a tall striking man who was clearly the leader. It had been a disaster. Philippe's men were either dead, had changed alliances, or had surrendered. Philippe stood defiantly. "I am Prince Philippe of France. Unhand me." When asked where Lady Jilliand was, Philippe snarled, "I have no idea. You should check her castle." Rurik glanced at the Viking men now surrounding him and Philippe.

"The perfect offering," Rurik noted coldly. "Now. This will be done now." He walked slowly toward Philippe. Fear choking him and despite the men holding him, Philippe tried to struggle away. The fear he felt was justified. The blood eagle sacrifice began.

When Philippe's screams finally faded away, Rurik asked about Jilliand. None of Philippe's band knew where she was. Some knew she had ridden away, trying to get back to her burg, they believed. None had seen her since then and much time had passed. Rurik ordered the men to set up camp and search the area. He would ride back to her burg. *If she is on horseback, she could have gotten away. The gods would not play with me again, surely. I must get to her before her brother leaves with her.* Rurik returned to Jilliand's burg with two laden horses in tow.

King Aethewulf was in council chambers when a message was brought to him. Thoughtfully, he stood. "We are through until tomorrow." Each man with him noted his response to the messenger and in silence the room emptied, but for one of his pages. "I will speak with this man in private. Bring him to me."

Rurik was taken to Jilliand's private study where the king waited with his page. When Rurik entered, the page was dismissed. Rurik did not kneel, but stood watching the king. King Aethewulf stood eyeing the tall man before him. Neither spoke for a moment.

King Aethewulf spoke first. "I hear much about you. You have a fearsome reputation. You are Rurik, the prince of Rus, a land great in size. What brings you this far south?" *What can I tell him about Jilliand? I know not if Alexander was successful.*

Rurik noted the attention Aethewulf gave him, the challenge in his eyes, how much like Jilliand he appeared. His mouth was the same; the eyes were the same.

"I come for a woman." Rurik would not tell what he now knew—Jilliand was not here and, as yet, was not safe.

"We have many women, as I am certain you noticed," the king replied dryly. "Describe her." Aethewulf knew well the woman Rurik sought. He was not certain how to tell the Viking that Jilliand was no longer with him.

"She is more beautiful than any other. Her eyes are like emeralds of great value. Her hair is red as the sunset, her temper fiery as the sun. I think you know her and know her well." His voice had softened. Rurik looked squarely at the king, his eyes unwavering. "This woman looks much like you."

Aethewulf replied, "What is your business with the king's sister? She is more valuable to me than gold."

Rurik's disdain at this statement was evident. "As she is to me. I thought her dead for a long time. I hear she lives. She is my wife." A curious sadness filled the deep-blue eyes looking at the king.

Aethewulf walked slowly around the room, his mind racing. Aethewulf spoke of many things. At last he spoke of the deadly raids against his land and people. Rurik listened without comment. Losing patience, Aethewulf challenged, "I am not certain I will allow Jilliand to see you. Vikings have long been a thorn in my side."

Better a thorn than a sword, Rurik thought. Aloud, he noted, "I think you would talk with me of matters about your kingdom. I am willing to listen." He glanced at the man walking around him.

"Lady Jilliand is not here. She was taken hostage eight days ago during a siege on her castle. When we arrived, they had taken her away. Sir Alexander and his men have ridden to take her back." King Aethewulf stood with his arms crossed over his chest, waiting. The Viking before him might be forced into his service, if the king spoke well.

Rurik stepped to the door and spoke to another page standing in the hall. When Rurik turned again to Aethewulf, he carried a sack. The sound of Aethewulf sucking air into his lungs sliced through the room. On the floor lay Alexander's sword, his blade, and a leather pouch. "The man you speak of is lying outside. I brought his body to you. He was outmanned," Rurik noted coldly. "When we got to him, the fight was well on. He was already dead. Some of the men with Alexander survived: They are with my men." Rurik picked up the satchel and shoved it into Aethewulf's hand. "The body of the man we fought is outside, also. He left with Lady Jilliand headed for the southern coast. We drew him to us."

Aethewulf froze. Rurik stood watching him closely, waiting for the questions he knew would come. At last Aethewulf spoke, "My sister? She is safe?"

"If I find her," Rurik responded quietly, "I will care for her."

Aethewulf nodded slowly. He suddenly felt old and tired. "She looks just like her mother, only more so," Aethewulf told Rurik. He sank into a nearby chair. "You should know, I tried to get her to marry. Not a good thing: woman like her, alone. She refused. She was waiting for you."

"I know." Rurik's face softened. "Our time has come again." He walked to the door, then stepped back—turning to Aethewulf he spoke, with his voice carrying the unmistakable note of finality. "If I find her, we will not be back. Our place is not here."

Aethewulf nodded. "I have loved her and cared for her."

"That's what I am told," Rurik acknowledged. "She is your sister. She is my world." With that, he was gone.

EPILOGUE

DARKNESS COVERED THE FOREST. TALL evergreens swayed above, pushed by a slight breeze. Under one large tree, Jilliand sat cold and alone. For several moments, the sound of approaching horses shaking the very ground nearly went unnoticed.

Jolted by the sound of someone calling her name, she raised her head to listen. The sounds of men and horses surrounded her. Again, she heard the sound, "Lady Jilliand!" Dare she hope the caller was not with Philippe? Slowly, she tried to stand. Her heart beat as if she would die. Her breath came so quickly that she had to grasp the tree trunk she leaned against.

"Who hails?" Jilliand tried to reply. Her voice seemed not to carry. Again, she tried. "Who calls for me?" This time, louder. "Here, I am here," she yelled, after taking a deep breath. Silence. Then, a voice spoke.

"Keep shouting, Lady. We come for you." The answer was in Norse. Jilliand's heart beat faster. Could it be Philippe's men had deserted him? A knot pulled at her stomach. Or maybe the Norseman is with Philippe.

"Here, I am here," Jilliand cried out again. She could hear horses snorting, riding gear jingling, and men coming toward her. Taking a breath, she stepped out, cautiously. There, coming toward her, were men in her brother's colors and the Norseman previously with Philippe. Had Aethewulf come for her? An older man dismounted and hastened to her side. He scooped her up and set her on his horse, mounting behind her.

"We can make camp further in. We wait for two days, and then . . . " He stopped. Jilliand only knew Philippe was not with them. That was all that mattered. When the party stopped, a small tent was set up for her. Soon, there was a fire burning in a pit inside. The man brought a thick broth to her and some wine. "You are safe here, Lady. If you have need of anything, call out. We are all around you."

"Alexander?" she asked, watching the soldier. He shook his head. "The Frenchman cannot find me?" Again, he shook his head, and this time a slight smile passed over his face. "Thank you." Jilliand hardly knew what to do next. Suddenly, she was exhausted, cold, and hungry. She dreaded seeing her brother again, but it was better than seeing the French court. This night, she would sleep as one who is safe, not afraid of what the night might bring. After drinking the broth, she lay down on a padded mat. The sounds of camp slowly faded from her mind.

Jilliand slept that night and most of the following day. After eating, she slept again. The low sound of the men talking was comforting. She did not ask why they stayed. She had no desire to see Aethewulf. Logically, she understood why he would not come for her. It still stung. Somehow, Alexander had managed to save her—somehow.

On the afternoon of the third day, Jilliand ventured outside her tent and walked among the men. A few she recognized from her brother's soldiers. The rest she knew had ridden with Philippe. Yet here they were, protecting her—or so it seemed. Seeing the young man that wore her cloak, she asked, "Why did you ride with the prince? I do not believe you are French." She spoke softly to him, in Norse. He stared at her so long, she decided he would not talk.

As she turned away, he replied, "I was promised freedom for my brothers." When Jilliand turned back to him, he looked hard into her eyes. "It was easy for him to promise such a thing. They were already free—they were both dead." Jilliand started to speak. He spoke first. "It does not matter, Lady. Life goes on. The gods have other plans for me." He smiled at her. "And for you too, I think," he added.

"Perhaps." Jilliand, smiling sadly, nodded. "Perhaps." She wandered around the area, and then returned to her tent. Closing the flap, she sat cross-legged near the fire. Its warmth felt good, but still her heart was heavy. She closed her eyes. Remembering every detail of her burg, she tried to imagine it as home again. She knew it could never be. Aethewul⁻ would never care enough for her to protect her. Worse, he would now insist she marry. Word of what had happened would spread, and it would surely happen again. She had become fair game. *What do I do now? Where can I go?* She sat staring into the flames, empty and alone.

The sounds of a rider coming into camp made Jilliand stand up. Holding her breath, she waited. The men were laughing and visiting. The rider was obviously known to them. She started to sit back down, when she heard a man's voice.

"It is him!" Jilliand opened the flap of her tent. Men throughout the camp had begun to gather. Following his voice, she found him.

When Jilliand stepped into the light near the fire, she saw only the Viking. Rurik turned to her. Their eyes met for a heartbeat, and then her feet were moving as in a dream. She cared little that it would be unseemly to run to this man. He had been her husband, her lover, the father of her child. She would feel his arms about her once more, if only for a moment.

Rurik moved toward her as a path opened through the throng of men. Only he and Jilliand existed now. He reached out to her as she ran into his arms. He could feel her against him; her arms wrapped around his neck. He could smell her hair and feel the tears flowing from the emerald eyes he had longed to see. "Jilliand . . ." He held her fast. Time stood still. "Jilliand, I have dreamed of you just this way, for so long." His voice was low, husky with emotion.

The men watched this woman some hardly knew and the man they all now served. The camp was hushed. At last, Rurik straightened. With his arms still around her, he softly spoke into her hair, "Tell me, is it true? Do you still wait for me?"

"I told you I would, Viking," she whispered into his ear. "My word is all I have left to me. I keep it." With one motion, Rurik scooped Jilliand up and walked toward her tent.

NOTES FROM THE AUTHOR

WHILE RESEARCHING MATERIAL FOR THIS novel, I looked for names that fit the time period. For the heroine, I chose Jilliand, an Old English name meaning child of the gods. For the Viking, I came across the name Rurik, which was easy to remember, short, and of the correct time period. I next researched all I could regarding Rurik to be certain there was not a dark history to the name. What I discovered was a legendary man. He is credited with founding what we now call Russia, although nothing was written about him until three hundred years after his death.

It is difficult to tell what is fact and what might be fiction. A document, known as *The Russian Chronicles*, tells of a Viking sea king who settled Novgorod, and two other men, Dir and Askold, who settled Kiev. However, to this day, while some Russian people believe they have Rurik's DNA, scholars differ on whether he even existed. Some feel he is storied but never lived; others believe he lived.

I do not have an opinion on his existence. However, if he did indeed live, I cannot believe a man who accomplished all that he is believed to have accomplished simply gave his holdings to a good friend, left his only son of record with that same friend to teach how to be a leader, and then quietly went away to farm. If he did even some of the things he is credited with, I cannot, in my mind, marry his colorful career and his sudden disappearance from such a life. It is believed, and certainly very likely, he was a pagan. If so, his ideology was such that he would much rather have wished to die fighting. It is almost as if because little else was known about him, someone filled in the blanks to close his story. I hope I will be forgiven for taking the liberty of allowing him to have a different ending to his life.

One of the articles I found about Rurik tells of a possible marriage to an English princess. My story is the fictional story of a strong lady—one who rose above what might have become her life. I must remind my readers: She and everyone in the book are the products of imaginative writing.

Before sitting at the computer to write this book, I researched the Vikings and life in that period extensively. That research continued during my initial writing and during each re-read. My research revealed them to be a people much more complex than our common stories and movies portray. I believe we have done a grave injustice to the Vikings. It would seem the "berserkers'" actions may have colored much of what we see in our mind's eye. Some historians believe the berserkers were warriors with a fanatical devotion to the god Odin; men who dressed in bear or wolf skins and fought with a frenzy, striking fear in the hearts of the enemy. In many writings by Christians, the stories of these men were based on legends. However, one must remember, the exploits of Vikings and their raids were written by the people upon whom those raids crashed. Their lives and goods were taken, and their homes, monasteries, and whole villages were destroyed.

Yet, research and archaeological finds tell us more. There is another very important side to the Vikings. Archaeologists have uncovered a great deal of evidence that Viking men and women were clean and particular about their appearance. Items found in ancient graves also speak to Viking skills in jewelry design, stone carving, textile creation, and even tools such as ear spoons used to keep the ear free of wax. Yes, the Vikings were clean, family oriented, and hard working. Research reveals they had strong family ties, not much different from those in England and France. As a general rule, every Viking man was in great physical shape. His day-to-day activities assured he would stay that way.

Captives who were initially taken as slaves were required to learn the language and adopt the religious beliefs of the Vikings. Many were free people by the next generation. Many Viking clans converted to Christianity, while others remained pagans. Volumes of texts tell of Viking supremacy in shipbuilding, navigation, and, of course, fighting. Fighting was not only a way to capture lands, peoples, and plunder but also a way to survive. Their fighting skills were unmatched for many years. Their navigational abilities are legendary.

King Aethewulf ruled Mercia from 839 to 858. One of his sons, Alfred the Great, is credited with turning Wessex into an effective kingdom and reviving intellectual and spiritual life.

It is my hope that my readers have enjoyed this trip with Jilliand and me.

ABOUT THE AUTHOR

CLARE GUTIERREZ, A REGISTERED NURSE, grew up on a cattle ranch in rural Colorado as one of four children. After living in Carlsbad, New Mexico, for twenty-eight years, she now lives in the Rio Grande Valley of South Texas. Together with her husband, Dr. Beto Gutierrez, they host first-class photographers from the world over at Santa Clara Ranch—a 300-acre wildlife sanctuary.

Other titles by Clare Gutierrez are: *Dancing with the Boss* (2012) and *Come Winter* (2014).

Annie Kirk leads a quiet life. But everything changes when she arrives at her family's ranch to visit her retired brother, Allen, for the summer. She is reluctantly drawn into Allen's relationship with the mafia and an assignment to break up a terrorist plot. As friends fall by the wayside, Annie must make drastic life-changing decisions—*Dancing with the Boss*.

Clare Gutierrez curates your voyage back to the Scottish highlands of ages past . . . a time and place in which simply staying alive constituted a noble adventure and becoming a patron of the oppressed and the impoverished could make you a hallowed queen—*Come Winter*.

GLOSSARY

AMULET: an ornament or piece of jewelry worn for good luck or to ward off evil.

ASGARD: home of the halls of the Norse gods.

BERSERKER: a particularly fanatical Viking warrior who fought with a deep rage.

BLOOD EAGLE: a sacrificial rite to Odin performed by cutting the victim's ribs at the spine so that they resembled an eagle's wings; the lungs were then pulled out. The rite, while doubted by some scholars, is reported in sagas.

BURG: (also burgh) structure with a massive series of banks, fronted by a wide ditch or moat. The bank was typically faced and timber riveted. This was topped by a wooden palisade of stakes up to ten feet high, with a walkway. Castles, as we know them today, were not built until around 1066, with the Norman invasion, specifically, William the Conqueror.

CAULKING: a fibrous mixture of animal hair and tar that is packed between two overlapping stakes in a ship, making it watertight.

FREYA: fertility goddess.

JARL: Norse for nobleman, "earl."

KNARR: a Scandinavian ocean-going cargo ship.

NORMAN: derived from medieval Latin, *normanni*, meaning "northmen."

NORNS: the three sisters of fate: Urd (past), Verdandi (present), and Skuld (future).

ODIN: supreme god noted for his ecstatic powers in battle.

RAGNARÖK: the final doom, when the gods and monsters are destroyed in a great combat. A new world will be reborn then.

RUNES: the Viking alphabet was composed of only 16 runes. Runes had magical and numerical value and were sacred to Odin.

THOR: sky god of Odin who was a friend of mankind. His symbol was a hammer that he used to smash other gods.

VALHALLA: hall where heroes feast until Ragnarök.

VALKYRIES: female spirits who select the fallen for Valhalla; they also direct the course of battles.